A Scandalous Bargain

"Of what benefit am I to you, then?" Celeste asked.

He bent close to her, which, in an already confined space, brought him *very* near. His scent surrounded her, a thrilling mix of woodsmoke, leather, and herbs, and she could see how stubble already shaded his chin. If he bent just a little closer, she could kiss him.

Involuntarily, she dipped her tongue to her bottom lip. What would he taste like? Surely something forbidden, and delicious.

As if he could hear her thoughts, his gaze dropped to her mouth. She could have sworn that his eyes darkened, and the column of his throat worked.

And wouldn't *that* be thrilling? To be kissed by rakish Kieran Ransome in the fitting alcove of Madame Jacqueline's modiste shop?

He blinked, straightening, and disappointment thudded in her chest.

"You're the most respectable woman I know," he said.

"I'm the *only* respectable woman you know," she countered.

By Eva Leigh

The Wicked Quills of London
FOREVER YOUR EARL
SCANDAL TAKES THE STAGE
TEMPTATIONS OF A WALLFLOWER

The London Underground
FROM DUKE TILL DAWN
COUNTING ON A COUNTESS
DARE TO LOVE A DUKE

The Union of the Rakes
MY FAKE RAKE
WOULD I LIE TO THE DUKE
WAITING FOR A SCOT LIKE YOU

Last Chance Scoundrels
THE GOOD GIRL'S GUIDE TO RAKES

The Good Girl's Guide to Rakes

Last Chance Scoundrels

EVA LEIGH

An Imprint of HarperCollins*Publishers*

This is a work of fiction. Names, characters, places, and incidents are products of the author's imagination or are used fictitiously and are not to be construed as real. Any resemblance to actual events, locales, organizations, or persons, living or dead, is entirely coincidental.

First Avon Books mass market printing: February 2022

Print Edition ISBN: 978-0-06-308627-2
Digital Edition ISBN: 978-0-06-308263-2

Designed by Amy Halperin
Cover illustration by Paul Stinson

FIRST EDITION

Printed in Lithuania

22 23 24 25 26 SB 10 9 8 7 6 5 4 3 2 1

To Zack, who always saw that I was much more than merely a Good Girl

Acknowledgments

❖

Thank you to Jackie Barbosa, for keeping me accountable and making sure the words actually get on the page. Thank you, also, to Rose Lerner, Sierra Simone, Isobel Carr, and Dr. Ros Clarke, for advising on matters factual and historical. Any errors are my own, though let's just pretend they're artistic liberties and entirely intentional.

Thank you to the legendary and gracious Beverly Jenkins, who agreed to have a cameo role in this book. There would be *no* historical romance without Ms. Bev.

Thank you to my agent, Kevan Lyon, keeping me in contracts and consequently coffee for fifteen years. And thank you to my editor, Nicole Fischer, who doesn't balk at historical heroes in eyeliner and never, ever tells me to tone down my sex scenes.

This book was written during a very challenging time in our collective history, and it gave me a sense of adventure and optimism when such things were in short supply. I hope it gives you, Dear Reader, the same experience.

The Good Girl's Guide to Rakes

Chapter 1

❧*❧

London, England
1818

The wedding hadn't happened yet, and already the marriage was a disaster.

Kieran Ransome and his family stood beneath the portico of St. George's before entering the church's vestibule, and as his mother briefly lifted his sister's veil to brush away a stray lock of hair, he caught a glimpse of Willa's face. Her cheeks were ashen, her lips drawn into a thin, tight slash. The countess twittered and fussed with Willa's gown, yet his sister barely uttered a word.

Last night, the family had enjoyed a prewedding supper, and Willa had been almost mute then, as well. She'd had two and a half glasses of wine instead of her usual one, picking at her food rather than displaying her typically robust appetite. The groom had slumped in his chair, offering up grunts when spoken to, and had declined Kieran's offer of a post-meal drink at their favorite chophouse.

Something was clearly wrong.

"Something's clearly wrong," Kieran's brother Finn whispered into his ear.

Kieran shot a glance toward their father, the Earl of Wingrave, who stood close by, chatting with Simon, his eldest son. Alice, Simon's wife, hovered at her husband's side. The earl and the countess ignored each other, which was unsurprising, but what did astonish Kieran was the fact that no one seemed to notice how anxiety emanated from the bride like a silent scream.

Ordinarily, Willa charged ahead into everything—places, discussions, opinions—yet this morning she was rooted in place.

"Do you think she wants to cry off?" Kieran asked lowly.

"Difficult to blame her," Finn returned. "Dom's been an utter ass these past weeks. Hell, the way he's been carrying on, *I* wouldn't marry him."

"She'd jilt Dom?"

Finn exhaled, and a rueful expression crossed his face. "I wouldn't take that wager, little brother. Remember how she insisted on eating a handful of sand when we told her she shouldn't?"

"She was five years old at the time."

"If anything, her stubbornness has only increased in the intervening years."

Kieran couldn't argue against that. He'd initially believed that Willa and Dominic Kilburn were perfectly matched. Two more obstinate beings didn't exist with arguments that involved slammed doors and broken porcelain. Yet Kieran had also seen the adoring way in which Willa and Dom looked at each other, how they always had their hands interlaced as if unable to bear a moment without touching. Surely, they would have a happy, if tempestuous, union.

He wasn't so certain of that anymore.

Something he *did* know for a fact was that churches made him deucedly uncomfortable. They were physical manifestations of temperance, solemnity, and quiet reflection—all conditions he studiously avoided. Merely standing outside St. George's caused restless energy to pulse through his limbs, and it was all he could do to keep from leaping onto the back of a passing dray and riding off toward a tavern or the theater or anywhere that wasn't soaked with staid gravity like this house of worship.

God knew he had no intention of ever standing up as a bridegroom in one of these places.

"Christ," he muttered to Finn, "I haven't seen this side of the daytime in years."

"Tompkins owes me five quid," his brother answered. "He said you wouldn't make it, let alone show up sober. But I knew that you'd make an appearance, if only to gorge yourself at the wedding breakfast."

"Thank you for your faith in me," Kieran said dryly. Louder, to his family, he said, "As groomsman, I'm off to check on Dom. I'll offer my early felicitations for joining his cursed line to ours."

"On this day of all days," his father said distractedly, "spare us your histrionic pronouncements."

His mother rolled her eyes, though it was difficult to say whether it was her son or husband who irritated her the most.

Giving the earl an ironic salute, Kieran wrested open the church doors. He raised a brow as Finn fell into step beside him.

"I've a wager with myself to see if you are struck dead the moment you set foot inside the church," Finn explained genially.

"There will be two charred spots on the floor, then. Yours beside mine."

The moment the doors opened, Finn threw Kieran a rude hand gesture, eliciting gasps from guests seated in nearby pews. Kieran shared a grin with his brother.

"A new part of the Ransome Brothers mythos," Finn murmured as they walked down the aisle toward the chancel. At least, Kieran *believed* it was called a chancel, but he couldn't be certain, as he hadn't been particularly attentive when schooled on the aspects of faith.

All of London's elite packed St. George's, drawn from the country's most esteemed and respected families. The groom's side of the church was filled with titans of industry and commerce, since Dom's kin was part of that world, and their elegant garments easily rivaled those worn by the aristocracy. Yet both the nobility and those with newly made fortunes stared uneasily at Kieran and Finn as they walked down the aisle. Perhaps they, like many in the city, had read of the Ransome brothers' exploits in the scandal rags. Everyone was eager to hear of someone else's misbehavior, if only to feel marginally better about their own paper-thin lives and spongy morality.

Kieran threw a roguish smile to the guests, delighting in the way the ladies' hands fluttered at their throats and the gentlemen puffed out their chests. What did their discomposure mean to him?

One particularly engaging woman on the bride's side caught his interest, her fingers dancing along the lace of her fichu, her lips curved upward in an intrigued smile. Kieran winked at her, and she batted her lashes.

"Hell." Finn's chuckle was dry. "Only you would attempt to arrange an assignation in a bloody church."

"I join a long and storied tradition of defiling houses of worship. But I've found someone even more captivating. Get a look at the neck on the one in the second row, groom's side."

It was a most enthralling neck. Sweetly curved, with just a hint of soft, chestnut-hued down where the hairline began. Kieran's mouth watered as he imagined gently nipping his teeth into that neck and hearing the lady's shocked, thrilled gasp of pleasure.

Some men loved breasts, others were enthralled by arses or legs. But Kieran could write stanza after stanza on the allure of a woman's neck.

The lady in question turned to the person seated beside her, presenting her profile.

Damn—Kieran knew her.

He swore aloud, earning him more censorious looks from nearby guests.

Finn laughed again. "Mentally seducing our best friend's sister. A new nadir has been reached."

"Don't tell Dom," Kieran muttered.

Though Dom accompanied him and Finn for nightly carousing, Kieran was the one who truly engaged every variety of wickedness known in London. For all his boisterousness, Dom remained on the side, placing bets, bellowing songs, yet eschewing female company. He *did* have a habit of getting into spontaneous brawls.

Given that Dom knew exactly what kind of a rogue and scoundrel Kieran was, he'd never countenance Kieran contemplating debauchery with his younger sister.

As if sensing Kieran's salacious regard on her, Celeste Kilburn turned in her seat, her gaze catching his. Her eyes widened slightly, then she offered him a tentative smile.

He did his best to return it as though he hadn't been mentally disrobing and seducing her moments earlier. It was a neutral smile, verging on fraternal. Several years ago, Celeste had returned from finishing school as a striking woman, no longer a girl. From the time of her debut to now, she was also the model of proper decorum, faultless in her behavior.

He always made certain to give Celeste a wide berth. Doing so remained the only thing in the whole of Kieran's existence that could be considered wise or safe.

Celeste tipped her head toward the front of the church, and he followed her direction, expecting to see her brother standing in front of the altar. That was usually the way with grooms, or so he believed in his limited experience, since he was never invited to weddings—or anywhere where respectable people congregated. Today was his first sortie as a groomsman, since Simon had asked a friend from Oxford to be his attendant, so he knew little about his responsibilities in this arena.

Instead of seeing Dom standing nervously but eagerly in his nuptial finery, awaiting the appearance of his bride, Kieran only saw the robed vicar. The vicar *did* appear somewhat uncertain, his attention shooting back and forth between something behind him before returning to the crowd, offering the assembly a smile.

It was the reassuring quality of that smile that gave Kieran pause. Just what was the vicar trying to reassure everyone of?

Warily, with Finn beside him, Kieran approached the vicar. He half expected the older man to glow with holy righteousness, or perhaps smell of frankincense, but the bloke was an ordinary man who had missed a tiny patch of whiskers underneath his ear during his morning shave, and he smelled of the starch of his robes mingled with mundane sweat.

"Something amiss, Reverend?" Finn asked.

"You seem to be short one groom," Kieran added.

"Nothing at all is amiss," the priest said heartily. Then, in a voice low enough so that only Kieran and Finn could hear it, he added, "Are you two . . . gentlemen . . . closely acquainted with Mr. Kilburn?"

"If by close," Kieran answered, "you mean have I seen him drunkenly challenge three sailors to a brawl and win? The answer to that is yes."

The priest stammered and turned lobster red, as Finn choked on a laugh.

"I'm also his attendant," Kieran added.

Once he had recovered enough to speak, the reverend whispered, "The groom is faring poorly. I put him in the vestry to collect himself, but when I suggested summoning a member of his family to assist him, he vehemently declined. Well, I assume that by throwing a footstool at my head, he was declining my offer."

Though lobbing small pieces of furniture at holy men did sound like Dom, doing so on his wedding day raised an alarm.

"Perhaps Mr. Kilburn might respond better to his groomsmen," the priest continued.

"Take us to him," Kieran said.

He and Finn followed the reverend through a small door near the chancel, and then through a narrow hallway, before they reached another door. Crashes and swearing came from inside, and a noise that sounded like a man attempting to hurl his body against something heavy.

The vicar shot Kieran and Finn a worried look, most likely concerned that his vestry—whatever that could be—was in the process of being destroyed. He knocked on the door gently.

"Mr. Kilburn," the reverend said tentatively. "It's Reverend Hodgson, and—"

"Piss off," Dom shouted within. "I don't want any of your homilies, and your wine is swill."

Reverend Hodgson blanched.

"Let me handle this." Kieran placed his hand on the vicar's shoulder and urged the man away from the door. He pounded his fist against the wood and bellowed, "Dom. It's Kieran and Finn. Stop acting like a ruddy ass and open the sodding door."

There was a long pause, before his friend muttered a grudging "Come in."

"Best to wait with the congregation, Reverend," Finn said.

The man shot Finn a grateful nod before dashing away, seeking sanctuary in his own church. Once the vicar was gone, Kieran opened the door—slowly, in case Dom had gotten his hands on some of the church's silver and attempted to hurl it at Kieran's or Finn's head.

Cautiously, Kieran stepped into the vestry and let out a low whistle. "I thought the damage you did to the Twin Bastards Taphouse was bad."

"Jesus, Dom," Finn added, "did you *kick* this bookcase apart?"

There was no answer except a low, animal groan that originated from a man crouched in a corner of the chamber. The man had to be Dom because few people with such massive shoulders wore exquisitely tailored coats straight from Bond Street. Those shoulders were a legacy of Dom's formative years spent laboring in the London docks.

"Fucking bloody hell," Dom growled without rising. "What a goddamned disaster."

It was a measure of how agitated Dom had to be because he'd reverted to the rough Cockney accent his family had tried to erase from their speech. The Kilburns had been mostly successful in eradicating traces of their humble beginnings, but when Dom was deep in his cups or especially upset, he reverted to the pronunciation he'd spoken with for the first eighteen years of his life.

"Ain't you going to chastise me for cursing in a church?" he threw over his shoulder.

Kieran chuckled. "If you're seeking penance, you've invited the wrong brothers into the vestry." He approached his friend warily, as one would approach a maddened bull. The question remained whether or not Kieran would have to shoot Dom to put him out of his misery. "Done a fair job of leveling the church, though, so I commend you for that."

"I don't possess the observational brains of a Bow Street runner," Finn said slowly, picking up a few pieces of a shattered table, "but it appears you're a trifle agitated."

Dom made another bestial noise.

Carefully, as if he was truly facing a feral animal, Kieran laid his hand upon Dom's shoulder. Dom immediately shook free of his touch.

"Don't be kind to me," he snarled. "Don't you fucking dare be kind to me. I don't goddamned deserve it."

Kieran shared a mystified, worried look with his brother. Given that Finn made and lost fortunes at the gaming tables by hiding his emotions behind an unreadable facade, the fact that he didn't bother to hide his concern served to ratchet up Kieran's own unease.

Kieran drew in a breath, trying to catch a whiff of spirits that surely wafted up from his friend. If Dom was cup-shot, it might explain his behavior, since, with enough strong drink in him, he had a tendency to become even more pugnacious. Mystifyingly, no smell of whisky or gin clung to him.

However, a touch of alcohol might help steady what surely had to be a common case of anxiety before a wedding. Reaching into the inside pocket of his coat, Kieran pulled out a slim flask and tapped it against Dom's back. "A better medicine than being bled."

Dom took the flask in his shaking hand and swiftly downed a swig before he handed it back to Kieran, who took his own sip before offering it to Finn.

"Don't drain it, you son of a bitch," Kieran muttered as his brother tipped his head back to drink deeply.

"How dare you call our mother a bitch," Finn said, throwing the now-empty flask at Kieran, who snatched the vessel before it struck his chest.

A clock on a shelf struck a quarter to the hour. Given that the wedding was supposed to happen in fifteen minutes, the fact that the groom was hunkered in a ravaged vestry and continued to make incoherent sounds of distress did not bode well. A little inducement to get started might be in order.

"You should see Willa," Kieran said cheerfully. "Pretty as a raven against a snowfield. All this turmoil will have been forgotten once she's your wife."

At the mention of his future bride's name, Dom leapt to his feet, and threw his fist into a nearby cabinet. The furniture trembled and listed, but Kieran shoved it upright before it could collapse.

"It's a mistake," Dom growled. "This whole thing is one enormous sodding mistake."

For a moment, Kieran was stunned into silence.

"Like hell it is," he finally said. "You and Willa are mad for each other. Have been for years, even before her come out. Whenever she walks into a room, you stare at her like a lion eyeing a gazelle. Unless . . ." He straightened as an alarming prospect struck him. "You don't want her anymore."

"I'd kill for her," Dom snarled.

Kieran silently exhaled. At least there was no shortage of deep emotion between his friend and Willa. Since childhood, Kieran had witnessed the distance between his parents, and their icy disdain for each other. They never addressed each other directly, and when they did, it was always "my lady" or "my lord," but never their names of John or Aoife. Only when Kieran overheard a pair of housemaids gossiping did he learn that the match between an English earl and an Irish heiress had begun as a tempestuous love match, until in time they'd come to despise each other.

He'd had vague memories of his parents' loud arguments, which had terrified him as a small boy. But by the time Willa had been born, his mother and father had barely acknowledged each other. That selfsame chill frosted the entire family. Simon had been treated decently, as he was the heir, but Finn and Kieran were afterthoughts—which was fine because it permitted Kieran all the freedom he desired.

Willa, though, was like a flame burning through the frost. She didn't sit in the biting silence that reigned in the family, and was surprisingly adored for it. Whomever she was going to marry would have to be able to hold his own, or else be flattened like so much grass beneath her bootheel. Dom seemed to be the perfect match for her.

As the daughter of an earl, Willa *had* to marry, yet there was no expectation for Kieran to do the same, and thank God for that. How could he anchor himself to one woman when there were so many people out there in the world?

"Then go out there and marry her, you dolt," Finn said.

"I can't." Dom shuddered as he covered his eyes with his hand.

"Why the fuck not?" Kieran demanded.

"She's too goddamned good for me."

Kieran stared at his friend in disbelief. "This can't be the same man who swaggers into each ballroom as if every person within it isn't fit to button the fall of his breeches."

"It's the truth, you bastard," Dom snapped. "Even if she wasn't a sodding earl's sodding daughter, she's so much better than me. In all possible ways, she's better than me. I'm just some bloody longshoreman, and the things I've done—"

"Who hasn't got a bit of mud on them?" Finn asked mildly.

"You wouldn't understand," Dom threw back. "Both of you, to the manor born, never knowing what you got to do to survive. The depths you got to sink to in order to lift yourself up. How can I touch her, with these"—he held up his hands—"that have committed the worst crimes? How can I be the right kind of husband for her? The right kind of *man*? She's ruining herself by becoming my wife, and I can't live with myself, knowing that.

"Don't you see?" He turned imploring eyes to Kieran. "Marrying her is the worst thing I could ever do to her. She'll be miserable. Worse. I'll destroy her, and I ain't going to let that happen. But if I call it off, I'll be wrecking her reputation."

Kieran absorbed his friend's anguished words. The pain within them had been tangible, like running a hand through a bowl full of broken glass.

There were things about Dom's past Kieran didn't know, but he'd seen the raw hurt that flashed in his friend's eyes, and could only speculate that he'd endured some of life's worst. And it pained Kieran to see Dom so wretched on this day, which should have brought his friend happiness.

"A moment," Kieran said, motioning for Finn. When his brother stood close, he whispered, "I'd say he's talking rubbish, but he and Will *have* been driving each other mad. The fights. The tears. Do you think he's right? That she'd be miserable as his wife?"

"Entirely possible," Finn murmured. "And if the marriage is a catastrophe, there's no undoing it. She'll be shackled to him for life. Like Mother and Father."

"If she didn't want him, though, she could have cried off."

Finn fixed Kieran with a dry look. "And own that she'd made a mistake in her selection of bridegroom?"

The two brothers were silent as they contemplated their only sister ruining her life because she was too obstinate to admit an error in judgment. Kieran remembered the day she was born, and how he'd snuck into his mother's bedchamber to get a glimpse of Willa as she'd lain in her cradle. He'd been prepared to hate this new squalling creature who'd demanded the household's attention, but he'd taken one look at the red, wrinkled thing who, within hours of her birth, already tried to pick up her head—and that determination had made him fall in love with her immediately.

That hadn't prevented him from tormenting and teasing her mercilessly over the years, but between siblings, what was a little ink in the hand whilst napping? It didn't mean he wanted her to permanently lash herself to a man who might obliterate any chance of her happiness.

He'd seen what had befallen his parents, and the way that poison had leeched into every branch of the family.

Was that what awaited Willa? God, he prayed that wasn't so.

But . . . her reputation if Dom jilted her . . .

There was a tap at the door, and the priest said hesitantly, "Beg your pardon, sirs, but we're to begin the ceremony shortly."

A strangled groan tore from Dom.

"Five minutes," Kieran called through the door.

After a long pause, Reverend Hodgson said, "As you wish, sir."

Kieran understood what had to happen. It was appalling but perhaps there was no choice.

He and Finn shared another look, one fraught with the unspoken communication that they had shared over the course of their lives. For all Finn's ability to disguise his thoughts and emotions, Kieran had twenty-seven years of experience as Finn's younger brother, so he knew how to read Finn.

Should we? Finn silently communicated to Kieran.

There's no other choice, Kieran answered wordlessly.

Finn stared at Kieran. *There may be hell to pay.*

Better that than the alternative. Besides, we're doing Willa a favor. She'll be grateful.

In a whisper, Kieran added, "We can't consign our sister to what's surely a tremendous mistake, and following down the path our parents took."

"But she'll be too stubborn to take the necessary action to prevent it from happening," Finn added darkly.

Kieran nodded at his brother, then took a breath, preparing himself for what needed to come next.

"There wasn't room for all of us in the carriage without crushing Willa's gown, so Finn and I rode here this morning," Kieran said, turning to Dom. "My horse is in the mews."

The would-be bridegroom gaped at him. "The hell are you saying?"

"Move quickly, and don't attract attention to yourself." Kieran gestured toward a door that led to the outside.

Walking to the door, Finn pushed it open and glanced out. "No one's about so now's the time."

Dom swung his head back and forth between Kieran and Finn as he seemed to gauge whether or not the brothers were in earnest. Kieran gazed back, trying to imbue his expression with all the gravitas that the rest of Society seemed to believe he lacked.

A rare look of terror crossed Dom's face, followed by a flash of sorrow.

"The world will know *she* changed her mind," Kieran said. "It's a scandal, but not so bad as *you* jilting her."

Dom immediately nodded. "No one will blame her when you let everyone know I was a drunken lout with the manners of a starved dog."

"You *are* a drunken lout with the manners of a starved dog," Kieran noted.

"Say whatever you have to," Dom answered. "Drag my name through the mud, only make certain she emerges clean from this whole debacle."

"You've only heard the insults I've spoken to your face," Kieran replied. "Rest assured I will be inventive in the ones I say behind your back."

Dom's expression turned stony before resolve took its place. He strode to the threshold, pausing briefly to look back at Kieran and Finn. "It's the right thing to do. For Willa's sake."

"For Willa's sake," Kieran answered. She would be safe, and protected. He had to ensure that happened. Pointing toward the door, he said, "Go. Finn and I will take care of the rest."

"Tell Willa . . ." Dom swallowed hard. "Tell her . . ."

With one last glance, ripe with agony, he hurried out. A fine rain had begun to fall, staining the shoulders of what would have been his wedding coat as he raced toward the mews.

Finn shut the door, and crossed his arms over his chest. "Suppose we ought to tell Willa that she's rejecting her groom."

"She'll thank us. Surely Mother would have thanked anyone who kept her from marrying Father." Kieran glanced around the vestry. "Looks like Rome after being sacked by the Visigoths."

"The Vandals sacked Rome."

"Who *didn't* sack Rome?" Kieran glanced warily at the door that led to the church.

Something tightened along his limbs, and it was only as he headed out of the small, devastated chamber and toward where his sister awaited a wedding that was not going to take place, that he could name the feeling: dread.

Chapter 2

❖*❖

Two weeks later

Steps approached the door, and the handle rattled as the person on the other side fitted their key into the lock. From his position flanking the door, Kieran exchanged a nod with Finn, who stood on the other side of the entrance to the rooms they shared with Dom. Out of readiness, Kieran had deliberately worn some of his older clothing, lest one of his favorite garments be torn in the scuffle. His allowance as a third son was generous, but he'd rather not dip into it in order to repair an extant coat.

The door swung open, and though the light was low, there was no mistaking the size and shape of the man who crossed the threshold.

"Now!" Finn commanded.

Kieran flung himself at the man, and Finn did the same. Both he and his brother spent several days a week at a pugilism academy, yet even after extensive work maintaining their strength and physical condition, it took both of them to wrestle the newcomer to the ground.

"What the fuck is this?" Dom snarled. "Get off me."

"We'll stop," Finn panted, "if you agree to come quietly."

"Come quietly *where*?" Dom demanded. "What the blazes is going on?"

"The honor of your presence is requested." It wasn't easy to attempt an explanation when busy trying to avoid a behemoth's massive fists in significant parts of one's anatomy.

"If you agree to be docile," Finn added, evading an elbow to the windpipe, "we'll get up. And afterward, we'll all go to the Eagle for some pints, and everything will be rosy."

"After *what*?" Dom's struggles didn't cease.

"Can't tell you that," Kieran said. "But it's going to be quite simple and easy and utterly painless."

After a few more futile attempts to throw Kieran and Finn from him, Dom stopped struggling. "You could've just *asked* me to accompany you somewhere."

"Given that no one has seen you in a fortnight," Kieran said, his words breathless, "and the last time we did, you were running like hell away from the altar, we weren't certain what your response might be."

"An ambush in our shared rooms seemed the most sensible option," Finn noted, also winded.

"Entirely sensible," Dom echoed sardonically.

The fire popped in the grate as the three of them lay on the floor, valiantly attempting to regain their breaths. A moment passed, and then another. Finally, they staggered to their feet.

Briefly, Kieran debated whether or not to make his friend change his rumpled garments before they headed off on their errand, but now that he and Finn had managed to capture Dom, it was best not to dally. Already, Finn was scribbling a note, presumably to send ahead to the interested parties. The sooner Kieran and his brother delivered Dom to the destination, the sooner they could resume normal life.

"Best we move along," Finn said, heading to the door.

When they reached the pavement outside their rooms on Henrietta Street, Finn gave the note and a coin to a waiting boy, who raced off to deliver it, while Kieran hailed a cab.

"Don't think about it," he warned Dom as his friend eyed the stretch of road, clearly considering flight.

"I'm bigger," Dom said on a sigh, "but you two are faster."

A cab pulled up, and Finn called to the driver, "Cavendish Square."

Dom's brows climbed. "We're going to your family home? Won't *she* be there?"

"Willa's abroad," Kieran answered. "She left the day after the wedding."

Seemingly resigned, Dom got into the cab, with Kieran and Finn following. Silence reigned in the vehicle for a long while. It was early evening, and the lamplight cast flickering patches of illumination into the interior of the cab, giving Kieran more of an opportunity to study his friend. Dom truly did look like he'd been to hell, and had yet to make the return journey. Dark circles ringed his eyes. Within the span of a fortnight, he appeared to have dropped half a stone, his face haggard and gaunt, the image of a man who had loved and lost.

Watching others tumble into that morass of emotion was the closest Kieran had ever come to it. Truthfully, it wasn't that he couldn't feel it himself, but there was always a new person, a new sensation and adventure, and tethering himself to anyone for any extended period of time simply didn't make sense. Better to remain unencumbered, open and ready to experience anything that came his way, and whatever and whomever he sought out.

Love also had a disastrous habit of turning rancid, as he'd seen with his parents, and now with Willa and Dom. While the initial pleasure might be great, in the aftermath love cooled and congealed like spilled blood. The stronger one loved, the greater the despair that followed its inevitable retreat.

"How is she?" The question tore from Dom as if he'd had to lure it out like an animal from its hiding place.

"She's . . ." The last time Kieran had seen Willa had been a fortnight ago. He and Finn had gone to her as she'd waited in the vestibule, their family standing with her as they prepared to begin the ceremony. Finding the right words had never been problematic for Kieran, but at that moment, facing his little sister to tell her that he'd assisted in the flight of her groom, he'd been unable to speak. It hadn't made sense. He and Finn had acted in her best interest, and yet as he'd stared at Willa in her wedding finery, the veil obscuring her face but the gauzy fabric rising and falling with her quick breaths, for the first time, he'd doubted whether or not they had done the right thing.

Willa had lifted her own veil and stared at him. Her face had been pale as paper, and written across that paper was terrible, icy resolve.

He'd wished she had railed at him. Thrown something as she shouted opprobrium. But she'd been still and quiet in a way he had never seen in all of Willa's twenty-three years.

"I'm sorry, Will," Kieran had managed to croak.

"Sorry? Sorry for what?" his mother had demanded, her Irish accent thickening with her distress.

"Dom is gone," Willa had said. "And Kieran and Finn helped him go."

"He says to tell everyone you called things off," Finn had answered.

"As if that makes everything better," the earl had snapped.

Willa hadn't spoken to him again after that. They'd left the church and she'd gone up to her room, not coming out all day and all night. In the morning, when Kieran and Finn had stopped by for breakfast, she'd left, with only a note from their parents saying they were seeing Willa off.

"I don't know how she is," Kieran answered, realizing that Dom waited for a reply. "If she's sent any letters home, none have been to me."

He shifted on the cab's seat, but the squabs were worn from countless passengers, and the uneasiness twisting in his belly remained.

"I'm to be met with a firing squad, I suppose," Dom said lowly.

"All I know is that we're to deliver you to the Green Parlor," Kieran said. "Though it's doubtful you'll be greeted by a row of rifles. My mother's fond of the wall coverings in the Green Parlor."

"Comforting," Dom muttered.

Yet surprisingly, when the cab stopped briefly to permit a wagon to pass, Dom didn't attempt to leap from the vehicle and run away. It was almost as if he was reconciled to whatever punitive measures were likely waiting for him. Or perhaps, in some way, he welcomed them.

A taut silence fell, and Finn attempted to fill the quiet with chatter about a new gaming hell that had just opened on Moreton Place in Pimlico. Kieran hadn't been to it yet, but he joined in the conversation. It was a way to pass the time, and kept his thoughts from shifting toward that morning in the church, and the awful stoicism on Willa's face when she'd learned that her groom was gone, and that he was responsible. But he'd done the right thing, saving her from a lifetime of misery. Hadn't he?

The cab finally stopped outside Wingrave House, and Finn tossed a coin to the driver as they emerged. From the street, the earldom's city residence radiated importance, evidenced in the lights that blazed from many windows. Kieran had never given the amount of illumination much thought, until the first time he'd brought Dom to his family's home, and his friend had cursed in wonderment that they could afford so many candles, and so much glass in the casements.

Of course, Dom's family's fortune nearly matched that of the earl, but he hadn't been born into wealth.

Kieran, Finn, and Dom marched up the steps that led to Wingrave House's front door, which opened to reveal Vickers, the butler.

Tension collected in helixes in Kieran's stomach, though he'd no reason to be uneasy. All he had been tasked to do was bring Dom, so his friend ought to be the anxious one. Yet that apprehension trailed after him as he walked the well-known hallways of his family home. He glanced at Finn striding beside him, but if his brother shared his discomfiture, he did his usual expert job of hiding it.

Kieran didn't envy his brother's ability to conceal how he felt. Unlike Finn, he didn't spend the majority of his time at the gambling tables, so he'd no need of such disguising. And life was simply too delicious to spend suppressing your responses to it.

Voices came from up ahead in the Green Parlor. It was a strange symphony of the smooth, cultured timbre of his father, his mother's more musical tones that still bore the lyricism of her native Galway, and the heavier, rougher angles of Ned Kilburn's East London cadence. At the sound of his father's voice, Dom's steps faltered, but he kept moving toward the parlor like a man unflinchingly determined to meet his fate.

Kieran stopped in the doorway of the chamber. His father stood in front of the fire, hands clasped behind his back in his typical posture, whilst his mother sat on the divan, with the usual amount of distance between herself and her husband. Neither of his parents greeted Kieran, and he realized that this was the first time he'd seen them since the wedding. They hadn't met for their weekly stilted Thursday night dinners after that day, and he'd received no summons.

"Father," Kieran said, coming into the parlor. "Mother."

Heavy lines bracketed the earl's mouth as he pressed his lips together, and his mother barely inclined her head to receive Kieran's kiss on her cheek. Ice crystallized along his spine. Relations between him and his parents had never been especially warm, yet this was a new tier of distance.

"Mr. Kilburn," Kieran added with a nod toward the other man.

The grunt that Ned Kilburn gave him was almost identical to Dom's. Though the elder Kilburn was approaching middle age, his shoulders remained wide as a marathon, and despite his costly clothing, it was an easy feat to imagine him hauling cargo in London's docks. The man had made his fortune leasing warehouses to shipping companies, his beginnings humble but his ambition extraordinary.

His glance at Kieran was icy, just as it was when Finn greeted him. Yet his eyes blazed when his son entered the parlor.

"Da," Dom growled.

Another grunt came from Ned Kilburn.

Kieran eyed the cut crystal decanter on a small table against the wall. It was decently full, and his father's cellar was excellent, but there wasn't time to down a glass. The sooner Kieran left this room, the easier he'd breathe.

"Our responsibilities end here," he announced. "Dom's been delivered, so I bid you all good night.

Finn, shall we?" He bowed, but the smirk he gave his parents surely undercut any of the bow's deference.

Yet as he and his brother made to leave, Vickers appeared in the hallway, closing the door in his face. Kieran stopped abruptly, blinking at the butler's disrespect. True, Kieran had never been a model of filial decorum, but the servants had always been polite and deferential, even after he and Finn had moved into their bachelor lodgings.

He pulled open the door to find two hulking footmen blocking his exit.

Spinning around, Kieran met the blisteringly cold stares of his parents. "You set a trap for three."

"Yet again with your dramatic pronouncements," his father clipped. "But, yes, my son, there's to be a reckoning. All of you, sit."

Dom slouched into a chair, and Finn draped himself on a divan, but Kieran remained standing. He planted his feet wide, folding his arms over his chest. His father's face pinched in displeasure—a look Kieran knew as well as he knew his own boots.

"I'm assuming the duo in the hallway are here to enforce your will," Kieran drawled. "Such physical intimidation is beneath you, Father."

"What *is* beneath me," the earl snapped, "is the fact that two of my sons assisted in their own sister's jilting." He glared in turn at Kieran, Finn, and Dom.

"The whole town's talking of what happened," the countess said tightly. "Fortunately, we were able to avert the absolute worst scandal by letting it be known that the groom arrived intoxicated to his own wedding, causing Willa to halt the ceremony."

Dom's expression remained stony, yet a muscle in his jaw flexed.

"Even so, it's on everyone's lips," the earl went on. "Surely you've noticed."

"The places I go aren't much concerned with the doings of polite society," Kieran noted. In the rare moments that he was out during daylight hours, he might have observed genteel folk steering wide of him and whispering to themselves, but that wasn't especially noteworthy.

"A good thing Lady Willa isn't suing for breach of promise," Mr. Kilburn added, glaring at his son. "She'd be well within her rights to do so. Instead, she's gone on holiday until the whole ruddy mess has quieted. Bad enough that we're not born into the gentry. Scandals like this only reflect poorly on folk like us."

"What the deuce were you thinking?" the earl demanded. "Causing a scandal of such immense proportions?"

"And hurting your sister so abominably," the countess added with a glare at her husband.

Mr. Kilburn threw in, "And leading my son into making such a bloody huge mistake?"

"I made my own decisions," Dom snarled.

"Abetted by these two overbred miscreants," Mr. Kilburn said sourly, shooting a look at Kieran and Finn.

A moment passed, and Kieran saw that the questions weren't rhetorical. When his parents stared at him, he blurted, "Why aren't you asking Finn? He's older."

"We know better than to expect anything intelligent from him," his father said dismissively. Though his mother almost never agreed with the earl on anything, she nodded at his disdainful comment.

Despite his parents' wounding words, Finn looked unperturbed, but Kieran knew better than to trust the lack of emotion in his brother's expression.

"Don't talk about Finn like that," Kieran said hotly, hating the way his parents spoke of and to Finn as though he were a dullard.

"Don't deflect," the countess replied. "What made you do such a horrendous thing as to aid Mr. Kilburn in jilting your own sister?"

"We were *helping.*" Kieran waved toward his parents. "It was clear that Willa and Dom were headed down the same disastrous path as you two. We had to keep that from happening."

His father reddened, and burning color also appeared in his mother's cheeks.

With a wary glance toward Mr. Kilburn, the earl said, "Our marriage is none of your concern."

Finn laughed bitterly, but said nothing, his gaze directed toward the middle distance.

"It's clear that we've let you all have your own way far too often," their father continued, "and the results were nearly disastrous. It's time for a remedy."

"Remedy," Finn said, sitting up with a frown.

"Ameliorate. Put to rights." Their father made an impatient noise, not an uncommon occurrence whenever he conversed with his second son. Kieran's father strode back and forth in front of the fire, and spoke in an uncompromising voice. "We've given you handsome allowances so that you haven't had to seek employment. Clearly, however, such indulgent actions have yielded a crop of thorough scoundrels. No longer. The time has come for all of you to reform, beginning immediately."

Before Kieran could open his mouth to object, Mr. Kilburn spoke. "It's a simple process. To demonstrate that you've changed for the better, you'll need to marry."

A disbelieving laugh escaped Kieran, and Finn swore under his breath. Dom was as still and wordless as granite.

"And not simply marry any jade you meet in the sordid places you habituate," the countess said. "Your brides must be *respectable.* That, above all. These women must be of the most faultless moral character with nary a reproach against them."

Kieran gave another stunned bark of laughter, causing both his parents to scowl.

"Me, marry." He chuckled. "Granted, neither of you are known for your wit, but surely you're jesting."

"No jest, my lad," Mr. Kilburn gritted. "Find yourself an upstanding wife, or else you're not getting a single ha'penny from your generous parents."

Kieran stared at the man, then swung to face his mother and father. Incredulously, he demanded, "You're cutting us off?"

"It's time you faced the consequences of your actions," the earl replied.

"And forced marriage to some debutante is the means by which this will happen," Kieran threw back. He shook his head. "Like hell."

His mother sucked in a breath at his foul language, but he'd be damned if his parents would coerce him into doing anything.

"Think you'll find yourself a profession?" his father jeered. "You're seven and twenty, Kieran. What skills do you have? You possess no abilities besides carousing and causing infamy wherever you go. Do you honestly think you could ever make a living from that poetry you used to scribble?"

"I'm more sodding adaptable than you've ever believed, *Father*," Kieran retorted. He barely prevented his hand from touching the small notebook he kept tucked in his inside coat pocket, filled with his latest verses. The last time his father had found such a notebook on him, the earl had thrown it into the fire.

"Language," his mother cried.

"Forgive me if I'm not employing my most polite and restrained discourse," Kieran said tautly. "But up until this moment, you've had no use for either Finn or myself. Suddenly, we're expected to heel like a pair of spaniels."

"We've tolerated your escapades but that tolerance is over," his father said, his back stiffening. "You and your siblings hounded me to divest from the Caribbean. I've done that. You insisted I support abolition. I've done that. Now it's your turn to do something for *me*."

"Acting in support of decency and humanity doesn't require compensation," Kieran answered.

His father's face was rigid. "The harm you've caused your sister—"

"I regret that," Kieran muttered.

"Doubtful," the earl said. "You act with no thought to repercussions, and that ends now. *Each* of you will find the aforementioned respectable brides or . . ."

Kieran steeled himself, calculating what possible threat his father could level that might make him accede to his parents' demands.

"*None* of you will receive a single cent more," Mr. Kilburn finished.

Kieran jerked as though someone had rammed an elbow between his shoulder blades. He stared at the earl and the countess, then Mr. Kilburn, barely hearing Finn's and Dom's string of profanities.

"All of you must find respectable wives," Kieran's father pronounced, "or you are all cut off. The rooms you keep, payment of your bills, your access to Wingrave House—completely gone. Further, you will inherit nothing upon my demise. The same goes for Dominic. When Mr. Kilburn passes, there's to be no bequest."

His head spinning, Kieran staggered toward the divan and sank down onto it, next to Finn. It was one thing to defiantly throw his parents' demands in their faces if it affected only him, but by refusing to obey, how could he consign his brother and best friend to penury? Outside of the bubble of London's elite, this was not an easy or comfortable world. It didn't give a rat's arse if you were an earl's third son. Either you scratched out a living or you drowned. Could he accept seeing his brother sink into poverty? Could he sleep knowing that Dom had risen from the direst penury only to be thrown back into it?

"Respectable brides aren't thick upon the ground like autumn leaves," Kieran croaked. "And none of us are welcome in venues where we'd find such paragons."

He could hardly remember the last time he'd made an appearance at a reputable ball—it had to have been at least five years, if not more, and any memories he had of it were muddled by time and the amount of spirits he'd imbibed before attending. He did have a vague recollection of attempting to filch one of the potted palms that lined the ballroom, and betting Finn that said plant would reach the bottom of the stairs within sixty seconds.

Sadly, he couldn't remember whether or not he'd lost that bet. Finn would recall, though. His brother's memory was always excellent.

"Your first task," his mother said, "is to determine some way to overcome the stains of your wickedness. If you want to demonstrate your adaptability, Kieran, now's your opportunity to do it."

"Meantime, my boy," Mr. Kilburn said to Dom, "you're to move back home. The decision to allow you to room with *them*"—he shot a sour glance at Kieran and Finn—"was the worst of my life."

Dom muttered, his jaw jutting forward belligerently, but he didn't argue with his father.

"Are *we* to return to the nest, as well?" Kieran asked acidly.

The earl gave an undignified snort. "This is your sister's home, too. She'd stay away indefinitely if she had to share a roof with you reprobates again. You can remain on Henrietta Street—for the time being."

Sour regret churned in Kieran's stomach. He'd truly believed that liberating Willa from marrying Dom had been to her benefit, sparing her their parents' fate, but clearly, she didn't share his opinion. Was it worth writing her, knowing that she'd likely consign his letter to the fire without even reading it?

"What are the chronological parameters of this edict?" Finn asked. "Assuming that your largesse can only last so long, what's it to be? Two years, three?"

"Twelve months from today," their father answered.

Kieran shot to his feet. "Madness. You expect us to go from social pariahs to upstanding husbands in one goddamned year?"

"Time constraints will provide necessary motivation," his mother said, tapping her fingers on the inlaid tabletop beside her.

Kieran glanced at Finn, who lifted his eyebrows slightly, signifying his resignation. When Kieran threw a look at Dom, his friend curled his lip as if to say, *What the fuck can we do?*

Burning cold fury coalesced in Kieran's chest as he turned back to his parents and Mr. Kilburn. They stared back at him, their expressions implacable. He could rail, he could tear the Green Parlor apart, but it wouldn't make a difference.

He had to face the icy, brutal truth. There truly was no alternative. He, Finn, and Dom would have to find respectable brides, or lose everything.

Trouble was, the only respectable young woman he could think of was Dom's sister, the extremely decorous Miss Celeste Kilburn. Aside from their transitory encounter at the disastrous and abortive wedding, he hadn't seen her and *would not* see her. She moved in dreadfully polite circles, and meeting with her would require a goodly amount of strategy and subterfuge.

It was a fortunate thing, though, that when it came to behavior, he possessed almost no scruples.

Chapter 3

❧*❧

Another day, another bloody shopping excursion.

Celeste Kilburn ought to be grateful, she truly should. She still had memories of the early years when the family had lived in Ratcliff, and the many nights when she'd gone to bed still hungry because supper had been one small pie divided amongst four people. She could still feel the cold of the floor on her bare feet because there hadn't been enough money to afford new shoes for her *and* Dom. Because Dom had been the one to work alongside Da, and Celeste remained at home helping with the piecework Ma took in, Dom had required the shoes more than she had.

Eleven years since they'd left that grinding poverty behind, Celeste owned so many pairs of shoes—including soft kidskin boots and delicate dancing slippers adorned with satin ribbons that could only be worn once before falling apart—she couldn't keep count of them all.

Da insisted she needed to be seen making purchases in Pall Mall at least twice a week, so here she was, standing at the counter of a shop, waiting for her unwanted shoes to be packed up.

"What acquisitions have you made today, Miss Kilburn?" a genteel female voice behind her asked.

"Nothing of consequence, Lady Jarrett." Tacking a polite smile onto her face, Celeste turned to face the baron's wife.

"Do satisfy my curiosity." Though her words sounded pleasant, the older woman's eyes were sharp and calculating.

Celeste forcibly relaxed her jaw rather than give in to the urge to clench it. "Please show Lady Jarrett what I've purchased," she said to the shopkeeper.

The man removed her slippers from their boxes and held them up for Lady Jarrett's inspection.

Removing a lorgnette from her reticule, the baroness studied Celeste's purchases. Celeste made herself breathe steadily in and out, as if she was perfectly calm and not at all afraid that her choices would be ridiculed by one of the ton's most discerning—nay, judgmental—figures.

"Quite satisfactory, and the blue satin with the cream ribbons are especially elegant," Lady Jarrett finally pronounced as Celeste silently exhaled. "I commend you for your use of such a restrained color palette. You should have seen the garish footwear Miss Findlay wore last week to the Earl of Ashford's ball." She shuddered.

The implication was clear: Miss Findlay's family had made their fortune in wall coverings. They, like the Kilburns, were not part of the aristocratic elite, and, as such, their every action was thoroughly scrutinized, down to the color of Eliza Findlay's shoes.

Celeste *had* wanted to pair the blue satin of her new slippers with persimmon ribbons, but thankfully, she'd gone with the more muted cream instead.

"I hope they will continue to meet your approval when I wear them at Lord Hempnall's musical recital," she answered.

"So long as they're paired with a suitably harmonious gown," the baroness answered with a cool little smile. She glanced at the shopkeeper. "I believe I have my own order to review."

"Right away, my lady." The man snapped his fingers and an assistant came forward to finish wrapping Celeste's purchases, while the proprietor himself led the baroness to a gilded and ornately upholstered chair.

"Enjoy the rest of your afternoon, Lady Jarrett," Celeste said once her bundles were packaged up and handed to her waiting footman. "As always, it was a pleasure to see you." *You cheerless martinet.*

Busy examining half a dozen pairs of shoes, the baroness gave a small, distracted wave of her hand.

Celeste exited the shop with her maid trailing after her, while her footman brought up the rear as he cradled her latest acquisitions. The encounter with Lady Jarrett had been typically harrowing, yet all Celeste could manage was the barest glimmer of excitement at the prospect of wearing her new slippers.

What did it matter? What did any of it matter? When you lay on your deathbed, and the priest gave you your last rites as mourners crowded around you, were you truly going to say with your last breath, "I never drank sparkling wine in one of Mongolfier's balloons, and I never had a torrid affair, but, by God, I owned so many shoes"?

She squeezed her eyes shut as Pall Mall traffic swirled around her.

"Miss Kilburn, I believe we have a one o'clock appointment at Madame Jacqueline's. She's promising some beautiful gowns for you, and plenty of gossip."

Opening her eyes, Celeste looked into the patient face of her maid, Dolly. They had been together for many years, ever since Celeste had left finishing school, and Dolly always knew when Celeste's mood turned gray.

"Not that you indulge in gossip, miss," Dolly added wryly.

"In the absence of my own scandals," Celeste answered, "other people's will have to suffice." She began to walk toward the dressmaker's, since it *was* almost one, and Celeste hadn't been able to adopt the genteel habit of lateness, especially where appointments with tradespeople were concerned. Playing loosely with others' valuable time was something she'd been incapable of doing. Fortunately, Dolly had stopped attempting to prevent her from being on time.

"Your brother makes enough scandal for both of you," the maid said, falling into step beside Celeste.

"With generous assistance from the Ransome brothers." Even though neither of the brothers would be near Pall Mall at this hour of the day, Celeste still lowered her voice to speak of them. Finn Ransome and Kieran Ransome didn't give a fig about gossip—as evidenced by how often their exploits filled the pages of the scandal rags—but she didn't want word to reach them that their close friend's sister had been spreading tales about them.

Doubtful that they'd care. Especially not Kieran.

Merely thinking his name made Celeste's belly flutter, which was preposterous. During the few times she'd crossed his path, Dom's friend barely acknowledged her existence beyond a polite nod and perhaps a respectful "Miss Kilburn." That was all, and while it was somewhat dispiriting to be considered so utterly unworthy of interest, it was for the best. Wherever Kieran Ransome went, infamy followed, and her family had gone to great lengths to ensure that her reputation was above reproach.

More's the pity.

A trip to Madame Jacqueline's was supposed to be the cure for ladies' despondency, and Celeste tried to lift her spirits when the dressmaker's storefront appeared ahead.

The bell chimed as she entered the shop. She was greeted by the scent of rosewater and a cheerful chorus of French as madame herself came forward, trailed by an assistant.

"Mademoiselle Kilburn," the modiste sang. "Prompt as always."

Celeste attempted a smile, but her spirits sank lower. It didn't help her current dour humor to think that, aside from her charity work, every aspect of her life remained regimented and completely devoid of deviation or any sort of variety. Per Ned Kilburn's dictum, Tuesdays and Fridays were for shopping.

Her father had made his fortune, and they'd moved from Ratcliff to Cheapside and then finally to Hans Town, their clothing growing steadily finer, their servants more plentiful. Celeste, like Dom, had been given elocution lessons to cleanse all traces of her East London accent, and then she'd been packed off to finishing school to ensure that she comported herself with as much dignity as any aristocrat—even *more* dignity, in truth. One had to rigidly adhere to proper conduct when your money was newly made and not the byproduct of landed estates.

Her teachers at finishing school had said as much. Daughters of the nouveau riche were held to a higher standard, lest they accidentally reveal their humble origins.

So Celeste had been told, and been impelled to live her life in the most respectable manner. She went to the same places every day, saw the same people, talked about the same things, and never, never, never did anything that could be considered remotely improper. Not even wear blue slippers with persimmon ribbons.

She'd been born into poverty, but now she lived in a cage. Granted, it was a cage full of beautiful things and abundant food, but it was nevertheless a cage. All she could do was let her song float out between the bars, yet no one heard her tune.

"We have the gowns you ordered," Madame Jacqueline continued, unaware that her client stared down the barrel of a crisis of existence. "Please, will you try them on?"

Was it Celeste's imagination, or did the dressmaker and Dolly exchange a look?

It *had* to be Celeste's fancy, because nothing remotely interesting ever happened to her, including some kind of secret between her modiste and her maid.

Familiar with the layout of the shop, Celeste headed toward the back where the fitting area was located. There was a row of alcoves, each shielded by a heavy curtain for the customers' privacy as they disrobed. All three curtains had been drawn, however, which indicated that the alcoves were currently occupied.

"In here, Mademoiselle Kilburn," Madame Jacqueline cooed, gesturing to the last nook. "I have it reserved exclusively for you."

This was a new development, since the modiste rarely played favorites with her clientele, but it hardly signified. Celeste ducked around the thick brocade and stepped into the fitting alcove.

Only to come face-to-face with Kieran Ransome.

She bit back a yelp as he pressed a finger to his lips.

Her pulse thundering in her ears—it wasn't every day that she encountered astoundingly handsome rakes in a modiste's fitting room—she managed to whisper, "What in heaven's name are you doing?"

"Waiting for you." He flashed her a smile so devastating in its charm and attractiveness, she pressed herself into the corner of the little chamber.

And it *was* a very small area, barely more than five feet by five feet. Hardly any distance separated her from Kieran. He wasn't exceptionally tall, and possessed a lean frame, but he still managed to take up most of the space by sheer presence.

"How did you get back here?" she demanded lowly.

His smile widened. "They know me at Madame Jacqueline's."

"Little surprise," Celeste muttered. A man with Kieran's reputation was likely familiar with the fitting rooms of every ladies' shop between here and Paris. "And you bribed Dolly and madame, of course."

"Of course." The rascal actually winked at her, and her perfidious heart sped up in response.

"It's almost admirable, your network of cohorts and conspirators." She was rather impressed with how she managed to keep the giddiness from her voice, but it was not an inconsiderable struggle. She'd never been alone with Kieran Ransome before. Every part of her, from her body to her mind, was in eager disarray.

It truly *was* a problem that he was so handsome. He'd inherited his mother's black wavy hair and dark eyes, over which slashed a pair of dramatic and thick brows. His mouth was wide and full, as arresting as his other bold features, including a strikingly proportioned nose and hewn jawline.

Both Ransome brothers were exceptionally attractive, but it had always been Kieran who made her feel dizzy and breathless and aware of every inch of skin on her body.

She envied her brother for many reasons—his gender, which permitted him a freedom she could never have, and his ability to push against Society's constraints by doing whatever he pleased, whenever it pleased him. But she also envied Dom's time spent with Kieran Ransome. She could never hope to spend more than five minutes alone in Kieran's company, not if she wanted to maintain her own rigidly patrolled reputation.

Today, however, was proving the exception.

"I cannot fathom what might possess you to engage in such a complex scheme," she whispered.

"They aren't precisely throwing wide the doors to the Kilburn home," he answered. "Not to me, at any rate, and not in the current climate between our families."

"I do recall my father using some language to describe you that harkened back to his time on the London docks."

"I've earned every single one of Mr. Kilburn's epithets." A corner of Kieran's mouth hitched up. "And in such a pungent atmosphere, I deemed it wisest to reach you through more secretive means."

It was rather thrilling, to have him go through such lengths for *her*. And to be unescorted with him like this, so clandestinely.

Still, half a lifetime of behaving in the most circumscribed manner made her ask, "Are you certain you haven't mistaken me for one of your sophisticated paramours?"

"Impossible." His disbelieving laugh was *not* flattering, with all of its implications.

"Why seek *me* out?" She folded her arms over her chest.

His expression sobered. "You're aware of the ultimatum your father and my parents have placed on me, Finn, and Dom. That we all must find brides of good repute within a year or we're to be cut off."

"I'm aware."

How could she not be? Dom had moved back home a little over a fortnight ago, and thunderous arguments between him and their father had ensued. Since their mother had passed away five years ago, the lack of Ma's soothing, mitigating presence was acutely felt whenever Dom and their father were together. The trouble was that Dom and Ned Kilburn were far too much alike, and loved each other deeply, resulting in almost constant conflict. Though Dom was poised to join the family business, contention was ever present between father and son, especially because Dom seemed to enjoy flouting convention at every opportunity. His preferred methodology had been tearing a path through London's wilder corners with the Ransome brothers, but now that carousing had to come to a stop.

Not that it *had*, not for Dom.

"Then you understand my need for a respectable wife," Kieran said.

She held up her hands, warding him off. "*I'm* not going to marry you."

"Oh, *God*, no," he answered at once.

Well, that was also exceptionally unflattering.

"Dom knows precisely what manner of scoundrel I am. If I married you, he'd use my entrails as a necklace."

Peculiar how this statement made her feel a trifle less terrible.

"Of what benefit am I to you, then?" she asked.

He bent close to her, which, in an already confined space, brought him *very* near. His scent surrounded her, a thrilling mix of woodsmoke, leather, and herbs, and she could see how stubble already shaded his chin. If he bent just a little closer, she could kiss him.

Involuntarily, she dipped her tongue to her bottom lip. What would he taste like? Surely something forbidden, and delicious.

As if he could hear her thoughts, his gaze dropped to her mouth. She could have sworn that his eyes darkened, and the column of his throat worked.

And wouldn't *that* be thrilling? To be kissed by rakish Kieran Ransome in the fitting alcove of Madame Jacqueline's modiste shop?

He blinked, straightening, and disappointment thudded in her chest.

"You're the most respectable woman I know," he said.

"I'm the *only* respectable woman you know," she countered. "Not including your mother and sister."

"Which signifies," he persisted, "that it's a simple matter for you to gain entry into all of London's upstanding events, wherein a man might make the acquaintance of a substantial number of reputable, marriageable women."

She stared at him as his intent became clear. "You want *me* to get you into these gatherings."

He beamed at her, and she didn't want to be gratified that she'd pleased him.

"I haven't been invited or welcome at anything virtuous for years. But if *you* gain me entry, it will show Society that my reformation into an upstanding gentleman is well underway. It will also serve my purpose wherein I will be able to meet the sort of woman our families would approve of as a potential bride."

"I'm a means to an end." Impossible not to feel dispirited by Kieran's request. He had never truly seen her until she was useful to him, and only then as a stepping-stone to some other woman.

An immediate refusal sprang to her lips. Yet she didn't speak it right away as she contemplated how to tell him to *piss off* in her most ladylike manner.

In that silence, Kieran spoke. "You needn't give me your answer immediately. Although . . . sooner rather than later would be preferable, as I'm on something of a tight schedule."

"Given that you convinced my brother to flee the altar—yes, I learned the truth from Dom's own lips—and must now face the repercussions of your own actions, I hardly think you're in the position to make demands of me. *Your* injudicious behavior doesn't constitute *my* urgency."

He inclined his head. "Apologies. Would it help at all to consider that what I'm attempting to do will benefit Dom as well as myself?"

"Not especially. Pleas of your altruism don't ring quite true."

His smile flashed, and something that resembled respect gleamed in his eyes. "I'll take my leave of you."

"That would be for the best." She hadn't heard anyone rustling in the other fitting alcoves, so there was a chance they were empty, but she had tested her luck enough for one afternoon. If Kieran Ransome was spotted slipping out of this tiny space they currently shared, there was no doubt that scandal would follow.

Women had very little for themselves in this life. Their worldly goods were usually the property of husbands or male relatives. Their bodies counted as a man's property, as did any children. Females' reputations belonged to everyone. At the least, everybody seemed to care what happened to those reputations, no matter *who* that woman was.

Kieran Ransome might be considered a paragon of virility if he was seen coming out of her fitting room, while she would face ostracism and utter ruination.

"But be careful when you leave," she said pointedly.

"I always am."

"Untrue. I just read about your latest intrigue with Lady Selwin in *The Hawk's Eye*. Especially the part about you almost being shot by her husband as you fled her bedchamber."

Kieran lifted one brow, and she realized she'd revealed too much of her interest in him. Yes, she found him fascinating, but *he* didn't need to know that.

Clearing her throat, she glanced at the curtain, indicating that it was time for him to go.

He sketched an ironic bow, which was no small feat given the narrow confines of the space they shared, and then, after checking to make certain no one was about, disappeared behind the curtain.

Alone, she leaned against the wall and let out a shaky exhalation. Though it had been the most extensive exchange of words she and Kieran had ever shared, it hadn't been a very long conversation, and she half believed what had transpired had been merely the product of girlish infatuation combined with excessive fantasizing of all the scandalous things she'd like to do if she wasn't . . . who she was.

And now here was Kieran Ransome, with a proposition that was unfortunately the opposite of scandalous. She might as well be a lamppost or a bedside ewer, an object that fulfilled a purpose—but no one ever thought about what the lamppost or ewer desired for itself.

She did her best to put the encounter with Kieran Ransome from her mind as she finished her fitting at Madame Jacqueline's before heading home, as she always did after her usual shopping outings. At the least, after luncheon she would be able to spend several hours sorting clothing for an upcoming charity bazaar. *That*, in any case, was a worthwhile task.

Moments after she stepped into the foyer and handed Dolly her bonnet and gloves, her father approached.

"Showing them toffs we got as much blunt as they do." He nodded with approval at her footman laden with packages.

"How unexpected to see you home." She lifted up on her toes to kiss his cheek. "You're usually at your offices at this hour."

Would her father know that she'd just been ensconced in a fitting room with Kieran Ransome? It wasn't as though there was a scarlet handprint on her breast.

Even though Kieran hadn't touched her bosom, she glanced down just to be certain there was no telltale mark that she'd spent a good ten minutes completely alone with London's most notorious rake.

No sign of his presence was left on her—thank goodness.

"Came by to pick up a few papers," her father answered. "A good thing, too, because I met Lord Montford at our door. He's waiting in the parlor."

"Lord Montford?" She blinked. "The earl usually calls on Wednesdays."

"His mother wanted you to come for tea today and try her cook's new recipe for iced biscuits." Her father chuckled. "Look at us now, eh? A marchioness impulsively inviting you over for tea like you were already part of the family."

"But . . . but . . ." Celeste frowned at this unwelcome news. "I'm supposed to head to the meeting hall and help sort clothing for next month's charity bazaar. I'll have to tell Lord Montford to send my regrets."

Her father's smug expression dropped away, and he appeared confounded. In a low, angry voice he hissed, "Do you think invitations from marchionesses are thick on the ground like fallen leaves? That they mean so little to people like us that we can shove them aside?"

People like us. Poverty and hard work, versus inherited wealth and privilege. It always came down to that, didn't it?

"Lady Stretton will understand." Celeste patted her father's hand, but he snatched it away from her.

He held up a warning finger. "Listen, my girl. Our reputation in Society is already precarious. Dom's marriage to an earl's daughter would have gained us more security, but that's thrown into the rubbish. It's a dangerous waltz we dance with the ton, and *you're* the Kilburn everyone sees on the dance floor. Being engaged to Lord Montford protects us—"

"Not officially," Celeste corrected, but that wasn't the right thing to say, because her father's face darkened.

"Officially unofficially engaged," he snapped. "Lord Montford told me just now that he plans on proposing just before the Season ends."

Something invisible wrapped around Celeste's throat and tightened. The end of the Season was less than two months away, and her acceptance of Lord Montford's suit was clearly a foregone conclusion. It didn't matter what *she* wanted for herself. It never did.

"Think of the honor, my girl," her father added. "He's *the* one every grasping mama wants for her daughter. And if you don't land him now, be assured there are dozens of chits ready to wed him."

When Celeste still didn't speak, her father leaned close. "All the sacrifices I made, working twenty hours a day, even on Sundays, hardly seeing your mother and you kids, the deals I made to fight my way to the top and send you to finishing school and buy this fine house—it was all for *this*. For *you*."

"*Is* it for me?" she asked plaintively.

Her father's brows drew into a heavy vee. "Think of it, gel. You'd be a countess, and then a marchioness. The girl who sewed fancy ladies' petticoats wouldn't have to lift a finger for the rest of her life. That's what I want for you." His voice thickened. "I remember how

I'd come home after midnight and you'd be curled up on that tiny pallet on the floor, and I'd brush your hair out of your face and pray to whoever was in charge of such things that one day, you'd have a decent bed with clean sheets and you'd be just as fine a lady as those women you sewed petticoats for. And that's almost here, gel. It's almost yours."

Celeste swallowed around the edges of whatever had lodged in her throat. She was an ingrate, surely, to desire more for herself than endless leisure. It beckoned to her now, that perpetual ease and privilege. In less than two months' time, her path would be set forever, and that's what she was supposed to seek. Wasn't it?

Whatever she desired for herself, that didn't signify. Once her father had made his fortune, her path had been set, and there was no straying from it, no matter what other roads she wanted to take. She was like a blinkered carriage horse, except she could just glimpse possibility beyond the blinders—which made it all the harder to relentlessly plod forward, driven onward by her father's doggedness to gain the ton's acceptance.

"I'll meet Lord Montford in the parlor," she said, attempting to sound pleased rather than resigned. "I'll tell him how honored I am by the invitation, and if his mother wouldn't mind postponing our tea until tomorrow so I may attend to my duties for the charity bazaar."

"You'll *accept* the marchioness's invitation," her father corrected. "The charity bazaar can wait."

"Da." She took a deep breath, fighting to keep her

tone even. "When I wanted to establish a foundation that helped the people of Ratcliff, you said no—"

"We don't need any association with that place," he answered tightly. "It's our past, but we're looking to the future."

"At the least, let me go today and do the work I promised." She inhaled as she battled frustration. It had been a bitter disappointment to abandon her hopes to assist the families of her old neighborhood, yet she'd done so, burying her own ambition to help her family.

"Go up to the parlor now, and tell Lord Montford you'll join the marchioness presently." Her father folded his arms across his broad chest, the sign that the argument was settled—in his favor, as usual.

The very thing that had ensured Ned Kilburn's financial success was the same quality that made it impossible for Celeste to deny her father's command. Besides, Da and Dom were counting on her to keep their family circulating through the highest ranks of Society. Declining Lady Stretton's invitation might insult both the marchioness and Lord Montford, imperiling the Kilburns' standing and dashing her father's hopes, when he'd done and given up so much for her and her brother.

The entryway of their home in Hans Town could contain their old room in Ratcliff. There were parlors and chambers she never used, and spare bedrooms that no one slept in. And yet, for all the size of this house, the walls now loomed close and it felt impossibly cramped.

"Yes, Da," she said at last.

His dark expression cleared, and he beamed fondly at her as he patted her cheek. "There's my Star. I'm back to my offices, but I'll see you for supper tonight."

Before she could say anything more, he strode away.

She turned to the mirror hanging in the foyer and smoothed her hair, trying to make herself look as composed and flawless as her father wanted. Her locks always were a little unruly, which was why Dolly had to use fistfuls of pins to keep everything straight and tidy, the hair of a perfectly respectable young lady.

On their own, the pins didn't weigh very much, but when employed en masse, they were impossibly heavy. Her scalp ached every night when Dolly slid them from her hair, and never fully recovered by the morning when it was time to put them back into place.

A smiling, familiar face appeared behind her, and she made herself smile in return as she turned to face Lord Montford.

He was a tall man, and she had to tip her head back slightly to look into his blue eyes. There were small lines around those eyes, as befitting someone who spent a goodly amount of time in Rotten Row on the back of a horse, or shooting the birds beaters scared from hedgerows. In truth, Lord Montford *was* an attractive man beyond his fortune and title, yet her heart didn't speed up whenever he was near. He never gave her the roguish grins or winks that came so easily to Kieran Ransome, the ones that made her fluttery and warm.

"Forgive me for not waiting for you in the parlor," he said with the smallest of bows.

She curtseyed. "I was on my way to join you, my lord."

"I keep insisting you call me Hugh, Celeste." He chuckled indulgently. "After all, you're almost my wife."

We're not even engaged, she thought with annoyance.

"However," he continued, "I grew impatient to pass on my mother's generous invitation. I know that you typically do charity work on Tuesdays after your shopping, but of course you'll join Mother and myself since she's most eager for you to try her cook's recipe for lemon biscuits."

"Surely her opinion on the matter of her vases carries more weight than mine," Celeste objected.

"She's always eager to guide you in matters of connoisseurship and taste," he said warmly. As if bestowing a great compliment, he added, "Mother sees your potential and would hate for you to waste it."

Oh, for fuck's sake. Celeste opened her mouth to tell Lord Montford what she'd like to do with her *potential*, but how could she, when her father had made it quite clear how critical it was to maintain cordial relations with the earl.

She fought to inhale, but the cage around her chest made it almost impossible to breathe. Everything pressed in on her, smothering her, and there was nowhere to run, no means to keep herself from being crushed. In the end, she *would* be pulverized, as her father and Lord Montford gathered around the dust of her remains to congratulate themselves on their accomplishments.

There had to be some way out. Some means of relief—even if it was only temporary.

"I'll have my carriage brought around," he said, "to convey you to my home."

"Very kind of you." Evidently, there was no concern that Celeste might refuse.

His responding smile made it clear that he, too, thought he was being very kind.

Dolly approached with her bonnet and gloves, clearly having eavesdropped on the conversation between Celeste and her father. As Celeste donned the items, she kept her expression mild and pleasant while her mind spun.

Once she returned home from tea with Lady Stretton, she would write Kieran Ransome with instructions as to where and when to meet.

The scoundrel wanted her for her spotless reputation, and nothing more. But perhaps . . . just perhaps . . . he might have something that *she* wanted . . .

Chapter 4

❖*❖

Kieran eased past the queue of people outside Catton's bakery, and he couldn't be certain whether or not their astounded looks in his direction were because the customers believed him to be cutting the line, or because Kieran Ransome was rarely seen in such an upstanding, sanctioned place.

He paused just inside the threshold of the famed pastry shop, next to the sign that proclaimed that all sugar used in the production of its cakes and biscuits was exclusively grown by free men. The air was laden with vanilla, butter, and the aforementioned sugar, but equally thick in the atmosphere was women's chatter. To be sure, there were some men enjoying a pot of tea and some iced cakes, but largely the patrons of Isabel Catton's shop were female.

Kieran recognized some of the women—young widows and more adventurous married ladies—yet many of them were unknown to him, which was precisely his dilemma.

Hopefully, today would set him on the right path toward remedying that situation.

Glancing around the pastry shop, he searched for one woman in particular. Occasionally, he caught the eye of a lady, who either stared at him in affronted surprise or else lowered her lashes in the timeless sign of a female who liked what she saw.

Celeste Kilburn's surprising note had arrived yesterday afternoon stipulating that he was to meet her today at Catton's. He'd truly believed after their discussion in the fitting room that the subject was closed. Yet in a neat and precise hand, she'd given him instructions to convene at this bakery. He'd smiled at the addendum at the bottom of her note: *Dress like a respectable gentleman.*

At last, he spotted her seated alone at a table, though her maid hovered nearby, chatting with another servant.

Something within his chest knocked against his ribs. Peculiar.

Yesterday had been the longest amount of time he'd been in Celeste Kilburn's company. Certainly, he'd never stood in such close proximity to her. God knows he'd done far more outrageous things in his life besides have a chaste discussion with a woman in a fitting room, or meet her in broad daylight in a busy bakery. Seeing her across the room was, in truth, hardly noteworthy. And yet there went that thudding of his heart.

Celeste caught sight of Kieran, and while she didn't precisely smile, her heavy-lidded hazel eyes brightened when she recognized him. She was already a striking person, with high cheekbones and a stubborn chin, but to witness how excitement made her light up from within transformed her into someone he couldn't look away from.

Come to think of it, he'd never witnessed her exhilaration before. She often looked mildly disinterested, or her gaze was faraway, as though she had taken herself somewhere else . . . somewhere more interesting than the place she was at the moment.

Not so now. She appeared very much engaged in the present, and her gaze was keen as she watched him approach her table. She ran her hand across her brow, smoothing her reddish brown hair.

He paused in front of her, removing his hat and holding his arms at a slight angle as he presented himself for inspection. "Have I met your requirements? You said to come looking as much like a respectable gentleman as possible."

Her gaze glided down him, from the top of his head, along his face, down his torso—lingering slightly at his groin—and then lower. He *was* wearing his most sedate garments, and not one of his favorite flamboyant waistcoats. For the love of Christ, he'd even shaved this morning.

Celeste's perusal was thorough, as if she saw past all his temporary polish to the uncivilized man beneath.

The room was suddenly rather hot. He tugged at his neckcloth.

"It's sufficient," she allowed. "I needed to see whether or not you could, in fact, *look* the part of someone who's respectable."

He pulled out a chair and dropped into it as elation careened through him. "Then you'll help me?"

"For a price."

He frowned. This was not what he'd anticipated.

She clearly read his confusion, because she said, "You truly assumed I would assist you simply out of the munificence of my heart? Don't answer that. I can see that's precisely what you believed."

"I thought ladies commonly practiced charity."

"I'm not a lady," she pointed out. "Certainly not by birth."

"By action and public perception, however, you are certainly one. The work you do with sundry altruistic organizations is proof."

"Which brings us to why, precisely, you've requested my aid." She nodded as a server approached with a tray laden with a pot of tea, two cups, and a plate of miniature cakes. As the refreshments were laid out, Celeste remained silent, though her gaze shot to him when he chuckled.

"That's a rueful sound," she said when the server left.

"My domestication has already begun," he noted. "When I have meals like this, there's likely whisky in that teapot, and the cakes are baked into erotic shapes."

She selected one tiny dome-shaped cake and set a glacé cherry atop it so that the confection resembled a woman's breast. "That should make you feel more at ease. As for the spirits, I believe we can wring brandy out of the fruitcake."

A startled laugh burst from him. Since she'd returned from finishing school, he'd found Celeste physically alluring, but never had he anticipated that she possessed a wicked wit. What a delightful development.

"What *is* your price?" he asked, intrigued.

Briskly, she said, "I will gain you entry to all the best parties, and introduce you to the most respectable and marriage-minded women. In exchange . . ." She leaned closer and lowered her voice. "In exchange, *you* must take me to all the places where disreputable, scandalous people go."

Stunned, he stared at her, the voices surrounding them fading away. She simply gazed back at him, unblinking, as if insisting that a known scoundrel accompany her to London's most immoral venues was as ordinary as requesting another cup of tea.

He liked to believe that he had a certain facility with language. He loved the sounds of words, their shapes and textures, and their infinite variety. Yet now all he could do was stammer, "You *want* to go to such places?"

"Why wouldn't I?" She tilted up her chin.

"Because . . . because you're . . . *you*." When she continued to gaze levelly at him, he went on, "Gaming hells and dissolute parties aren't where good girls go."

"There's so much in that sentence I hate." She made a face as if eating an unripe persimmon. "Firstly, I am three and twenty, and well past girlhood. Secondly," she said, planting her gloved hands on the table, "I am *so tired* of being 'good.' Everything about it is suffocating. But you wouldn't know anything about being forced into a tidy little pen, like a prized pig. You and your brother and my brother can do whatever you please, whenever it pleases you."

He could hardly believe the diatribe pouring from her in a hushed, urgent whisper. Still, he felt compelled to say, "Not anymore."

She rolled her eyes. "Up until now, and that would have continued in perpetuity if you and Finn hadn't idiotically shoved Dom out the vestry door. Yet the fact remains," she continued determinedly, "that you've lived a life completely unencumbered by expectation and obligation, unlike me. For years, I've heard and read about your exploits but haven't ever had an exploit of my own. But if you agree to my terms, all that is going to change."

A shocked, pleased laugh burst from him. It was more of a shout than a decorous chuckle, which caused many heads to turn in his direction. In response, he leaned back in his chair, his legs sprawling wide, the picture of insolent indolence.

"I'd no idea," he said after absorbing her words. "Never had I suspected that beneath Celeste Kilburn's sedate exterior beat a wild heart."

"There are many things about me you don't know," she answered crisply.

"So it appears."

"If you truly want to amend your public reputation," she said, her brow arching, "you'll stop your impression of a dissolute rogue and sit up like a gentleman."

His first impulse was to slouch lower, but she did have a point. With great reluctance, he straightened in his chair and planted his feet on the floor. He exhaled once he'd corrected his posture. This wasn't so bad.

"There's the matter of your reputation," he pointed out. "If I take you, an unmarried woman, to some of London's more notorious places, your standing will be damaged. Even if that damage isn't irreparable, it would still take considerable time to remedy it."

"A disguise shall conceal my identity," she replied primly.

"You've given this thought." Which made it all the more difficult to dissuade her from holding him to his end of the bargain.

"Considerable thought." She leaned forward, her expression grave. "I don't expect you to understand how much I *need* this. But I do, Kieran. Very much."

He studied her, this woman he hardly knew. Her eyes were filled with yearning and demand, the depths of which he hadn't expected. She was Celeste Kilburn, societal paragon, as esteemed as she was proper. Yet the stipulations she insisted upon indicated that there was far more simmering beneath her reserved surface than he'd ever believed.

Resolve also shone within her gaze.

"If I said no . . ." he ventured.

"Then our business with each other is concluded," she answered firmly. "You'll have to find some other woman of irreproachable character to gain you entrance to Society."

He rapped his knuckles meditatively on the tabletop as he pondered. She'd been made aware of the risks, but was determined to carry out her scheme. He truly *didn't* know any woman who could vouch for his character, so his alternatives to help pave his way into the good graces of the ton were exactly nothing.

"What choice do I have?" he said under his breath. Then, louder so she could hear, "I agree to your terms."

"Excellent," she said with the kind of trim propriety that didn't indicate the scandalous nature of their bargain. She pressed her lips together as if fighting a smile.

Relief poured through him, cool and reviving. Having Celeste's assistance would be invaluable, and he could marshal himself for the time it took to locate a suitable bride. Yet the relief was tempered by the fact that he'd just entered into an outrageously improper agreement with his best friend's sister.

If anything was to happen to her, if her reputation *was* hurt because of this . . . no amount of penance could undo that.

He'd simply have to be very, very careful. For the first time in his life.

She studied him. "Do you *want* to marry, or is your bride hunt impelled by no other reason than our families' ultimatum?"

"In truth," he said, tracing his finger on the lacy table covering, "I've no eagerness to wed."

"A rake's prerogative," she murmured. "Why tether yourself to one person unless by necessity?"

"You must be getting second thoughts about me," he said with the smile he used often to get what he wanted.

She opened her mouth, then closed it. Debating. "You'll always give me second thoughts and third ones, and fourth ones, too. But I'll do what you ask, so long as you do what *I* require in exchange."

He exhaled, then held out his hand. Yet she shook her head slightly, and he withdrew it.

"When are we to begin?" he asked. "Soon, I hope. The choice of respectable venue is at your discretion, though I believe a—"

"Before that is settled," she interrupted, "we will begin with you taking me somewhere scandalous."

He frowned. "Ought you take me to a reputable gathering first?"

"As you said, I'm a *good girl*, which makes me trustworthy. You, however, are a scoundrel and utterly unreliable." Her lips curved beguilingly.

"I showed up relatively on time for this appointment," he pointed out.

"One self-serving act of dependability hardly negates a lifetime of suspect behavior." She took a sip of tea, then removed her glove to break off a piece of iced cake and nibble on it. He tried not to watch her fingers touching her lips.

"I'd say you slander me," he drawled, "but everything you've said is accurate."

"Then you understand why I need a show of good faith that you'll do what you've promised." She narrowed her eyes. "However, you never intended to uphold your end of our bargain."

He smiled ruefully. "Injurious as your words are, they are also correct. My hope had been that you'd get me in the door at some sanctioned event, and I'd make the necessary connections to obviate our arrangement."

"Once a scoundrel . . ." she said with annoyance.

To prove his point, he took the cake that now resembled a breast and licked off the icing before popping the whole confection in his mouth.

She no longer looked irritated. A fascinating stain of pink appeared in her cheeks, yet she didn't avert her gaze or fidget.

Arousal shot through him, hot and direct as an arrow.

He frowned in surprise. Damn. There were few things he denied himself, but this growing interest in Celeste Kilburn was going to be one of them. Dom would be highly displeased with a known rake and rogue like Kieran sullying his sister.

"Tell me," he said, brushing crumbs from his lips, "how long can you lend me your assistance on this endeavor?"

Her expression darkened. "Until the end of the Season."

"What happens then?"

"It doesn't signify," she said with a wave of her hand. "That should be enough time to enact our plan of attack."

"And you've already mapped out our tactics."

"No wise general goes into battle without strategy." The darkness in her face retreated as she gave him a tiny, self-satisfied smile.

How delightful, this proud and cunning side of her. "What are our marching orders, General?"

"The first thing we need to accomplish is introducing you to some of the ton's most upstanding figures." She spoke crisp, precise words, every inch the superior officer. "You'll come to an open event as my escort, thus indicating to those in attendance that I vouch for your integrity. Once we're there, I will secure you an invitation to a gathering where you will meet young women of the most sterling reputation."

"Neat, targeted strikes," he said with a nod. "Glad one of us knows how to manage this."

She arched a brow. "Since my coming-out, I've done nothing but manage my role in Society. At least now that useless knowledge has a measure of purpose."

Useless. The word snagged in his mind, hinting again at her sense of dissatisfaction with her life. Yet it stood to reason that if she was satisfied with her life, she wouldn't have put the screws to him and insisted he take her to the disreputable side of London.

"It will take some time before your standing will be repaired," she went on. "I'll endeavor to secure you more invitations to more events, and there you shall meet more eligible and reputable young ladies. We'll have until the Season's end, at which point you may not be engaged to anyone, but the groundwork will be laid for you to call on a lady with the intention of proposing to her."

"And if my character hasn't been mended by that time? It's not a considerable span, barely two months, and I've done some very, very bad things." He couldn't stop himself from grinning at the thought of some of those bad things.

Celeste Kilburn, however, appeared unimpressed. "Then there's nothing I or anyone could have done to fix your reputation," she said dryly.

"Very good, General." He saluted her. "We have our plan to assist *me*, but if you're insisting on me honoring my end of the bargain—"

"I am," she said, her tone even and firm.

"Where would you like to go on your first scandalous foray?"

"Vauxhall," she replied at once.

"You cannot be serious." He rolled his eyes. "Vauxhall is for tourists."

She scowled as if annoyed, and a little stain of what appeared to be embarrassment colored her cheeks. "Then I want to go to a gaming hell." When he didn't answer right away, she tipped up her chin. "I've heard my father yelling at Dom because he goes to gaming hells. Now it's *my* turn to visit one."

"Very well," he said gruffly. "I'll send you word tomorrow evening as to where to meet me."

Her eyes brightened excitedly. "I shall be properly disguised."

"However," he added, and her shoulders sagged. "If you *are* intent on going to London's most notorious dens of iniquity, I require proof that you can hold your own amongst the profligates."

"What sort of proof?" She tilted her head in curiosity.

"That's for you to determine." He spread his hands. "You desired a chance to live a little recklessly, now's your opportunity to demonstrate just how far you're willing to go. Here. Now." He threw out the challenge, half in jest. Perhaps he could finally dissuade her from insisting he take her to the unruly parts of town, yet part of him ached with curiosity to see precisely what respectable Celeste Kilburn would do.

"This is a public place in the middle of the day," she objected. When he merely smiled in response, she huffed out a resigned breath.

She glanced around the shop, as if calculating precisely what she could do. Observing the play of thought and calculation across her face was more engrossing than any stage spectacle.

What was that strange voice in his head? Oh, God, was it . . . was it his *conscience*?

He suppressed a shudder.

Unaware of his internal struggle, Celeste continued to scan Catton's. The rise and fall of feminine conversation was punctuated by a higher shrill voice.

"This is unacceptable," a woman said as she sat at a table with two other ladies. She had blond hair in a stylish coiffure, and her clothing was elegant, but her most notable accessory was the pinched look on her face. "I demand to speak with whoever manages this establishment."

"My lady," the mortified server said placatingly, "I will be most happy to replace your tea with something warmer."

"It shouldn't have come out cold in the first place," the blond customer insisted.

"I didn't think it was cold, Lady Carenford," one of her companions ventured.

"It was as icy as the Serpentine in winter," the complainer insisted. Glaring at the server, she spat, "Fetch me your superior at once."

Face reddening with embarrassment and, Kieran suspected, anger, the server curtseyed before hurrying off to get the proprietor.

"Hell," Kieran growled, "if this is polite, respectable society, I'm happy to consort with villains."

"She deserves the blunt end of a teapot in the face," Celeste muttered. "I'd settle for a pencil and paper, though."

Reaching into his coat, he produced a slim notebook. He opened it, searching for a blank page, and didn't miss how her gaze raked eagerly over the verses within, though it wasn't possible for her to read precisely what he'd written.

And she wouldn't read them. Not ever.

As soon as he found a page without writing on it, he tore it out of the notebook, and handed it and a small pencil to her. For a moment, she hesitated, and then bent over the table to write something on the paper. He tried to read it, but she folded the page up before he could make out the words.

"Excuse me for a moment," she murmured, rising.

He recalled enough of his manners to stand as she stood, and then he lowered himself back to seating as, transfixed, he watched her wend her way toward Lady Carenford.

Interestingly, she did not directly approach Lady Carenford to give the woman a much-deserved set down. Instead, she seemed to purposefully bump against another table, causing a metal tray balanced on the edge to fall to the floor. The loud clanging clatter drew Lady Carenford's notice as well as the interest of her two companions. As her attention was diverted, Celeste dropped the slip of paper onto the woman's plate, and walked back to Kieran.

She eased into her seat, her expression smooth and enigmatic.

Lady Carenford turned her attention back to her own table. She frowned as she espied the paper on her plate, then squinting, read the note.

Her face turned waxen. Her head whipped around as she looked around the shop, and as she did so,

Celeste kept her gaze on Kieran and calmly sipped her tea.

A dark-haired woman in a neat apron approached Lady Carenford's table, the server beside her. "I am Isabel Catton, my lady," she announced evenly. "Vera tells me you wanted to speak with me. Something about the temperature of your tea, I believe."

Lady Carenford fabricated a smile that stretched across her face, making her resemble a death's-head. Her eyes were fever bright and her voice loud as she said, "Everything is fine. Absolutely nothing to complain about. You have my sincerest apologies for any inconvenience I may have caused. In fact . . ." She fumbled in her reticule until she produced a coin, which she held out to Vera. "This is for you. Such excellent service. Please take it, with my compliments."

Vera reluctantly took the coin from Lady Carenford, and both she and Mrs. Catton looked on with bemusement as the lady lurched to her feet and hurried out the door. Her mystified companions trailed after her, though one of them grabbed a biscuit and tucked it into her reticule before leaving. Mrs. Catton shrugged and assisted Vera in clearing the table.

Kieran swung his attention back to Celeste, who appeared entirely unmoved by the bizarre spectacle that had just transpired.

"What the hell was in that note?" he demanded gleefully.

"I merely reminded Lady Carenford that if she did not immediately apologize to the server, Lord Carenford would be most interested in the fact that Maestro Olivari is doing far more than teaching her how to sing. Given that Lady Carenford has yet to produce an heir, her husband would be rather displeased by this development."

"And *how* do you know this?"

Her smile was enigmatic. "Possessing a sterling reputation has its benefits, including the fact that I hear all of the latest gossip. Everyone thinks I'll keep the secrets to myself, when in fact I'm simply storing information for a time when it can be advantageously deployed."

Kieran had seen and done things in the course of his life that would make most decent people blanch, or perhaps cause them to envy him. Shocking him was not something that happened often.

Yet he could only gape at Celeste Kilburn, who looked as virtuous as always.

"My God," he breathed, delighted to his marrow, "no one has any idea, do they? About who you truly are."

"No idea at all," she agreed placidly.

Mute, Kieran sat back in his seat, surrounded by London's most esteemed women as they took their afternoon tea. He'd come to Catton's today believing that Celeste was going to make a deal with the devil—namely, him. But, in fact, she was far more dangerous than he'd ever believed. If anyone needed protection, it was *him* from *her*.

Chapter 5

❖✻❖

Celeste's gaze excitedly moved back and forth between the note on her dresser and her reflection in the mirror.

The brief letter had arrived earlier that evening, just after supper as she and her father had been in the parlor. Fortunately, Da had been too engrossed in the late edition newspaper to notice the footman bringing a missive to Celeste. She'd known what it was before even reading the masculine and slashing penmanship that had declared simply: *Corner of Hans Street and Pavilion Road. Midnight.*

There had been no signature, not even an initial, but there was no doubt who had sent the note.

Now, hands trembling with exhilaration, Celeste dabbed on the last of her cosmetics before examining her reflection in the mirror atop her dressing table. She turned her face from side to side, contemplating her handiwork.

"What do you think, Dolly?" she asked her maid, who stood behind her.

"Put the wig on, miss," Dolly urged. "I'll help."

Celeste did as her maid suggested, tugging on the black wig so that it covered her own wild chestnut hair. Dolly fussed with the false tresses as she arranged them, then pinned the wig into place.

"Give your head a shake, miss."

Celeste did so, and was pleased when the wig remained fixed to her head. "That should suffice. Am I adequately disguised?"

"Oh, miss, I'd hardly believe you were you."

"Such is my intention." After parting company with Kieran Ransome yesterday, she'd sent Dolly to the theatrical supply shop to purchase cosmetics and a suitable wig, and had spent the intervening hours between then and today practicing the application of both.

Looking at herself now, she couldn't stop a surge of pride. At least the painting classes she'd been forced to take at finishing school had a genuine use now. Through careful shading, she'd narrowed her nose and made her mouth appear smaller and thinner. She had also created a false dip in her chin and lowered the angle of her cheekbones. With the black wig secured, she truly didn't resemble herself.

If she did her job properly, no one tonight would recognize her. Would Kieran? A thrill skimmed down her spine, envisioning his response to her transformation.

"The gown next," Dolly said.

Of course—that was part of Celeste's metamorphosis. She stood and her maid helped her into a dress. Once, when Celeste had been desperate to escape from her sedate, modest wardrobe, she'd ordered this gown from Madame Jacqueline, but her father had forbidden her from wearing it due to its phenomenally low bodice and the bright emerald satin fabric that clung to her body. In the intervening year since she'd had the gown made, she had gained some weight, so it was even more figure-hugging than before, her breasts pushing up into the neckline.

She had once dreamt of stepping into a ball wearing this dress, fantasizing about all the scandalized looks she'd receive, perhaps even some attention combined with flirtatiously wicked repartee. Those dreams and fantasies had to be packed away, like the gown, because of her father's decree.

With her wig, her cosmetics, and this entirely improper gown, she hardly recognized herself. But now she was to give free rein to all her most forbidden wishes, with this gown as the passport to a secret, midnight world.

"Your father and brother would suffer an apoplexy if they saw you in this," Dolly said cheerfully.

"Thank goodness they *aren't* going to see me," Celeste answered. Hopefully, since Dom was supposed to reform, he'd avoid all the places she intended to go.

The clock on her mantel chimed quarter to midnight. She had fifteen minutes to make her escape from her house and meet Kieran at the designated rendezvous point. Dolly handed her a dark hooded cloak, and Celeste's heart pounded as she draped it over her shoulders. Nerves danced along her skin, her mouth going dry.

"I can't believe I'm going to do this," she murmured, adjusting the hood so that it covered her wig.

"About time, too," Dolly answered. "The short leash your family's got you on would choke a hound."

Celeste quirked a brow. "Did you just call me a bitch?"

"I don't even know the meaning of the word, miss," her maid said pertly. "Now let's get you out of the house."

Opening her bedchamber door, Celeste peered into the hallway. A footman bearing a lamp made a patrol down the corridor, and she ducked back into her room until the servant passed. Once he was gone, she eased out into the hall, with Dolly close at her heels. Both Celeste and her maid crept through the dark, using their sense of touch to guide them as they inched down the back stairs.

Dolly took the lead once they reached the ground floor. The door to the butler's pantry stood open, casting light into the corridor. Mr. Mooney, the butler, had to be up late, going over the latest order to restock the wine cellar. Dolly pushed Celeste deeper into the shadows as she craned her neck for a better look, causing Celeste to jostle against a broom that had been left in the hallway. It fell to the floor with a clatter that sent ice through Celeste's veins.

Her adventure was over before it had even begun.

"Who's there?" the butler's voice rang out.

"'Tis Dolly," her maid said, stepping into the doorway of the pantry. She moved farther into the room, and from Celeste's vantage point she could see Dolly standing in front of Mr. Mooney's desk. "I saw a rough-looking character loitering in the mews this afternoon, and thought you might like to know."

As her maid spoke, Celeste took advantage of Mr. Mooney's distraction and hurried past the open door as noiselessly as possible.

"Thank you, Dolly," he said. "I shall have Sam and Henry keep a lookout in case he comes back. But shouldn't you be abed? Miss Celeste rises fairly early."

Hearing her name on the butler's lips, unease slithered through Celeste. The risk she was taking was considerable, and the punishment would no doubt be severe if word reached her father that she'd been caught sneaking out of the house in an immodest disguise. Her father had never had cause to punish her, so she'd no idea what it might actually entail, but Ned Kilburn could be a ruthless man in his business dealings and it stood to reason that he'd be similarly severe when it came to the discipline of his children.

Given what Dom was being coerced into doing, Celeste could only imagine what she'd have to endure.

"I was worried about that man skulking," Dolly answered. "But I feel better now knowing we've got two big bruisers of our own on the case. While I'm up, I may peek into the larder for a late-night nibble. Good night, Mr. Mooney. Don't you stay up too late, either."

"Good night, Dolly."

The butler bent to his labors as the maid returned to the corridor. She motioned for Celeste to follow her as they headed toward the kitchen, and the exit that led to the outside courtyard. The way out beckoned like a hand offering freedom. Celeste tempered her impatience as Dolly checked to make certain the way was clear, and when her maid waved her forward, Celeste darted toward the exit. Dolly grabbed a hooded cloak from a peg as she stepped through the doorway.

Much as Celeste wanted to hurry out, she had to be cautious, so she opened the door slowly to ensure there would be no betraying squeak of the hinges. Cool night air met her as she crossed the threshold, welcome and liberating. Though she'd never been in the courtyard at this late hour, she couldn't spare a moment to take in the details of a familiar place made unfamiliar.

Dolly closed the door behind them, raised her hood, and together they walked quickly down the mews. Once they were on the street, they hurried down the pavement, the darkness punctuated here and there by lamplight.

Celeste's breath came fast and quick. Was she truly doing such an act of defiance and daring?

Her breathing sped up. What would her father think? And Dom?

She didn't give a rat's arse what Lord Montford thought. No—that wasn't entirely true. He was key to her family's status, and she couldn't afford to scandalize the earl.

But she was here, on the street, *now*, and the novelty of it went to her head like wine. The pavement beneath her feet wobbled, but she kept striding forward. Doubt and fear wouldn't slow her steps.

Since she'd come of age, she had never been on the sidewalk after nightfall—not counting the brief minute between alighting from a carriage and going inside for a dinner party or an assembly—and she looked around eagerly to experience Hans Town in the nighttime.

Most of the windows that fronted the street were dark, though here and there some illumination spilled out from between curtains. She longed to stop and peer through the windows to see precisely what the people within the homes were doing. But she had to meet Kieran at midnight, and if she was late, no doubt he'd simply leave without her. He was that sort of man.

A man she was going to be alone with tonight. Her already choppy breath grew even more erratic. Since she'd first come out, there had been a handful of moments that she had been briefly unaccompanied with prospective suitors, which included Lord Montford. A minute on a darkened balcony talking of the weather was hardly the same as spending the entire evening with one man, however, especially a man who was a dreadfully handsome, thoroughgoing rogue.

Her already thrumming pulse sped up even more. How ridiculous to feel any kind of excitement about being with Kieran. He'd been quite plain in stating his lack of intentions—dishonorable or otherwise—toward her. Most likely, he thought of her as though she were his sister.

Though . . . the way he'd eaten that naughty bosom-like cake at Catton's . . . and the look he'd given her as he'd done so . . .

Impossible. He probably flirted the way other men took snuff. Purely habit, and nothing more.

She shook her head at herself. Here she was, about to embark on her first real wicked adventure, and she was spending far too much time mooning over Kieran Ransome. She ought to take advantage of this rare opportunity and simply absorb what it meant to finally be out of her house as midnight approached.

Freedom, true freedom. For the first time since her father had made his fortune, Celeste could do whatever she pleased. Where to begin? There were so many options—almost too many. But she'd embrace all possibilities because, for now, she was beholden to no one.

A stunned, giddy laugh broke from her lips. Dolly shot her a wry look of understanding.

They passed few people, and those they did were either too intoxicated or too intent on reaching their own destinations to pay Celeste and Dolly any mind. Fortunately, the streets were free of watchmen, which might have alarmed her if it wasn't so convenient for her purposes.

Up ahead was the intersection of Hans Street and Pavilion Road. A cab waited beside a lamp, with a black-haired man in a rather elaborately embroidered coat and waistcoat leaning against it. His long, lean form was unmistakable, even at this distance. Once more her heartbeat sped up.

"That Mr. Ransome is a wicked-looking one, to be sure," Dolly murmured beside her.

"And yet you gladly accepted his bribe so he could await me in the fitting area at Madame Jacqueline's."

Her maid winked. "He's wicked in the very best ways, and in any event, I knew he'd behave himself or else Mr. Dominic would have words with him—at the least."

It was slightly comforting that Celeste's brother was so protective of her. Yet even the most protective instincts were smothering if they were applied with too forceful a hand.

Pushing back her hood, she approached Kieran. He glanced in her direction, and then his head whipped back to her as he looked again. A slow smile spread across his face as his gaze touched on the glimpses of skin and brightly hued satin that appeared from beneath her cloak. There was no mistaking the carnal interest in his dark eyes. Something hot and alive kindled to life in her belly. She'd had men look at her with admiration before, but never with such sexual energy.

Kieran Ransome all but radiated with erotic possibility.

"A fine night, beauty," he murmured to her, his voice rich as wine. "Finer now that you've arrived."

Dear God. He didn't recognize her.

"What do you propose we do on such a fine night?" she asked, pitching her own voice lower and employing a hint of her old accent.

His smile turned devilish. "We'll compose verses and then whoever fashions the better poem is at liberty to claim the prize of their desiring."

"Are you a poet, sirrah?" She could hardly believe she was trading outrageous badinage with Kieran Ransome. If it was a dream, it was the very best one she'd ever had, and she prayed she didn't wake soon.

"When the muse is kind, I can be most inspired." He took a step toward her, then froze, his smile vanishing. "Good Christ. *Celeste*?"

"It seems my disguise is effective." She tried for her own saucy grin, but the horror on his face undercut her effort.

He dug the heel of his palm into his eye. "Do not, under any circumstances, tell Dom about what I just said to you."

"The poetry bit? Or the part where you were propositioning me? Incidentally, *are* you a poet?"

"Don't tell him *anything*," Kieran said through gritted teeth. He reached out to flip back the front of her cloak, and, once she was revealed, his gaze ran down the length of her. It was the least gentlemanly perusal she had yet experienced in the whole of her life. Everywhere his regard touched, she went hot and sensitized.

Yet . . . his expression verged on angry.

"It doesn't please you?" she asked.

"Not a bit." His jaw tightened as he tugged the cloak back into place.

"I haven't got anything else to wear." She fought against dejection. "Nothing suitably disreputable."

"This is definitely disreputable." He pinched the bridge of his nose, and exhaled. "God help me. I don't suppose it's worth trying again to convince you to drop this outrageous scheme?"

"It isn't," she answered as firmly as she could.

He exhaled. "Get in the cab."

"We're dropping Dolly at a Mayfair home on Chesterfield Hill along the way," she announced. "Her sister works there, and Dolly will spend the hours we're out with her."

"After that, onto Jenkins's," he declared. "If that particular gaming hell meets with your approval."

"I expect you know these things better than I," she said.

"If you've other ideas, I'll happily yield to them." He smirked. "This is your mayhem, sweetheart. You're the one in charge."

Two things struck her: she didn't enjoy how much she liked him calling her *sweetheart*. The other thing was how much it pleased her to have command of her life ceded to *her* instead of someone else.

Where *did* she want to go? Her head spun with the possibility. She had the whole of London after midnight at her disposal, and yet what that actually meant, she'd no idea. It was one thing to imagine all the secret, depraved places that existed under cover of darkness, but when it came down to it, she couldn't think of a single one.

"Jenkins's sounds perfect," she said at last.

"Fine. Let's go."

"Could you sound a bit less like an adolescent being dragged along to visit an elderly relative?" she asked irritably.

"There's nothing *adolescent* about me, love." His gaze shifted, growing hotter as he glanced down at her revealing gown.

Her limbs went suddenly languid but she wouldn't let his instinctive flirtation distract her from her purpose—finally experiencing London's scandalous side for herself.

After she gave the driver the address on Chesterfield Hill, Kieran helped her into the cab. Astonishingly, he provided the same service to Dolly, though she was a servant. He climbed in the vehicle, shut the door, and knocked on the roof. The cab shuddered as it lurched into motion, and the rest of the ride to Mayfair was similarly jouncing.

She refused to complain about the hired vehicle's poor springs, though judging by the wary look Kieran kept throwing her across the cramped interior, that was precisely what he believed she would do. At last, they reached the home where Dolly's sister worked, and Dolly climbed down from the cab.

"Last chance," Kieran said to Celeste. "Before your maid leaves, I can take you both home now and no one will be the wiser."

"Gaming hell, or I don't gain you entrance to a single afternoon tea. And don't try to dissuade me again."

He sighed. "Obstinance runs in the Kilburn family, clearly."

"How late can I return for you?" Celeste asked Dolly.

"Haven't seen Lily in an age, miss," her maid answered through the window. "I expect we'll be up half the night talking. Come back for me whenever you please, but we both need to be home before five in the morning. That's when the kitchen staff stirs."

"I'll do my best," Celeste said, hardly able to fathom what it must be like to come home as the sun had begun to rise, still wearing last night's finery.

Dom and the Ransome brothers did it all the time, and if she could, she'd have the same experience.

Once Dolly was making her way down the mews, the cabman called to Kieran, "Where to, gov?"

"Corner of Shepherd and Hertford Streets," Kieran answered.

The driver clicked his tongue, urging his horse into motion. Soon, she and Kieran were on their way. He sat opposite her, but the interior of the cab was quite cramped, and their knees kept bumping. She shifted, trying to avoid the small collisions, but whenever she moved, she seemed to encounter more of him.

"What are you playing at?" he demanded.

"It's not my fault you have such long legs," she fired back.

"Next time," he drawled, "I'll remove them and set them beside the driver."

A taut silence fell. She'd half hoped that their first carriage ride alone together would be full of charged awareness, building on the sensual promise that he'd shown when he had first beheld her in her disguise, but instead, they seemed to wear on each other's nerves. A disheartening beginning to her night's adventure.

"What am I to call you?" At her questioning look, he explained, "I can't very well announce to all and sundry that you're Miss Celeste Kilburn, which would cause a tiresome scandal, so an alias is required."

"Call me . . ." Her mind spun with possibilities, all of them tantalizing. Finally, she said, "Salome."

"The woman who danced for Herod and when he said he'd give her anything she wanted, she demanded the head of John the Baptist."

"Yes, Salome." She folded her arms across her chest. "This is my opportunity to name myself rather than be called something that someone else picked for me. I absolutely *loathe* my name," she added dourly.

"Celeste is a lovely name," he said.

Much as his praise pleased her, she explained, "It's too precious. Too . . . celestial."

"You'd much rather be a woman of earthly flesh, than some ethereal ideal. Salome connotes a woman who brings men to their knees."

She started. Of all the people to recognize and understand her need to be something, some*one* other than who she was—her need to be a woman with power—she hadn't anticipated it would be him.

When the cab came to a stop, he leaned forward. "Time to experience your first gaming hell, Salome."

Chapter 6

This is a spectacularly terrible idea, Kieran thought as he climbed down from the carriage in front of Jenkins's. After the trip in the cramped cab, he tugged the wrinkles out of his favorite gold-and-black embroidered waistcoat.

And yet, for all his misgivings, when he turned to help Salome/Celeste from the vehicle, his skin buzzed with anticipation. Her cloak billowed as she stepped out, revealing peeks of her vividly green gown, and while he'd seen women in far more immodest clothing, the fact that *she* wore such a garment made his skin even more sensitive.

True, he'd been entranced by Celeste when he hadn't recognized her earlier. Perhaps that's why he now watched the play of emotions on her face. He was still caught in the spell of her masquerade. It had nothing to do with the fact that her eyes glimmered with anticipation, or that the layers of paint she'd applied didn't hide her eager yet poignantly anxious smile.

He was merely reacting to her disguise.

Still, he found himself looking at her as she stared at the front door of the establishment on Shepherd Street. He wasn't certain what she expected to see, since the place looked quite ordinary. The two-story structure had a columned portico, reached by a short flight of stairs, and the door was simply painted wood sporting a simple brass knocker.

"I was anticipating something a little more sinister," she admitted to him. "Demons beckoning us into a mouth of flames."

"That's on the inside."

"Truly?" Excitement vibrated in her voice.

"Not truly," he said indulgently. "But I shan't spoil your sense of discovery."

It wasn't his responsibility to ensure she enjoyed herself, and yet . . . She'd insisted that she *needed* to take this risk. What caused such desperation, that she was willing to take chances with her reputation? What pressures was she under that drove her toward their mad agreement?

Whatever those burdens were, she'd set them aside tonight, her face brilliant with anticipation.

He'd been to many gaming hells many times, knew them and their pleasures as well as any scoundrel could. Yet, beholding the eagerness in her expression and the way her eyes gleamed in expectancy, something in his own chest lifted up.

"Come." He offered her his arm.

She put her hand on his arm, and started.

"Something amiss?" he asked.

"It's merely . . ." She cleared her throat. "I didn't expect you to feel so . . . firm."

He ought to receive some kind of commendation from Prinny himself for not making a lewd comment in response. But the bigger struggle was keeping his head from filling with thoughts of her softness against his firmness, her fingers brushing over other—unclothed—parts of him.

"You went a little strong on the rouge," he said as they approached the gaming hell's door.

Her fingers flew to her cheeks.

"I'm excited to experience my first gaming hell," she replied. "Are *you* wearing rouge?"

"Not tonight." He should have lied and attributed the hotness in his face to something other than sudden, unexpected desires.

She arched a brow. "But you *have* worn cosmetics?"

"Never underestimate the dramatic impact of a kohl-lined eye." Better to brazen it out than let her realize she affected him. As they neared the building, he said, "There was another gaming hell a few years ago, so exclusive it didn't even have a name. You would have liked it—the manager was a woman named Cassandra, elegant as crystal. The place shut down and no one knows what became of Cassandra . . . though she does bear a resemblance to a very influential duchess." He shrugged as they climbed the stairs. "Jenkins's will do for your beginning foray into the world of gaming hells. It's exclusive and the proprietress won't tolerate unruly fools."

Before he lifted his hand to use the brass knocker, the door swung open. A massive liveried footman appeared. The servant's gaze flicked impassively over Kieran and then turned to Celeste.

He watched her battle indecision, as though picking the proper strategy for how to interact with the footman. Of course—she had no idea what women did when they entered such places. Finally, she lifted her chin with cool disinterest, though a flare of uncertainty still glinted in her eyes.

Something struck him square in the chest, a sensation he couldn't quite name. Yet it swelled and ached to see her deliberately, purposefully encountering a frightening, unknown situation, yet facing it directly. There was a courage in her he hadn't anticipated.

The footman stepped aside, permitting them entrance.

Kieran and Celeste crossed the threshold but as they did, a tiny tremor passed from her into him. Entering a gaming hell was an everyday occurrence for him, but for *her* it seemed to mean something more.

Again, the thought gnawed at him: Why would she take this risk? What impelled her to gamble with her reputation?

A maid came forward to take Celeste's gloves and cloak, revealing her vivid, snug gown, and how it adhered to her body like emerald water. Dragging his gaze away took far more effort than he liked. Even so, it would be a long, long time before he could get the glowing afterimage of her in that dress out of his mind.

Fortunately, she didn't seem to notice him leering at her as she took in their surroundings. The foyer blazed with light from a chandelier, and nearby huge Chinese vases held palm fronds as they stood sentinel. The antechamber itself was not very large, but just beyond it lay an enormous room with an extremely high ceiling and equally tall windows. Even more massive chandeliers were suspended from the ceiling. Crowds of people in evening finery moved through the room, though one couldn't see precisely what they did. The cacophony emanating from that chamber was terrific.

"It's noisier than Billingsgate," she said to Kieran.

"The language is worse here," he answered with a grin, "especially as the night wears on and the losses pile up. But, as I said, fools are not tolerated and anyone who causes unruly scenes is summarily escorted off the premises. Ah, Mrs. Jenkins, how you sparkle tonight." He beamed as a mature Black woman in regal azure silk came forward.

"Mr. Ransome, you bestow flattery with a generous hand," Mrs. Jenkins answered. "'Tis my sapphires that sparkle, not I." She fingered the strand of impressive gems around her neck and shook her head to make her jeweled earbobs dance.

"Those are cold rocks of minimal value and negligible beauty compared to you." He bowed over her hand as she chuckled throatily.

"How glad I am that I've a rule against dallying with my establishment's patrons," Mrs. Jenkins said, her lips curving. Her regard turned to Celeste. "This sweet plum is newly harvested from your orchard."

"Mrs. Jenkins," he said, nodding at Celeste, "may I present Salome."

"Salome what?" the proprietress asked.

"Just . . . just Salome," Celeste replied.

Mrs. Jenkins raised a brow. But then the woman nodded, as if well used to her patrons using pseudonyms.

"Welcome," Mrs. Jenkins said. "As this is your first time here, and as Mr. Ransome is a particularly generous patron, I am happy to stake you ten pounds." She snapped her fingers, and another liveried footman hurried forward with what looked like a folio of banknotes.

"You are kindness itself," Celeste murmured, taking the cash and tucking it into her reticule.

"My duties require attention," Mrs. Jenkins said, "so I will bid you both a good evening, and wish you luck at whatever venture you decide to play." She sent a meaningful glance between Kieran and Celeste, and then, smiling enigmatically, glided away.

"An extraordinary woman." Celeste watched the proprietress as she went into the gaming room and wove through the crowds.

"None more extraordinary." Kieran offered Celeste his arm once more. "But we'll gain nothing if we don't enter the fray."

"This is it," Celeste said under her breath as she set her hand on his sleeve.

He laid his hand over hers—his intent to offer comfort. But the feel of his bare hand covering hers was anything but comforting. Embers of awareness glowed into being, illuminating all the shadowed corners within him.

Her eyes widened at the contact. She felt it, too. *Damn.*

Theirs was a relationship of mutual usefulness, and nothing more. He had to remember that.

They went into the main gaming room, and noise and heat met them, solid as a bulwark. He tried to see the place through her eyes, as though experiencing all of it for the first time. People shouted while standing around numerous tables arranged throughout the room, cries of elation mixing with yells of dismay, and the cheers of onlookers encouraging the bettors. Everyone was dressed in evening regalia, with more than a few ladies in silk and jewels gleaming amongst the gentlemen's dark finery. Liveried servants circulated with trays bearing glasses of wine, admirable in their deftness in avoiding collisions with unthinking patrons. Adjoining the gaming room was another, smaller chamber where people took refreshments, ranging from plates of roast beef served with potatoes, to an array of cakes accompanied by sparkling wine.

A set of French doors led to a balcony, where the glowing tips of cheroots hovered in the night.

Curses blended with the round vowels of the upper classes, and he glanced at Celeste.

"The language is as unbridled as the game play," he said, feeling almost embarrassed that she should be audience to such profane words.

"You forget I'm the daughter of a former longshoreman," she answered, though her round eyes showed she *was* taken aback. "It's rather novel, to catch the sounds of elegant ladies and esteemed gentlemen swearing worse than any stevedore."

"Places such as this *appear* relatively genteel," he said.

"A closer examination reveals more raffish details," she replied lowly.

Once more, he tried to experience the place as if for the first time. Several men had loosened their neckcloths, revealing glimpses of skin shining with sweat. A dowager openly fondled the buttocks of a young dandy, who appeared to enjoy her attentions. The laughter was louder as guests tipped back their heads to unleash full-throated guffaws, no attempts at polite, restrained chuckling. Anger was in fuller display, too, as a pair of men beside a vingt-et-un table shoved at each other until another burly footman separated them.

"It's as though someone has amplified the volume of more respectable gatherings," she said. "Granted, no one is drawing blood over a feud or copulating on the floor."

He chuckled, though it was wiser not to tell her that he'd been to many a gathering where both of those things had happened, and *he'd* been the one doing them.

"Mrs. Jenkins would doubtlessly forbid such crass behavior," he said. When Celeste continued to look around, her expression intent, as though she wanted to commit everything around her to memory, he urged, "Tell me what you're feeling."

He didn't know why he needed to know. Only that it mattered.

"There's a palpable sense of wildness," she said after a long pause. "As if the tight leashes that bind everyone to a strict code of propriety has been loosened, leaving the guests to indulge their more primal impulses."

"Is that what brought you here?" he heard himself ask. He grabbed two flutes of sparkling wine from a passing server and handed one of the glasses to Celeste. "Indulging your more primal impulses?"

Her cheeks went pink, and yet she answered, "Would you be shocked if I answered yes?"

"A little," he admitted. "I've no idea what dwells beneath your well-mannered, proper surface."

"I . . ." Her gaze held his, and a current passed between them, electric and edged.

Someone shouted, fracturing the connection between Kieran and Celeste.

He took a sip of wine, letting the sharp taste and effervescence on his tongue bring himself back to where he was and who he was with. Flirtation with Celeste Kilburn was a gargantuanly terrible idea.

"We're here now," he said in his most jaded voice. "What do you propose to do?"

"First, I'd like to . . . more than anything, I want to . . . I . . ." She shot him a rueful look over the rim of her glass. "I have no idea."

He lifted a brow. "Coming here was your plan. Surely you have some notion as to what would transpire once you got here."

"I've never truly known what goes on in a gaming hell," she confessed. "Da's forever taking Dom to task for coming to places such as this one, so it always seemed forbidden and dangerous. Other than wagering on games of chance, I don't know what or how it happens."

He guided her around the room, letting her see what choices were available to her.

"Whatever you imagined," he said simply as they walked, "do that."

She stared at him. "Not difficult for *you*, but for me, it's another matter."

"Perhaps for the other self you left behind," he pointed out. "But you're Salome now. Whatever Salome wants, Salome can have."

Still, she hesitated, and her brow furrowed as if in frustration. "All this time," she muttered, "I believed other people kept me in line, reining me in, but perhaps they've done such an effective job of telling me what I can't do, now I tell *myself* what's impossible."

"Implanting the seeds of doubt in you, so they barely have to do the work themselves." He twisted his mouth sardonically while shepherding her around a gentleman intent on drinking as many flutes of sparkling wine as the establishment would permit. "Seems to be the ways of families."

"They're not bad, my father and Dom. They want what's best for me."

"You defend those that keep you fettered."

"Love's a complicated thing," she said. "It seldom exists in its purest form."

He was quiet for a moment, studying her. She *was* far more than a sheltered miss.

"Being here now is what you want, correct?" he asked gently. "If it isn't, say the word, and we'll depart immediately. But the choice belongs to you."

"Thank you," she said after a moment. "I'm . . . not used to having my wishes taken into consideration."

Damn her family—Dom included.

"To hell with everyone else," he said. "Live for yourself. Be who *you* want to be."

She nodded, then straightened her shoulders and raised her chin as she did so. "To the gaming tables," she announced.

Painting was not one of his skills—he was far more adept with quills than brushes—but he possessed a keen eye for both the beautiful and the captivating. As Celeste rallied herself, finding that inner core of strength and adventure, she transformed far more than she had with the cosmetics she'd applied earlier. Resolve shone in her eyes, and an appetite for the world's experiences. She looked like a woman on the verge of transformation, a phoenix that would emerge even more magnificent from its own flames.

He'd been attracted to her when he'd made that horrendous error earlier, believing her to be someone else. But this Celeste, the true Celeste, snared his attention and refused to let him go.

"Where to begin," she said, surveying the room. "There's faro, and vingt-et-un. Or maybe I should try hazard."

"You can play any of those games. But before you do, I direct your attention to the people surrounding the tables."

She did so, and looked puzzled. "Many appear to be wagering, too. But it doesn't look as though they're playing. What are they betting on?"

By way of explanation, he drew closer to the throng of guests encircling the vingt-et-un table. A quintet of bucks actually played the card game. They were tiresome men full of braggadocio that Kieran knew from his usual haunts. He tended to avoid them as much as possible. There was one man observing the players, however, that interested Kieran.

"Hedgerly," he said, turning toward the older, bespectacled man. Lawrence Hedgerly had made his fortune in manufacturing, and while he was not often a habitué of gaming hells, he did occasionally indulge.

"Ransome," Hedgerly said with a distracted bow. Then he bowed more deeply for Celeste. "Madam."

"Sir," she replied with a slight Cockney accent.

"How goes the play tonight?" Kieran asked.

"Engaging, and profitable," Hedgerly replied. He gave a short huff of laughter. "These dandies think they can best me, but I didn't become the owner of three country estates by relying on charm alone."

"I know you better than that," Kieran countered. "And I'll wager you twenty pounds that Lonsdale will scratch his nose when he's dealt his next hand."

Beside him, Celeste softly drew in a breath, as if surprised that he'd place such a wager.

Hedgerly raised a brow. "How certain you sound, Ransome."

"How uncertain you sound, Hedgerly."

The older man's mouth hitched. "Goading me into betting is beneath you. And yet I'll take your wager."

Kieran, Celeste, and Hedgerly all turned their attentions toward Lonsdale, the florid dandy awaiting his next hand. Tension mounted as other players' cards were dealt, Celeste's hand squeezing on his forearm as she waited.

The press of her fingers on him brought his body to attention. Suddenly, he didn't give a damn about the wager. He was far more intrigued by the feel of her excitedly clutching his arm—bringing to mind other activities where she'd hold tightly to him.

Focus, goddamn you, he snarled at himself.

Finally, the dealer set cards before Lonsdale. Even Kieran held his breath and then . . .

Lonsdale scratched his nose.

"Damn," Hedgerly muttered.

Celeste bounced once on her feet, which did intriguing things to the neckline of her bodice, but Kieran tried valiantly not to notice. Instead, he turned to Hedgerly, his hand outstretched.

The older man amiably grumbled, but he stuffed a small stack of pound notes into Kieran's palm.

"Parched in my defeat," Hedgerly said wryly, "I'll hie myself off to the refreshments." He bowed again before ambling away.

"How did you know?" Celeste demanded once Hedgerly had gone. "That Lonsdale would scratch his nose? Did a fly alight upon it?"

"He possesses an obvious tell when his hand is poor," Kieran explained, drawing her away from the table. His arm still blazed with the feel of her hand on him, and that sensation burned through his body.

"Given the way his hair and clothing were in disarray," he continued, attempting to cage his wayward body's response, "he'd been steadily losing all night, which makes him play recklessly. He called for another round of cards, so it was reasonable to assume that he'd go over. Thus, my wager."

She stared up at him, and a snug little bubble of awareness enclosed them.

"I'm not certain what's more surprising," she said softly. "The fact that people are betting on things that aren't actual games, or the fact that you're an expert at it."

"Because a scoundrel such as myself couldn't have a skill?" He grinned at her, and her lips quirked in response.

"Because you're so modest about it," she returned. "Were it me, I'd be crowing from the top of my phaeton that no one can best me at seemingly random wagers."

His smile widened as the bubble surrounding them shrank. "Boasting about one's gambling prowess tends to scare off those who would wager against you. And if you want to see true expertise in gambling, you'd do better to study Finn. My brother's facility with gaming borders on brilliance."

"Finn?" She looked dubious.

Kieran's spine stiffened, even though it made sense that she might question his assertion. Finn himself never bothered to contradict those who saw him as a dull-witted rake, a persona that had been affixed to him since Eton, where his academic efforts had been disastrous. In truth, Finn seemed to encourage others to believe that he was brainless.

But then she said, "We're not always who the world believes us to be."

He looked into her eyes, a mix of green and brown

and gold, and the ground beneath his feet went unsteady, as if unmoored by her perceptiveness.

Seeking stability, Kieran glanced away. He recognized his brother's dark-clad presence at the periphery of the gaming hell. It wasn't a surprise, encountering Finn here. What *was* unexpected was the fact that if Finn noticed Kieran, he didn't approach, which was fortunate. It would be unlikely that his brother would correctly guess Celeste's identity beneath her disguise, but better to avoid him altogether and not take that risk.

Even so, he and Celeste ought to keep moving so as not to tempt fate.

"The games of chance at the tables are adequate," he said, "but if you're in search of deeper play and more substantial excitement, seek side bets from the spectators. That's where the sport truly happens."

"And it's a matter of studying the players at the tables," she noted. "Watching them, tracking how their games proceed, and how they behave."

"Precisely."

She glanced toward the hazard table, and a smile of eager potential bloomed across her face. Her expressions were so dynamic, so emotive—impossible not to wonder what such responsiveness might mean in a bed partner.

Speculate all you want, Ransome. It's not going to happen.

"Time to try my luck." She gave his arm a slight squeeze before walking away.

He didn't plan on watching her go, it simply happened. He couldn't stop himself from staring at the bitable curve of her neck, and as she headed toward the hazard table, more than a few heads turned in her direction.

Point your attention elsewhere, he instructed himself. He headed toward a hazard table but drew up when he heard a very young male voice say with strained good cheer, "Just wait here, Antoinette—I need to speak with the pit manager but I'll be back presently."

Turning, Kieran saw a pale boy who couldn't have been more than eighteen hurrying away from an equally young woman in deep blue silk. The moment the boy left the woman's side, his desperately merry expression fell away, leaving terror in its place. Wringing his hands, the boy glanced around in a panic, a sheen of sweat glistening on his ashen skin.

Kieran strode to the boy's side. In a low voice he asked, "How much are you down?"

"P-Pardon?" the lad gulped.

"You've bet beyond your means," Kieran said, careful to keep a jaded, disinterested look on his face. "Lost your quarterly allowance on deep play to impress the lady."

The boy scrubbed a hand over a chin that sported a single blond whisker, not enough growth to warrant regular shaving. "I didn't want her to think I've no ruddy idea what I'm doing."

"The world's most common blunder." Kieran's chest twinged in sympathy. When he'd been this lad's age, how often had he done something similarly stupid?

He dug into his pocket and, stepping close to the boy, shoved a wad of pound notes into the youth's hand.

The boy's eyes went wide. "Th-Thank—"

"Enough." Kieran refused to meet the lad's gaze. "Take Antoinette home to safety, away from the jackals." He glanced over to where the woman in blue anxiously stood, surrounded by avaricious men. "And cease your injudicious gaming. A sonnet is far more effective at seduction."

"Sir," the boy said earnestly. "I'm so grateful, so very grateful."

"Go on, now," Kieran answered, already walking away. His lips twitched mirthlessly. He'd given the lad nearly all his blunt for the night, and though he could get credit if he so desired, he didn't like to play someone else's coin.

Looking for Celeste, he espied her near another hazard table. She seemed in the midst of a wager. The earlier uncertainty she'd appeared to wrestle with was gone, newfound confidence bright in her eyes and steady in the set of her shoulders. A trio of men hovered nearby, clearly more interested in her than the game, but she didn't seem to notice.

Kieran took a step in her direction, only belatedly realizing that his hands had knotted into fists. Puzzled, he looked down at them as if they were subject to someone else's emotions.

But they were *his*. And this unexpected protectiveness he felt toward her, that was his, too.

Celeste sauntered up to him a moment later, waving a stack of banknotes as though it was a fan, and beaming. Her eyes were bright as she struck a pose like a fashion plate.

"Felicitations on your successful efforts," Kieran drawled, fighting for composure. She certainly didn't know that he'd been ready to commit violence against anyone who might dare harm her. "I hope you sufficiently drained everyone's pockets."

"A whole fifteen pounds," she said, and laughed. The husky sound wrapped around him in a velvet caress. "I wagered that the lady playing hazard would cough when the gentleman player to her right cast the dice."

"What led you to the conclusion that she'd do such a thing?"

"I watched the table and saw that the gentleman had been winning, whilst she'd been losing, and didn't look overly pleased about it. It stood to reason that she would attempt to sabotage his play—and she did. Resulting in this." She waved her winnings.

He quickly covered her hand with his and the heat of her skin permeated his, rich and heady. His body responded at once, the darker, baser part of himself jostling forward to demand action.

She drew in a breath, the hazel of her eyes eclipsed by her widening pupils. The cosmetics she'd applied with a liberal hand didn't hide the fresh redness in her cheeks, and that color in her face matched the heat rushing through him.

Fuck. This was inconvenient.

"Careful," he said, his voice a deep rasp. Slowly, he released his hold on her. "This may be a gaming hell, but even here you don't want to tempt people into doing something they shouldn't."

She swallowed, and when she spoke, her words were throaty. "They must be held accountable for their own actions."

They stared at each other for a long moment, the air between them taut with things unsaid, and urges that shouldn't be acted upon.

"With that newly won blunt," he said, "you'll want to keep playing."

She blinked, surfacing from the thrall that had encircled them. "Oughtn't I stop whilst the odds are in my favor?"

"That's precisely when you should test the limits of that good fortune." When she looked surprised, he chuckled. "If you're in search of someone to advocate temperate behavior, you'll need to look elsewhere."

"God, I've had enough of that from everyone else," she said, her mouth twisting wryly.

"Then let's be intemperate, Madam Salome." He held out his arm.

"Indeed, let us." She set her hand on his arm and smiled up at him, but it wasn't the polite, respectable smile he'd seen her dole out at sundry social events over the years. This one was enigmatic, sly, as though both she and Kieran were possessors of a very naughty secret.

This was not Dom's sister—she was her own woman. The realization seemed to hit Kieran and Celeste at the same time, drawing them closer while she discovered the very beginnings of her own power.

He led her back to the gaming tables, and for the next hour, she placed wagers both on the games themselves as well as the people watching them. She wasn't always successful, losing almost half of her money before recouping the loss, but none of it dimmed her enthusiasm. Her smiles, too, were contagious.

His face actually hurt a little from the amount of smiling he'd done tonight.

"Why aren't you scowling and cursing your fortune?" he asked her when a bet with a woman in pearls resulted in a substantial loss.

"Whatever comes of this," she answered, handing the woman two pounds, "I've learned, and experienced, and I never would have done either if I'd stayed quietly at home. But you surprise me."

"Predictability is anathema to foolhardy men such as myself." Though he had no idea what it was about him that she found surprising. In truth, he surprised himself by remaining vigilant at her shoulder lest anyone—any *man*—attempt to accost her, rather than leaving her to fend for herself.

Naturally, he'd tend to her welfare. If any harm came to her, surely Dom or the elder Mr. Kilburn would seek him out and demand vengeance. It was simple self-preservation.

"I assumed you'd join me in all these wild wagers. Instead, you play devil on my shoulder but leave all the risk-taking to me."

"My taste for gambling is minimal. A few bets here and there are enough to slake my thirst." She did *not* need to know that he'd given the pale boy most of his money.

Her gaze turned shrewd, but then she started. She looked over his shoulder, and her cheeks faded into pallor. Kieran turned to see what had snared her attention.

A tall, blond man stood at the entrance to the gaming room. He was fair skinned, possessing the kind of English handsomeness that resulted from similarly featured people mating and producing attractive progeny, and his broad shoulders filled out his expertly tailored coat.

"Oh, hell," Celeste muttered. Her face remained pale.

"You know him?" Kieran demanded, protectiveness rising again in him.

"I do. He's the very last person I wanted to see me here. And," she added, her voice strangled, "he's coming this way."

Chapter 7

✣✻✣

Celeste's heart thudded painfully as Lord Montford strode in her direction. She should have expected that at some point in her foray into London's freer side, she'd encounter a familiar face. Yet, of all people, she hadn't expected Lord Montford.

What was he doing *here*? And for the love of all that was holy, why was he heading her way?

His attention seemed focused not on her, but on Kieran.

"Good evening," the earl said as he neared. "We've met once, but briefly. I'm Lord Montford."

"My lord," Kieran said without interest.

"Have you seen your brother?"

Kieran made a vague gesture with his hand. "I may have seen Finn here tonight."

Celeste barely kept herself from blurting, *You did?* Hopefully, her disguise did its job and concealed her identity.

"Ah, no, not Finn." Lord Montford offered a suitably sheepish yet charming smile. "Your eldest brother. Simon." The earl's gaze moved to her, and Celeste's throat closed.

Would he recognize her?

If Lord Montford identified her beneath her wig and paint, disaster would follow. She didn't know much about gaming hells, but she was confident unmarried women didn't frequent them, certainly not in the company of one of London's most notorious scoundrels, and absolutely not in a figure-hugging emerald dress that revealed more than it concealed.

Lord Montford *did* stare a little too long at her cleavage, and then his attention rose higher, to her face.

Oh, God. Oh, God.

"Have we met before?" he asked, tilting his head.

What was the *opposite* of something respectable, reserved Celeste Kilburn might do?

"Doubt it, ducks," she said, speaking with her old Ratcliff accent. "I'd remember a pretty face and soft hands like yours. Like milk, them hands."

Kieran made a low, choked noise and looked suspiciously on the verge of laughter, while Lord Montford glowered at her.

This was it. The earl would know her voice, and then realize who she was. He'd tear off her wig and point at her, declaring to everyone at Jenkins's that she was none other than Celeste Kilburn, daughter of dockyard magnate Ned Kilburn—ruining her and her family's reputation for eternity.

Scarlet rimmed her vision. Madness, that something as useless as *reputation* had value, and that it threatened her entire existence. Not only that, someone like Lord Montford had it in his power to completely destroy her with a few words.

She vibrated with the effort to keep her terror and fury invisible.

"*Is* Simon here this evening?" Lord Montford asked impatiently as he turned to Kieran.

"Places such as this are not to my elder brother's more sober tastes," Kieran replied dryly.

"I'd hoped to ask him his opinion on a matter of business, but you're correct. He's not the sort to frequent these locales. Enjoy the rest of your evening." Lord Montford sketched a bow at Kieran, nodded at Celeste, and then was gone.

"Prig," Kieran muttered. "Are you well?"

Celeste hadn't realized that she'd sagged against him until that moment, leaning into his side and using his strong form to stay on her feet. "The heat of the room has gone to my head."

"And the fact that you knew him and were paralyzed with terror that he'd identify you." Despite his wry words, his arm came up to support her. "Take comfort, he'd no idea who you were."

"For now." She straightened, appreciating that he didn't continue to hold her when she could stand on her own. "Much as I'd like tonight to continue, it's wiser to leave before we encounter him again."

"Excessively starched," Kieran said, glancing at Lord Montford, who talked with an older man at the entrance to the refreshment chamber.

It was with some relief that she accompanied him to the foyer. She kept glancing nervously over her shoulder as a footman brought Kieran his coat and her cloak. As he slid his arms into the sleeves, he said, "How did you find your first foray into disreputable London?"

"My heart's still pounding. And," she realized with surprise, "not all from fear." She accepted her cloak from the servant.

"You did splendidly." His smile was wide and gleaming, a scoundrel's smile that made her pulse spike. "More courage than a lioness."

She didn't want to savor his praise, yet it was as warm and luxurious as being wrapped in velvet. "I worried everyone could tell how nervous I was."

"Perhaps at first," he allowed, "and it's to be expected. But you rallied and devoured the night like it was a feast."

They stepped out into the street, and, much as she wanted to remain in the sublime chaos of the gaming hell, she had to be strategic. Retreating before Lord Montford possibly recognized her meant that she'd have another opportunity to venture out into the night. With Kieran.

Her thrumming pulse sped even faster.

Yet she had to keep her head, and something he'd said earlier snagged in her memory. "You didn't say that Finn was here."

"He didn't see us, so it didn't warrant mentioning."

"Please don't filter that kind of intelligence from me," she replied, annoyed. "I get enough of that from everyone else. 'Don't trouble yourself over unpleasant business matters.'" She made a face.

"I'll not hide anything from you in the future."

As he hailed a cab, she glanced at him surreptitiously. Throughout the night, he'd shown her remarkable consideration. No one, not even her own family, had ever truly heard her. Yet this handsome rogue had done so, and it had been all the more delightful because it had been so unexpected, like taking a bite of meringue and instead of it dissolving on her tongue, she was nourished and sated.

A cab pulled up to the curb, and Kieran handed her in. She'd neglected to put her gloves on again, so the brush of his fingers against hers sent a shiver through her body.

This cab was a bit more commodious than the last. Their knees didn't knock against each other, even as he sprawled with the kind of long-limbed insouciance only men could enjoy.

"Much as I dislike employing strategy," he said, rocking with the motion of the vehicle, "we'll need to consider it for the next step. My perceived reformation is in your capable hands."

She glanced down at her hands folded in her lap and the image of them wrapped around his bare biceps leapt unbidden into her mind. Shaking her head to knock the picture from her thoughts, she said decisively, "I've selected a venue that's known for its prestige but is open to the public. There's someone attending this event that I shall introduce you to. If everything goes well, and you suitably play the role of a respectable gentleman—"

"Emphasis on *play the role*," he noted wryly.

"You did say *perceived* rather than *actual* reformation."

His laugh was full and rich, covering her in its rough

silk. She shivered at the sensation even as her laughter joined his.

"Pray, continue with our strategy, General," he chuckled.

"The person I intend you to meet is hosting an exclusive gathering, and it is my hope to gain you an invitation to this gathering. If you make an appearance *there*, with me at your side, Society will consider you honorable."

"When we both know that's the furthest thing from the truth," he added sardonically.

"Is it?" She arched her brow at him. "I saw what you did at Jenkins's. What you did for that very young man," she explained when he looked at her with puzzlement.

At her comment, his expression went carefully blank. "That was nothing."

"It wasn't," she insisted. "You prevented him from being embarrassed in front of his lady, and protected the woman, too. *That's* why you didn't gamble," she said with sudden realization. "Because you gave him all your money."

To her astonishment, Kieran made a dismissive flicking gesture with his fingers as he slouched in his seat. "A fanciful whim, that's all. Don't paint me with too kindly a brush. I'm an inveterate rogue, capable only of thinking of myself."

"Why are you so determined to cast yourself in a negative role?" Curious, frustrated, she found herself leaning forward as if she could somehow physically impel him to accept her praise.

"It's the role I've played my whole life," he drawled, his expression sardonic. "Careless, thoughtless, the usual assortment of delightful descriptions for a younger son."

"Younger son," she repeated. It suddenly became clear to her just *who* called him those terrible names. "They're wrong, you know. Your family."

He jerked as if she'd slapped him. "I said nothing of my family."

"But I'm correct, aren't I?" At his obstinate silence, she moved across the cab to wedge herself beside him. "I have a very distinct memory of going to Wingrave House. I was visiting your mother, and you came into the room. She didn't even greet you—merely accepted the kiss you gave her on her cheek and continued talking as if you weren't even there. And then Simon came in, and she extended an invitation to him to accompany her to an artist's atelier. She made no such invitation to you."

"You've a prodigious memory for trivial events," he muttered.

"It wasn't trivial," she insisted, looking intently at his shadowed face. "Not by a league. Because you suggested that you might also accompany her to the atelier, and she said, 'You won't find any wine or opera dancers there, Kieran. Hardly the sort of thing that would interest someone like you.'"

He flinched. Minutely, almost imperceptibly. But he did, recoiling from the memory of his mother's cruelty. Just as he'd flinched that day in the drawing room at Wingrave House.

Celeste's chest ached, and she took Kieran's hand in hers. It was much larger than hers, but beautifully made, like the hands of Michelangelo's *David*. She could have studied it for hours—some other time.

"Ever since my father made his fortune," she said softly, "I've been forced into a box. Celeste the Keeper of the Kilburns' Honor. Celeste the Respectable. It's so exhausting, being in that box. No one asking who *I* am, who *I* want to be. No one truly seeing me. But," she went on in a low, urgent voice, "*I* see that you're a kind and generous man. For whatever my opinion's worth, I see that in you."

She squeezed his hand tightly. For a moment, he let it lay passively between her palms. But then he very gently squeezed back.

Silence fell, and with it the realization that she sat with her leg pressed tightly to his, his hand snug in hers. His gaze fell to her lips. Her own attention was riveted by the hunger darkening his eyes and tightening his jaw.

It became much more difficult to breathe in the very warm, very small interior of the cab.

His own breathing turned slightly uneven, and he straightened, tension transferring from his limbs into hers.

"I think," he said, his voice very low, "you'd better get back to your seat."

"Right. I should. Quite cramped in here." Awkwardly, she shifted to the other side of the cab, but it didn't do anything to ease the tension. It continued on, crackling and tight. At last, she could stand the quiet no longer, and said in too loud a voice, "The next time, if you would be so good as to again pick the venue. We've already established that my knowledge of London's seamier side is rather . . ."

"Pedestrian." When she scowled at him, he chuckled. "No shame in it, sweetheart. You've led a sheltered life."

"Not always," she felt obliged to point out. "In some ways, I know the city's darker corners better than you."

"Have you ever any desire to see them again?" he asked with what sounded like genuine curiosity.

"I see them with my charity work. But as for Ratcliff itself, I did go back, shortly after Ma died." Celeste stared out the carriage window. The shadowed streets passed by, but they were West End streets, and the threats they held could never match the riverside slum's menace. Most of the people of East London were hardworking families, but there were others, more malevolent, more predatory, who also called it their home. When she had returned following her mother's passing, she had made certain to go at noon, and in her plainest garments. A footman had accompanied her, too, but she'd asked him to wear his own clothing rather than livery.

"Just after I came back from finishing school, I went by our old place," she continued softly. "We had two minuscule rooms at the very top of a tenement that sweltered in summer and froze in winter. When I visited, another family was living there—a woman and her three babes, and they stared at me like I was daft for wanting a look around. It was like being my own ghost, haunting my memories. I could still see the echo of Ma, bent over her mountain of sewing. It stole her beauty, that life."

"If you and she bear a resemblance," he answered quietly, "she must have been beautiful, indeed."

Heat slipped into Celeste's face, but Kieran was an unapologetic flirt, and his flattery shouldn't have meaning. Yet it did.

"I always thought that things would be so much better once we got out of that garret." She continued to watch the streaks of light from the streetlamps they passed. "But Ma got sick and died in Hans Town. The French lace on her cap, the Irish linen bedsheets, the Ceylon tea, and Royal College of Physicians sawbones—none of them saved her."

She turned her attention back to Kieran, who watched her intently from the other side of the cab. "When Ma died, I understood something. How fleeting and illusory all of this is. And I vowed that day that if I ever had the chance to seize control of my own life, I'd take it." She gave a hollow, cold laugh. "I never had the chance, or the nerve. Until now."

"Thus, our bargain." His next words were deep and she felt them within her as surely as if he'd caressed her with his hand. "Know this—I won't try to cheat you out of your experiences. We'll help each other get what we require. You *can* rely on me."

His words soaked into her with unexpected gravity. At each turn this night she'd encountered more and more surprises, but none more astonishing than him.

Up to now, her fascination with Kieran Ransome had been the kind of insubstantial infatuation based on what she'd believed him to be. Scoundrel, rake. Libertine. The sort of man who filled gossip rags but had no true dimension beyond the chaotic engine of scandal.

But he was more. So much more. There were depths to him, nuance and complexity that would ensure she would stay up far too late this evening, fascinated by everything she'd learned.

"I *do* hope I've given you a night to remember," he said, almost shy.

"There's no doubt of that." Something expansive opened in her chest as she thought of her walk through the darkened streets to meet him, to setting foot inside Jenkins's, conversing with the proprietress herself, and winning her first ever wager outside of a polite game of piquet. Gaming, with Kieran beside her. There had been that rather frightening moment when she'd encountered Lord Montford, yet even this brief terror added to the thrill of doing so many things that she'd yearned to do for so long.

None of it would have been half as wonderful without Kieran. He'd trusted her, encouraged her, in ways she'd never experienced before. And that alone was worth any possible scandal.

It was all temporary, of course. She had less than two months before the Season ended, before Lord Montford formally offered for her hand. And she had her end of the bargain with Kieran to uphold. She'd already plotted out her strategy for getting him invitations to the right parties where he'd be introduced to the right young women, one of whom would eventually become his bride.

She and Kieran were destined for other people, their time together was brief. Which meant that, while she still had the opportunity to live her own life, she would enjoy every moment to the fullest of her ability.

Yet, looking at his lyrically handsome face half in shadow, half in light, as he smiled at her with the joy of shared pleasure, worry coiled in her stomach. She had to be somewhat wise, and keep her heart safe. That, she suspected, would be an even greater challenge than avoiding social disgrace—and would hurt her far more than any scandal ever could.

Chapter 8

❧*❧

Kieran tried to slow his steps that took him toward Regent's Park, but his feet refused to obey. They sped him quickly toward where he was to meet Celeste, regardless of the fact that such haste went against the languid principles of a bona fide rake. In theory, scoundrels were far too jaded by their debauchery to hurry anywhere.

Yet here he was, darting around slower-moving pedestrians and dodging vehicles as he crossed New Road to reach the park. He could have ridden or taken a cab, but it seemed much faster to simply walk than bother with all that.

It had been two days since Kieran had taken Celeste to Jenkins's. On the ride home, she'd mentioned that she had a specific venue in mind for his debut as a reformed rake, and this morning, he'd received her note telling him to meet her at the park.

Hopefully, his clothing wasn't too disorderly from his quick journey here. Of course, he needed to look presentable to meet whomever Celeste wanted to introduce him to, but more importantly, what would *she* think of how he looked?

He came to a sudden stop.

"The deuce," a man behind him said in annoyance, stumbling around Kieran to keep them from colliding.

"Get stuffed," Kieran answered distractedly.

Only one night with Celeste at a gaming hell, and he was losing sight of his goal. She was a means for him, a way to enter the realm of respectable society so he could find an equally respectable bride. It didn't matter that watching her bloom beneath Jenkins's many chandeliers had been far more enjoyable than any gambling he'd ever done. It hardly signified that she had called him kind and generous—something *no one* had ever done—or that the press of her hand against his had lit fires throughout his entire being.

It didn't sodding matter. They had separate paths to tread. And it was highly, highly unlikely that Dom would take kindly to a scoundrel like Kieran having designs on his sister.

But what *did* matter was that he was almost late for meeting Celeste. He strode into Regent's Park and approached the designated meeting point.

"Goddamn it," he muttered to himself, "why is it so *bright*?"

Yet the sunlight skipped along the surface of the park's lake, as if someone had scattered a handful of golden coins atop the water. The image was so unexpectedly lovely, he almost forgot why he was at the park at this ungodly hour, and for what purpose. Yet he couldn't lose sight of the fact that he was here for two reasons: to show polite society that Kieran Ransome had mended his rakehell ways and, in so doing, find himself a bride.

Just as Celeste had indicated in her brief missive, a large pavilion stood beside the lake, and he steeled himself as he strode toward it. His steps quickened when he caught sight of her at the water's edge, watching the waterfowl gliding upon the surface.

Today, instead of that salacious green gown, she wore a perfectly demure pale blue redingote over a white dress, and instead of a dark wig, she'd covered her reddish brown hair with a bonnet of straw, trimmed with matching pale blue ribbons. The sweep of her bare nape riveted him.

She looked just as captivating today as she had two nights ago. It would be far more comfortable if she attracted him only in her Salome guise. Any man, and many women, would find her alluring in that rig.

To want to nuzzle her neck when she was dressed so primly did not bode well.

Christ, he was in trouble if only one night in her company and merely holding her hand set his head to spinning. Because he needed her and her social connections, so he'd have to find some miraculous way of holding himself in check around her.

Of course, keeping Celeste *out* of trouble was his intention. Well . . . *public* trouble. She seemed quite enthusiastic to experience as much private trouble as possible, and damn him if he didn't look forward to the prospect. He'd simply have to forget about how she'd been so insightful, so compassionate, or how good it felt to touch her, even briefly.

Impossible.

As if she could feel his regard on her, Celeste turned and waved at him. He saluted her in return and continued on his course in her direction. A small distance away he espied her maid, but the servant was busy chatting with a burly groundskeeper.

"I'm awake again while the sun still hangs high in the sky," he said, coming to stand in front of her. "It's slightly alarming how regular this occurrence is becoming."

"You'd better develop a callus where daylight is concerned," she replied, "because there's quite a lot of it whenever polite society decides to convene."

"Good Lord," he said, making a face, "with such unforgiving light, it's a wonder anyone manages to breed."

"We're supposed to close our eyes, rely on imagination, and consider our duty. And besides," she added, giving him a once-over, "you look equally handsome at noon as you do at midnight."

His chest broadened, and he fought the smug little smile that tugged at the corners of his mouth. He'd heard more elaborate compliments before, but her simple words warmed him.

"Be advised that I'm fully committed to this endeavor," he said, striving to stay focused. "Since our excursion, I haven't set foot outside my door after ten o'clock in the evening. Not to the theater, not to a single private gathering." His bed had been empty, too.

"Such noble sacrifice." Yet her lips quirked.

A wider smile spread across his face. There was something so bloody delightful about her willingness to make sport of him.

"And what's my sacrifice to be today? That pavilion strikes fear into my heart. It seems so . . . wholesome." He shuddered.

"An event which is fortunately indiscriminate in who it allows to enter. You've no need of an invitation to participate, so it's ideal for your first sortie. Before we breach its ramparts, I must ask—do you sneeze in the springtime?"

He frowned. "We're answering riddles now?"

"Reply to the question, please."

"Cloves make me sneeze, but not the springtime."

She nodded. "Then you're fit for battle."

"Once more unto the breach, et cetera." He extended his arm to her, and she set her hand atop it. This was only the third time they'd walked together like this, and it was far too pleasurable. He couldn't get used to having her on his arm.

They approached the pavilion, Celeste's maid trailing many paces behind them. The air grew thickly floral, but the scent could also have come from the respectable society matrons, decorous young ladies, and dandified bucks who also made their way toward the tent. Many speculative looks were shot in his direction, some of them scandalized.

"Don't," Celeste warned lowly.

"Don't what?"

"Give them a rude hand gesture or make a face or any of the other thousand things I imagine you want to do."

"I'd never," he said, affronted. A moment later, he said, "All right, I wanted to. But I didn't, and that should count for something."

"Felicitations on being slightly less appalling than normal."

"My thanks."

They reached the entrance to the pavilion—people nearby keeping ample distance between themselves and him—and Kieran finally understood why Celeste had pressed him about sneezing.

A banner within read REGENT'S PARK HORTICULTURE EXPOSITION, 1818. Tables laden with plants of every description were arranged from one end of the tent to the other, and some larger potted specimens sat upon the ground, including miniature fruit trees and tropical palms. Colorful flowering plants made the warm atmosphere rich with fragrance, and their colors shone against the more sedate hues of the attendees' garments. Men and women stood beside many of the plants, wearing eager expressions that clearly indicated they wanted to talk all things botanical with whoever would engage them on the subject.

"This isn't an orgy," Kieran murmured as he and Celeste entered the pavilion.

"Did you expect it would be?" she asked archly.

"A man can hope. What do we do now?"

"Now," she said, moving toward the first row of tables, "we see and are seen. By and by, I'll introduce you to the man who's our goal. But we can't go directly to him, lest we appear importunate."

She nodded in greeting at people they passed, some of whom acknowledged him, while more than a few either stared at him in shock or else pretended not to see him. It wasn't quite a cut direct, but being ignored hardly signified anymore. Unless he was being shot at or, to a lesser extent, punched in the nose, he didn't care.

The atmosphere within the pavilion was humid and close, both from the horticultural specimens as well as the people admiring them. Yet the tent was even more redolent with the weight of propriety and expectation.

"Remember that you aren't to spit on the floor," she said lowly, "and try not to proposition anyone no matter how flirtatious they are in conversation."

"I'm not *utterly* feral," he muttered sullenly.

She raised an eyebrow. "I read about what happened at the theater."

"Ah, yes." Then, "Which theater, and what night?"

A stunned laugh burst from her. "My gracious, you're the definition of *incorrigible*."

"You say that as if it's a negative characteristic."

"If we're to amend your reputation," she said primly, "it can be a liability."

"You were my defender the other night in the cab back from Jenkins's." His words were light, yet a small throb of hurt crept in. "Yet now you're casting me in the same scandalous light as everyone else."

She turned her gaze to his, contrition in her eyes. "Apologies. You deserve better."

"Thank you." His chest tightened. Unexpected for anyone to own their mistakes, and even more unexpected for it to matter that she cared about his feelings.

"Good afternoon, Miss Kilburn," a gray-haired woman said politely as they passed. She eyed Kieran warily, and he was seized with the impulse to make a suggestive comment to her simply to see Celeste's aggravation.

But he wasn't *that* perverse to undermine their efforts at reformation.

"And a very good afternoon to you, Lady Newstead," Celeste answered. "How fares your grandson?"

Lady Newstead beamed. "He's learned his letters already."

"But he must be hardly two years old," Celeste exclaimed.

"Two years and three months," the older woman answered proudly. "Takes after his mother's side." Lady Newstead's gaze drifted once again to Kieran.

"Lady Newstead," Celeste said, "perhaps you know Mr. Kieran Ransome. The earl of Wingrave's son."

"My lady." Kieran bowed.

Both the older woman and Celeste appeared mildly surprised that he could execute the maneuver. He fought to keep from rolling his eyes. For fuck's sake, like any aristo's son, he'd had a dancing master. He kept his expression placid and pleasant, however.

"Once your grandson moves past hornbooks," Kieran said civilly, "he might enjoy reading the stories about Samuel the Pirate. Rousing tales of adventure, but with solid moral lessons."

Lady Newstead barely contained her shock at his recommendation before saying with a pleasant smile, "How delightful. I shall pass your recommendation on to my grandson's nanny."

"Enjoy the rest of the horticulture show, my

lady," Kieran replied, bowing again as Celeste led him away.

They were a few steps away when Celeste murmured, "Marvelously done."

"As I said, I'm not utterly feral." Still, he enjoyed the admiration in her voice. "And how is it that you know so many details about my escapades? Dom's been garrulous."

She was quiet for a moment, before she said, "I read about you."

"The things that pass for entertainment." His brows climbed higher. "Why would you waste your time reading that?"

"As I've said," she replied, pausing to gaze at a spray of pink roses, "you have the privilege of leading the life I want for myself."

He studied the line of her profile as she examined the flowers. "Then it isn't me you find fascinating."

"I didn't say that." A tiny smile appeared in the corner of her mouth, and the pad of his thumb itched with wanting to run it across her smile so he might learn the softness of her lips, her skin.

"Admiring my Celsiana," an equally rosy-cheeked gentleman standing beside the flowers said.

"Such magnificent blooms, Lord Hempnall," Celeste replied.

The man then launched into a detailed and protracted monologue about the cultivation of the rose, including the difficulties in maintaining adequate drainage, and the appropriate time to prune. Celeste listened with an attentive manner, while Kieran did his best to mirror her expression, though he couldn't help but remember the opera dancer who'd shown a remarkable inventiveness when it came to the application of rose petals.

"I must say, Mr. Ransome," Lord Hempnall added just as he concluded his speech, "I'd little expectation of ever seeing you here, amongst us horticulture enthusiasts. For you I imagine it's a trifle, er, sedate."

"There's such inspiration to be found amongst the botanical world, my lord," Kieran replied. "'*I'll not leave thee, thou lone one / To pine on the stem; / Since the lovely are sleeping, / Go, sleep thou with them.*'"

"That's quite clever," Lord Hempnall exclaimed.

"The credit belongs to Thomas Moore." Kieran wouldn't recite his own verses on flowers here—these people at the horticultural exhibition were not his preferred audience.

"Considerable erudition." Lord Hempnall nodded approvingly at Kieran.

"And to have such sophistication and intellect amongst your musical recital's guests would undoubtedly add to the success of the event," Celeste added. "It's next week, isn't it?"

Well played, Miss Kilburn, Kieran thought. It was all he could do to keep from elbowing her in the side and grinning slyly at her.

"Indeed," the older man said with a nod. "So it is. Do say you'll join us, Mr. Ransome."

"I'm deeply grateful for the invitation." Kieran bowed again. "Will you be honoring your guests with a performance?"

Lord Hempnall chortled. "An unwell goat bleats better than my own attempts at music."

"When I come to your home," Kieran vowed, "I shall bring a remedy for the goat."

The gentleman laughed again, and Celeste looked quite pleased.

"I shall provide you with Mr. Ransome's address so your secretary can send him the formal invitation," she said. "Now he and I will bid you farewell so that you mayn't tire of our company before we see you again."

Kieran bowed to Lord Hempnall before he and Celeste moved on.

"Bravo, my general," he said in a low, appreciative voice. "Our campaign progresses."

"Many young women of excellent families and outstanding reputation will be in attendance at the viscount's recital. You won't be able to declare your intentions to court one of them so quickly, but I'll introduce you, which is an important step."

"And what if I'm not courting someone by the time the Season ends and our bargain is over?"

She sent him a wry look. "Between my vouching for your character, your unspeakably handsome face, and your ability to recite poetry, I'm certain you'll find some woman who will happily be home to accept your calls."

"Unspeakably handsome, am I?" He strutted, pleased by her admiration, however unwillingly it was given. "And you're blushing."

"It's dreadfully warm in here." Her hand climbed to the front of her neck, and he couldn't look away from the long lines of her fingers against her throat.

"Someone's selling lemonade next to the lake.

While it isn't the rich and holy blood of virgins, I'll drink it."

They turned to head toward the pavilion's exit, but the predictably handsome Lord Montford stepped into their path. He gave Kieran a genteel nod, slightly cool in its brevity, but when he turned to Celeste, it was as though he'd forcibly turned up a lamp to shine brighter.

"Miss Kilburn," he said smoothly, bowing over her offered hand, "how charming to see you here today."

"Good afternoon, Lord Montford," Celeste answered, and while her words weren't precisely dripping with affection, there was something in her tone that bespoke a certain degree of intimacy. "I believe you know Mr. Kieran Ransome."

As the words left her lips, Celeste looked as though she wanted to grab them and stuff them back into her mouth.

"At Jenkins's," Kieran said offhandedly. "But let's not talk about such immoderate places in front of Miss Kilburn, when we've such a delightful horticultural exhibition that absolutely demands every ounce of our attention."

Lord Montford looked a trifle puzzled, but Kieran smiled at him with easy conviction, adding a nod for good measure. Soon, the other man smiled and nodded as well, likely half-convinced that they ought to study every plant and flower with thoroughgoing zeal. Kieran had learned the trick of convincing someone through positive reinforcement from Finn, who'd used it to outstanding effect in the gaming hells across London.

Then Lord Montford's attention fell on Celeste's hand, resting atop Kieran's sleeve. The other man's focus sharpened, turning proprietary as he looked up at Celeste.

Very subtly, her posture changed, turning more rigid.

"Mr. Ransome's family is very intimate with mine." Celeste's words were nonchalant, perhaps deliberately so.

"Ah, of course," Lord Montford answered congenially. "I dine with the Kilburns often." He turned to Celeste. "Do you remember, the other day, when you took tea with my mother? She said you enjoyed the lemon biscuits, and will be happy to have our cook share the recipe with your cook."

"That would be delightful," Celeste replied and though her tone was genial, her eyes remained cool.

Tension coiled in Kieran's spine, along with the urge to safeguard her. The earl wasn't overtly threatening, yet something about him seemed to steal the joy from her.

"We'll see you and your father next Wednesday for supper, won't we?" Lord Montford asked.

"My father would be loath to miss it."

Lord Montford grinned. "Charming. And I'll be sure there are lemon biscuits to conclude the meal."

"Delightful," she said.

"Good to see you again, Mr. Ransome." Lord Montford inclined his head, his expression perfectly amenable, and then he was gone.

Kieran and Celeste stood together for a moment, and she didn't move or speak.

"What do you need?" he asked protectively.

"Lemonade," she croaked.

He quickly escorted her outside, and in short order, they both held mugs and stared out at the lake. A child attempted to sail a boat upon the water's surface, though his insistence on placing stones on the toy vessel's prow kept it from floating. The sky had turned pale gray, as it so often did in London this time of year, and cool wind toyed with the ribbons of Celeste's bonnet.

"At the onset of our arrangement," Kieran said after taking a drink, "you didn't mention you had a suitor."

"It wasn't of consequence," she replied, distant. Then, more firmly, she said, "No, that isn't so. It's absolutely of consequence. Lord Montford is the rest of my life, and I needed something for myself before I'm forced to spend my days at horticultural exhibitions and tea with his mother where she insists I adore her cook's dry lemon biscuits."

"Are you engaged to be married?"

She was quiet for a moment. "Not yet."

"Soon, though." Something hard and cold knotted itself between his ribs.

"My father told me Lord Montford will make a formal offer for me by the end of the Season."

"Do you have feelings for him?" Her approaching engagement was and wasn't a surprise, but that didn't make the news any more palatable.

"What's more important are my father's feelings," she answered, her voice flat. "He's eager for me to become an earl's wife, and eventually holding the title of marchioness."

"I see now," he said, rubbing his hand against the odd feeling in his chest. "Why you set the terms and time limit for our arrangement."

She made a quick, humorless noise that resembled a laugh. Turning to Kieran, she said with sudden vehemence, "You must understand. If I refuse the earl, the Kilburns and their gauche new money won't be accepted into the upper ranks. We must at all times appear grateful to be part of Society. We cannot have a trace of scandal. Which is why, when Dom jilted Willa, it became even more important that I perform my role as perfect young lady."

"The burden all falls on you." His muscles tightened. "I want to run all the way to Hans Town to find both Ned and Dominic Kilburn and bellow at them that it's not fair to put such a responsibility entirely on your shoulders."

"When has fairness ever held sway on how the world works?" she asked wearily. "Regardless of what I want, I'm going to have to marry the earl, and that will be that. My function in Society will be encased in amber, forever preserved, never changing. Perfect wife, mother of great men, facilitator of someone else's dreams."

"Which is why you wanted to experience all you desire of disreputable London while you still could." His hand ached with wanting to thread his fingers with hers, a small way to show her that she wasn't as alone as her damn family forced her to be.

"Thus far," she said with an attempt at a smile, "you've been an excellent guide. It's far better than my pointless shopping trips and dull morning calls."

He faced her. "If you could have anything, anything at all for yourself, what would it be? Please, don't hold back," he said when she started to speak and then stopped herself. "If there's one belief I want you to hold, it's that you can always speak your mind with me."

For a moment, he feared that she wouldn't or couldn't trust him, but he wanted that. He truly did.

"When Da found out I visited Ratcliff," she finally said, "he was livid. He didn't want us to have any connection to where we'd come from. It was fuel for the toffs' fire to treat us as if we were lesser beings."

"As if the source of the ton's wealth was without stain." Kieran snorted.

Her own expression was wry. "My father still aspires for us to join your ranks. And when I proposed that I wanted to start a foundation that worked directly with families in Ratcliff to improve their lives, Da flatly forbade it. He said I should stick to charity bazaars and other genteel ways of being charitable that don't involve *dirtying my hands* with real work.

"But," she went on, "if I could bring tutors and teachers to Ratcliff, hornbooks and slates so the children and adults could learn their letters, they'd be able to find better-paying employment. They'd secure good housing and not fear being taken advantage of by the unscrupulous. I saw it so many times when I was growing up there. Men and women getting swindled out of their wages because they'd signed something they couldn't read. Children stuck in the same cycle of poverty as their parents. I myself didn't learn to read until I was eleven. If it wasn't for Da making a fortune leasing warehouses and then being able to get me a governess, I'd still be unable to read. I'd still be doing piecework and living from coin to coin."

A shadow passed over her face, likely the ghost of what might have been, and Kieran ached for the hopeless young woman she could have become.

"I don't want that happening to anyone," she said tightly. "Most in Ratcliff aren't as I've been. Yet my dream of helping them won't ever come to pass."

The miserable resignation in her voice and her face shot straight through him.

"Oh, love," Kieran said, his throat burning. "I'm so sorry."

"There's nothing for *you* to apologize for," she said with a forlorn little laugh. "I used to weep about it, yet that only makes my head ache without actually changing my circumstance." She glanced at him wryly. "I don't suppose *you* cry about your family's treatment."

Now it was his turn to give a humorless chuckle. "Displays of any emotion—lachrymose or otherwise—are treated like mud on the Axminster carpet. First blame is assigned, and then they're scrubbed away as quickly as possible."

Her hand lifted, as if she, too, struggled with the urge to touch and offer comfort. He held his breath in anticipation, but then she lowered her hand to her side, and they both looked at each other with hard-won understanding.

"I've just the antidote to all this confining propriety," he said, waving toward the pavilion.

He was rewarded for his efforts by the light returning to her eyes. Excitedly, she asked, "What's it to be? Vauxhall, finally?"

"Far better," he vowed. "Far freer. But I want it to be a surprise. Do you trust me? No, don't answer that. The gentleman part of me will be disappointed if you answer in the negative, and the rake part of me will be disappointed if you answer in the affirmative."

"Then I do trust you—up to a point." Her smile was full and genuine, unlike the ones she'd proffered to the attendees of the horticultural exhibition.

"An excellent compromise." Her joy affected him just as potently as any liquor—even more so, because he could ingest gallons of her smiles and still crave more.

What if she were mine? What if I could make her smile like this every day and every night?

The thought whispered through him, and he jolted.

No, no, no. He pushed the dangerous idea away. Because even if he could somehow truly make her care for him, she was essentially promised to another. He could never make her his. The best he could do was give her what joy he could, for as long as he was able.

Chapter 9

The following day, Celeste was finally able to help sort clothing for the charity bazaar, though it was a Sunday rather than her usual Tuesday. She joined a dozen other ladies in Lord and Lady Blakemere's ballroom, where numerous long tables held heaps of laundered but slightly worn garments. It was slow-going, but Celeste didn't mind her labors because it meant impoverished people could have warm, clean clothing.

"Reminds me of helping Ma do mending," she murmured to her friend Rosalind Carew.

"Mind the volume of your voice," Rosalind replied wryly, her Welsh accent making her words musical. "We can't have the fine ladies know we come from people who actually *work*. Did you hear what happened to Lydia Hearne?"

"Do I want to?" Celeste remembered the mild-mannered girl from Miss Hadstock's Finishing School for Refined Young Ladies. Like the other pupils, Lydia came from a family that had amassed a fortune through business and commerce, and like the other students, she'd endeavored to gain entry into the world of England's elite families.

"Her mother was at a dinner party a week ago and scandalized the other guests by accidentally revealing that she still does her own cooking." Rosalind clicked her tongue as she held up a petticoat for inspection. "The invitations have slowed to a trickle since then."

"Poor Lydia," Celeste said sadly. She examined the seams on a child's jacket and saw that they still held. Since the jacket could be donated, she put it in a large basket at her feet.

Rosalind shook her head. "These toffs are more treacherous than any copper mine. It's a good thing Lord Montford fancies you—"

"Like a pretty vase to display on his mantel," Celeste added grimly. "A thing that he can show off and display and put precisely where he wants it. I'm commanded to walk with him in the park after this."

Celeste was *not* anticipating seeing the earl again and mouthing pleasantries, or feigning attention, when all she wanted to do was ponder just where Kieran intended to take her on their next excursion.

"*That's* a pleased smile," Rosalind noted playfully. "And I doubt it's because you're promenading with Lord Montford. Although," her friend went on, peering closely at her, "the flush in your cheeks is the variety that's usually attributed to a sweetheart. That can't be the earl, could it? Unless you find bland blonds exciting."

"It's *not* the earl," Celeste said.

"But there *is* someone else. Oho," Rosalind crowed, "you're getting redder, so I'm correct. Who is he?"

"There's no one," Celeste insisted.

Yet she could still picture Kieran at the horticultural exhibition, and how he'd been both dangerously handsome and unexpectedly well-behaved amidst the blooms and leaves and ladies and gentlemen. She might have anticipated that he could charm whomever he met, but most surprising, most incredible, was his concern for her. Especially when she'd revealed her circumstances with Lord Montford.

If you could have anything, anything at all for yourself, what would it be? If there's one belief I want you to hold, it's that you can always speak your mind with me.

She didn't regret telling him about her longed-for work in Ratcliff, but it brought back sharp, painful memories of what could never be. Still, no one else asked her what she desired for herself. No one offered her the kind of trust and security that Kieran did. A fortnight ago, she wouldn't have believed that such a scoundrel could have given her so much—but there was far more to him than she'd known. Including the fact that he, too, was forced into a persona assigned to him by his family.

The nuance and layers to that man continued to unbalance her. Learning more about him only increased her fascination, and that was a state she could not encourage developing.

She caught herself stroking the palm of her hand, as if his touch continued to linger there, a day later. It had been foolish to touch him in that way, creating a sharp hunger where before she'd merely wanted a taste. Yet, much as she should, she couldn't bring herself to regret it. Life was a collection of moments, and she'd have that one to clutch close in the years ahead.

But by the end of the Season, she would be engaged to Lord Montford, and a lifetime of marriage to one man while simultaneously pining for another was a tragic circumstance.

Refusing the earl was impossible. Not only would her father be furious if she declined him, Lord Montford would be outraged that a girl from new money refused his suit, and the Kilburns would become societal pariahs.

She'd have to accept, but until then, she would enjoy every stolen moment of freedom—with Kieran beside her.

"Given that you're staring into the ether like a woman who's eaten a considerable amount of opium," Rosalind said dryly, "I strongly doubt that there's no one. That's all right, Celly. Tell me if and when you're ready. God knows you had to endure my impersonation of a gothic heroine when I thought I was in love with Justine Powell."

The urge to confess swelled within Celeste. She'd been so good about keeping her bargain with Kieran secret, and while she did talk about certain aspects of it with Dolly—though not too much, to create a defense of plausible deniability should things fall apart—sharing this thrilling episode of her life with her dearest friend was irresistible.

"I need a moment of air," Celeste said in a normal conversational tone. When she headed toward the ballroom's balcony, she motioned for Rosalind to accompany her. Once she and her friend were outside, and once Celeste had ensured that they were entirely alone, she explained her arrangement with the notorious Ransome brother, careful to pitch her voice as low as possible so no one could hear her, just in case there *were* any curious ears about. As she spoke, Rosalind's eyes grew wider and rounder, until they nearly eclipsed her face.

Unease iced along Celeste's nerves. Would Rosalind chastise her? Call her foolish, willful, or worse? Their friendship had been forged in the depths of their hatred for Miss Hadstock's lessons, creating a bond over their desire for more than a life as a useless ornament. If Rosalind condemned her, she could lose her dearest and most beloved confidante.

"*Salome?*" her friend asked in a whisper when she'd concluded. "You call yourself Salome?"

"You have another name in mind?" Celeste replied stiffly.

"Salome danced and brought men to their knees. Even cost a chap his head." Rosalind's grin was wicked. "Your scheme's utterly perfect."

Celeste sagged in relief against the stone balustrade. "You aren't going to try to talk me out of it, or tell me I'm a madwoman for doing this?"

Rosalind enfolded her in an embrace. "The world has expectations for us, and all of them are confining. We need to take every opportunity to do something exclusively for us. We owe it to ourselves." Her friend stepped back enough to look her in the eye. "Do be careful, Celly."

"Admonitions of caution," Celeste said, wry, "when you've just been encouraging me to chop off men's heads?"

"I don't care about their heads." Her friend spoke earnestly. "It's your heart that needs protection."

"Kieran Ransome is a rogue and scoundrel of the first water. I'd be a fool to get my heart involved."

A corner of Rosalind's mouth turned up. "That's the trouble with hearts. They involve themselves, whether we want them to or not."

OVER THE MANTEL the clock chimed eleven, which was usually the hour that Kieran was nestled at his favorite chophouse, dining robustly to fuel himself for the night's adventures. Instead, he was home, sitting next to the fire with a book balanced on his thigh, sheets of paper resting on the book. He paused with his quill hovering above the foolscap, trying to come up with precisely the proper combination of words.

They burst into his mind—*She prowls amongst timid hothouse flowers*—and he hurriedly scribbled them onto the paper. It wasn't easy to write on so precarious a surface, but he scrawled the line and looked down at it with satisfaction.

"Quite right," Finn drawled as he crossed the room. "Desks are inane and overvalued when writing."

"I do my best work when there's an element of danger in the composing." Kieran resisted the impulse to hunch protectively over his work. Finn was the one person he trusted to know that he still wrote poetry, yet even so, it was a challenge to unlearn habits long ingrained. He'd lost too many of his poems when his father or Simon had discovered them and torn them to pieces or burned them.

Finn ambled closer, and peered over Kieran's shoulder. "*Who* prowls amongst timid hothouse flowers?"

"My fanciful muse," Kieran answered, striving for an indifferent tone.

"No one in particular?" his brother prodded.

"I take my inspiration wherever I find it," Kieran replied. "Never from any particular person."

Or he had . . . until now. Because who else could the woman in his poem be, but Celeste? And why did he want to find words that rhymed with her name? Or find precisely the right simile for the color of her eyes?

Those eyes filled with the light of a thousand stars when she was joyous, and it crushed him to see that radiance dim when she talked about her unwanted engagement and marriage. How could anyone steal her brilliance? It was a crime.

Finn dropped into the seat opposite his. "What were you doing with Celeste Kilburn at Jenkins's?"

Kieran started. "The woman with me wasn't Celeste Kilburn."

His brother raised one of his eyebrows. It was remarkable how that tiny expression spoke so eloquently, but then Finn was always adept at managing what he showed and to whom. Kieran was one of the fortunate ones whom Finn entrusted with his thoughts and emotions, which were bestowed the way a fairy king gave out enchanted gifts.

"I wasn't sure you'd seen us," Kieran said. "You didn't approach or say anything."

"Given that you were with Miss Kilburn and she was in disguise," Finn replied dryly, "it seemed prudent to steer clear of you both."

"How'd you work out that it was Miss Kilburn? No one else recognized her."

"There are tells." Finn added when Kieran motioned for him to explain, "She has a particular way of holding her head, unlike anyone else I've met. It's as though she's attempting to work out a complex equation."

Kieran sat back in his seat. Thinking on it now, Celeste *did* often seem as though she was carefully, thoroughly assessing the situation, which, given what she'd been saying about her particular social position, made perfect sense. She had narrow paths to navigate, with far more limitations imposed upon her than he'd ever know.

"What—"

Kieran barely uttered a syllable before the front door to their rooms slammed open. Heavy footfalls stalked across the floor, headed in his direction, and a moment later, Dom stood in front of him, his arms crossed over his massive chest.

"What the fuck are you doing with my sister?" Dom demanded.

"How did you—?" Kieran shot a glance at Finn. "Why the hell did you tell him?"

Finn used the poker to stir the fire. "I didn't."

"Lord Montford stopped by and said he'd seen you and Celeste at some damned flower show. Explain yourself," Dom gritted.

"I'm not saying a bloody word until you cease looming over me like some East End Colossus of Rhodes," Kieran answered. At the least, Dom knew nothing about Salome. He tucked the sheets of foolscap into his book, and, setting it aside, he answered, "I'm trying to fix our collective goddamned problem."

"How is squiring my sister fixing the problem?" Dom challenged.

"I'm not answering you until you sit down," Kieran snapped in response.

Glowering, Dom stomped over to a chair at the dining table and picked it up as easily as if it were made of reeds. He slammed it down on the ground, turned it around, and straddled the seat, bracing his arms across the back of the chair.

"Talk," he ground out.

"Don't understand what you're so scorched about," Finn murmured. "You were engaged to our sister and neither of us were sent into a roasting fury about it. Not even when you jilted her."

A contrite, wounded grimace flashed across Dom's face. "You *helped* me jilt her."

"Now I wonder at the wisdom of that," Kieran said darkly.

"And my intentions toward Willa were always honorable," Dom muttered.

"Until you jilted her," Finn added.

"Until then," Dom said, grim. "From the moment I met Willa, I was true to her. Whereas you," he went on, pointing a finger at Kieran, "are the biggest slut in London who wouldn't know the meaning of constancy if it sucked your cock. So, I won't have you toying with Celeste whilst you amuse yourself with others."

"I haven't shared a bed with anyone in weeks," Kieran protested. He blinked in astonishment as the truth of that statement struck him.

He rose and stalked to the shelf where they kept the decanter of whisky, then poured three glasses. He bolted back his first tumbler, then poured himself another before turning to his brother and Dom.

"I'm not serving you like a ruddy footman," he clipped.

Both Dom and Finn rose and came forward to take their glasses. They all studied each other over the vessels' rims, wary as any soldier expecting an ambush.

"In any event," he continued in the taut silence, "I'm not ruining her. Everything she's doing is by her choice, which is a fuck more than what you and your father are giving her. Forcing her to marry Lord Montford." He glared at Dom.

To his credit, a look of surprise crossed Dom's face. "Forcing? She always seemed happy to be in his company."

"Because she *has* to," Kieran said darkly. "Your father's grand plan of making her into a countess, and then a marchioness. Ned Kilburn's great victory. And if she refuses him, then you and your father can bid adieu to your social prestige and cachet." He shook his head, disgusted. "Fuck's sake, it's all so goddamned medieval."

Compared to an earl who would one day be a marquess, what was Kieran? Merely a third son who would never have a title or inherit ancient land.

"Damn," Dom muttered. "If it's *my* cachet she's protecting, she needn't bother. I don't give a fig."

"Your father seems to," Finn noted before taking a sip of his drink. "And if it is of significance to him, she apparently feels she hasn't a choice in the matter."

Dom's shoulders rose and fell. "Well, hell. But that doesn't explain what she was doing with you," he said to Kieran.

"We all must marry," Kieran answered, "or none of us gets a cent. Yet no one's going to consent to be our brides with our godawful reputations. Celeste is helping me remedy that."

Dom finished his drink in one swallow and slammed the glass onto a tabletop, then stuck his finger in Kieran's face. "I don't like having you near Celeste."

"It isn't up to you," Kieran said tightly.

Dom took a warning step toward him, but Kieran wouldn't flinch or back down.

"This isn't how ten years of friendship ends," Finn said, slipping between them with his hands upraised. "In this skirmish, consider me the sapper, disarming you both. Step back, take a sodding breath, and collect yourselves like goddamned grown men."

Kieran and Dom glowered at each other before they both retreated to opposite sides of the parlor. As his brother had advised, Kieran hauled in a serrated breath. His hands hung at his sides, lightly shaking with unexpected anger. But that made no sense. It wasn't as though he and Dom were unused to having rows, given that they were both men of strong natures and even stronger opinions. A handful of weeks ago, they'd nearly come to blows over the outcome of a knife-throwing competition, but then, as now, Finn had stepped between them and in short order they were toasting each other over many pints of ale.

But this anger now surged through him, as fierce and possessive as a dragon guarding its hoard.

Was he angry . . . for Celeste's sake? Even now, Dom didn't seem to understand the depths of his sister's strength. He remembered how she'd said that her family refused to see her for who she truly was, and didn't that just stick in Kieran's craw like a choking bone?

Her fight had become his fight, and by God, he'd be sure she got everything she desired.

"Fine," Dom finally said through clenched teeth. "If you mind your fucking manners, I'll allow Celeste to help you."

Kieran exhaled a rueful laugh. "No one *allows* Celeste to do anything. She's her own person, and her choices belong to her alone."

"Well," Dom hurled back, "I choose not to shoot you in the face."

"You—"

"Like grown men," Finn said warningly. "You asses."

"How do you intend to enforce your will, Finn?" Dom retorted. "I can bludgeon you with a teacup."

"There are more effective means of defeating a man than through blunt force," Finn replied with surprising cheer. "I know all of them."

"Crafty bastard," Dom said.

"How approving you make that sound," Kieran noted, and snorted in amusement.

A moment later, Dom's rumbling approximation of laughter sounded, followed by Finn's smooth, cool chuckle.

It was a truce, of a sort, but Kieran knew that when it came to his relationship with Celeste, he couldn't allow himself to simply follow his impulses, as he'd done so often in the past. The cold truth of it was that she might inspire his poetry, yet he could be nothing but a footnote in the story of her life. It wasn't so much that she couldn't be his, but that she didn't belong to herself. And she deserved better than being a pawn in others' games.

At the least, he could do something only for her. He'd already planned their next nocturnal outing together—but now he had another destination in mind, a place to take her where, if he couldn't give her all the freedom she desired, she might still have a measure of joy. That would have to be enough.

Chapter 10

Two nights after she'd confessed to Rosalind about her arrangement with Kieran, Celeste sat across from him in a hired carriage that sped through the darkness. They'd met at the same designated spot as they had the night he'd taken her to Jenkins's, but this evening's destination was unknown.

"Where are we going tonight?" she excitedly asked him. "You said it was to be a surprise but I can stand the suspense no longer."

Difficult to know whether her racing pulse was because of where they might be heading, or because of the man seated opposite her. Since her conversation with Rosalind, she had tried to remind herself that she ought to be more careful with her emotions when it came to him. Yet here she was, perfectly happy to spend the entire night in the carriage simply riding around town, so long as it meant being with Kieran.

"A private party." His smile promised all sorts of wickedness. "Given by Oliver Longbridge. You're likely already familiar with him."

"I am." Longbridge was the son of a Black West Indian father and a white English mother, and had made a fortune through a combination of inheritance and strategic investments. He'd become a fixture in Society as an arbiter of taste and elegance. "But I've been to Mr. Longbridge's assemblies before. They're hardly the sort of gathering that would attract your notice. Negus and quadrilles, all of it quite respectable."

Kieran's smile widened, and her belly leapt in response. "You only know half the story. When the whim takes Longbridge, he hosts fêtes of a very different character."

She raised her brows. "Pray, go on."

"That would rob you of the pleasure of surprise and discovery, and I'd hate to do that."

"What an insufferable tease you are," she said, pretending to sulk.

"When I tease," he said, his voice lowering so that she could feel it stroking over her flesh, "you'll know it."

Her cloak became quite warm, and she had to open it wider to let in some night air to cool her suddenly feverish skin. But when his appreciative gaze slid along her body, nothing could bring down her temperature.

"A new gown," he murmured approvingly.

"Funded by my winnings at Jenkins's." She smoothed a hand over the bronze silk that, unlike the green gown from the other night, had been specifically made for her nocturnal adventures, and fit her far better. All the clinging fabric was deliberate, the low bodice purposefully showing more of her décolletage rather than happenstance caused by the changes in her figure. She'd paired the dress with a topaz pendant and earbobs, and Dolly had artfully placed golden brilliants in her hair.

If only she could wear such a garment without having the need to paint her face to disguise her identity. Still, she could tolerate the discrepancy if it meant seeing Kieran gaze at her with barely disguised interest. Tonight, he'd actually darkened his eyes with kohl, so he was all shadow and mystery.

A damned nuisance, this fascination with him. Because it could not and would not lead to anything. It would have been easy to dismiss her growing obsession as merely physical, yet there was distressingly more to her fascination than simply wanting his gorgeous mouth on hers.

Oh, God. Her hand flew to her lips.

She wanted him to *kiss* her. Wanted to know what he would feel like, and how he'd taste. Would he be soft and tender, or rough and commanding? Perhaps a little of both?

Her body warmed even more. Try as she might to will it to some semblance of calm, it flatly refused to obey.

She needed to focus on what *was* possible, and that was tonight's escapade.

"Can you at least give me a hint about what awaits us at Mr. Longbridge's?" she asked.

"I'll say nothing, but I hope that your maid is a dab hand at cleaning silk, because there's a high degree of likelihood that your gown will require attention."

"That could mean anything," she objected.

By way of reply, he merely smirked.

Yet while he didn't answer her question, his words made her anticipation for tonight soar even higher. All kinds of delicious possibilities filled her mind . . . and the fact that Kieran would be beside her, also taking part and never judging her for her choices only made her eagerness sharper.

The cab came to a stop outside Mr. Longbridge's impressive Mayfair residence, just as a trio of finely dressed people stepped down from a lacquered carriage and made their way to the front door. As with Jenkins's, the exterior of the mansion appeared perfectly ordinary—if one could consider a mansion ordinary.

After Kieran and Celeste climbed out of the cab, they also headed toward the entrance. The door opened ahead of them to admit the trio of guests, and raucous music pouring out broke the quiet of the night, making Celeste's heart thud in anticipation. Whatever her future held, however constrained her remaining life was to be, at least she'd have memories of tonight to console her.

The door remained open to permit Kieran and Celeste to go into the entry hall. A stoic footman took her cloak and Kieran's coat, completely unmoved by the fact that a pair of women's drawers were draped over a marble bust nearby.

A woman raced through the entryway, chasing a gentleman. Neither of them wore shoes, and they slid and careened across the polished floor, laughing boisterously.

Celeste stepped back to avoid colliding with the pair, and was met by a firm, warm wall. She tottered, on the verge of losing her balance, when an arm encircled her.

"I've got you," Kieran murmured in her ear.

Her eyes drifted closed at the feel of his breath fanning across her skin. The last time he'd been this close, they'd held hands. She wanted more, so much more.

"Ransome, you rat-eaten brute," a voice called out. "Who the hell let you in my home? I don't know whether to sack them or raise their wages."

She opened her eyes to see Mr. Longbridge approaching. And while the gentleman was always attractive when he appeared at Society functions, tonight he verged on dangerous. He'd lost his cravat—or perhaps he'd never put one on—revealing the deep brown skin of his throat, and instead of a jacket, he wore an elaborately embroidered banyan that flowed behind him as he strode toward Celeste and Kieran. In one of his hands was a glass of amber-colored spirits, while a cheroot dangled between the fingers of his other hand.

"Longbridge," Kieran answered with surprising warmth, given how the other man had just insulted him. "It would take cauldrons of burning pitch pouring down from the ramparts to keep me away."

"I'll put in an order of flaming pitch with my housekeeper." Mr. Longbridge eyed Celeste.

For a moment, she debated whether or not to curtsey, as she had when they'd encountered each other before, but remembered that in disguise, and in this place, at this hour, she could liberate herself.

She plucked the glass from Mr. Longbridge's hand and took a drink from it, letting the smoky flavor coat her mouth and warm her throat. With traces of her old East London accent, she said, "I'm Salome."

The host threw back his head and guffawed. "Welcome to my home, Salome. You're free to do whatever you like, so long as all parties are willing."

"Duly noted," she answered, relieved that Mr. Longbridge hadn't recognized her.

"And *this* rogue is willing to do anything," Mr. Longbridge added, arching a brow at Kieran. "Did you ever return that suit of armor?"

"It was left on its owner's front step," Kieran answered, his eyes glinting, "more or less as I found it. Save for the codpiece."

Celeste pressed her fingertips to her lips to stop herself from laughing, but then, wasn't the point of these expeditions to live as wildly and openly as she pleased? She gave a loud, unladylike chortle. "You *must* tell me that story."

"Another time," Kieran said. "Tonight, we're going to test the limits of Longbridge's hospitality."

She started to return their host's drink, but he waved it off. "Keep it. There's an abundance in my cellars. Which I'm sure Ransome will drain. Godspeed, my children."

Putting his cheroot between his teeth, Mr. Longbridge sauntered off. As he went, a woman hurried up beside him, wrapping her arm around his waist. His low chuckle drifted back to where Celeste stood with Kieran.

"The very best of blokes, that Longbridge," Kieran said, guiding her up the curving stairs. "Don't tell him I said that, or else he'll ban me from his house."

"Never would I have guessed that he's the same man I sat opposite at the Earl of Ashford's dinner party three weeks ago. His manners were so polished, the earl himself *almost* suffered in comparison."

"None of us are precisely who people believe us to be." At the top of the stairs, an array of decanters and glasses were arranged on a sideboard, and, after topping off Celeste's beverage, Kieran poured himself a drink.

"We certainly aren't." She tapped the rim of her glass against his, then took another drink as giddiness danced along her limbs.

"I can't believe I'm about to advocate temperance," Kieran murmured, "but have a care with how much of that you imbibe. While Longbridge insists his guests respect consent, sometimes people forget themselves and try for too much."

"I'd no idea when I impressed you into service that meant you'd also act as bodyguard. Don't scowl. I'm flattered . . . possibly."

"I trust you," he grumbled, "but not others."

In sisterly affection, she patted his cheek, but she wore no gloves and the feel of his stubble against her palm was far from fraternal. He went still beneath her touch, his shadowed eyes hot. Despite her decision to act uninhibitedly, she snatched her hand back, curling her fingers in—whether to preserve the sensation of his beard on her flesh or to erase it, she couldn't tell.

They both took long drinks from their glasses. Kieran pulled a cheroot out from an inside jacket pocket and used a provided flint to light it. He drew on the cigar, yet he was careful to blow the smoke away from her. The rich smell enfolded them both.

She couldn't stop from staring. Even her father and brother adjourned to a different room when they took tobacco, and to see a man smoke openly in front of her was another first.

He held the cheroot out to her.

Cautiously, she plucked it from his fingers, then put it to her lips. Feeling like the most sophisticated woman in the whole of England, she inhaled.

And promptly coughed so violently that she dropped the cheroot. He ground the smoldering end beneath his boot while patting her on the back.

"S . . . sorry," she choked.

"Did the same thing when I had my first smoke," he said affably. "Perhaps we'll save the tobacco for another night."

Two men approached, one with massive shoulders and impressive height, while the other was much leaner, his face angular and his pale eyes incisive. As they neared, she glanced down and saw their hands were intertwined. Even Rosalind had to be cautious with her public displays of affection for other women, so for these men to openly show their attachment to each other spoke volumes about the tolerant atmosphere at Mr. Longbridge's party.

"Curtis, Rowe," Kieran said warmly. When the larger man gripped his hand and gave it a shake, the force had to be bruising because Kieran grimaced with a chuckle.

"Ransome," the big man said, and his companion nodded by way of greeting. They both nodded at

Celeste, but didn't ask for her name, which seemed more designed as a measure of her protection rather than to exclude her.

"Theo convinced me to take a night off from work," the angular man explained.

"Will's going to burn his eyes out like candles and his hands will wear to stubs with the amount of writing he does," his companion grumbled.

"There are always more political causes that need articulate voices," Kieran said with a smile. "Enjoy yourselves."

The couple moved on, and Celeste watched them go.

"Are you shocked that men love men?" Kieran asked neutrally.

"The world's a beautiful and expansive place," she answered. "Their affection for each other is enviable."

He smiled in response, making her heart leap. "Let's hunt down the source of the music."

After she took his arm, they followed the melodies from the landing into a ballroom, where colored lanterns hanging from the ceiling gave the massive space a more intimate, enchanted feel. Situated on a dais was an octet playing music Celeste had never heard before, but it made her toes tap. Like more typical balls and assemblies, guests filled the dance floor. Unlike those balls and assemblies, however, they were not performing any dances she'd witnessed.

Intimate was a tame word for it. Not even the waltz could match this dance for suggestiveness. Couples were draped over and around each other as though they were wet silk, moving in time with the music. Here and there as well, she spotted men dancing with men, and women with women.

It was indeed a measure of how careful and protective Mr. Longbridge was that his guests felt that they didn't have to hide their true selves, and she warmed with appreciation that such a place existed.

"There isn't a better orchestra in London," she said above the music. She swayed as it washed over her, its rising and falling notes transporting her.

Kieran downed the last of his drink and put the glass on the floor. He held out his hand. "Dance with me, Salome?"

She stared at his ungloved palm as Eve surely stared at the apple.

After she threw back the last of her drink, she slid her fingers into his. The languorous tension in his body seeped into all the corners of her being. Together, their gazes only on each other, they walked onto the dance floor.

Once in place, he took her in his arms. Her skin sparkled with awareness as one of his hands clasped hers, whilst his other hand cupped her waist. Never had she felt so alive in her own body as she did at that moment.

Then he began to move, effortlessly guiding her across the floor. She gave in to the urge to laugh. Dancing with Kieran Ransome, at last. No longer a girlish fantasy but a woman's reality.

"What's your first memory of pleasure?" he murmured.

Her gaze flew to his. "My what?"

"Was it a food? Feeling an object? Or did you see something that filled you with unfamiliar pleasurable sensations?" He snuggled her closer to his body and her mouth went dry.

"When I was a little creature toddling around on wobbly legs," she said softly, her palms molding to the broad plain of his back, "Ma had to wrap my hands in batting because whatever I touched, I put in my mouth."

His lips curved. "I like this fixation of yours. Keep talking."

"One day," Celeste went on, "my mother was busy, and forgot to wrap my hands. I found a boiled sweet she was saving for Dom, and of course, into my mouth it went. She fished it out right away, but that burst of sweetness . . . I'd never had anything like that. It was as if the sky filled with light and my body soared up to meet it." She wryly glanced at his expression, but instead of looking bored, he seemed enraptured. "Surely you're disappointed that it wasn't more prurient."

"Pleasure is pleasure," he answered, turning her in his arms, and her heart spun within her. When she faced him again, his eyes were intent and dark as he stared down at her. "However we find it, and whatever bestows it. I'll never sneer at pleasure."

"You wouldn't, would you?" She liked hearing the word *pleasure* on his lips, as if it was not merely a sensation but a spiritual pursuit. It must be something wondrous to share pleasure with such a man. With *him*.

A ripple of desire moved across her skin and settled in the deep, secret places within her.

"So long as no one's harmed in its getting," he said, his voice low, "we ought to be free to find our joy where we can. God knows that in this life, none of it's guaranteed."

"Is that why you pursue it with such dedication?" she asked breathlessly.

He was quiet for a moment before answering. "Depending on others to bring us happiness leads to disappointment."

"Thus, you give it to yourself," she said with approval. "A wise strategy."

His eyebrow quirked. "If you call me wise, I'll deny it to my last breath."

"I should call you something else, instead." How fascinating that he refused to believe anything positive about himself. A piece of her stung for that boy he'd once been, the child who had been forbidden from showing emotion, and the rakehell who now gave himself the comfort that no one else thought he deserved.

"*Impulsive*," he said sardonically. "Or *undisciplined*."

"Perhaps that's how you want people to perceive you," she insisted. "Yet I've tangible evidence of your generosity. And you could have done the bare minimum in our bargain. If you truly didn't care what I experienced, you would have taken me to Vauxhall or somewhere just as commonplace. But here we are at this extraordinary party because it's unlike anything else in London. You're giving me precisely what I need. Because you're a good man, Kieran."

Their bodies moved seamlessly together in the dance. Strange how she could be so ablaze with exhilaration, and yet also feel as though she'd finally found her home.

"My minimal efforts are hardly worth praise." His voice was dismissive, yet there was a searching in his eyes, as if he craved her approval.

"I can see you're going to impede me at every turn," she replied with a smile. "Has anyone ever called you *obstreperous*?"

"*Pigheaded arse* is employed with more frequency."

"I'll endeavor to call you that, the next time we're in polite company. 'Do pass me the biscuits, Pigheaded Arse.'"

The way he smiled, a mixture of boyishness and virile charm, shot heat through her. But it was the way he held her that made her heart race. His arms were secure but not too tight, as though he wanted her close but trusted her to be able to stand on her own.

"It will be a challenge not to call you Salome when we're in less disreputable company," he said, his gaze heavy-lidded.

"You must resist the temptation," she answered, alarmed by the notion.

"I will, only I've come to realize something over the course of our bargain." His voice dropped even lower. "Salome isn't a disguise."

"No one has recognized me thus far," she pointed out as he turned her again.

"What I mean is that Salome isn't merely paint and scandalous dresses, although," he added, with a sly half smile as he glanced down at her clingy bronze gown, "I'm entirely in favor of scandalous dresses. Salome, I see now, is *you*. She's part of you. Bold. Daring. A touch naughty, and completely in command of herself. I can even hear you in her voice, that touch of Ratcliff that your father wants to repudiate but is so important to who you are. All of that has always been within you, but as Salome, you can finally embody that part of yourself. You're setting Salome free."

Celeste started, absorbing his words.

It was a good thing that he held her so securely, or else she would have stumbled from the impact of Kieran's insight.

Was it true? When she painted her face, donned her revealing clothing, and spoke with her old accent—was she playacting, or was she allowing herself to be the woman who dwelled inside her?

"I've changed my mind about you," she said, slightly dazed from this revelation. At his curious frown, she added, "You're generous *and* perceptive, and anyone who doesn't value that is a damned fool."

"You are no fool," he said warmly.

I am, she thought. *For you.*

The feel of his long, taut body pressed to hers made her head spin, far more than the turns of the dance. Even if they had danced at one of the assemblies that clogged up the Season's calendar, they never would have been able to touch each other this way, with only the barriers of their clothing between them. The silk and wool were both too heavy, and hardly anything at all. His thighs were firm, his torso unyielding, and he radiated penetrating heat.

She clasped her hands to his shoulders, loving the play of muscle underneath the fine wool of his coat. Their faces were mere inches apart, close enough for her to see the widening of his pupils and feel the subtle accelerated shift in his breathing. His gaze lingered on her mouth.

Growing up in Ratcliff meant that the harsh realities of life were ever present. She'd witnessed many things there, both brutal and beautiful, but never had the luxury of swooning. One always had to keep their wits. Yet having Kieran so close, reading the hunger in his face and body, wanting him as feverishly as she did, Celeste nearly gave in to the urge to swoon.

Yes, this. She tilted her head, inviting him in for the kiss she wanted so badly to experience.

The tempo of the music abruptly changed, turning from dreamy and sensual to unrestrained and fast. At the first few notes, the other dancers broke into rowdy applause, hooting and cheering.

Kieran straightened, his brow furrowing as though he was regaining consciousness. He looked at the dancers, who now spun in a frenetic, frenzied pace far wilder than any typical country dance. The taller dancers picked up their shorter partners and swung them around, causing giddy laughter, especially when the ladies' skirts flew up to reveal ankles and calves.

And then Celeste was spinning, too, Kieran's arms around her waist as he turned with her. She laughed as the room whirled around her, light and color streaking as if she was in the depths of a dream. The last time anyone had spun her around, she'd been a little girl in her brother's arms. Yet now she was a grown woman, being turned by Kieran Ransome, in the heart of a bacchanal.

He set her back on her feet and they continued to dance, joining hands as they capered across the floor.

A sandy-haired, rather handsome man appeared behind Kieran. The man smiled as he tapped Kieran on the shoulder, and motioned toward Celeste in a wordless question. Whoever this person was, he wanted to dance with her.

Kieran shot her a questioning look.

Should she? She adored being in Kieran's arms, but if his words were true, if she *was* Salome, she needed to explore everything about that part of herself. Soon, she'd be Lord Montford's property, and might never have the chance again to experience this freedom.

Kieran trusted her to know what she wanted for herself, as she needed to trust herself.

She inclined her head in agreement. The man's smile widened as Kieran handed her to him. Her new partner had already begun to twirl her around as Kieran bowed before retreating.

Celeste lost sight of Kieran after that, too caught up in the rhythm and movement to keep track of his whereabouts.

"I'm Frank," the man said to her above the music.

"Salome," she answered, feeling the strength behind owning that name for herself.

"You're the most spectacular being I've ever beheld, Salome," Frank said as they danced. "The way you laugh . . ."

She favored him with her laughter, making him grin delightedly. This was precisely what she'd wanted for herself when she'd come up with this mad scheme. It felt like her first taste of that boiled sweet so long ago.

And yet . . .

Dancing with Frank wasn't as wonderful as being in Kieran's arms. Frank was pleasant enough to look at, and capable of partnering her, and while he looked at her with interest, he fortunately didn't try to steal any kisses or groping touches.

But Frank wasn't Kieran. It was like staring at the sun through many layers of gauze. There was brightness, but it was far dimmer—and less dangerous. Yet she craved the burn, and the searing afterimage in her mind and body.

When the song ended, she immediately looked for Kieran. She saw him standing in the corner with a glass of wine.

Watching her.

She nodded her gratitude to Frank, but her attention was fixed entirely on Kieran, and she went to him. Because tonight she followed her heart, and it wanted the man she couldn't have.

Chapter 11

✣✻✣

Kieran watched Celeste head to him, and though the ballroom was alive with color and motion and an abundance of sensory details that would have usually drawn his attention, she was his sole focus.

It wasn't as though her walk had changed. Her hips had always swayed in an intriguing fashion, her spine was as upright as ever, and her shoulders as straight as a confident woman might hold them. Yet there was an intangible quality about her now, her courage fully manifesting. She was tasting what the world had to offer her, and hungered for more.

Hell, how he wanted to be the man to give it to her. When that damned blond oaf had cut in on the dance floor, Kieran had had to will his hand to uncurl from a fist and remind himself that these midnight outings were for Celeste's benefit. If she wanted to dance with another man, by God, he'd ensure that happened. And the blond buffoon had done Kieran a favor.

Because he'd wanted to kiss her. No, he'd needed to *devour* her. He ached to cover every inch of her body with his, surround her with himself. Be inside her.

Stepping aside so she could dance with someone else gave him the distance he required. His levelheaded self—the one he seldom listened to—reminded him of who she was, and why he had to keep some semblance of detachment from her.

"A shame to stand on your own," a woman in violet said, sidling up to him. He recognized her as Mrs. Cochrane, a widow who was well-regarded for her creativity in the bedroom. She and Kieran had never become lovers, though the potential had always been there. "Especially a man who can dance so expertly."

Mrs. Cochrane glanced meaningfully toward the dance floor, where more pairs had gathered as another slow, sensuous tune began.

"If it's a partner you seek," he said lightly, "you've your choice." He directed her attention toward a hale silver-haired gentleman watching her from one side of the ballroom, and then looked over at a woman in ruby velvet, who also had fixed her attention on the widow.

The woman in question gave him a smile of rueful understanding. "Another time, Ransome."

She moved away, motioning for both the silver-haired man and the lady in ruby velvet to join her on the dance floor.

Kieran barely attended this because Celeste now stood before him. A light film of sweat made her skin shine, especially the tempting curve between her shoulder and her neck, and he longed to taste her salt on his tongue.

So much for detachment.

"Weary of dancing?" he asked.

"I'm in search of a new experience."

"Come with me." He offered her his arm, and smiled to see how readily she took it. Leading her from the ballroom, down a dimly lit corridor, they passed many couples kissing and fondling each other. Though their activities weren't as overt or explicit as they were at the Lily Club, where masked guests gave in to their every erotic impulse, the kisses were passionate. Hands roamed freely over bodies.

He stared at Celeste as she avidly watched the couples. She trailed the fingers of her free hand across her collarbone in an unconscious caress, and he bit back a growl.

He hadn't enjoyed a lover since he'd entered into this bargain with Celeste. Now he paid the price. He was as randy as a stallion scenting a mare, body aching with need. Ironic, given that he was currently surrounded by people yielding to their lusts, while he remained frustratingly chaste.

If Celeste had appeared shocked, or uncomfortable, by such public sensual displays, he would have taken her straight home.

But the hell of it was, she looked intrigued.

Familiar with the layout of Longbridge's home, Kieran took Celeste down a back staircase to the ground floor, then led her to the dining room. More guests congregated here, sprawling in chairs or each other's laps as they ate and fed each other from the spread of delicacies laid out upon the table. There were sugared fruits sparkling like gems, and cakes, and haunches of meat beside wedges of cheese, and, naturally, oysters. A barely dressed woman had even seated herself in the middle of the table, putting grapes between the diners' lips.

"Ancient Romans would be proud," Celeste murmured as they circled the room.

"He isn't reading Pliny the Elder," Kieran said, tipping his chin toward a young man seated at the head of the table, who held an open book and read aloud from it, with many of the diners paying close attention.

"'*As his mouth opened over mine*,'" the young man recited, "'*his hand delved between my legs, finding me as slick as a summer storm, and eager for him*.'"

A startled-sounding laugh burst from Celeste. "That's from *Midnight with the Bandit*, by the Lady of Dubious Quality."

It was Kieran's turn to chuckle in surprise. "You're familiar with her work."

"You aren't?" She arched a brow.

"I've had to purchase multiple copies when the bindings have failed after many perusals."

The man who had been reading passed the book to the woman seated beside him, and she read the next line aloud before handing the book to the man in the next chair. And so it went, until the book reached a lady seated in front of Kieran and Celeste.

The woman turned in her seat and waved the volume at Celeste. "Have a turn, my lovely."

For a long moment, Celeste only stared at the book, her eyes wide.

"Refuse if you want to," Kieran murmured into her ear. "You're under no obligation."

She hesitated before waving off the offered book. He exhaled. Certainly, he'd never expect her to do anything she didn't desire. Their nocturnal outings were for *her* pleasure, after all and if she—

"'*His mouth trailed down my neck,*'" she said, her voice soft, "'*with little stinging bites and slick swipes of his tongue. By the time he reached the hollow of my throat, I burned with need.*'"

Kieran gaped at her. She wasn't reading from the book. She *recited* it.

She noticed him staring, and the corners of her mouth turned up. All of the dining guests turned their wondering attention to her, many of them appearing delighted that this newcomer was so familiar with the book in question she could repeat it from memory.

Smiling, Celeste strolled around the table. Her voice growing in volume and confidence, she continued. "'*Clad as I was in only the thinnest of shifts, his hand on my breast seared me, and when he pinched my nipple between his fingers, I gasped with desire. His other hand worked between my legs, caressing my hot, glossy petals that opened like a flower in the spring.*'"

She paused long enough to pluck a wineglass from a man's fingers, take a drink, and then return the glass to his hand. The stunned expression on his face surely mirrored Kieran's own astonishment.

No, *astonishment* was too pallid a word for what roared through Kieran right now. Hearing such delightful filth on Celeste's lips—words she'd *memorized*, by God—aroused him beyond reason. His cock was harder than it had ever been, and while this company was no stranger to the sight of an excited man, he couldn't very well present Celeste with his raging erection.

He interlaced his fingers and placed his hands in front of his groin. It didn't fully hide the massive ridge in his breeches, but better that than let her see how much she affected him.

She continued circling the table, clearly aware that everyone watched and listened avidly. "'*He wasted no time in gathering up my skirts in his massive hands, and when he lowered to kneel between my legs, I gave way to my most sensual urges and moaned like the strumpet I was.*'"

She stopped to pluck a berry from a guest's plate and pop it in her mouth. "'*Grinning like a demon, he lowered his head to my cunny and gave it one thorough swipe of his tongue. My dew soon coated his cheeks as he made a meal of me, and I the willing feast.*'"

Celeste sipped from another guest's glass. Everyone, Kieran included, was in thrall to her masterful performance. It was a magnificent agony to listen to her, to watch her, bold and confident. Salome. No, not merely Salome, but Celeste, as well.

All he wanted was to lead her to some darkened corner, hold her neck with his teeth, and sink into her.

She can't be yours, so think of something else. Anything. Cold porridge slipping down the back of your shirt.

"'*When I had given way to no fewer than three deluges of release, he freed his cock, and thrust—*'"

"A stirring recitation, Salome." Unable to withstand this torture any longer, he looped his arm with hers and pulled her away from the table. "Yet there's much more for us to see, and you're so captivating, the guests are neglecting their supper."

Celeste appeared momentarily stunned as they moved out of the dining room. "I was just getting to the best part."

"Apologies, but it was either end your performance or else make a spectacle of myself in front of the entire company." He steered them down the corridor and toward the back terrace, passing more guests engaged in revelry. "Mind, I've happily made a spectacle of myself numerous times in the past, but I'm not fully prepared for *you* to observe that."

"Preserving your dignity?" She smirked.

"What little of it remains."

They stepped onto the terrace, which opened to a spacious garden. Here, too, the celebration continued, with guests chasing each other around the hedges, and half a dozen people cavorting in the fountain. The air was warm, but he dragged it into his lungs. Hopefully, it was brisk enough to cool the heat searing him from the inside out.

"I wish I could join them," Celeste said, staring longingly at the men and women in the fountain, splashing each other.

"This is your night to do as you please." He propped his elbow on the stone railing that ran the perimeter of the terrace, affecting a lounging pose that was far more relaxed than he felt.

She gestured toward her face. "My paint would run, and of all the scandalous things we've witnessed here tonight, the scandal of proper, virginal me being discovered here would eclipse them all."

"A virgin who knows filthy literature by heart."

Her smile was ripe with secrets. "The masculine gender hasn't cornered the market on dimensionality and contradiction."

"We men like to believe ourselves the apotheosis of complexity, but we're just crawling infants in comparison to the women running past us. All we can do is gurgle and hope we don't soil ourselves."

Her laugh plucked along his nape and trailed under the folds of his neckcloth. "What a way with words you have."

His chest puffed—he'd been commended for his verbal and linguistic skills before, but having *her* praise him far outpaced any other compliment.

"I warrant," she continued, "that you've developed a fine set of skills as part of a rake's seductive repertoire."

"You can talk a fine game, but if you can't see it through to the end, then all devices—rhetorical or otherwise—ultimately fail. Nothing speaks so well of one's abilities than the satisfaction of prior lovers."

There her hand went again, trailing along her neck, as if the minx had no idea that the sight of her fingers on her throat drove him to madness.

He didn't want this time with her to end. And he prayed that the additional excursion he'd planned for them would give her some happiness.

Below, the revelry continued, with more guests romping in the fountain. A woman in a diaphanous yellow dress rode a horse through the garden, up the stairs to the terrace, and then past them and through the double doors that led into the house.

He took her hand and led her back inside. They peeked into a sitting room, and inside, Curtis and Rowe were splayed across a sofa, kissing with tender passion. Wanting to give the couple privacy, Kieran escorted her to the next room.

Her hand was still laced with his, and when they passed a group of guests shouting as they kicked a football back and forth along the hallway, he urged her into an alcove to avoid the commotion.

He angled his body to shield her from the boisterous tumult as she pressed her back to the wall. Two of the men began to argue as they debated who tripped whom.

"It's getting wilder as the night continues," he noted, glancing over his shoulder as the argument grew more heated. Turning back to face her, he murmured, "I should take you home."

"No," she said quickly. "Please. It's disorderly but I'd rather be in the midst of disorder than feel nothing at all."

He looked down at her. Hardly a few inches separated their bodies, and he was so close he could see the flutter of her pulse in her neck and feel her breath on his face. Her eyes were wide, pupils nearly swallowing the forest hues of iris, while rosy color stained her cheeks. The atmosphere in the alcove was close, humid, and thick with awareness. Her tongue darted out to wet her lips.

Desire hit him so acutely he nearly buckled from its force. Centuries of wanting her built up to this one moment, with the rest of the world disappearing to leave only Kieran and Celeste in this small space, carved specifically to fit just them.

You can't do this, he reminded himself. But he didn't move away, even when the quarrelsome people in the hallway had gone.

"Is that what you're feeling?" he asked lowly, his gaze fastened on her mouth. "Disordered?"

"In the best possible way," she whispered. "You've given me so much, yet there's one thing I haven't yet experienced."

"What's that?" He felt his own voice vibrating deep within him.

She slicked her tongue over her lips again, and he fought to keep from groaning. "I've never been seduced."

He squeezed his eyes shut as a shudder of longing moved through him. "Never?"

"When would I?" she asked huskily. "*Good girls* lead frustratingly chaste lives. Not like rakes." She looked up through the fringe of her lashes.

"Which I am." He chuckled, though there wasn't much humor in it, not when he ached with this hunger for her. Each moment in her presence only sharpened his appetite, and even when they weren't together, he still craved her. More poems about her filled his notebooks, his thoughts, his body. "What you're asking of me—how can I give you what you want when we both know you're destined for someone else?"

"The things I do with my body are *my* choice." Her eyes flashed. "This time as Salome, it's taught me that. Not long from now, I *won't* be in command of myself, but for now . . . for now I am. And I want to be seduced. I want *you* to seduce me."

"It's a terrible idea."

Hurt flashed across her countenance, and she turned her face to the side. "Because you don't want me."

"Because," he said, gently using his fingertips so she looked at him once more, "I truly *want* to seduce you. And the only things I ever want are unwise."

A touch, a taste, and he'd need more. That was certain.

"We can be unwise together." When he was still and silent, she offered tentatively, "Perhaps you don't have to actually do it. You could simply *tell* me what you'd do to seduce me. But if you truly don't want to, we can leave this alcove and pretend that the desire between us doesn't exist."

Could he? The thought of walking away, of never yielding even just a fraction to this powerful yearning hollowed him out. Emptiness without her flooded him. Ahead of him lay a lifetime deprived of her company, her smiles, her energy.

Was it selfish of him to do this? Very possibly. But at this moment, in this place, with her looking at him with such authentic, honest desire, he couldn't bring himself to give a damn.

She would never be his. Yet for now, for now he could give them what they both craved.

Chapter 12

❖✻❖

Kieran's eyes darkened. Surrounded by the kohl, they became as fathomless as the midnight sky. Celeste stared into their depths, entranced. Her whole body was aflame as her youthful infatuation with a rake bloomed into a woman's need for this man. In all his complexity, she craved him.

"Oh, I want to, love," he said in a low rumble. "Shall I show you?"

"Please. Please show me." Her head was light as his words encircled her.

He raised one thick brow. There was a long, fraught pause. She feared he might have some last-moment change of heart, but then he planted his palms against the wall, bracketing her with his arms.

His gaze was hot and intent on her, and she felt it like a physical caress. "*If* I were to seduce you, do you know what I'd start with first?"

"A kiss?" she asked hopefully.

"That's the destination," he rumbled, "but there's a whole journey before that. No, the first thing I'd do is tell you how utterly obsessed I am with your neck."

"M-My neck." She became acutely conscious of that part of her body, and couldn't stop herself from resting her fingertips against the fluttering hollow of her throat.

He groaned. "All I want to do is bite that gorgeous neck of yours. I want to nip at it, sink my teeth into it. Lick it and taste you. My hands burn because they want to wrap around your throat and hold you still as I pleasure you."

She whimpered, and cast a longing glance at his hand pressed firmly against the wall, willing it to move and to hold her the way he'd described. Yet it remained frustratingly in place.

"Would you merely tell me these things," she whispered, "or would you do them?"

"All good seduction involves waiting, love. A little teasing builds anticipation, which is part of the joy of it. But," he went on when she was certain her body would be reduced to cinders, "after telling you what I want to do, I'd lightly, very lightly, stroke my lips along your throat. As gentle as a sigh, but you'd feel my breath against your skin, and then I'd touch the tip of my tongue to your flesh."

She closed her eyes, lost in the picture he painted. "Yes."

"I'd go higher," he continued, his voice deep and rough, "and scrape my teeth to the place just beneath your ear. Perhaps I'd give you the softest of bites, and you'd moan because it wouldn't be enough. Not nearly enough."

"Would you kiss me then?" she asked, hardly able to breathe.

His chuckle delved between her legs. "Oh, no, my love. As you tipped your head back, I'd stroke my thumb over your collarbone, and let my fingers drift lower across the skin of your chest. Your breasts would ache with wanting, but I wouldn't touch them right away. I'd watch you arch your back, offering yourself to me, just like you're doing now."

Glancing down, she saw she did exactly that, her chest curving forward. He stood close enough that the front of her bodice just brushed against the planes of his pectorals. It was a maddening taunt, hardly enough to satisfy her.

"I might want you to touch me," she murmured.

His gaze went even darker. "So I would. With my mouth. I'd kiss my way down until I reached the tops of your breasts, straining against the neckline of your gown. And when you could stand it no longer, you'd grab the back of my head and press me to you. That would be my invitation to finally touch you with my hands. I'd stroke your breasts and pinch your nipples."

"Oh, God," she whispered.

"And then I'd reach beneath your skirts to stroke up your leg," he went on in a relentless, velvet voice, "feeling all that delicious skin beneath my palm. After that, do you know what I'd do?"

"Wh-What?" she breathed, so dazed with lust she could barely form words.

"I'd go higher until I found your sweet little cunt."

She gasped at the word.

"Did I shock you with my language?" he murmured.

"I . . ." She swallowed hard. "I like it. I like hearing those words on your lips."

He made a dark feral sound. "You are exquisite."

"Because I'm crude?" She was feverish with embarrassment and pleasure.

"Because you're you." He nipped at her throat. "Your cunt would be wet, wouldn't it? You're wet now because you're as on fire for me as I am for you."

A whimper from her lips. How could he do this? How could he set her aflame with words alone?

"Kieran," she implored.

"Love?" he growled.

"I want to kiss you. Not in theory, but in truth."

He sucked in a breath and his nostrils flared. Earlier, when she had recited from the Lady of Dubious Quality's book, he'd appeared aroused, but now he looked on the verge of devouring her where she stood—and she welcomed it.

"I told myself I couldn't let it happen."

"So you don't want me to?" she asked, though she feared his answer. Because of all the adventures she'd had with Kieran, nothing made her feel the way he did. Awake, alive, potent. The gaming hell and this bacchanal were entertaining, yet *he* was the experience she'd longed for.

"God, how I want it." His voice was resonant, more a rumble than words that strummed across her skin.

Excitement and happiness bubbled through her. Yet he didn't move. Though he was willing, it would be up to her to fling them both into the fire.

Threading her fingers into his hair, she lifted onto her toes. He tilted his head to bring their mouths near, and she closed the distance, pressing her lips to his.

At last. He let her explore as she learned the feel of him. She'd read a good deal about kisses, yet all those words fled as she sank into exquisite reality. He *was* soft, but firm, and she could have spent decades simply touching her mouth to his. Desire had greater demands.

She stroked the seam of his mouth with her tongue. Growling, he opened to take her in. Their tongues met in hot, slick strokes that reverberated through her whole body. He tasted of wine and tobacco and sugar, and kissed her as though he'd been fashioned for this purpose alone. She was the center of his world, his one ambition, and he let her know it through his lips.

She clung tightly to him, holding nothing back as she fell into limitless pleasure.

Yet he kept his hands on the wall.

Needing more, she surged into him, pressing her body to his. He was tight and solid and deliciously male, such a welcome contrast to her own softness. Her hips met his, and she mewled to feel the hard length of his erection snug against her belly.

His kisses turned deeper, more demanding, and she met that demand with her own need. Reckless joy seized her as she tested the limits of freedom, made all the better because *he* was the man experiencing it with her. The man she'd wanted ever since she had first seen him, years ago. Now she knew so much more than that starry-eyed girl. She knew herself and she knew *him*.

"Touch me," she gasped against his lips. "I want you to . . . want you . . ."

With a fierce snarl, he tore his hands from the wall. At once, one of his palms curved around the front of her throat in a gentle but firm clasp.

He cupped his other hand over her breast. "Ah, love," he said in a deep rumble.

Even with the fabric of her bodice between them, he was hot against her flesh. As he stroked her, sensation gathered and traveled in hot currents between her legs. She could not keep still beneath him, shifting and arching. When he dipped his deft fingers beneath the neckline of her gown to find her nipple, she made a keening sound, the noise sharpening with pleasure when he pinched the tip of her breast. White gleaming ecstasy burst through her.

"Kieran," she gasped.

He was taut against her, his body deliciously unyielding. "Can I give you more, love?"

"Please."

As he'd promised, he scooped up her skirts with his other hand, until his hot palm found her leg. He caressed her through the film of her stocking, then went higher. He toyed with the ribbon of her garter. And then his hand went higher still, until he met the bare flesh of her thigh.

Until now, the only hand she'd ever felt on her thigh had been her own. But to have someone else touch her—to have *Kieran* touch this sensitive part of her—made the pleasure all the greater. He stroked over her flesh, surprisingly calloused fingertips lightly abrading against her flesh.

He pressed his face into the curve of her neck. "I want to touch you, love. Your cunt. May I?"

She opened her legs wider, willing to give him anything.

"Give me the words," he urged.

"I want you to," she said on a gasp. "Touch my . . . my cunt."

He snarled his approval.

Just as he had described, he slid his hand up until he reached her sex. She jolted with the sensation, but didn't push him away. If anything, she pushed herself farther into his touch.

"Ah, fuck," he rasped. "You're so beautiful." His fingers dipped between her folds, and she adored the slight roughness against her flesh. He traced the tender skin, his touch confident, deft and attentive. When he gently circled her bud, she cried out, lost to ecstasy. Pleasure built higher and higher, suffusing everything, as he stroked her.

A climax tore through her. She bowed up from the wall with the force of it, clinging to him as shudders racked her. He held her securely, yet did not relent in his caresses, not until she came once more, and then again.

At last, he slowed his hand, and then soothingly covered her mons with his palm. She held tightly to him, her body limp in the aftermath. He was solid as he held her up, and murmured wordless praise against the crown of her head.

"I want to return the favor," she whispered against his chest, and slid her hand down the length of his taut abdomen.

He let out a rueful chuckle as he stopped her hand. "Much as I desire that, love, I'm going to have to decline."

"Oh," she said, defeated. She wasn't experienced like his other lovers, so of course there was nothing tempting about her offer.

"Because," he explained, looking her in the eye, "if you touch my cock, that's all I'll ever want, and I have to make it through the rest of my life without it."

A pleased smile touched her lips, but her smile fell away when, gaze heavy-lidded, he dipped his fingers into his mouth, licking where she'd coated him with her arousal.

He wrapped his fingers around her wrist and kissed her where her pulse hammered beneath the delicate flesh. He did the same to her other hand. "Thank you."

"Shouldn't *I* thank you?" she asked as he tenderly smoothed her skirts down.

"You gave me such gifts, love. The gifts of your body and your trust." His eyes were warm but his lips turned down. "I'll treasure them always, especially because I'll never receive either again."

She didn't ask why—there was no arguing with the fact that she was all but promised to someone else, even if she had no affection for him. And it was wiser to stop this dangerous path with Kieran. Just this lone time receiving pleasure at his hands had already marked her, and, like him, the more she had of him, the more she would want.

"I should take you home." He stepped back, but his hands lingered at her waist as she eased away from the wall.

Though she stood steadily, her heart plunged. This wondrous night and all it had meant was drawing to a close. "I'll see you in three days, though. At Lord Hempnall's music recital."

"Would you object to a supplementary outing?" he asked in an unexpectedly bashful voice. "One that's apart from our bargain. No respectable gatherings intended to reform my reputation, no scandalous venues to explore."

"No objections," she said at once, grasping at the chance to be with him without the obligations of their pact. "Where are we going?"

"Another surprise. It will be during the day, and I advise you to dress plainly, something old that isn't the height of fashion. No need to paint your face as part of a disguise."

Her brows climbed. "You intrigue me. And I've some clothes I'd intended to give to Dolly, so one of those dresses should suffice."

"Superb. I'll meet you at our usual corner, and from there we'll proceed apace." He bent down and pressed his lips to hers. But the quick kiss at once turned hotter, deeper, his hands cupping her head as his tongue stroked hers.

Despite her shattering climaxes moments earlier, desire blazed to life again. She held tightly to his shoulders, kissing him back fiercely.

With a groan, he tore his mouth away. His breath came hard and fast, and it gusted over her as he rested his forehead against hers. Frustrated hunger ached within her as he seemed to fight with his own needs.

"We need to leave, love," he growled, "before I forget myself and fuck you against the wall."

"That sounds rather nice," she admitted.

His laugh was rueful. "It would be far more than *nice*, and that's why it can't happen." He stepped away and she resisted the overwhelming impulse to reach for him once more. Voice heavy with genuine regret, he said, "It's time to go."

HOW WAS SHE supposed to sleep that night when her body still glowed with the pleasure Kieran had given her? After returning home from the party, Celeste lay in bed and stared at her canopy as she relived every glorious moment from the evening. There were so many things she'd done that defied her wildest imaginings, yet nothing had been as wondrous as what she and Kieran had done in that alcove.

She hugged a pillow to her chest, but it did a poor imitation of holding Kieran. In truth, for the rest of her life she would never experience anything like him.

What if . . . what if *Kieran* courted her? What if they could turn their secret bargain into something real, something sanctioned?

The question kept her awake, teasing her with its possibility, until at last, gray light stole beneath her bedroom curtains. Wanting to give Dolly a few more moments of rest, Celeste dressed herself in a plain morning gown before stealing softly downstairs.

It came as little shock to find her father in the dining room, already shaved and prepared for the day. But from the surprised look on his face, he didn't anticipate seeing her.

"An early morning for you, Star," he noted from his place at the head of the table. A cup of coffee and a pile of newspapers were arrayed before him.

"Feeling industrious, Da," she answered as she went to the sideboard to pour herself some tea. After helping herself to toast and marmalade, she took a seat beside him.

"Young ladies of quality aren't *too* industrious," he cautioned.

As though she wasn't well aware of the rules, both spoken and unspoken, that regulated her behavior.

She nibbled on toast, and cast uncertain glances toward her father. "Da?"

"Mm." He didn't look up from his newspapers.

She swallowed her tea and trepidation. "Would a second or even third son do, instead of an earl?"

"What's this now?" he asked, setting *The Times* aside.

"Merely idle fancy." She traced the gilded edge of her porcelain saucer. "If, say, a nobleman's younger son was to offer for me, would that suffice? We'd still have the connections we want, and that's a fine thing, isn't it?"

"We don't need to concern ourselves with that," he answered. "Lord Montford's asking for your hand. He's no one's younger son. He's an earl, and the heir to the marquessate."

"If someone else came along before that," she ventured. "With not so great a rank, perhaps, but of a good family and with excellent connections . . ."

"Are you encouraging other suitors?" Her father's look was thunderous. Before she could answer, he said firmly, "You are promised to Lord Montford. It's as good as done—and if you think throwing him over in favor of some *younger son* will sit well with him, you're mistaken, my gel. Sorely mistaken. He'll call you a flirt and a jilt, and then the Kilburns won't be accepted in any stable let alone drawing room in Mayfair."

"It all rests on me," she said, grim. The weight of her burden pressed down on her, stealing her breath, robbing her of strength.

Her father's fingers wrapped around hers, and she looked up into his face. His expression was resolute, but not entirely unkind.

"It'll be a good life, Star," he said earnestly. "I vow to you, you'll want for nothing."

What about having purpose? What about affection and companionship and understanding?

But she said none of this. Instead, she fabricated a smile and sipped at her tea when he released her hand so he could continue to read his morning papers. Eventually, he finished his coffee and stood from the table.

"Be good, my girl." He dropped a kiss to her forehead before quitting the dining room.

She sat alone, her tea growing cold. The weariness she hadn't been able to find earlier now weighted down her bones. Perhaps she could simply lay her head down on the table and fall asleep here and now. But sleep wouldn't take away the fact that she had no choice in how the rest of her life was to play out. Her fate was settled, and that fate included nothing she wanted for herself.

She was too tired to even feel the urge to run

away. Instead, she slumped in her seat and looked out the window, hardly noting that fine rain pelted the glass.

The footman appeared, carrying a silver tray bearing a letter.

"This came for you, miss," he murmured. "The messenger said he'd wait for a reply."

"Thank you, Charles." It was still very early, so whoever had written the correspondence had either done so late last night, or first thing this morning. Perhaps it was Rosalind.

After she unfolded the paper and scanned the handwriting, her heart leapt, and her weariness was forgotten.

Couldn't wait. Meet this morning at 9? I flatter myself that my charm will override the importunity.

There was no signature, yet she knew at once who'd written it. She smoothed her thumb across the words.

"Tell the messenger that I shall be there," she said to Charles as he impassively awaited her response. "And give him a shilling for his trouble. I'll repay you after breakfast."

"Yes, miss." The footman bowed before departing the chamber.

Celeste made herself eat her toast, then finished her tea quickly. Wherever Kieran intended to take her, it would be ill-advised for her to journey there on an empty stomach. When she'd finished her breakfast, she took the stairs two at a time—

fortunately, Da had gone, so he couldn't scold her for such unladylike behavior—and went to her room.

She rang for Dolly, who appeared a minute later, dressed but rubbing her eyes.

"We're meeting Mr. Ransome at nine this morning," Celeste said without preamble.

"Cor," her maid mumbled. "Nobody's about at nine."

Celeste's exhaustion was gone. Effervescent excitement took its place as she strode to her wardrobe and threw it open, in search of her oldest and least ostentatious dress. "Today, we are."

THE HOUR WAS unfashionable and the weather inclement enough that no one was about when she met Kieran at their usual rendezvous spot.

She tried not to feel a burst of pleasure to see him loitering on the street corner, leaning against a lamppost, but her heart didn't listen, and so she was wreathed in smiles when she and Dolly approached him. He wore clothing in subdued shades of dun and brown, the fabric more serviceable than modish, yet he still looked exceptionally handsome as he straightened when she drew closer.

Only a few hours earlier, he'd been pleasuring her in an alcove, and she'd loved every moment of it. Now here he was, in the daylight, just as sinful as he'd been when he'd licked her essence off his fingers. He'd said they couldn't dally with each other again, but perhaps he might be convinced otherwise.

"Where we're going isn't half as salacious as what you're picturing." He grinned wickedly, then laughed. "The look of disappointment on your face."

"I hope I'll find today's outing worth it," she said, taking refuge in a lofty tone rather than admit that she truly did wish for a repeat performance. How shameless she'd become. And how she adored it.

"That's my hope, as well." He glanced up and down the street to make certain it was mostly empty of anyone who might see them, before helping her and Dolly into a waiting cab. As they pulled away from the curb, he said, "I shan't say where we're going, but it might become evident in due time."

Curious, she kept her attention focused out the cab's window as they journeyed east. By and by, the buildings grew closer together, their facades older and more careworn. The people on the streets likewise grew more numerous, and their clothing and accents struck a familiar chord within her. When the sharp smell of the river reached her, she sat up straighter.

Then the cab came to a stop on a familiar street.

"I know this place," she exclaimed. She turned to Kieran, whose face was carefully neutral. "You've brought us to Ratcliff."

His expression remained impassive, as if he was uncertain of her reaction. "So I have."

"But . . . but why?" She peered out of the vehicle's window to see the tenement where she and her family had once lived. It looked older, shabbier, smaller. Craning her neck, she could just make out the narrow windows that fronted the rooms in which she'd dwelled long ago. The flowerpots were gone, replaced by a line that held a row of minuscule shifts clearly meant for a child.

"You've been forbidden from coming here," he said, and she swung back to look at him. He watched her carefully. "From helping the people who live in this neighborhood. That's what you want, isn't it?" At her nod, he went on. "Now you can take the first steps."

She stared at him, hardly able to believe what she heard. "I'm to set up a charity *today*?"

"Not precisely." He looked at her levelly. "But you have a plan already, do you not? We can set it in motion now. You're an exceptionally capable person," he added, and she thought she detected a hint of pink in his cheeks.

Possibility and pleasure filled her, yet she had to say, "My father won't be pleased."

"We can leave right now, if that's your wish. But," he said, reaching across the cab to clasp her hands in his, "if this is something you truly want for yourself, and something you want for the people of Ratcliff, will you let him stand in your way? You're doing everything else to please him, but this could be for you. We'll make it happen."

We, he'd said. Not *you*, but *we*.

She blinked back tears, her heart overflowing. "No one's ever given me a gift such as this."

"That's *their* failing," he said vehemently. "You deserve whatever you desire. Everything. Anything."

Celeste was faintly aware of Dolly slipping out of the cab, yet her fullest attention was on Kieran. He continued to watch her carefully, as though he still wasn't certain how she'd respond to what he'd done.

She flung herself at him, wrapping her arms around his shoulders and pulling him tightly to her as she pressed kisses to his face, his hair.

"I take it you're pleased," he laughed, his hands around her waist.

"It won't be easy to manage," she said between kisses. "There will have to be subterfuge where my father's concerned."

"Does that make you uneasy?"

"It does," she admitted, "but, as you say, I'm already doing so much for Da. I cannot be expected to give up everything for the sake of his social climbing. He may be livid if he finds out, but I'm his daughter, and made of the same steel as he is. I was too afraid of what he thought to push back and fight for this. My time as Salome has shown me that I'm stronger than I'd ever believed." Her mind had already begun to spin with plans and notions and all the necessary elements that would be required.

"Don't forget," he said, lips to hers, "I'm here, too. Wastrel scoundrel I may be, but I can make myself useful. Speaking of which," he went on as he carefully set her back on her seat, "we ought to get out and get started."

Once she and Kieran had reassembled themselves, he opened the vehicle door and helped her down. The cabman barely waited for them to reach the muddy pavement before driving on. She couldn't quite blame a West End driver for hurrying away quickly from Ratcliff—he wouldn't collect wealthy passengers here. But she barely spared the cab another thought as she stared at the building that had once been her home.

A woman with graying hair and a small child on her hip approached. "Celeste? Is that you?"

"It's me, Susan," she answered, smiling to see her

former neighbor. Waggling the child's bare foot, she asked, "And who's this?"

"Freddie, my grandson," Susan said proudly. At the mention of his name, Freddie turned his face into his grandmother's shoulder. Susan laughed, but then eyed Kieran cautiously.

"Delighted to meet you, Susan," he said with a polite nod. "I'm Kieran, a friend of Celeste's."

"Sir," Susan replied with her own nod. Looking at Celeste, she said, "Didn't think you'd come back, not after that time years back."

"I can't stay away," Celeste confessed. She could hear herself slipping back into her old accent. "Ratcliff's always going to be a part of me.

"I have plans for Ratcliff," she said to Susan, "on ways to make things better for the families here. Plans that involve learning to read."

"Oh," Susan said, brightening, "that would be wondrous. There's many here who don't know their letters. But how's that going to happen?"

"I've got it worked out, but before I move forward, I want to talk to the people here and make certain it's what they want for themselves. It's much more important that the people these decisions affect have their own say in the matter."

Susan brightened. "When it comes to opinions, I've more than my share. Come inside, and we can talk." She climbed the steps leading into the tenement.

"Shall we?" Kieran held out his hand, and she took it.

She exhaled, grateful and proud beyond reason. Anticipation rose with each step into the tenement. At last, she was going to realize her dream. The power to bring it to life had always been with her, but by bringing her here, Kieran had helped her to see that, and reminded her how much Ratcliff meant to her.

Yet beneath this joy was a darker, bleaker truth. She might be able to find a way to keep her work with Ratcliff going, even after her marriage to Lord Montford, but sooner rather than later, this wondrous time with Kieran would come to an end.

Chapter 13

❧*❧

A fortnight earlier, if anyone had said to Kieran that he would have voluntarily been sober and awake at nine in the morning, sitting on a rickety chair in a tenement in one of London's humblest neighborhoods, transcribing plans for an aid organization . . . well, he wouldn't have even bothered laughing, the notion was too ludicrous.

Yet he'd spent all of yesterday morning and into the afternoon doing precisely that. As Celeste and the woman he came to know as Mrs. Susan Vere talked in Susan's cramped set of rooms, he had volunteered for the role of stenographer. Celeste had first gone out to bring many people into the conversation, and at her urging, they'd offered their thoughts on her intention to bring literacy to Ratcliff.

Celeste had facilitated the discussion, ensuring that everyone's voice was heard, and taking all suggestions into consideration. She'd run the talk smoothly, coming up with solutions to problems and making recommendations when something seemed too difficult to attain.

Damn Ned Kilburn for denying his daughter what was so clearly important to her.

Kieran's intention was only to show Celeste what was possible. He hadn't the ability to bring her dream alive himself, yet it seemed much more potent, more formidable, that she realized her own vision.

At the end of the meeting with the people of Ratcliff, Celeste emerged with a purposeful fire burning in her eyes and determination in her step. They hadn't been able to hail a cab in Ratcliff, so a walk was necessary.

"I'll contact the Duchess of Northfield immediately," Celeste said decisively as they skirted around a dray that had stopped in the middle of the road. "She does exceptional work with her schools for girls in the East End, and I'm certain she'll be amenable to donating hornbooks and quills to our cause."

"I'm on good terms with the Earl of Ashford," Kieran volunteered. "His wife runs *The Hawk's Eye*, so she would be an excellent resource for providing more literacy materials."

Celeste came to an abrupt stop. She wheeled to face Kieran, her expression intent. "Thank you—again."

"The hard work is yours," he protested, "and Susan's, and the other people of Ratcliff. I merely sat around decoratively."

"You did far more than that." She glanced up and down the busy commercial street before pressing a kiss to his cheek. "You've helped them, and made me very happy."

It was as though he'd gotten drunk on pure sunshine. His head spun and light seemed to emanate from his skin. What was this feeling? He couldn't place it, but managed to say with a modicum of rationality, "I'm glad."

But there wasn't time to linger on the streets of Clerkenwell. She took his arm and together they made their way west, until Kieran was able to hail a cab and take her back home.

TWO DAYS LATER, Kieran faced his reflection in the glass, watching his valet adjust the already perfect snowy white folds of his neckcloth and check that his equally white waistcoat was entirely free of lint.

"A subdued ensemble, sir," Wesham said, flicking away a speck of dust from the shoulder of Kieran's dark green coat, "compared to your favored garb."

"We do what we must as circumstance compels us." Kieran glanced toward his clothes press, which held a kaleidoscope of waistcoats and coats in an abundance of colors and fabrics, but, much as he would prefer to sport any of those garments, they weren't precisely acceptable to the rarefied company he was to keep that afternoon.

"Sir, you're fidgeting," Wesham admonished gently as he adjusted Kieran's cuffs.

"I'm a grown man," Kieran answered, "and grown men don't *fidget*. We are *moodily restless*."

"Your moody restlessness is preventing me from doing my job, sir."

"Very well." It was no good taking his humor out on his valet, but, damn it, merely thinking about seeing Celeste again after pleasuring her and after seeing her happiness in Ratcliff sent his mind and body into an uproar.

How was he supposed to play the smooth, sophisticated roué in her presence? The taste of her continued to linger on his lips, and the feel of her still burned his hands. And her joy . . . her joy brought *him* joy.

It scared the hell out of him.

Because he couldn't have her, *shouldn't* have her. He'd already done a shit job of staying away, but he had to do better.

He ought to stay home this afternoon, find an excuse and beg off. It wasn't as though he relished the thought of spending several hours with his arse growing numb as he listened to Mozart. But the whole point of this bargain he'd struck with Celeste was to put him in circulation as a possible bridegroom to Society's most esteemed figures. Today, in fact, she was supposed to introduce him to respectable young ladies, thereby laying the groundwork for him to pay calls on and eventually court one of them.

Kieran scowled. He didn't *want* to meet any respectable young ladies. The only thing he looked forward to today was seeing Celeste again.

What the hell was happening to him?

"I believe that completes your toilette, sir," Wesham said, stepping back and surveying him with an approving nod. "You will surely draw the attention of many eligible ladies, and perhaps those that are a trifle less eligible."

Finn poked his head into Kieran's room, knocking his fist against the doorjamb. He was clad in only a shirt and a pair of breeches, his feet bare on the floor. "Are you done with Wesham? I'm to meet Dom at the club by four o'clock."

The valet turned a questioning look to Kieran, who waved him toward his brother.

"I'll just prepare the things to shave you, sir," Wesham said on his way out.

Finn ran a hand along his jaw. "Damn. Here I thought I'd done a fair job of scraping off my whiskers."

"Doubting Wesham is a grave error to be repented at length," Kieran said, striding to the desk he kept in his bedchamber. Books and sheets of foolscap covered its surface, with quills scattered here and there, but atop the whole chaotic affair was a slip of paper bearing the bold cursive of Celeste's handwriting.

> *At the recital, I will introduce you to no fewer than three respectable debutantes. Alas, no one will be reading from the Lady of Dubious Quality or frolicking in a fountain but there might be cake.*
>
> *—C.*

He ran his fingers over the words, picturing her bent over the paper, perhaps with a stray tendril of hair caressing her cheek that she unconsciously brushed aside, only to have it slide along her skin once again.

What he wouldn't give to be the one to stand behind her and bend down to press a kiss to her nape.

"I can only speculate on what has you wearing the guise of a respectable gentleman," Finn said, breaking into his ruminations. "Perhaps you intend to rob a jeweler's shop and need to look presentable to get in the door."

"A bank, in fact," Kieran answered. "They won't let me into the vault if I appear too raffish."

His brother leaned against the doorframe, crossing his arms over his chest. "Where *do* you intend to go at this godforsaken hour, and in such staid regalia?"

"Musical recital at Lord Hempnall's." Kieran fussed with his neckcloth, even though Wesham had tied it perfectly. "Celeste wrangled me an invitation, and she's meeting me there. Have to look suitably virtuous if I'm to be thought of as a viable bridegroom by the mamas in attendance."

Finn was mute.

"What?" Kieran demanded as he faced his brother.

"I said nothing."

"One of your weighted silences always signifies that you've an opinion on something." He glowered at Finn.

"How many outings have you had with Miss Ransome?"

"Just the one," Kieran answered, tugging on his cuffs. When Finn continued to wordlessly stare at him, Kieran growled, "One sanctioned event during the day. Two at night. And a small outing yesterday."

"Telling you what to do is a fool's errand," Finn said, pushing away from the door, "but I'd advise you to be cautious, Key."

"I'd tell you that I'm always cautious but we both know that to be a lie."

"Where Celeste Kilburn is concerned," Finn said mildly, "you'll need to employ that underdeveloped skill. You have a responsibility to her."

Kieran marched up to his brother. "I'm aware of my goddamned responsibilities."

That selfsame accountability had been the only thing that had kept him from yielding to his desire for her. But Finn didn't need to know that Kieran and Celeste had kissed with an incendiary passion that continued to echo hotly in his body. He could still feel the silk of her most intimate places on his fingers.

Close as Kieran was with his brother, he'd never tell Finn that he ached with wanting Celeste Kilburn.

"I need to go," he said, striding toward the door. He didn't wait for his brother's response before quitting their rooms.

Half an hour later, Kieran stood on the curb outside Lord Hempnall's home on Green Street, smiling and nodding at the elegant people passing him on their way inside. Some of the guests looked at him with puzzlement, whilst others politely returned his bows. Even so, there were others that gaped at him as if they couldn't understand how the Thames had flooded its banks and deposited garbage on Mayfair's pavement.

He fought a sigh. Lasting change couldn't be wrought quickly, so he ought to be grateful that Hempnall hadn't sent a footman out to chase Kieran away.

Still, if Celeste didn't arrive within the next quarter of an hour, Kieran would seek his solace in the closest tavern. God knew he was far too sober. A pint would round off the afternoon's hard edges.

"Have I kept you waiting?" Celeste asked, hurrying up to him.

His heart squeezed when he saw her, dressed in a pretty saffron-hued gown trimmed with cream ribbon, but he manufactured an ironic smirk. "The fault's mine. I arrived *early*—a distressing turn of events."

"Oh, that's terrible," she said, her lips quirking. "You'll have to do something to atone for your atrocious behavior, such as drunkenly pass out on a church altar."

"That will be my next order of business."

She smiled up at him, and the damned sun chose that particular moment to emerge from a cloud, so that her face was bathed in golden light. He clenched his jaw, certain that nature itself conspired against him.

"Already, I've heard from the Duchess of Northfield," she said excitedly. "She's pledged no fewer than five dozen hornbooks. And Lady Ashford wrote to me to say that she'll provide chalk, ink, and quills. This is truly going to happen, Kieran." Her smile widened, enfolding him.

"We'll plan to meet in Ratcliff next week," he answered. "Can you circumvent your father's dictum again?"

"I'll find a way," she said with determination. She glanced past him toward the door to the elegant home behind them. "For now, Lord Hempnall's is our goal."

"I have my invitation," he noted as they approached the door. "Should anyone demand to see it."

"The fact that you're here is enough assurance to the footman that you're an invited guest." Now standing in the entry hall, she nodded at the footman who stepped forward to bow a greeting. "This is an exclusive event, so interlopers seldom try to wheedle their way in."

"My thanks for managing to gain a miscreant such as I entry." He bowed as a marquess and marchioness walked past, and, shock of shocks, they both inclined their heads to acknowledge his presence. How novel to be seen.

He and Celeste followed the guests down a corridor that was replete with stylish, expensive objects and stylish, expensive people.

"Good afternoon, Mrs. Lapley," Celeste said to a ruddy-cheeked woman in pearls. "This is Mr. Kieran Ransome, a family friend."

"Madam," Kieran murmured, bowing.

"Mr. Ransome," Mrs. Lapley replied politely, but Kieran didn't miss the appraisal in her gaze, far more commercial than sensual.

Kieran and Celeste passed other guests on their way toward the back of the house, and she introduced him, making certain to either indicate that his family was friendly with hers, or overtly stating that he was the son of an earl. He watched as the genteel guests' distrustful expressions turned interested.

He stopped abruptly, coming face-to-face with his mother and eldest brother. Both members of his family stared at him uncomprehendingly, as if trying to ascertain how he'd suddenly grown a pair of dragonfly wings.

"Mother, Simon," he said neutrally.

"Lady Wingrave." Celeste dipped into a curtsey. "Lord Greville."

His mother continued to look at him with puzzlement, but Simon managed to collect himself enough to say, "This event is by invitation only."

Celeste made a quiet, sharp inhalation, clearly not expecting his brother's rudeness. For better or worse, Kieran *had* expected it.

"And here is mine," he answered, holding up the piece of paper. "Issued by Lord Hempnall himself."

"That is . . ." The countess blinked. "Bewildering."

Why should her words wound him, when he'd endured similar from his mother his whole life? Still, something sharp slipped between his ribs, and he pressed his lips together to suppress any noise to show that she'd caused him pain.

"Kieran, that is, Mr. Ransome, made quite a favorable impression on Lord Hempnall at the horticulture exposition the other day." Celeste's tone was polite, but there was steel beneath her words. "Wherever he goes, he gains admirers. But that should come as no surprise to his own family." Her smile was more a baring of teeth than a friendly expression, stunning both his mother and brother into silence.

"The program will commence shortly," she continued loftily. "If you'll excuse us."

As soon as Kieran had led her away a safe distance, he murmured, "It's impolite to kiss you in public, but damn if I don't want to."

She cast a glance over her shoulder and scowled. "I see a physical resemblance between you and your family, but thankfully that's where the similarity ends."

"Never had a defender before." He coughed as his throat tightened.

"Why is it that the people we share blood with are the ones who understand us the least?"

"Because the universe thrives on irony." Yet he covered her hand with his own, wishing he truly *could* kiss her. "Now it's my turn to thank you."

"You deserve better," she insisted, color high on her cheeks. "We both do."

They reached the capacious saloon, at the center of which stood a lovely pianoforte, currently unoccupied, as well as three chairs and music stands placed close to the large instrument. Seats were arranged in a semicircle around the instrument, but the majority of them were taken, so Kieran guided Celeste toward the back of the chamber to stand with other attendees. When a footman passed by carrying a tray bearing glasses of wine, Kieran didn't hesitate to grab two. Celeste, however, politely waved away his offer of a beverage.

He'd have to drink both. Alas. What a horrendous predicament. After finishing one glass and handing it to another servant, he took his time with the second.

His gaze roved over the audience as he sipped surprisingly fine burgundy, finding some familiar faces and lesser-known ones. It was a decent mix of male and female guests, all of them supremely distinguished as they gossiped and fanned themselves, waiting for the music to begin. Several times, Celeste smiled in recognition at a person, or murmured a greeting to someone walking past, making certain to introduce him in the process.

"At the conclusion of the music," she said to him after another introduction, "I'll take you to some of the young, unmarried ladies."

The wine soured in his stomach. Naturally, the whole purpose of coming to this event was to present him to suitable women he might be able to court. Yet none of them would be half as fascinating as Celeste. None would have her zest for living, or possess her incisive and clever mind, or burn to create real change in the world.

Polite clapping sounded as four musicians took their places in the middle of the room. They remained standing as Lord Hempnall stood in front of the guests, wearing the expression of a man who believed himself to be the height of generosity.

"Welcome, welcome," the older man said, waving for the attendees to quiet their applause. "Today's program was selected by myself, and I'm sure you will find it delightful. Without further delay, let us begin." He shot a meaningful look at the pianist, who lifted his hands in preparation.

Once Lord Hempnall had deigned to remove himself from everyone's vision, the recital itself began.

Kieran attended the theater and opera often. In those venues, his focus remained on the activity in the pit or the boxes, and he seldom paid much heed to the performances, let alone the instrumental accompaniment. Here, however, nothing distracted him from the music itself.

His knowledge of specific pieces was limited to mostly bawdy tunes or tavern songs, so when a lyrical, lilting tune poured forth from the quartet, he was wholly unprepared. The work began with a kind of martial air, then shifted into something flowing and soft. There was an aching tenderness in it, as though striving to reach the source of its happiness. It evoked sunlight and shadow, a heart longing for recognition—and it reverberated deep within him.

Something damp trailed down his cheek. He reached up to brush it away, and discovered his fingers wet.

Dear God, he was weeping.

It was as though the composer had transcribed Kieran's own hidden self, the part of him that he'd once guilelessly displayed to the world. The part that had impelled him to write poems, which he'd foolishly shown his parents, proud of his work.

Those poems had been crumpled up and tossed to the floor. When Kieran had wept at their loss, his father had shaken him. *Men don't cry*, the earl had spat, and his mother had sent him to his room to collect himself.

Kieran's gaze sought out his mother and brother. Thankfully, they were seated and couldn't watch him now, silently crying in the middle of a music recital.

He glanced at Celeste, and, thank Christ, she didn't seem to notice that he'd been moved to tears. Lord knew he did not want anyone observing what a tenderhearted fool he was beneath his rake's polish.

Discreetly, he wiped at his cheeks.

That motion seemed to catch Celeste's attention. She glanced curiously at him—so he acted quickly.

Leaning closer to her, he whispered in time to the flute player's notes, "Listen to me play / What a fine chap I am / Bleating on my pipe / Like a sickly lamb."

She snorted, causing a seated dowager to shoot Celeste a glare. In turn, Celeste glowered at Kieran—though mischief danced in her eyes.

"Here I saw on my fiddle so nice," he continued softly, matching the violin player's melody. "Hee haw hee haw. I need to scratch / 'Cause I'm covered in lice."

Celeste clapped her hand over her lips but a titter escaped between her fingers.

"Shh!" the dowager hissed.

In response, Celeste removed her hand from her mouth and offered the older woman an apologetic smile. The dowager sniffed and turned back to the musicians.

"Stop," Celeste whispered urgently to Kieran. "Or you'll get us both thrown out, and undo all my hard work."

"A thousand most heartfelt apologies, miss." But he caught the impish humor sparkling in her gaze, and let out a noiseless exhale. She didn't suspect that he'd been overcome with emotion. His distractions had worked. He was safe.

"Where did you hear those rhymes?" she asked.

He shrugged. "Made them up just now."

That seemed to catch her by surprise, and she appeared as though she wanted to press him for more details, but the dowager had appointed herself the recital's prefect, and threw Celeste and Kieran another acidic glare.

There was nothing left to do but listen to the concert. He composed more nonsense verses in his head to distract him from the music, lest it led to another embarrassing and unwanted display of sentiment.

Celeste nudged him with her elbow. Then she tipped her head in the direction of someone seated. He followed her gaze toward a middle-aged woman with ash-blond hair, who had turned slightly in her chair to regard Kieran.

Perhaps she sized him up as a potential amour, which wasn't an uncommon occurrence. But then the lady gave the younger woman beside her a poke. She directed her companion to look at Kieran, and the resemblance between the two was such that it was evident the young woman was somehow related to her.

"Lady Caunton likes what she sees for her daughter," Celeste murmured in his ear. "Very nice. Miss Goswick comes with eight thousand but more importantly, you won't find a more respectable young lady in London. Spotless family reputation, too. Ideal for your purposes. I'll introduce you two at the recital's conclusion."

"My thanks," Kieran said quietly, bowing to Miss Goswick and her mother. Yet within him, something grew heavy and dour even as he reminded himself again that the whole purpose of this excursion was to pair him up with a young lady. Yet having Celeste point him toward other women, women that he might potentially *marry* . . . There went that weight in his gut again.

Whatever troubled him, he'd have to find some way of subverting it. His family's ultimatum was ever present—and if he didn't take a wife while Finn and Dom *did* find brides, then he'd cost all of them their inheritances, a burden too heavy to bear.

After the recital, he *would* meet Lady Caunton and Miss Goswick. That's what he had to do.

He caught himself staring at Celeste as she resumed listening to the music. The curve of her neck continued to fascinate him. Yet, more significantly, she'd defended him against his family, her words continuing to reverberate within him. *You deserve better.*

He wasn't certain what he deserved, but what he *wanted* remained out of reach.

Chapter 14

❧ ✲ ❧

There was no denying it: Celeste had seen Kieran weep during the performance of Beethoven.

The sight nearly moved *her* to tears. She wasn't familiar with the sight of adult men crying, save for her father's unguarded moment when Ma had died. Dom *never* wept, not ever.

But something had brought tears to Kieran's eyes, and it made her throb with the need to offer comfort.

She'd been about to reach for his hand when he'd abruptly started reciting silly rhymes. They'd been humorous enough to momentarily distract her, which she suspected had been his intention. Should she say anything to him about what she'd seen? Let him know that there was no shame in having emotions? Or would he deny it, and insist she was mistaken?

Men were peculiar, prideful creatures, but then again, the world didn't rise up and applaud whenever a man displayed his feelings.

She waited until the recital finally concluded, but this public place didn't seem to be conducive to heartfelt conversations. Seeing Lady Caunton and Miss Goswick stand up from their seats and move to mingle with the other guests, she was reminded of her responsibility.

"Never say I don't honor my obligations," she said to Kieran. "We have work to do."

Yet her feet seemed made of stone as she walked with Kieran toward the two women. Mother and daughter stood together, observing the other socializing guests. This was precisely why Kieran had approached her in the first place. It was not for the pleasure of *her* company, and she had to remember that. After he upheld his end of the bargain, it would be downright churlish of her not to assist in his quest for a wife—much as it filled her mouth with a bitter, acidic taste.

"My lady, Miss Goswick," she said, curtseying once they had reached the mother and daughter. "May I introduce you to a family friend, Mr. Kieran Ransome?"

"One of the Earl of Wingrave's sons?" Lady Caunton asked with more curiosity than suspicion.

"Indeed, my lady," Kieran said, bowing over her hand. "I am the youngest of three sons, but I believe the first two were trial runs before my parents finally got it right."

Lady Caunton laughed, though Miss Goswick looked to her mother first before permitting herself to giggle.

"How did you find the recital, Mr. Ransome?" Lady Caunton inquired.

"Inspiring, my lady."

Celeste regarded him, searching for a telltale sign

that he'd been emotional during the performance. Yet his eyes were as dry as his tone.

Even so, her lips quirked as she remembered the funny little nonsense rhymes Kieran had improvised during the music. It oughtn't have astonished her that he could spontaneously come up with a clever turn of phrase. He was an intelligent man, and playful, and every now and again he said something especially poetic.

Come to think of it, when they had met at Catton's, she'd observed the slim notebook he carried with him, and that there were lines written within it. Unlikely that Kieran was the sort of man who wrote down lists of things he intended to do each day, as her father did. What *did* he write in that little book?

It didn't matter, because she had to stop her appalling fixation on the man. Never mind that he'd brought her to Ratcliff for no other purpose than she wanted to be there. She had to forget the taste and feel of his kiss, his lips on her neck, and how he'd touched her with expert reverence in her most intimate place. It didn't matter how his dark eyes turned the shade of deepest midnight when he was aroused, or that he was sharp-witted, occasionally whimsical, generous, and unexpectedly sensitive. He was meant for someone else.

"Do excuse me for a moment," Celeste said, her eyes suddenly hot. "I believe I see someone I've been meaning to speak with."

She curtseyed before hurrying away, though she had no particular person or destination in mind. All she knew was that she had to be somewhere else, and give Kieran the necessary space to appear a potential suitor to Miss Goswick.

Celeste wove between chatting guests, heading toward the terrace at the back of the house. A tiny parcel of time on her own would help her gather her thoughts, and rein in her emotions.

She reached the terrace, where a handful of other guests had gathered in small groups to converse, discuss the musical program, and naturally, gossip. Chatting with these people, some of whom she knew, required more fortitude than she had at the moment, so she went to stand on her own near the balustrade.

Lord Hempnall's gardens were well maintained, though a trifle too formal for Celeste's liking. Back in Ratcliff, she and her mother used to tenderly nurse a miniature collection of plants that they set on the narrow windowsill. Ma often dreamt of a green growing space of her own, somewhere that didn't require careful balancing on a cracked sill, but when they finally had enough money to establish themselves in Hans Town, Da had insisted that their staff would manage the gardens.

"You're here with him again," a familiar voice said behind her.

She turned to face Lord Montford, whose pleasant countenance was slightly marred by the crease of displeasure between his brows.

"Good afternoon to you, too, Lord Montford," she answered. "I didn't know you were in attendance at the recital today."

"The engagement I had prior to this one ran late, so I came in after the concert had begun. This is the second time I've found you in Mr. Ransome's company."

"I thought the selection of music to be charming," she said, facing the garden once more. "Granted, my tastes are somewhat less cosmopolitan than many others', but I can appreciate a pretty melody."

"Miss Kilburn," Lord Montford said as he stepped closer. "Celeste. Are you going to answer my question?"

"I didn't hear a question, Lord Montford. Merely a collection of statements."

His jaw went tight. "Ah, you are in one of your humors."

"If having opinions and beliefs of my own might be considered as such, then yes, I am in one of my humors. Tell me, precisely, what you want to know." Irritated beyond measure, she continued to only offer him her profile.

"Does he have any intentions toward you?"

"His family and mine are on intimate terms," she answered tautly. "It's perfectly reasonable to expect that Mr. Ransome and I might be sociable together without drawing conclusions that he might have wicked designs on me."

She wouldn't speak of the fact that only three nights ago, Kieran had kissed her senseless and that his hand had been up her skirt.

Lord Montford opened his mouth, then closed it. He drew in a breath, as if marshaling his patience—which only increased Celeste's annoyance. She did not want to be *dealt with*.

He visibly smoothed out his expression and attached a mild, indulgent smile to his face. "If you want to maintain a friendship with Mr. Ransome for the sake of your families, I shan't prevent you. In truth, I find it refreshing that men might form platonic relationships with females. We can't live at the club and talk exclusively to other men, or else our conversations will grow stagnant."

"How fortunate that *females* are here for you to prevent that from happening."

He laughed as if she'd made a jest. "Truer words, my dear. I do hope you forgive my brief sojourn in the land of jealousy, but I'm so eager to make you mine that I see any other man as a potential threat."

"Rest assured that no one is more concerned about my welfare than I am," she answered. God knew if she didn't look out for herself, her life would consist of almost exclusively pleasant, empty diversions where nothing she did or said had any significance.

"I nearly forgot," Lord Montford went on cheerfully. "I want you to dine again with my parents next Friday, say, seven o'clock."

She didn't miss the fact that he'd issued a command, rather than a request. Clearly her time belonged to him, and they weren't even married yet.

Kieran approached, all polish and sophistication. He nodded at Lord Montford with perfect politeness, but was there a shard of hostility in his gaze?

"Delightful to see you again, Ransome," Lord Montford said.

"It is," Kieran answered.

Celeste pressed her lips together.

"Well," Lord Montford said in the ensuing pause that stretched on, "I must go take supper, before going to the Marquess of Hursley's ball tonight. Quite an exclusive event, you know, but the marquess insisted I make an appearance. Will I see you there, Ransome?"

"Alas, I am engaged to attend the theater this evening," Kieran drawled.

"Pity," Lord Montford replied.

Kieran made a noncommittal noise, but when Lord Montford continued to look at him, his expression slightly puzzled, Kieran said, "I believe you were off to take supper, Lord Montford."

"Yes. Right. My dear," Lord Montford said as he bowed over Celeste's hand for what seemed like an inordinately protracted amount of time before striding away.

Once she was alone with Kieran, she permitted herself the luxury of a full, unabashed scowl.

"Is there no way to discourage his attentions?" Kieran asked, studying her.

"None that wouldn't result in my family being effectively shut out of Society," she answered grimly.

"Hellfire," he said, his frown matching hers. "I wish Dom and your father didn't lean on you so heavily."

Her anger winnowed away, leaving her drained, with a faint headache pulsing behind one eye. "We share that sentiment—but I have no idea what to do to alter my circumstances. There truly isn't anything to do."

"I'd change it for you if I could." His eyes were dark and sincere.

It was too much, and yet not enough. Because she wanted more of him, this man who listened to her and honored the fact that she was a fully formed being with thoughts and emotions of her own.

"How fared your conversation with Lady Caunton and her daughter? Are you expected during calling hours?"

He frowned slightly at her change of topic, but she had to remind herself of the reasons why she and Kieran were occupied in this scheme of theirs.

"They aren't slaughtering the fatted calf in anticipation of my arrival," he said dryly. "The lady said she looked forward to seeing me again at one of the Season's events, and her daughter seconded that sentiment."

"It won't be long now before they're anticipating you leaving your card with the footman." She shouldn't be pleased that Lady Caunton wasn't throwing wide her doors to permit Kieran's courtship of Miss Goswick just yet. Shouldn't. But was.

"In the interim," he said with a smile, "you and I have a nocturnal adventure to undertake."

Lord Montford and Miss Goswick fell away, as excitement rose at the prospect, dispelling the confining truth of her future. "Is it to be another surprise?"

"Tonight, we are going to the theater," he announced.

She deflated slightly. "I've been to the theater."

"Not like this." Lowering his voice so only she could hear, he said, "Wear your usual garments for a respectable evening, but bring with you all the elements necessary to make your transformation into Salome. Is there a friend you can bring with you?"

"Our adventure is to include my friend?" This was growing more and more curious.

"You will attend with them, and then, at the conclusion of the performance, you'll part company with your friend and go with me to the next stage of the evening."

"I'm intrigued." Her heart already pounded with anticipation.

His smile was enigmatic and alluring, and she couldn't look away from him or the shadowed mystery that encircled him. "You should be."

CELESTE JOINED THE applause as the performers of Lady Marwood's latest burletta took their final bows. The work had been incredibly involving. She'd almost forgotten that she was here at the Imperial Theatre for some scandalous event. It was a testament to Lady Marwood's writing skills, because ever since Kieran had told her that *something* was going to happen at the theater this evening, she'd been in a state of breathless excitement.

"That was marvelous," Rosalind said beside her, adding to the ovation. "When the thief said to the princess that he'd love her until the last diamond turned to dust . . ." She sighed. "Thank you for inviting me to join you tonight."

"Thank you for accompanying me. My father never would have permitted me to come alone."

"How can I resist the opportunity to be part of a nefarious scheme?" Rosalind asked, eyes glinting.

The audience began to filter out of the theater, and Celeste and Rosalind stood to join the queues of people leaving.

"What are we to do, precisely?" her friend asked on a whisper.

"Kieran said to wait for him in the lobby. Beyond that, I have no idea. I do feel a trifle strange being the only woman in attendance who brought a small valise." At least she had been able to find one of the theater's staff to hold on to her bag during the performance. A generous tip of a whole pound had helped secure the discreet service.

"A good thing that the theatrical life is one that's accustomed to less than respectable behavior," Rosalind remarked as they headed down the stairs.

The crowds were thick and full of chatter after an evening of varied performances. There had been several singers, acrobats, even a trained bird that could spell by pecking at a deck of alphabet cards. The highlight had been the burletta, which had certainly been worth the wait as it alternated between comedy and pathos.

As she had during the performances, Celeste scanned the crowd in search of Kieran. She thought she'd caught a glimpse of him once, his dark hair gleaming down in the pit with the other raffish young men, but she'd blinked and he'd disappeared. She thought she'd also spotted Dom amongst the blades, but he'd likewise melted into the throng.

She and Rosalind reached the lobby and stood off to the side as the audience headed toward the exit.

"Seems strange that he wanted to meet you *after* the performance," Rosalind said.

"I've no idea what he's planning, or why I'm supposed to be at the theater at all."

"A mysterious creature, your Mr. Ransome."

"He's not *my* Mr. Ransome," Celeste said, her attention fixed on the multitudes of people moving past her. "He belongs to no one."

"Not *now*," Rosalind noted, "but if your plan works, at some point he will."

Celeste snorted. "Even when men take wives, they're no one's property. The same can't be said for women."

"Makes me grateful I'll never have a husband."

Was that Kieran amidst a group of bucks? No, just a man who bore a passing resemblance to him. Waiting was intolerable, especially because she'd no idea what awaited her. Knowing Kieran, it would surely be something extraordinary.

"Is that him?" Rosalind asked. "Esgob Dafydd, he's a handsome one."

It didn't seem to signify how many times Celeste saw Kieran. Every time he appeared, her belly gave a tiny flip and her head went light. He emerged from the multitudes and moved toward them. Unlike the restrained garments he wore when attending the recital earlier today, now he'd donned a waistcoat of gold, worked all over with ornate embroidery, and his beautifully fitted coat was made of claret-hued velvet. She couldn't stop from watching the flex of his thigh muscles beneath his snug buckskin breeches, which were tucked into tall black boots that shone like obsidian mirrors.

His hair, too, was worn slightly differently. It had been sleek and smooth at the recital, but now it lay in wild curls that tempted her fingers to feel their texture. She'd felt his hair's softness when they had kissed at Mr. Longbridge's party—but she wouldn't think about that now.

Alas, he hadn't put kohl around his eyes, but that was something better suited to more private gatherings.

He strode to her and Rosalind, wearing his sly smile that promised so much.

"This is my friend Rosalind Carew," Celeste said when he reached them. "Rosalind, this is Mr. Kieran Ransome."

"Miss Carew," he said, bowing. "Your assistance tonight is invaluable."

"Anything for Celeste, Mr. Ransome," Rosalind answered. "Including acting as alibi when necessary."

Kieran's smile widened. "You are a delight, Miss Carew."

"I know," Rosalind answered pertly.

"Back at finishing school," Celeste confided, "Rosalind frequently encouraged me to misbehave."

"As I recall," her friend replied, "*you* were the one who advocated that we sneak out after bedtime and swim in the pond. And *who* encouraged me to steal Miss Hadstock's keys so we could liberate her sherry? They found us in the morning asleep on the front lawn."

"So there's a precedent for your misbehavior?" Amusement danced in Kieran's eyes as he gazed at Celeste. "I'm wounded—I thought I was helping you break ground. However, we ought to be moving along to tonight's mischief."

He glanced at the now almost empty lobby, whose few occupants consisted of two inebriated men leaning on each other as they staggered toward the exit, and a trio of staff sweeping up programs, orange rinds, and other debris. "Did you bring your . . . ?"

"I'll fetch it." In short order, and with another generous tip, Celeste had her satchel that contained all the necessary components to transform her into Salome. Kieran took the luggage from her since, as he explained, it would look the height of boorishness to have him empty-handed whilst a woman carried her own bag.

With her disguise secured, they joined the remaining audience members clambering into carriages and cabs. Kieran hailed one, then held the door open for Rosalind.

"Are you comfortable heading home on your own?" Celeste asked as her friend climbed into the vehicle.

"I grew up with brothers," Rosalind assured her. "Which means I know how to throw a punch. And I know the vulnerable bits to hit."

Kieran winced as he closed the door behind Rosalind. "I've a younger sister, and I can vouch for the fact that she aims her punches with vicious accuracy. Good night, Miss Carew."

"Good night, Mr. Ransome," Rosalind said, poking her head out the window. "Enjoy yourself, Celeste." She punctuated this statement with the world's most obvious eyebrow waggle, before Kieran knocked on the side of the cab and it pulled away.

"The theater's closing," Celeste said, looking back toward where a burly man was shutting and locking the front doors. "I assume that means we're headed someplace different."

"We *are* going someplace quite different, but it's right here."

She shook her head. "You've turned into a sphynx."

"The solution is close at hand. Follow me." He headed toward the side of the theater, and she trotted after him. When he turned into the alley beside the building, her steps slowed, yet when she did, he called to her, "You're on the right path. Keep going."

He took long strides deeper into the alley.

Muttering about dark-haired scoundrels, she hurried in pursuit. It was not a very remarkable alley, with crates scattered here and there, and the usual puddles shining dully in the half-light. She found Kieran waiting beside a nondescript door with an even more nondescript sign above it that read PERFORMERS AND STAFF ENTRANCE.

Still wearing that inscrutable smile, Kieran rapped on the door. But it wasn't a regular knock. It had a strange rhythm to it. *Tap. Tap-tap. Tap. Tap.*

The door swung open, revealing a female dancer still wearing the cosmetics she had clearly worn on the stage. From behind her came the sound of a fiddle and a drum, the wild melody combining with laughter. The woman looked first at Kieran, but her brows rose when she studied Celeste.

"She's with me, Lottie," he said.

"Not your usual sort," the dancer remarked.

"Tonight, I am," Celeste replied.

Lottie tipped her head back and laughed. "All right, love. Come on in. We're just getting started."

"Another party like Mr. Longbridge's?" Celeste asked Kieran.

He smirked. "You aren't going to find anything like this anywhere in London. As Lottie said, we're just getting started."

"I certainly hope so," she replied. Nervousness prickled along her skin since she hadn't yet donned her disguise. Hopefully, no one would recognize her.

"Through the gates we go to Inferno or Paradiso."

"Which is it to be?" she pressed, abuzz with curiosity and excitement.

"Whichever pleases you most." Kieran held the door open for her, looking like the veriest devil inviting her into the depths of sin. Yet she didn't care what punishment followed her transgression. As long as she made her own choices, and he was beside her, she would face the consequences.

Chapter 15

❧*❧

Set pieces loomed over her as she stepped inside. They truly did look like the entrance to the caves of the underworld, with Kieran and his wicked grin leading her deeper into its depths.

There were so many possibilities here. What precisely did one do in a theater once all the patrons had gone?

"This way." Kieran guided her through the maze of painted scenery and other accoutrements that were stored in the darkened wings that flanked the stage. She cast a glance toward it, from where the music and laughter seemed to emanate, but heavy curtains blocked most of her view. "Careful. Easy to trip or get lost in this place."

Kieran wove through a mystifying labyrinth, passing a few people who carried blankets and flagons, until they were in a long corridor lined with doors. He knocked on one, and when there was no answer, opened it to reveal a narrow chamber that was filled with vanity tables and mirrors. A scarf-draped chaise longue stood in one corner, while clothing in a dizzying variety of colors were hung on racks next to a shelf of mannequin heads wearing wigs from every era. Shoes and stockings were flung about the room, as well as baubles, feathers, flowers, and, bafflingly, an iron frying pan—though there was no hob on which one might set it. A trio of cats lounged atop a mound of discarded costumes.

The chamber carried the scent of face paint, perfume, and the slight tang of sweat.

"This is where the actresses don their costumes?" Celeste asked, gingerly entering after Kieran.

"And receive their admirers after the performances." He set her satchel beside one of the dressing tables. "It will suffice as a place for you to transform into Salome. Can you manage on your own, or shall I ask Lottie to assist you?"

"I made certain to wear gowns that I can change in and out of without assistance."

"Then I'll leave you to your metamorphosis." With that, he moved into the hallway, shutting the door behind him.

Though she was impatient to join him and see what, precisely, was planned for the evening, she couldn't resist nosing around the dressing room. In Ratcliff, there had been a dance hall performer who had lived on the floor below Celeste's family, and Polly had often let Celeste sit on the floor when she'd come home from a night's work to putter around her room and unwind. Polly hadn't been especially fond of the place where she danced, but at the time, it had seemed so glamorous to little Celeste.

Yet to be a performer at the Imperial had to be quite different. True, the dressing room was cluttered and cramped, and was likely even more so when it was full of women preparing to go on the stage, yet it fascinated Celeste just the same. This was where the actresses and dancers got ready to perform.

And receive their admirers, Kieran had said.

Celeste glanced toward the chaise, its upholstery slightly faded and more than a little threadbare. Doubtless it had held more than its share of lovers.

Her cheeks heated as she imagined herself telling Kieran to stay in the dressing room as she disrobed. She'd seat him on the chaise, watch his eyes blacken with desire as she removed her clothing, garment by garment, and then, when she was clad in nothing but her shift, she'd straddle him and . . .

A knock sounded at the door. "Everything all right?" Kieran asked. "Things are almost underway out here."

"I'll be right out," she said, dragging her mind back from dangerously salacious images.

She'd become proficient in quickly transforming herself into Salome, and twenty minutes later, opened the door to find him leaning against the wall in the corridor. He straightened when she emerged, a smile unfolding across his face. "Ah, there she is."

"You only like me this way because my garments are practically indecent."

His smile widened. "Much as I adore your scandalous clothing, when you're Salome, you become the woman who's been inside you all this time. I do love to see her."

She needn't have bothered with rouge because surely her cheeks were red as poppies. Yet his words inspired her. Perhaps she truly *was* Salome, expressing part of herself that she'd been forced to keep hidden.

More music eddied from the stage, with laughter and chatter adding to the merriment. "That must be the next step in tonight's adventure."

"Let's join them." Instead of offering her his arm, he reached out and threaded his fingers with hers. The feel of his bare palm against hers was a hot bolt streaking through her, so that by the time they reached the stage and a group of nearly two dozen revelers, she was fever hot and more than a little dizzy.

When she and Kieran stepped onto the boards, they were greeted by wild cheers. There were women she recognized as dancers and actresses, who had changed from their costumes into a mixture of gowns and loose-flowing robes, as well as other women who hadn't performed tonight. Most of the men had removed their coats and undone their neckcloths, and one of them sported silk wrapped around his head like a turban.

The merrymakers lounged on mounds of pillows that were scattered across the stage—four people passed a long pipe back and forth between them—while a woman on the fiddle strolled from group to group, accompanied by a man playing a small Celtic-looking drum. Flagons of wine were everywhere and handed freely from person to person. More than a few of the revelers had brought pads of paper and were busy sketching the others.

"This is Salome, everyone," Kieran said, presenting her like a treasure he'd claimed on an expedition.

Another round of cheers rose up, and Celeste gave a small curtsey, though it felt a little silly to be polite with such a gathering of freethinkers.

"Oi, Lottie," a freckle-faced man hooted cheerfully. "You and Salome could be sisters."

Lottie had been lounging on cushions, but at the man's observation, she rose and swayed over to Celeste. She eyed Celeste, and it was indeed like looking into a smoky mirror because Lottie's hair was the same shade as Celeste's wig, their heights and figures very similar, and even the way Celeste had painted her face was a close approximation of Lottie's own features.

Wrapping an arm around Celeste's waist, Lottie cooed, "Ever think about a life on the stage, chicken? We could make a fortune as a sister act. And afterward, the men would knock our door down into splinters."

"There can be only one you, Lottie," Celeste demurred.

The other woman laughed. "True enough, but too much of a good thing is an even better thing. Just think about it, chicken." She pressed a kiss to Celeste's cheek. "Blimey, I've never kissed myself before."

"A dream come true," a pale woman in blue shouted.

Lottie made a rude hand gesture before returning to her place on the cushions.

"Who *are* all these people?" Celeste asked Kieran quietly.

"Some are performers. We've poets and artists—that woman in the coral dress is one of the finest sculptors you'll ever meet—and composers. Some are idlers like me, but to a one, everybody brings a little talent and unconventional thinking to the festivities. And once a month, after the theater empties out, we gather together to see where the night takes us."

"Stop hovering at the edges and join the party," Lottie shouted at her and Kieran.

"Are you ready?" Kieran asked her with a wicked gleam in his eye. Yet she thought she detected a hint of nervousness beneath his swagger. What on earth could he be uneasy about?

"I'm past *ready*," Celeste answered, "and I've moved into *breathless with anticipation*."

Kieran winked at her—incredible how such a tiny thing could send sunlight careening through her belly—and together they went to sit with the others. Celeste made herself comfortable on a stack of pillows as Kieran stretched out like a lounging cat. The laughter and conversation flowed, especially as the wine was poured. Though to her surprise, Kieran declined the offered pipe, so she followed suit.

"Growing dull in your old age, Ransome?" one man wearing a printed scarf jeered.

"Some of us don't need the crutch of the pipe to reach the Muse, Darwen," Kieran answered smoothly.

Hoots rose up from the group, and though Darwen joined in the laughter, his jaw tightened.

"A duel, a duel," someone cried.

"Give us a duel!" the crowd chanted.

Alarmed, Celeste stared at Kieran. "Will you *really* duel each other here?"

"Not in that way. But," he added with eager expectation, "it appears we're going to have to give the people what they want." He kissed her hand—her belly jumped at the sensation of his lips on her skin—but again uncertainty flickered in his eyes. Before she could ask him about it, the apprehension was gone, and he stood.

Darwen also got to his feet, and as he and Kieran stalked to the middle of the stage, the cushions and pillows were pushed back to give the men room. Kieran pulled off his coat and threw it carelessly to one side before he and Darwen began to pace, circling each other.

Mystified as to what exactly was about to happen, Celeste could only stare.

"Who goes first?" a gorgeous Black woman in a flowing yellow gown asked.

Kieran mockingly bowed at the other man. "I cede the floor to you. Show me how it's done, Darwen."

After clearing his throat, Darwen struck a pose, one hand on his hip, the other lifted up toward the heavens.

"The ebon' sky doth shine like ink,
Whilst here on earth, I raise my face,
And were I to bow, sigh, and shrink
The night etern' would lose its grace."

The crowd clapped politely, and Celeste joined them, even as she blinked in surprise. This was a *poetry* duel?

Kieran joined the applause, though his expression seemed underwhelmed. "A decent effort, Darwen."

"Decent?" The other man's face reddened. "And you can do better?"

His posture relaxed, yet, his deep voice resonating, Kieran said:

"On time's great voyage, I have lost my way,
Adrift, unmoored, eyes to horizon trained.
All stars I seek fade with the light of day
Yet to this cold prow my body is chained.
Each question I pose, one answer is true—
My guide is the constellation of you."

The audience shouted and clapped its approval as Celeste could only gape at Kieran.

He . . . he was a poet.

Of all the secrets he kept, of all the facets to his personality she'd yet to discover, this above all was the most wondrous, the most unexpected, and yet the most fitting. She should have known that a man with such a depth of feeling wrote poetry. He was a libertine, and perhaps in that seeking of pleasure and sensation, he reached out to the profundity of experience to channel that into verse.

The woman in the yellow gown got to her feet and strode over to Kieran and the other poet. She held her hand over Darwen's head, and more restrained clapping rose up from the guests. The woman then held her hand above Kieran, and the crowd exploded into loud applause and whistles.

Kieran was the winner.

Darwen scowled, but he grudgingly clapped for Kieran. The two men shook hands before they returned to their respective places on the cushions.

As conversation and the music resumed, she turned to Kieran as he stretched out. "Does your family know that poetry is one of your talents?"

"Finn knows," he answered after taking a drink of wine. "And Willa. Dom—though he's not blood kin. But I keep it hidden from Simon and my parents." He gazed at her cautiously, as if assessing her response.

"I hope you aren't embarrassed."

"No need for embarrassment," he answered, still reserved. "I only share that part of myself with people I trust. People who've earned it."

"They've earned it?" she asked, glancing toward the revelers.

"They take me as I am." He continued to regard her warily. "And you?"

This was why he had brought her here tonight—to show her this part of himself. Her heart expanded within her chest as she realized what an incredible act of vulnerability this was for Kieran.

"I am touched that you trust me this much." She stroked her hand down his cheek, and he leaned into her touch, his eyes warm with gratitude. "Have you ever considered publishing your poems?"

He gave a wry little laugh as he sat back. "Who would pay for such gibberish?"

"It isn't gibberish," she insisted. "It's wonderful. And anyone who says otherwise will have to contend with my wrath." She shook her fist menacingly.

"Do you truly believe people would want to read my poems?" he asked with uncharacteristic shyness.

"I do," she answered fervently. "At the least, consider the possibility of releasing a volume of your work."

"I will." He was contemplative for a moment before saying softly, "Thank you."

A thrill shot through her body, a mixture of excitement and, strangely, pride. Pride to know that she'd given something to him that he seemed hungry for.

Yet he wasn't and would never be hers. *Remember that.*

"Who is the 'constellation of you'?" She needed to ground herself in the truth of the situation. "A lover?"

"Something I never lack is imagination." His smile was wry.

She didn't mean to exhale, yet her breath left her. "And a very rich imagination it is."

Still—what would it be like to have him write a poem for her. *About* her?

"Kieran Ransome," she mused. "Another Byron."

He rolled his eyes. "Don't talk of that histrionic, self-absorbed clown. Not to mention he does things that even *I* find reprehensible."

"Haven't seen you before, Salome," a handsome man with thinning brown hair said, interrupting her thoughts.

"My first time here," she admitted.

"Oho, a virgin!" the man exclaimed to the company. "She's got to face the initiation."

"Ah, leave her be, Hyde," Kieran chided. "She doesn't have to do anything she doesn't want to."

"What *is* the initiation?" Celeste asked.

"You've got to dance with us," Lottie explained.

"I can dance," Celeste said at once. She'd even done some of the more risqué variety at Mr. Longbridge's gathering.

Knowing chuckles went up, and she tried not to feel too gauche.

"It's not your typical dancing," Kieran explained.

"Here, we'll show you." Lottie snapped her fingers at the musicians. "Give us something to move to."

The fiddle player grinned and launched into a spinning tune, with the drummer giving a steady, thrilling accompaniment.

Lottie got to her feet, and three other women and one man joined her. She nodded at each of them before they began to dance. It was bawdier than any of the performances that night, with more swiveling hips and legs being bared. Yet it wasn't *entirely* shocking.

Until the dancers started removing their clothes. A woman suggestively peeled off her gloves and let them drop to the boards, while Lottie and another dancer picked at the fastenings of their draped gowns, loosening them to reveal a peek at a shift and even bared flesh. The other woman untied her garters and tossed them into the cheering crowd.

The man, too, shucked his waistcoat and flung away his neckcloth, which landed on Hyde's shoulder.

Celeste stared in mingled shock and delight. The expressions on the dancers' faces were nothing short of revelatory. Because while they were the ones taking off their clothing, they also held astonishing strength as the audience watched them, enrapt.

Even Kieran watched the dance, though there was a touch more remove in his countenance. He seemed almost as interested in *her* reaction to it, glancing back and forth between her and the performers. Perhaps he expected her to be shocked. Surely that couldn't be the case—not after all they had seen and done.

But had she done *enough*? She and Kieran had a limited time together. Already he had made tremendous inroads into being accepted by respectable Society. Her heart plummeted. It wouldn't be much longer before he didn't need her anymore . . . and the Season was coming to a close. Lord Montford would offer for her soon. Then she would be forced into an even more constrained, circumscribed existence.

How many more opportunities would she get to express herself, to do something that frightened and challenged her?

She turned back to the dancers, shimmying and spinning and holding their audience captive.

What would Salome do?

Before she could think better of it, she surged to her feet, toed off her slippers, and joined the performers. She squeezed her eyes shut—it was too soon to look at anyone, especially Kieran—and fell into the music's spell. There was a moment's ungainliness as her limbs felt stiff and inflexible. But then she concentrated on the melody and rhythm and began to sway. She imagined herself the queen of a kingdom underneath the hills, a creature full of enchantment. Her body twisted with the music and she half believed something magical simmered beneath her skin.

Opening her eyes, she saw the revelers watching her, and she briefly panicked before pushing her self-consciousness away. The other dancers encircled her, inviting her to join them. She was a maenad now, freed from the tethers that lashed her to ideas of propriety.

The only person watching that truly mattered was Kieran. His gaze burned her as she moved, and more strength surged inside her. She bent down to grab the hem of her skirts, gathering up the fabric and twitching it in time to the music as she bared her leg.

Her heart pounded. One distant corner of her mind cried in warning—*Good girls don't show their legs*—but the melody drowned it out. By the time she reached her garter, all of her inner admonitions fell silent, and there was nothing but the pounding of the drum and her heart as she untied the material and flicked it away.

Kieran snatched it out of the air. And pressed it to his lips.

The crowd bellowed its approval.

Immersed in her power, she unrolled one stocking and kicked it off, then did the same to her other garter and stocking. When she shook her skirts in time to the music, its fabric brushed against her bare legs, and air caressed her naked skin. She still wore drawers, so she wasn't *entirely* exposed, yet her whole body was aflame with the knowledge that not only was she showing herself to strangers, she showed herself to *Kieran*.

But could she go as far as the other dancers? The male dancer's shirt was gone, and Lottie had stripped down to her shift, her breasts plainly visible beneath the sheer cotton, while another woman unfastened the brooch at her shoulder that held a drape of fabric across her chest. A moment later, the woman's chest was completely bare.

Celeste's fingers halted at the fastenings of her gown. Could she? *Would* she?

The music came to a stop. The crowd booed, but the musicians merely smiled apologetically.

"We need refreshment," the drummer explained as someone lobbed a pillow at him.

A man brought wine to the musicians. Meanwhile, some of the dancers reassembled their clothing while others remained partially dressed. Lottie stayed in her shift as she reclined on several cushions, her face flushed and triumphant as three men surrounded her, begging for a moment of her time.

Celeste scooped up her discarded stockings, and one garter, before returning to where Kieran continued to lounge. His eyes were hot and black as she lowered down to sit beside him.

"I'll want my garter back," she said brazenly, holding out her hand.

"I claim it as my prize." He patted his chest.

"What have you done to merit such a prize?" she challenged.

"The fact that I didn't haul you off the stage to ravish you in some darkened corner deserves some recognition."

"Men think that they're champions if they *don't* behave like beasts. Hurrah, you've done the absolute minimum." She smirked at him, even as her heartbeat became a roar.

"Believe me, love," he rumbled, "what I'd like to do with you is the maximum."

"*Are* there things you'd like to do with me?" she asked, finding it difficult to catch her breath.

He sat up and prowled close, his breath warm on her cheek and spiced with wine. "Many, many things. And I'm having a very difficult time convincing myself that we shouldn't do them."

Chapter 16

Kieran fell into the profundity of Celeste's gaze as she stared back at him. In those hazel depths, he saw arousal, but more than that, he saw acceptance. He'd revealed his most secret self to her, and she not only accepted him, she celebrated who he was.

Soft warmth flooded his body, even as he tightened with need for her. What he'd said to her was true—he ached with desire and for the life of him, he couldn't remember why they had to stay away from each other, or why they shouldn't yield to the attraction that crackled between them.

Her lips parted, and her pulse fluttered frantically at the base of her throat. Though she had just been dancing, her breath accelerated even more at his words.

"You'll drive me to madness," he snarled when she stroked a finger down her neck, "if you keep touching yourself like that."

"I thought poets welcomed madness," she said huskily.

"I'm suitably inspired without it."

She glanced down, and her eyes widened even more when she saw how his cock surged inside his breeches. There was no sense in pretending that she didn't affect him, and there was something so delectable about her knowing what she did to him.

"Watching you dance," he murmured, "I truly did lose my mind."

"Surely you've seen more than a flash of bare leg."

"Everything I've seen before now doesn't matter." He leaned even closer, narrowing the distance between them to mere inches. "It was watching you free yourself. You loved it, and I loved to see it."

He paid no attention to the celebration that continued to unfold around them. The music started up once more. Later, he would pay Opal the fiddle player and Quintin the drummer at least a pound for having heeded his silent request that they stop playing before Celeste had disrobed entirely. Perhaps she had been ready to strip in front of the crowd, but *Kieran* certainly wasn't ready for that.

He'd never, until this moment, wanted someone as much as he wanted her. Hunger for her had taken him over, replacing every part of him. The beat of his heart was now desire, and his lungs were fiery need. He was acutely aware of every inch of his body, just as he was aware of every inch of hers—the beads of perspiration along her cheeks, the widening of her pupils.

"Perhaps it's time to leave," she said, low and husky.

It was a disappointment and a relief. He didn't want this night to end, and yet it was better if it did, before either of them did anything that they'd regret. He typically didn't allow feelings of regret—the present moment was all that existed—yet he needed to consider more than himself.

"As you like," he answered.

"Take me back to the dressing room." She rose and slid her bare feet into her slippers.

Did she realize that she'd issued a command instead of a question? This imperious side of her was delicious.

He didn't bother with saying goodbyes to the other celebrants, too focused on the sway of Celeste's hips as she wended her way off the stage to head toward the dressing rooms. The corridors were draped in shadow, yet he followed her unerringly, as though she was indeed the constellation of which he'd written.

He'd never counted prescience as one of his talents, but perhaps in his Irish lineage there was some seer who read the future in bones and stars. For how else could he have known that she was indeed as celestial as her name, and that he would be guided by her? The destination was unknown but he welcomed the journey.

She stepped into the dressing room yet lingered steps away from the open door. He leaned one of his shoulders against the jamb and crossed one boot over the other.

"I'll need your assistance to remove my gown," she said huskily.

It was a lie and they both knew it.

Should he? Should *they*? God knew how much he wanted her. And she wanted him. At that moment, nothing mattered more than that.

A battle raged within him, to yield to this passion or to walk away. Their time together was running out, and he was selfish enough to seize the provided chance. Yet he could give her so much, and damn it, he burned to give her everything. He *would* give her all that she desired.

He straightened, and shut and locked the door behind him before approaching. Her breath came fast and shallow, as did his when she turned and presented him with the fastenings that ran along the side of her bodice. He undid the hooks, fingertips brushing against her revealed stays.

"God how I wish women weren't compelled to wear such restrictive garments," he muttered. "I want to touch your skin."

"I want that, too."

With the last hook finally undone, she moved away just enough to remove her gown, and then she wore only her stays, shift, and drawers. Her breasts rose up above the top of her stays, the thin fabric of her shift providing no barrier so he could look his fill of her.

She stared at him with undisguised lust. His cock was as hard as iron, his breath moving in and out roughly.

Celeste took a step toward him. To his astonishment, he stepped backward.

She frowned, then moved forward once more. Once again, his body disobeyed him, and he moved back. The chaise bumped against his calves, halting his progress.

"Don't you . . ." She wet her lips, the sight of which arrowed heat through him. "Don't you want me?"

"God, love," he rasped, "I want you so much I'm half-blind with it. But . . ." Was he actually going to do this? Apparently, he was. "We need to talk first."

"Talk?" She blinked. "In the books by the Lady of Dubious Quality, they almost never talk *before*."

"This is the real word, and in the real world no one can simply make assumptions about what the other person wants. Not without a conversation."

She set her hands on her hips, which had the unfortunate effect of making her chest thrust forward. How was he supposed to be rational when all he could do was salivate over her lovely breasts?

"Then let's have a conversation," she said.

"First and foremost," he answered as levelly as one could when presented with a half-naked woman within touching distance, "do you want this? I need to hear the words that you want to be intimate with me."

"I do," she answered at once. "And . . . what about you?"

"Can't remember wanting anyone more than I want you," he rasped. He knew what desire was, but never like this, never this all-consuming hunger to be inside someone, to *join* with someone.

A pleased flush stole across her cheeks and even spread across the bridge of her nose. Still, she said in a crisp voice, "I assume you know the basics of preventing conception." At his nod, she said, "Then we'll be safe, and fulfill our desires. It's what you and I want."

"And what about what your future husband wants?"

Her expression darkened. "This doesn't affect him. It's *my* body. I can do with it as I please. Besides," she added fiercely, "I can have sex and still marry. Men do it all the time."

"Much as I hate to point this out, it isn't the same. The horrible truth is that women are held to different standards."

"I reject those standards," she threw back. "Even in Ratcliff, my choices were never my own. But this," she continued, waving down to her half-clad form, "for now, this is mine. No matter what happens in the future, tonight, I want to rule my own body and my own pleasure. And I choose you for me."

"Because tonight you're the hedonistic Salome." Lust and yearning coursed through him—for *Celeste*.

"Because Salome is *me* and I'm her," she countered. "She's always been within me, and now I have the chance to inhabit all the parts of myself."

"I'm glad," he said in a low, urgent voice. "Glad that you don't have to live apart from yourself."

"For tonight, at least." She tipped up her chin. "We've conversed enough. Do you want to fuck me or not?"

He jolted with arousal even as warnings shouted in his mind. "A better man would say no."

"I don't want a better man," she said wryly. "I want you."

"Touché." He bowed, but when he straightened, all gentlemanly presence fell away. "Now turn around so I can get your stays off. If we're doing this, we're doing it right, and that means I want you naked. *Now.*"

Celeste's heart beat so fast she was nearly faint. But she steadfastly clung to consciousness as she presented Kieran with her back.

He quickly unlaced her, and the moment he finished undoing her stays, she tossed them and her shift aside and spun to face him. She wrapped her arms around Kieran's shoulders and kissed him. It wasn't the most graceful of kisses, more enthusiastic and eager than skilled, but he didn't seem to mind as his lips met hers with maddened need. Within a moment, they found their rhythm, a ravenous give-and-take. His tongue stroked hers and she opened eagerly for him, loving the animal rumbles of approval that reverberated up from deep within him.

His hands stroked along her back and then along the curve of her waist. One of his palms found her breast, his caresses summoning sensation so acute she gasped into his mouth.

"Holy fucking hell," he swore. "You feel so good."

"I want to feel you everywhere," she said breathlessly. She pressed her hips into his and panted with arousal when she felt the buckskin of his breeches against her flesh. He remained fully clothed while she was naked, and the erotic contrast between them made her dizzy. "I want everything."

"One thing at a time, love."

"How can you sound so calm?"

"Inside, I'm a riot." His chuckle was velvet against her. "And here, I'm a conflagration." He took her hand in his and pressed it to the thick bulge of his erection.

"Ah," she said excitedly, "this is the famed cock I've heard so much about." He growled when she gave it an appreciative squeeze.

"*My* cock, or just any cock?" Despite the insouciance of his words, his voice was rough and low.

"Definitely *your* cock." She stroked over it, learning its shape and size through the barrier of buckskin. "All those stories in the gossip rags, all those lovers fighting over you. I'd wondered for years what it was about you that drove them mad, and now I think I know."

"If you're that impressed with it in your hand, just imagine it in other places."

"*Oh.*" She pulled her hand back. How would he fit within her? Would it hurt?

"Easy, love." He stroked his fingers along her tight jaw. "This is your first time, isn't it? We can go as slowly as you like."

She ducked her head. "I've read so much about this."

"Reading and doing are different," he answered gently. "I want to make this good for you."

"I know you will." His gentleness and patience were soothing balms even as she shivered with needing him. "And it's *my* want to be good for you."

"Everything you do with me is exactly right. Whatever you've dreamt of, whatever feels good—it's all perfect." He bent and kissed her sweetly. "This is a safe and sacred place. Free yourself with me."

"I'm . . . a little afraid." She pressed her forehead to his chest as she shivered. "Not of the pain, but what it might mean if I truly did set myself free."

"I swear to you that if you fall, I'll catch you. But I know that you aren't going to fall. You'll soar."

Heart brimming, she pulled back to look at him. "I believe you."

"Now . . . if this truly is to be our one night together, I mean to take full advantage." Taking hold of her wrists, he guided her toward the chaise. "May I?"

"You can do anything you desire," she murmured.

"Trust me, love, I desire many things. And I'm going to ask for permission to do all of them." As he spoke, he gently urged her to recline against the chaise. "I want to look my fill of you. Can I?"

"Yes," she answered.

He stepped back just enough so that he could do as he'd asked, his gaze scorching across her nude body. Her first impulse was to cover herself—since she'd come to maturity, no one except Dolly had seen her completely unclothed—but she craved him seeing her. The way he looked at her, as if she were something to be both venerated and corrupted, made her heart pound and her sex wet.

Kieran sank down to his knees.

"Do you know," he said, his voice feral, "how long I've wished to see you like this?"

She shook her head, mute with arousal.

"For so very long." As he spoke, he leaned close, his mouth a mere inch from her skin. "My thoughts and body are consumed with desire for every inch of you. And this neck . . . your gorgeous neck . . ."

She shivered as he dragged his lips along her throat.

"I want to bite this neck," he growled. "Hold you still while I fuck you and fuck you. I want to mark you like I'm a goddamned beast."

Celeste cried out when his teeth sank softly into her skin, punctuation marks of pleasure. At the same time, his hands stroked over her belly and caressed her breasts and skimmed along her hips. He was everywhere, and pleasure was everywhere. The fabric of the chaise rubbed against her back, its roughness adding to the sensations.

He pinned her with his mouth and teeth as she writhed beneath him, her legs shifting restlessly as she sought relief from the growing need. She clung to his shoulder with one hand, and brought the other to her aching sex.

"I'd like to do that for you," he rumbled against her skin.

"By . . . all . . . means," she managed to exhale.

She arched up as his fingers replaced hers, stroking outside and then within her folds. Ecstasy rocketed through her—touching herself had always been something she enjoyed but to have *him* do it again made her pleasure soar even higher. And the way he touched her, softly at first and then with deliberate intent to wring out as much bliss from her as he could. His thumb caressed her clitoris in dizzying circles, and his fingers traced her entrance. When he sank one finger into her passage, she cried out.

"Too much?" he rasped, stilling.

"It's good . . . it's so good."

"There's my love," he said roughly. He stroked in and out of her, finding a spot within her that sparked with every thrust. "I want to give you more, to make you ready for me."

"Do it," she demanded.

He added a second finger to his first, stretching her. As he pumped into her, his thumb continued its exquisite attentions to her clitoris.

Release hovered close, so close she could reach out and grab it.

"Let yourself go, love," he urged her between bites. "Use me and fly."

She worked her hips onto his hand, until her climax struck with breathtaking force. Her cry broke free as her body bowed, born upward on sensation, shaped by his relentlessness.

He softened his hold on her neck, and licked the spot where he'd bitten her. "Beautiful, beautiful creature. But you'd like more. And I'll give you whatever you want. Anything. Everything."

"Everything?" She lifted her face.

His grin was wicked, knowing and eager to give her whatever she desired. "Tell me what you seek."

The impulse to dismiss it, to say that it was nothing, threatened to choke her. She'd done so many incredible, bold things tonight. Could she be even bolder? Could she do as he'd urged and free herself?

She could, with him.

"That scene I recited at Mr. Longbridge's party," she whispered. "The one from the Lady of Dubious Quality's book, where the man . . . the man put his mouth on the woman's quim."

Kieran's smile turned ferocious. "And you want that for yourself." When she nodded, he said, "Tell me. Let me hear the words."

"I'd like you to . . ." She gulped. "To lick my pussy."

His grin vanished, replaced by fiery hunger that made her pulse hammer. He kissed her deeply, his hands pinning hers to the cushions of the chaise.

Then he was gone, kissing his way down her neck—pausing briefly to bite her once more—before continuing on down her body. He lingered at her breasts, moving from one to the other as he sucked and tongued her nipples, then drifted lower.

She held her breath as his lips brushed across the roundness of her belly. He pressed kisses to the tops of her thighs, first on the outside, and then he kissed closer and closer to her sex.

He stopped moving, and she looked down. Arousal and embarrassment warred in her to see his shoulders between her legs, his gaze fastened on her quim.

The man in the Lady of Dubious Quality's book hadn't done that. He'd gone straight in to lick the woman's pussy.

"Is . . . something wrong?"

"It's perfect." He didn't tear his eyes from her. "If this is to be my one time looking at you like this, I want to remember everything. You'll be burned into my vision, so whenever I close my eyes, this is what I see. You, and your gorgeous, wet cunt."

"Kieran," she moaned. He, who knew how to speak so beautifully, undid her by using the crudest words.

"But there's a time for looking," he said in a deep voice, "and there's a time for doing."

He lowered to her. She cried out again as his tongue delved into her, tasting and feasting on her with single-minded intent. It was a wonder, his mouth upon her pussy, and when he sucked her clitoris between his lips, she had to grab the back of the chaise. She gripped it harder when he flicked his tongue against her nub, stroking his fingers into her passage.

He *fucked* her with his mouth, ferociously pleasuring her. It was a struggle to keep her eyes open, but she did so she could revel in the sight of him, still in his coat, waistcoat, and neckcloth, abandoning himself to fulfilling her fantasy.

This was so much better than anything she could have read or imagined. It was real, and he was real, and her body was real—just as her climax was real, shredding her into glowing fragments as it exploded through her.

She was certain with her orgasm that he'd stop, yet he didn't. He continued to eat her cunt and fuck her with his fingers until she came once more, and again.

"Kieran," she said breathlessly. "Stop."

He did at once, looking up at her, his face glossed with her arousal. "Love?"

"Let me see more of you." She issued her command thickly, half-drunk on pleasure.

He moved back just enough to rip off his coat. His neckcloth, waistcoat, and shirt followed, so that when he loomed over her, his torso was bare.

Her gaze moved hungrily over him. Each of his muscles were impeccably defined, from the planes of his pectorals to the taut rounds of his shoulders and the sharp ridges of his abdomen. Dark hair curled on his chest, and she couldn't stop herself from threading her fingers into it and giving a tug—gentle, but hard enough that it might have a teasing sting.

With her other hand, she stroked the thick bulge of his cock as it surged against his breeches.

His head tipped back and he groaned. "Should have known. Proper Miss Celeste Kilburn is a wanton."

"Good for her," she murmured.

"I want to fuck you now," Kieran rasped. "May I?"

She squeezed her eyes shut, letting the deliciously coarse words wash over her. This was what she'd sought all these years. To be fully in command over herself, her body, her desire, and to have a man willing to cede that command.

"Yes," she said on a sigh. Then, more firmly, "Yes."

He still knelt on the floor as he tore at the fastenings of his breeches, and she watched avidly as he freed his cock. Other than the erotic illustrations she'd secretly purchased, she'd never seen an erect penis before, and the sight of his fist wrapped around his upright shaft—and the bead of moisture at his slit—made her whimper with eagerness and a touch of uncertainty.

"It may hurt a bit at first," he said, his deep voice anchoring her. "I'll do my best so that the pain doesn't last."

"I trust you, Kieran," she said as she looked into his eyes.

He gave a deep rumble and then positioned himself between her open legs. The crown of his cock met her entrance, and she and Kieran panted heavily as he paused there. Was this what it felt like in the moments before the world utterly changed? She was a little afraid, but she desired that transformation more than anything she'd ever wanted.

"Hold tight to me," he said hoarsely.

She gripped his shoulders as her legs wrapped around his waist, her body slick and shaking.

"Kiss me," he demanded.

Bowing up, she brought her mouth to his. At the same time, his hips thrust forward and he buried his cock in her.

She couldn't stop the little yelp of pain that leapt from her lips. But when he moved to pull away, she held him tightly.

"Stay," she whispered. "Stay. Only—I need a moment."

"Is it too painful, love? I've never . . ." He huffed out. "I've never been with a virgin before. I'd destroy myself if I didn't make it good for you."

"It is, Kieran. You are." She blinked away the sudden appearance of tears. But his candid admission touched her, as did his desire to please. "I think . . . I'm ready to keep going."

"Like so?" As he spoke, he drew his hips back, and then slowly thrust forward once more.

Ecstasy pierced her. "Like so."

"And this? And this?" Each question was punctuated by another stroke of his cock, and every time more and more pleasure streaked through her.

"Yes," she moaned.

His pace increased, and she watched how his whole body went tight, his face contorting with bliss. She loved watching his devotion to pleasure, how his jaw slackened as he panted, his eyes mere slits fringed with dark lashes.

Then he brought one of his hands between them, caressing her clitoris in time with his thrusts. She didn't think it would have been possible to climax again. Yet she did, the force of it so intense her whole body locked tightly around his, her cry long and keening.

He moved his hips faster, and faster, and she looked down to see the gorgeous sight of his cock plunging in and out of her body.

A moment later, he pulled out. Gripping his cock, he gave it two hard pumps before his seed shot from him and across her belly.

He held himself above her as they gasped in the aftermath. Their eyes met. Something shadowed moved across his gaze, no doubt a reflection of her own stunned state. Her body was limp and sated, yet her heart pounded.

The Lady of Dubious Quality hadn't fully prepared Celeste for sex. Oh, she'd understood its more animal qualities, even the mechanical aspects of it. She'd hoped for and had received physical pleasure.

But these moments afterward . . . as she and Kieran stared at each other . . . as if the joining of their bodies had also aligned their souls . . . this intimacy was unexpected. And not entirely welcome.

Because whatever happened tonight, they had to go on as they had before, merely friends who had entered into a mutually beneficial bargain. He had given her access to a forbidden world of freedom, and she . . . she would help him find a bride.

Somehow, she was going to have to keep pointing him in the direction of eligible ladies, watch him select one to court, and then smile as he offered that lady his hand in marriage. God help her, she might even have to attend his wedding. To another woman.

There was every possibility that when that day happened, she would be the Countess of Montford.

She stared up into the face of the man who'd made love to her. Because of him, her first time had been extraordinary. There had been so much more than pleasure, and tenderness filled her to think of all that he'd given her. To think of him marrying someone else . . .

Oh, God. When she pictured his wedding day, the woman who stood beside him in front of the altar was *her.*

But that could never be.

Later, when she was safely in her own bed, she might allow herself to feel the jagged hurt that threatened to tear her into tatters. Right now, she simply needed to put on her normal clothing, remove the paint from her face, and go home.

Before she could do any of that, however, he grabbed his discarded neckcloth and used it to clean her belly. The starched fabric scratched a little, but she appreciated his thoughtfulness. He stuffed the soiled fabric into his coat pocket before tucking himself back into and fastening up his breeches.

She thought he might simply throw the remainder of his clothing back on and urge her to do the same. Instead, he stretched out beside her on the chaise, gathering her into his arms. As she snuggled against him, he pressed a kiss to the top of her head.

A shard of sweet pain lodged in her chest.

"Are you very sore?" he murmured against her hair.

"Some," she admitted, "but it's worth it."

"That was my hope."

"You're very good at that, you know." She shivered as a draft moved across her cooling, damp body.

"The advantages of practice." He reached down to pull a discarded shawl over her, its silky fabric sliding along her skin.

"But never before with a virgin," she noted.

"Well, no." Humor tinged his voice.

She shifted to look up at him. "I warrant half the virginal women of London would beat down your door if they knew you could make their first time so wonderful."

It was safer to retreat into badinage than say what she truly wanted: that she appreciated him, that she hated the thought of life without him, and that she would spend every moment after this dreaming of tonight. Dreaming of him.

"My landlady wouldn't appreciate that. And though I'm flattered that you think my skills would warrant such demand, I'm not in the market to initiate other people into the realm of sex."

"Yet you did with me," she pointed out, stroking her hand back and forth across the extraordinary sculpture of his torso.

"You're exceptional in every way." He caught her hand and pressed it to his lips, and her chest tightened.

"Will you write a poem about this?" she asked softly.

"It's already written here." He tapped one of his fingers against his chest. "But I won't put it to paper—it's for us alone." Quietly, he added, "I've written about you, though."

"Truly?" She gaped at him. "A satire about a seemingly respectable young woman, no doubt. I'm sure you found many things that rhymed with *dull*."

He scowled. "Nothing of the sort."

"Well, go on," she said when he remained frustratingly silent. "Let's hear it."

After clearing his throat, he began,

"She prowls amongst timid hothouse flowers,
The blooms surrounding her wilting, ashen,
And soft. They think her tamed yet still cower
Rightly fearful of her hidden passion.
Trembling, adoring, my lone sacrifice
Beats in my hand. To die is paradise."

She stared at him so long a blush spread across his face and down his chest.

"Our afternoon at the horticultural exhibition," she breathed. When he nodded, she cupped his face with her hands. "I've been given gems and gowns and every sort of luxury anyone could want, but never have I been given anything like that. Thank you, Kieran."

He smiled against her lips when she kissed him. "Whatever you want, love, you'll have it from me."

Every word of his was sincere. She knew he believed that. But what she truly wanted, he would never, could never, give her.

Chapter 17

✣*✣

The most difficult thing Kieran had ever done in the course of his twenty-seven years was help Celeste dress, put on the remainder of his own garments, and then take her back to their usual meeting point. What he needed, what he desired, was to bring her back to his rooms and make love to her all night in his bed. Instead, after hours of wakefulness he'd fallen asleep at dawn, alone, his arms aching with emptiness.

As he woke later in the day, he turned onto his stomach and stretched out in search of her, but encountered more of that emptiness beside him. He smoothed his hand over the other pillow, picturing her there, chestnut hair spread around her, eyes sleepy but sultry with desire as she reached for him.

Jesus God, how was he supposed to go on, knowing how good it was between them? She'd been so trusting, so open, so beautifully receptive and eager. It had been a privilege to pleasure her, a privilege he'd never again know.

His biggest risk last night had been revealing the fact that he was a poet. He'd been afraid of her response, yet it had felt right to show her this important, hidden part of himself. And his fear had been unjustified. The joy in her face and the praise she'd given him would keep him warm on the darkest days.

Already, new verses to her gathered in his mind. How would he describe the many colors in her eyes? What words would do them justice?

Hell—he was composing sonnets to a woman who was promised to another.

He rolled onto his back and, groaning, covered his face with his hands.

"Are you sick?" Finn asked, entering his bedchamber. He was half-dressed in breeches, a shirt, and a long black dressing gown.

"Only sick of you not bothering to knock," Kieran answered, peering between his fingers. "What time is it?"

"Time for you to get up and come for a ride with me." His brother threw a boot at him, but fortunately, Kieran caught it before it hit him in the face.

Sitting up, Kieran scrubbed his palm over the stubble along his chin. "Much as I hate to say it, we ought to go to Rotten Row."

"Impossible to get decent speed there," Finn countered. He glanced at the clock on the mantel, which read quarter to five in the evening. "Especially at this hour."

"We're not going for speed." Kieran pulled a discarded shirt off the floor and slipped it on before rising. "We're going to be seen. Given that I need to continue to amend my tarnished reputation—something which *you* need to do as well, dear brother—a sedate and decorous turn on horseback in Rotten Row's most fashionable hour seems a likely way of maintaining the process."

The damned thing was he didn't *want* to maintain the process. He'd no interest in meeting potential brides, and the thought of courting any woman who wasn't Celeste made his gut churn. Yet she was meant for the damned Earl of Montford.

Last night, as he'd held her in the aftermath of their sex, he'd been on the verge of suggesting that *he* might court her instead of sodding Montford. After all, he was an earl's son. Granted, an earl's third son without a title of his own, but surely his pedigree counted for something.

Yet Montford would one day be a marquess, which far outranked an earl's youngest male offspring. Even if Kieran could find himself gainful employment, he'd never have Montford's wealth, or land. And Celeste had said that if she refused Montford, the earl would endanger the Kilburns' social standing.

Kieran could never court Celeste, not with so much riding on her future betrothal. Which meant that, as repulsive as it was, he'd no choice but to seek out some other woman to be his wife. His family's ultimatum compelled him.

Unaware of Kieran's tormented thoughts, Finn let out a gusty sigh. "Must we?"

"Do you want Father to cut you off, or not?" Kieran fired back. At Finn's silence, he said with a surly tone, "Get dressed and look fucking presentable."

Half an hour later, he and Finn sat atop their horses, sedately walking the length of Rotten Row. Typically, Kieran avoided this place between five and seven in the evening. If he wanted to ride, he favored heading to Hampstead Heath and giving his horse the freedom to run as much as the beast—and he—desired.

"Can't get a good gallop here," he muttered to Finn, riding beside him. Kieran's mount was Dulcinea, his black mare, a beauty of an animal who loved nothing more than tearing up the turf. She snorted impatiently as he tugged on the reins, keeping her in check when she likely wanted to bolt for the horizon. He guided her between open-top carriages and cattle mainly bred for looks rather than speed or strength.

"Since you said that we're here to be seen, a gallop would defeat the purpose," Finn remarked from atop his sleek gray gelding. "Impossible to get a decent eyeful if you're whizzing past like a drunken comet."

"Needs must," Kieran grumbled.

"Good afternoon, Mr. Ransome," a ruddy gentleman called out as he rode past. In a slightly less friendly tone, he addressed Finn. "Mr. Ransome."

"Lord Hempnall," Kieran answered, touching his fingers to the brim of his hat.

"Who the hell was that?" Finn asked once the man had ridden past.

"Celeste—I mean, Miss Kilburn introduced me to him at a horticultural exhibition, and I attended a musical recital at his home."

Finn didn't press for more details about such a sedate event. Which was good because merely mentioning that day brought Kieran back to the dressing room at the Imperial, with Celeste in his arms as he'd recited the poem she'd inspired him to compose. He continued to feel the imprint of her warm softness against him. He could still taste her sweetness and spice, and see the eagerness in her face as she'd encouraged him to publish his work.

Pride surged through him. He'd wanted to ensure that her first time had been good, and thank God he'd been able to give her that. Pleasing his partners had always been important to him, but with Celeste, the weight had been all the greater. He'd bleed himself into a husk if it meant securing her happiness.

What a damned fool he'd been to think that one time with her would be enough.

"Greetings, Mr. Ransome," a duo of ladies said, waving at him from their carriage.

"Lady Caunton, Miss Goswick." He gave a slight bow as the women drove past, then glanced at his brother to snap, "What?"

"Miss Kilburn must have some fae blood in her to have wrought such a magical metamorphosis in your reputation. Perhaps she can conjure luck for me at the gaming tables."

"You already win big at nearly every game of vingt-et-un," Kieran said crossly. "No need for luck when you've skill on your side."

Finn shrugged dismissively. "How difficult can something be if *I'm* good at it?"

Much as Kieran wanted to debate that point with his brother, his temper was too frayed to present a decent argument.

"Yet Miss Kilburn has brought about a remarkable alteration in your social standing," Finn mused.

"Suppose she did." Kieran nodded at an older man, his wife, and their daughter as the trio waved from their carriage. He had a vague recollection of meeting them at the recital, but he couldn't be certain. One aristocratic family looked much the same as any other—a collection of pale-skinned, overbred people with the kind of myopia that derived from refusing to look past their own circle of acquaintances.

He supposed he ought to make conversation with them, particularly as the daughter was of marriageable age. The thought repelled him.

"Perhaps she can take me under her wing, as well," Finn said thoughtfully. "We could arrange a similar bargain as the one you have with her now."

"The fuck you will," Kieran snarled.

The tiny quirk of Finn's eyebrow conveyed more than a library stacked full of books.

"I only meant," Kieran amended, "she mightn't require the same sort of arrangement with you. There could be some other way of her providing you an entrée into respectable circles."

A way that didn't involve taking her to the forbidden side of London at night. A way that wouldn't have her spending hours in Finn's company while she wore the disguise of the free-spirited Salome.

Dulcinea gave another snort of annoyance as Kieran pulled back sharply on the reins. "Sorry, girl," he soothed, patting the horse's neck.

"Fear not, little brother," Finn said evenly. "The odds of me developing feelings for Miss Kilburn are a thousand to one. Unlike you."

It was a struggle to keep his hands loose on the ribbons, but hell, how he wanted to tug on them sharp enough to make Dulcinea rear up.

What he *wanted* to do was kick his horse into a full-out gallop and ride away, far from the countless eyes watching him here in Rotten Row, far from his own brother's perceptiveness.

"Talking rubbish," Kieran answered immediately, but could Finn see into his heart? It beat fiercely within the cage of his ribs, nearly robbing Kieran of breath. Because what Finn had said about Kieran developing feelings for Celeste . . . it was true.

"Talking rubbish is a common occurrence with me," Finn agreed pleasantly. "Yet in this instance, I don't believe I am."

"Don't say anything to Dom," Kieran said, shooting his brother a warning look.

"What, precisely, *would* I tell him?"

"That I . . ." Kieran guided his horse around a cluster of riders who had stopped in the middle of the path to talk. He struggled to find the right words, ones that could both describe what he felt for Celeste, and also what would protect her. "That I . . . care for her."

"So, I was right," Finn crowed. "I was merely bluffing, and you fell for it."

Kieran swore. "I'm going to pour treacle in your hair the next time you fall asleep."

"A change of subject won't deter me from ferreting out the truth. You've become attached to Miss Kilburn."

"Lower your voice, goddamn it," Kieran said tightly as he smiled at a mother and her two daughters in a barouche. He didn't give a damn about ruining his chances with the daughters, but he had to shelter Celeste from any speculation.

He nudged Dulcinea toward a quieter patch at the side of the path, and waited for his brother to follow. When Finn drew up close, Kieran said lowly, "It doesn't matter how I feel about her. She's on the verge of marrying someone else."

"Have you kissed her?"

Not trusting himself to give away too much, Kieran merely nodded. He wouldn't tell his brother that he'd done far more than kiss Celeste. And goddamn, had it been incredible. The most extraordinary in his long history of erotic encounters.

Finn muttered something under his breath.

"What was that?" Kieran demanded.

"I said you're a bloody fool," his brother said. "And a cad, to boot."

"Both sobriquets I've already given myself," Kieran answered. It would have been far wiser never to have touched Celeste. Wiser, perhaps, for both of their sakes. Yet how could he truly regret it when he'd given her such pleasure, and she'd made him so happy?

With a curse, he nudged his horse into an annoyingly sedate walk. His brother kept pace on his mount. They were silent for a moment as they continued to ride, passing more people who greeted Kieran or else eyed him with far more interest than he'd ever received.

"How does it feel?" Finn asked.

"Like I'm playing a role," Kieran answered. "They think me worthy of their attention now, yet it was a superficial alteration in my behavior. At the heart of me, I'm the same."

"I meant," his brother continued, "how does it feel to care about someone?"

Kieran glanced over at Finn, noting his brother's pensive expression. Like him, Finn had never kept a mistress, but unlike him, Finn was far less of a libertine, preferring to keep his focus on the gaming tables rather than romantic affairs. True, more than once Kieran had come back to their shared rooms to find his brother entertaining a woman—though hardly ever was it the same woman.

"It's . . . like developing a new sense," he finally answered. "I'm raw and overstimulated and I can't help but feel like I'm doing everything wrong. But no one is here to teach me what to do. God knows Mother and Father are no experts."

"Wish I could help," Finn said wryly. "But I'm as useless as a spoon tasked with carving a steak."

"There's poetry, of course," Kieran murmured, "which abounds with descriptions of emotion. Words, though, are sharp, delineated things. They only hint at something, something so profound as to exist outside language, beyond careful construction. You can very well say something pretty and evocative about living to see a smile bloom on someone's face—but until you've actually experienced the answering blossom of light in your own chest when you do behold that smile, a poem's nothing more than empty syllables."

"Goddamn it, you're in trouble," Finn muttered after a moment.

"I surely am, big brother. I surely am." He looked around at the crowds of riders and carriages clotting Rotten Row, but no one held any interest for him. "I've had enough of being seen. I'm ready to leave when you are."

"Thank God," his brother said with relief. "This respectability veneer is appalling. Only a liberal application of strong drink can remedy it."

In short order, they returned to Henrietta Street. As Kieran stepped across the threshold to their rooms, he noticed an envelope bearing his name in an unfamiliar hand had been slipped beneath the door.

"A court summons?" Finn asked, passing him on the way to the whisky.

Kieran broke the wafer and read. "An invitation."

"To a paternity suit," his brother guessed as he poured two drinks.

"To a ball, you ass." Kieran's brows climbed as he read. "The Duke and Duchess of Greyland request the pleasure of my company in two nights' time."

"A gala of considerable repute," Finn said, handing him a tumbler. "Even a scapegrace such as myself has heard of it. Receiving an invitation to the duke's ball is quite a coup, little brother. Miss Kilburn has indeed worked wonders with your reputation. Felicitations."

His brother tapped the rim of his glass against Kieran's and they both drank. The whisky burned its path down Kieran's throat but he was still damned cold.

"For someone who's just been invited to the social event of the Season," Finn noted, "you seem remarkably melancholic. You've *arrived*, Key. All the mamas at the ball will know you're a man of good standing and be eager for you to pay calls on their daughters."

"Precisely." Kieran threw back the rest of his drink and poured himself another, yet there was no amount of alcohol that could lighten his mood. "I'm well on my way to finding a wife. And I no longer have need of Celeste's assistance."

The whisky pooled leadenly in his stomach. There had always been a limitation on the amount of time he and Celeste were going to have together, but he'd truly thought—and hoped—that limitation would come later.

A tap sounded on the door, and when Finn made no move to answer it, Kieran went to see who it was.

"Miss said I was to wait for a reply," the messenger boy said, handing him a folded note.

The alcohol didn't lift his humor nearly as much as seeing Celeste's handwriting. He took the missive from the boy and read it quickly.

> *Meet at the park three blocks from my house, two o'clock tomorrow afternoon? Strategy session!*

"I'll be there," he said immediately. He handed the lad a coin for his trouble before the boy sped down the stairs. Only when the messenger had slammed out the front door did Kieran recall that there was no reason to meet Celeste tomorrow. As Finn had said, she'd done her job. There was no longer a need for her to gain him entrance to reputable gatherings or make introductions to suitable young ladies.

But how could he inform her of that? Worse, how could he put it in a letter, rather than say it to her face? He'd have to tell Celeste what had happened, though he dreaded it with every particle of his being.

Chapter 18

❧*❧

It was, perhaps, unwise of Celeste to suggest to Kieran that they meet in the afternoon when her morning was unfortunately commandeered by Lord Montford. The earl had insisted she spend the morning with his mother. Yet Celeste couldn't bear the notion of waiting until later. She *did* have important information to discuss with him regarding the next step in the reformation of his social status. Of course she'd need to see him on the sooner side.

However, she knew better. Her breathless impatience arose strictly from the opportunity to be near him. A day and a half had passed since their unforgettable tryst in the dressing room. It was too long ago, and yet she still felt him on her, *in* her. She shivered with the pleasure that continued to reverberate through her body and in her thoughts.

The way he looked at her, the way he touched her . . . He trusted her to know what she wanted for herself.

"So, when is it to be?" Lady Stretton demanded.

Celeste blinked as she surfaced from her reverie. The marchioness's tasteful parlor came into focus, including the portrait of Lord Montford that had been painted shortly after he'd returned from his grand tour. In the portrait, the earl stood beside an urn that he'd stolen from a Greek ruin.

Naturally, he was proud of his theft.

"Forgive me, my lady." Celeste composed herself by taking a sip of excessively strong tea. "When is what to be?"

"The announcement of your engagement to my Hugh, of course." Lady Stretton clicked her tongue in a way that would have earned Celeste a scolding from the teachers at her finishing school.

"I cannot say, my lady, as he has yet to ask me." Celeste had no appetite for the dry lemon biscuits, yet she made herself nibble on one rather than continue discussing the subject she dreaded most. Still, perhaps it might be possible to maneuver the situation. After swallowing around the overbaked crumbs, she said pleasantly, "It would be most charming to make such an announcement around Christmas—or perhaps at the commencement of the next Season. If not later."

"None of those options appeal to me. I'll confer with Hugh about it."

"As you like, my lady." God, if only Celeste could jump to her feet, upend the fragile little table that held their tea, and run from the parlor.

Instead, she endured an hour of Lady Stretton's chatter about dismissing a servant for being slat-ternly. At last, Celeste was liberated and could return home. She had enough time to change her gown before rushing out the door and toward the park.

"Do slow down, miss!"

Belatedly, Celeste reduced her speed so that Dolly might keep up, but it didn't seem to matter how much she told herself she was being unseemly, she couldn't stop herself from hurrying.

When she'd proposed weeks ago that he was to take her to all the forbidden corners of London, she'd never suspected that the greatest danger came not from footpads and crooked gaming tables, but from imperiling her own heart.

It was well and good to tell yourself that you wouldn't involve your heart. You could make all the grand pronouncements you desired, yet it was hubris, pure hubris, to think that having your lover gently and tenderly press a kiss to the top of your head had no repercussions. The physical pleasure had been incredible—but the sweetness that had followed seeped into every corner of her being.

She and Dolly reached the edge of the park, and she turned to her maid as she ran a hand down her skirts. "How do I look?"

"Like a woman breathless to meet her lover," Dolly said dryly.

Celeste stiffened. Even though she considered her maid a confidante, she'd said nothing to Dolly about what had happened in the dressing room at the Imperial Theatre.

"Be at ease, miss," her maid said in a soothing tone. She fussed with the ribbons of Celeste's bonnet, adjusting the bow beneath her chin. "No one but me knows, and I'll not go spilling any stories. Not even to my sister."

"I thought gossip was the preferred currency of servants."

Dolly clicked her tongue. "No denying it's worth a fair amount, but if word got out that my mistress dallied with a bloke under my watch, no one would ever hire me again, and there's the truth of it."

"You're protecting yourself as much as me," Celeste noted.

"Ah, I do care about you, miss," her maid replied with a smile. "But when you're on the other side of the dressing table, you've got to look out for yourself, too."

Celeste anxiously gripped Dolly's hand. "I can't let anyone know about what happened," she pled.

"Be at ease, miss," her maid said, eyes kind. "No one will hear anything from me."

"Thank you." Grateful, relieved, she fumbled with her reticule.

Dolly held up her hand. "No need for that. But when you're tired of your yellow gown, the one with the cream ribbons—"

"You'll have it," Celeste vowed. The dress was a meager price to pay for silence. She'd give Dolly her whole blessed wardrobe if that's what secured her and Kieran's secret. "As soon as we are home again, it's yours."

"There's Mr. Ransome." Dolly looked past Celeste's shoulder. "Cor, that's a tasty slice of a man."

Celeste turned to see Kieran striding into the opposite end of the park, looking wickedly handsome in his tall gray beaver hat, sienna-hued coat, gold waistcoat, and buff breeches. Even at a distance, he drew her gaze and stole her breath. She loved watching him move, like an elegant knife.

"Who could ever blame you for yielding to such a bloke?" her maid wondered.

"I didn't *yield*," Celeste noted. "I wanted, and he gave."

"Always did like a generous man." Dolly chuckled. "There, miss, no need to chase me off of him. There's someone else I've got my eye on, but I can appreciate a fine view."

Kieran hadn't spotted Celeste yet, so he stopped at a bench and sat down. But he was far from still, jogging his leg as he glanced around.

"Who do you fancy?" she asked Dolly as she headed toward him.

"My would-be beau is the eldest son's valet at the place where my sister's in service. His name's Mr. Bedworth. John Bedworth." The normally composed Dolly sounded giddy as she spoke.

"Take Saturday off and visit your sister," Celeste said. "Perhaps you might cross paths with Mr. Bedworth."

"Thank you, miss," her maid replied eagerly. "Just for that, I'll stand very far away from you and Mr. Ransome and I might not even notice a thing if you two wandered off together for a few moments alone."

"Might not be a good idea," Celeste said under her breath as she approached Kieran—because she had a sneaking suspicion that if she did get some time with Kieran, she'd grab him and kiss him like she was a sailor on leave.

He saw her and leapt immediately to his feet. The bow he gave her was formal, slightly stiff. Had he lost interest in her, considering her merely a conquest?

Yet when his gaze met hers, there was such warmth and pleasure there, as if he were truly glad to see her again, and her worry unknotted.

"Miss Kilburn," he said politely.

"Mr. Ransome." She sat down on the edge of the bench, and he lowered down beside her. He kept a respectable distance between them, which struck her as strange, since the last time she'd seen him, he'd done the most incredible things to her body with his fingers and mouth and . . . cock.

Her face blazed, as did the rest of her.

"It *is* warm out, isn't it?" Kieran murmured.

She'd done such a remarkable job of concealment around her family, breakfasting and dining with her father—Dom joining them just once—but she couldn't hide anything from him.

"Indeed, summer will be here shortly, and the heat will chase everyone to the country." Inwardly, she grimaced at their banal conversation. For God's sake, he'd been *inside* her less than two days ago.

Dolly discretely drifted away to a bench clear on the other side of the park, with her back to Celeste and Kieran.

Forget taking off one Saturday. Dolly deserved *every* Saturday off.

"I thought—" Kieran began.

At the same time, Celeste said, "It occurred to me that—"

"You go first," he urged.

"Oh, no, I spoke over you."

His lips twitched. "Put us both out of our respective miseries and say what you intended."

After clearing her strangely dry throat, she said, "Tomorrow night's the Duke and Duchess of Greyland's ball, one of the highlights of the Season. Every eligible young lady will be there. After the success of your appearance at Lord Hempnall's recital, I should have little difficulty obtaining an invitation for you."

"My thanks." In a slightly gruff voice, he added, "I've already received an invitation."

For a moment, she could only look at him, her face no doubt as blank as her mind. Seeing how he stared back at her warily, she fabricated a smile and hoped her voice was cheerier than she felt. "That's marvelous."

"It arrived yesterday," he said, as if searching for something to say.

Yet yesterday she'd also sent him her note suggesting they meet, and he'd agreed. Which made little sense. He didn't need her anymore.

If that was the case, there was no necessity to continue on in their bargain. Their daytime outings together were finished. As were their midnight adventures.

Was all of it over? Everything that they'd become to each other might be gone.

She pressed a hand to her stomach, but it felt as though she'd swallowed a millstone. Surely devastation was written across her face, and devastation showed in her eyes. But she couldn't let Kieran see either.

Celeste managed to push to her feet and smile at him when he also stood.

"I ought to be going," she said brightly. "I'm due at Madame Jacqueline's for a final fitting on the gown I'm wearing to the ball."

Fittings were horrendously dull, but at that moment, she reached for it as if she were a drowning woman grasping at a thrown rope.

"I still need you," he blurted. When she blinked at him, he said hurriedly, "A lone invitation to a ball doesn't mean that my reputation has been entirely redeemed. I'll continue to require being seen with you to assuage anyone's lingering doubts."

"Yes." Relief made her legs wobble beneath her. The sunlight, which had seemed so watery moments ago, now turned everything golden and warm. "Reputations can't be fully repaired quickly. It's an ongoing process."

"At least until the end of the Season. If not beyond." He nodded solemnly.

Her stomach plummeted again. With Lady Stretton urging the earl to formally propose, the best Celeste could hope for was the remaining month until the Season concluded.

Yet for now, she had these next weeks. Whatever the future held for her, she had this brief time with Kieran. There would be years for her to nurse her damaged heart once he found his bride, and she was shackled to Lord Montford.

Strange to know that she was inflicting a wound on herself that she wouldn't truly feel until later, stranger still that she saw it happening and didn't stop. Never had she considered herself the sort of person who enjoyed unhappiness, but here she was, flinging herself headlong into future misery.

"You'll save me a dance," he said.

"Naturally. Though," she added, "it won't be the same kind of dancing we did at Mr. Longbridge's."

More's the pity.

"They'd need a crate full of sal volatile to revive the other guests." She tried to smile, yet the precious, fleeting moment couldn't last.

"Good afternoon, Mr. Ransome." Dolly came trotting up. "Begging your pardon, miss, but we've an appointment with the modiste."

"Are you hurrying her there to meet another scoundrel hiding in the fitting room?" Kieran asked.

"You're the only scoundrel she knows, sir."

"Dolly!" Celeste exclaimed, but Kieran bit back his laughter.

Her maid feigned abashment, muttering, "Apologies."

"Tomorrow night, then," Celeste said to Kieran.

"My anticipation's already growing." He bent over her hand, and she didn't miss the wicked gleam in his eyes.

Her body responded at once, even as her heart cracked. At the very least, she and Kieran would spend more time together. This magic with him would end, but for a little while longer, it didn't have to. And for that, she was grateful.

"Don't see why I have to attend a sodding ball," Finn grumbled as their hired carriage slowly lurched forward, bringing them closer and closer to the front of the queue of vehicles waiting to disgorge their passengers.

"Because, you ass," Kieran said, "the stipulations in our family's ultimatum are quite clear. Unless you, me, and Dom *all* marry, *none* of us gets a farthing. And I might be mistaken, but eligible ladies aren't given out at gaming hells like chits."

"Thank God for that," his brother muttered, "or else I wouldn't go. Stop fussing like a colicky babe."

"As though *you* have experience with babes of any sort, let alone colicky ones." Ignoring his brother, Kieran brushed a hand down the sleeve of his deep gray coat, though his valet had already done an excellent job of making his appearance flawless before Kieran had left his rooms tonight. A strange, unwanted edginess danced beneath the surface of his skin, and keeping still seemed nigh impossible.

His mood had been restless and apprehensive since parting company with Celeste yesterday afternoon. There was no reason to be uneasy, not when they'd agreed that they would continue with their arrangement for as long as possible.

Yet it wasn't enough. He wanted *more.* More than these sanctioned events, more than stolen moments in between their nighttime adventures. A metamorphosis was happening within him, and he approached it both eagerly and warily, as if being granted the gift of wings. You could soar into the heavens, or fly too close to the sun.

At the bare minimum, he'd see her tonight, and he'd every intention of having that dance with her.

"Nervous?" Finn asked.

"No reason to be."

"Except," his brother drawled, "the last respectable ball you attended was years ago, and if I recall correctly, the host of that ball bodily threw you out *himself* after you shot at his chandelier with a dueling pistol. Left a bloody big hole in the ceiling."

"I only missed because some fop knocked into me when I pulled the trigger," Kieran said sullenly. "And *you* were the fop."

Finn seemed to ignore this last comment. "It stands to reason that going to a ball where all of Society is watching and judging your every movement and word might cause some trepidation."

"I'm not a bit anxious." He did need to appear properly reformed before the other guests, but with the right amount of bravado and a goodly helping of charm, he could manage them. But knowing he'd see Celeste tonight made his heart race and his body eager for movement.

Something had changed between them. He now knew the taste of her, and how she held him with a ferocious grip when he pleasured her, and the sounds she made when she came. He'd seen her dance. And he craved all of it, all of her. His mind was full of rhymes and metaphors, his notebooks bursting with new verses.

The hired carriage finally came to a stop, and a footman opened the door so Kieran and Finn could step down. When they did, they joined the line of people in tastefully ornate clothing waiting to enter the Duke and Duchess of Greyland's massive Mayfair home.

"Are you certain the duke's invitation extends to me?" Finn asked.

"His Grace wants one Ransome brother, he gets two of them."

"Care to wager how many people ask me what I'm doing here?"

Kieran snorted. "Betting against you is always a fool's proposition."

Finally, he and his brother crossed the threshold and went up the stairs to the ballroom. It was, as Celeste had promised, a crush, and he didn't know if the fact that he was beginning to recognize many of the guests was a good sign or something to cause dismay.

He scanned the crowd, his gaze going right past several genteel mothers looking at him eagerly as he searched in vain for Celeste.

"Damn," he muttered. Louder, to Finn he said, "I need a drink."

"Put that on my headstone," his brother agreed. "Don't see any servants handing out wine."

Kieran sighed. "Punch it is."

Together, they moved deeper into the room to hunt down the punch bowl. The guests congregated close to one side of the ballroom, so Kieran headed in that direction with Finn close beside him. Kieran barely noticed the interested glances in his direction as concern for Celeste gnawed at him. She'd said she'd be in attendance tonight, but perhaps something had happened to her. Maybe she was ill, or her carriage had thrown a wheel on the way over, and she was in need of help. If that was so, he ought to leave immediately and trace her possible route.

"How pleasant to see you, Mr. Ransome," a middle-aged woman in ivory silk said to him.

"Lady Parslow," Kieran replied, bowing as he remembered that Celeste had introduced her at the recital. "May I introduce my brother Mr. Finn Ransome?"

When Finn also bowed, Lady Parslow nodded regally. She glanced at the young brunette beside her, a tall woman possessing sharp features and even sharper eyes. "This is my daughter, Miss Tabitha Seaton."

"Sirs," Miss Seaton said coolly as the brothers bowed again.

"Excuse me for a moment, I see a friend I must greet," Lady Parslow said.

"I'll accompany you," Miss Seaton offered.

"Oh, no, dear, do continue your conversation with Mr. and Mr. Ransome." With that, Lady Montford blended into the crowd, leaving her daughter behind.

Miss Seaton glanced around the chamber, looking wholly unimpressed. "Do you think His Grace has a library? One that is more than decorative?"

"Books are better company than the guests?" Finn asked.

"In my estimation," she said dryly, "books contain actual knowledge, whereas most of the people in attendance here do not."

"I contain almost no knowledge," Finn answered cheerfully.

"Perhaps," Miss Seaton said, regarding him. "Yet you may prove useful if you can introduce me to Sir William Marcroft. He's here tonight and is the head of the Sterling Society—you've heard of it?"

Kieran exchanged a look with his brother. "I cannot say that either of us have."

"No," the lady said with resignation, "I don't suppose fashionable gentlemen such as yourselves are familiar with England's most esteemed intellectual society. Do excuse me, sirs. I'm sure you find me as useless to your company as you are to mine." She curtseyed before walking away.

Finn exhaled. "My God, Miss Seaton's a crucible. She'd make a perfect match with Dom."

"Not you?" Kieran asked, arching his brow.

"I haven't the fortitude," his brother said with a smirk. "Though *you* haven't settled on anyone to court, and you just might possess enough indifference to make Miss Seaton an excellent husband."

"I'll keep that under advisement." But the truth of it was, Kieran had no interest in Miss Seaton. He had no interest in *anyone* but Celeste.

It struck him then, as he was surrounded by London's most eligible young women, that there was only one person he could imagine spending the rest of his life with. He staggered, as if he'd been hit over the head with the butt of a pistol.

Christ almighty, he was in love with Celeste. So much so he ached with it. Every face he saw was hardly worth a glance because it wasn't her face. Anyone who spoke simply made meaningless sounds because it wasn't Celeste speaking. A moment without her was a moment without joy, without purpose.

"Can we get that punch now," Finn asked irritably, "or am I going to have to use my lock-picking skills to break into the wine cellar?"

Kieran's gut clenched in eagerness as Celeste appeared at the entrance to the ballroom. He barely noticed that her friend Miss Carew stood beside her—he saw nothing but Celeste.

Tonight, she wore a leaf green gown embroidered with golden vines, and a strand of golden silk leaves wove through her upswept hair. She was springtime itself, and verses in praise of her unfolded in his mind the way fresh vegetation emerged from winter's frost.

Love blossomed in his chest and spread its tendrils through him. He was dizzy with it, and she was the fixed point in his spinning universe, holding him steady.

He wanted to make Celeste his—before the eyes of the world. All the mad chasing of pleasure he'd done for most of his life, it made him understand that the greatest pleasure of all was being with her. Standing close to her. Seeing her smile and hearing her laugh and watching her joy as she discovered a new experience.

Perhaps . . . perhaps . . . he *could* belong to her. Joy filled him at the thought that they would have mornings and nights and days together, and years. All the years of his life. There were obstacles, huge obstacles. But surely if she shared his feelings, they might find a way. The world would belong to them, and he'd never take another step without her beside him. And he'd be the fortunate bastard to support her in her own journey.

"Jesus Christ," Finn muttered. "If Dom could see your face when you look at his sister . . ."

"Shut up, brother," Kieran answered distractedly.

Without thought, he moved toward Celeste because he couldn't see her and remain at a distance. Wherever she was, he needed to be.

Chapter 19

❧*❧

Rosalind was saying something to her, something about how many people had crammed themselves into the duke's ballroom, or perhaps she was talking about the impressive orchestra that had been hired for the evening—but the truth was Celeste didn't hear a word her friend said because she'd just caught sight of Kieran as he headed straight in her direction.

There was heat and purpose in his gaze, and he seemed to cleave through the crowd like darkness through artificial light. With each of his steps closer, her heart beat faster and faster, and she was convinced its drumming would provide a bass note to the music from that impressive orchestra.

"Also, I'm eagerly awaiting the indoor pyrotechnic display," Rosalind said cheerfully.

"Yes, me, too," Celeste replied, her attention solely on Kieran's approach.

Rosalind laughed and shook her head. "Given that Mr. Ransome is nearly upon us, I believe I'll escort myself to the cardroom and fleece a few toffs."

On her own, Celeste didn't move or breathe until Kieran stood before her. He bowed smoothly, while she gave him her best curtsey, and the room itself dropped away into shadow. The only thing she saw was him.

"Mr. Ransome," she said breathlessly.

"Miss Kilburn." His voice was low and deep, strumming across her body.

"Are you enjoying your evening?" She had to mouth polite, empty phrases rather than launch herself at him and fasten her lips to his, but it was a struggle.

"I wasn't," he said. "Now I am. Yet later will be even more enjoyable."

"Why is that?"

"Because," he said, leaning closer and speaking lowly, "Salome and I have another adventure ahead of us."

Excitement leapt along her limbs, and a rush of heat. If the hot promise in his eyes was any sign, then she would know his touch upon her naked skin once more. Her body ached to lie in his arms, to feel his embrace around her.

"She's to meet you at the usual time and place?"

"She is. And I promise that she'll have a night she won't soon forget."

"Where—"

"Miss Kilburn," a man's voice said politely. "Ransome."

Celeste fought the urge to shout in frustration at Lord Montford, who looked at her with a pleasant, anticipatory expression. "Good evening, Lord Montford."

"I believe you've promised me the next dance," the earl said, holding out his hand as the orchestra played the opening bars of a waltz.

She'd done no such thing, but to say so, especially as many of the guests were watching her, would have been extraordinarily rude. Besides, it didn't matter if she granted Lord Montford one dance, not when she and Kieran had the rest of the night to themselves.

Kieran glowered, yet she sent him a speaking glance that managed to keep him from planting his fist in Lord Montford's face. It did seem a struggle for him, though.

"Thank you, Lord Montford," she said, placing her hand on his.

She walked with the earl out onto the floor, taking their position with the other dancers. Lord Montford's expression was smooth like polished stone. Perhaps beneath that polish he was annoyed that she had been standing with Kieran, so she'd have to find some way to placate the earl.

The dance began, and she moved through the steps by rote. Being held by Lord Montford didn't stir her at all, so she allowed her mind to wander as they danced. Where would Kieran take her tonight? They'd already gone to a gaming hell, a wild private party, and the gathering of freethinkers at the theater. She *did* want to see Vauxhall, despite his insistence it was for tourists, but what she truly wanted was to be alone with him, preferably near a bed, and with ample time to explore each other. She'd been dreaming about hearing him recite his poetry, especially if he was naked, and—

"It's time we made official our engagement," Lord Montford said agreeably.

She started at this unexpected pronouncement. "Is that so?"

"My parents and I talked about it after your visit and we all feel that this moment could not be more opportune."

"My understanding was that it would wait until the Season concluded." Panic skittered along the nape of her neck. She wasn't ready yet, not when a few more weeks with Kieran beckoned.

"No sense in keeping you waiting," he replied with an indulgent smile.

"I . . ." How could she hold him back? How could she move forward as his future wife? She didn't like him, and she certainly didn't love him.

But she *did* love someone.

Kieran.

The realization of it broke over her like a wave, yet she'd loved him for a long time. Not the flimsy infatuation she'd nursed as a girl, but a woman's full and deep adoration. He brought joy into her life and the unshakable conviction that she could do anything. And she believed him. He helped her see that.

How could she tie herself to another man when she loved Kieran?

Ablaze with this knowledge, burning with the need to tell him of her feelings, she searched the ballroom for him.

"I know, Salome," Lord Montford said lowly.

She blinked. "Pardon?"

"You're a clever girl, but I'm clever, too," he said.

"It wasn't particularly difficult to ferret out the truth, especially once my man was on your trail."

"Excuse me," she said, trying to comprehend what the earl was telling her. "What, precisely, are you speaking of?"

For a moment, the gloss fell away from Lord Montford's face, leaving a twisting mask of outrage in its place. But then it was gone, and he was the lustrous earl once more.

"You've been cavorting around London with Ransome," he explained. "Wearing a disguise. Calling yourself Salome. Acting in a wholly improper manner."

She stumbled but he kept her upright. Fear the likes of which she'd never known crashed over her, engulfing her in ice. This was a disaster, an unalloyed disaster. Her mind whirled as the worst possible scenario played itself out in the middle of a crowded ballroom.

There had to be some way out.

"I can pay you," she said quickly. "Whatever amount you're after, I can secure it."

He looked at her with disappointment. "Do you think so little of me that you believe I'd resort to something as lowly as blackmail?"

"What else can this be about?" she asked in a panic.

"It is," he said as he turned her in the dance, "me saving you from yourself."

"I didn't ask you to," she fired back.

"Of course you didn't," he said easily, "which is why I felt it necessary to intercede. You were on the road to ruin, my dear, and the gentlemanly thing to do is prevent that from transpiring. A good thing

I'm intervening now, before anything irreparable occurred. Thus, my proposition."

"Which is what, precisely?" she snapped.

His words had the precision of someone who'd planned out a speech. "You are to immediately cease all interaction with the younger Mr. Ransome. Tomorrow, I shall speak to your father about finally formalizing our engagement. We can make it a short engagement, and marry after the banns have been read. And," he added with a chuckle, "my mother will want time to properly plan a wedding. She has been so looking forward to our nuptials, I'd hate to deny her that pleasure."

Celeste tried to tug her hand free from his, but he held her tightly, and unless she wanted to cause a horrendous scene in the midst of the ball, she had no choice but to keep dancing.

"I'm not marrying you," she insisted.

Lord Montford smiled as if he pitied her. "Do you think Ransome will? Everyone knows that he's cut off if he doesn't marry a respectable woman, and if you refuse me, you will leave me no choice but to go public with my findings. You and your family have worked hard to erase the stain of that slum from your blood, but all it takes is a word from a true gentleman, and everything will fall apart. Surely you don't want that for your family, do you?"

"Don't do this," she pled. Nausea churned in her at the hopelessness of her situation. She'd realized her love for Kieran, but it didn't matter, not when she was pinned beneath Lord Montford's bootheel.

He looked at her indulgently. "If you go running to Ransome, and he makes even the slightest threat to my person, I've already penned my letters to every scandal rag in London, along with instructions to mail them if I'm hurt in any way. The outcome is a given: you'll be ruined, Ransome can't wed you, and no one else will have you except me. My mother will withdraw her support of you, destroying your family's precarious social position."

"You can have any woman you want," she insisted frantically.

"I've set my sights on *you*, and I'm accustomed to getting what I want. Yet," he added pointedly, "what I do is truly for *your* benefit. A little gratitude might suit you better than this vulgar display of emotion."

Bile rose in her throat, along with the feverish wish that she could punch Lord Montford in the gut. Anger surged through her. Here was another goddamned man who believed he could control her, who manipulated her into doing what *he* wanted.

"I'm not a virgin," she said curtly, desperate for anything that could force him to relinquish his grip on her.

Lord Montford's steps faltered, yet he regained his footing and continued to push her through the dance. "No matter. So long as you aren't increasing on the day of our wedding, everything can proceed according to my intentions."

"I never knew," she said lowly. "I was foolish and thought you innocuous. But you're truly a bastard."

He scowled. "Language, Miss Kilburn. I won't have my future bride speak so crudely."

"I beg your pardon," she said, fluttering her lashes, "you arsehole."

"You can't goad me into breaking our engagement."

What could she do? There had to be some way to extricate herself, yet how could she? Lord Montford had effectively trapped her, with Kieran's future and the fate of her family held hostage to the earl's demands.

Time. She needed time. "A week. Then I'll give you my answer."

His brow lifted. "You seem to have mistaken this for a negotiation."

"Unless you want me fleeing to America," she ground out, "you will allow me a week before I come to any conclusions." When he tried to stare her down, she simply stared back, until he exhaled. "As you please. But it's bootless to attempt any maneuvering out of our arrangement. You *will* marry me, Miss Kilburn, and I *will* undo the damage that you so thoughtlessly wreaked upon your family."

His condescension infuriated her, yet there was nothing she could do but seethe.

The song finally came to an end. She barely waited for the last note before stalking from the dance floor, uncaring whether or not it appeared rude. A headache dug talons into her throbbing skull, and she fought through the pain to locate Kieran. She had to tell him, had to warn him what was happening.

She drew up short as she saw him surrounded by two matriarchs and three debutantes, all chatting pleasantly as the older women tried not to appear overly acquisitive. The girls fanned themselves and sent Kieran coquettish glances.

She was going to lose him. In despair, she realized she was also going to lose herself. Desolation consumed her and she felt minuscule and powerless in the face of what confronted her. Tears welled, but she couldn't weep in the middle of a ballroom, so she furiously blinked them back.

"Celeste?" Rosalind's worried face came into view. "What's happened? What's wrong?"

"I have to go home," Celeste croaked.

"Of course," her friend said. "Here, lean on me and I'll get you out of here."

"Thank you," Celeste answered. "I'll be fine."

As she and Rosalind hurried from the ballroom, Celeste wished that her words were true. All she needed was to make it back safely to her carriage, and then she could let the world fall apart around her.

Once she was in her vehicle, she allowed herself to give in to tears. Yet it didn't leave her with the sense of exhausted peace she sometimes got from weeping. Instead, she was a bundle of rusty wire, all jagged pieces and tension. She wanted to feel numbness, but pain and anger kept rising in drowning tides. There could be no way out of this situation, and she stared down the barrel of a lifetime of misery.

Chapter 20

❧✻❧

Two hours had passed since Kieran had left the Duke and Duchess of Greyland's ball, and he now waited impatiently beside the rig. He held the horse's bridle and strained to peer into the darkness for signs of Celeste's approach. Though his invitation to her had been spontaneous, he'd made a plan after leaving Mayfair.

He'd hired the vehicle for the whole night, his intention to drive it himself all the way to Hampstead Heath and spend as much damned time there as he and Celeste wanted. In the rig was a packed hamper of bread, cheese, apple cakes, and wine, as well as a blanket.

A midnight picnic wasn't quite as wild as some of their other adventures, but eagerness shot along his limbs and made his palms sweat. Because once he had Celeste out on the moonlit heath, he'd finally let her know that he wanted more from their brief arrangement. Something lasting—something permanent.

"Christ," he muttered in disbelief. He'd never have believed he could reach this point in his life, or meet someone with whom he wanted to spend the rest of his days. And yet it was precisely what he needed: a lifetime with Celeste. It was frightening, and wonderful.

She'd disappeared from the ball after her dance with the priggish Lord Montford, which had worried Kieran, but she likely had returned home to don her Salome disguise and make ready for tonight.

He forced himself to take a long, steadying breath. Maybe he was wrong, and he hoped like hell he wasn't, but she seemed to care for him. Surely, he could make a convincing case that they would be well matched.

But that didn't solve the conundrum of the earl, or her father's determination for her to marry Montford. There had to be some way to break Celeste's future engagement without causing her or her family irreparable damage, and avoiding Ned Kilburn's rage. The hell of it was that he didn't know what that way might be.

The clock struck a quarter hour past midnight, and anxiety clambered up his neck. Was it possible . . . she wasn't coming? She'd appeared so eager for another escapade.

He exhaled in relief when two cloaked female figures appeared a block away and headed straight toward him. As they neared, he frowned. The gown Celeste wore beneath her cloak was the same one she'd worn to the ball, and when lamplight fell on her face, it revealed that she hadn't worn her Salome paint.

He'd meant to say something wry or glib, something that didn't reveal quite how breathlessly eager he was for their excursion. Yet as she stopped in front of him, her eyes brimming with pain, all words dried up and flaked away. Fear clawed along his limbs.

At once, he took her hand and led her into the shadows. When they were in the mews of a house, with Dolly keeping watch from the street, he tugged Celeste close. She stepped into his arms without hesitation, and he held her snug to him, the tremors in her body working their way into his.

"What is it, love?" he murmured against the crown of her head. Protectiveness beat like a drum beneath his skin. She meant everything to him and he'd do whatever it took to shield her from harm. "Let me help."

"You can't. No one can." Her shudders stopped, and she stepped away from him.

Alarm turned him cold, but when he tried to hold her again, she evaded his touch. "If there's something I've done," he began, "some harm I've caused—"

"It isn't you," she said, her voice unsteady. "But . . . our arrangement has to end. All of our nocturnal excursions have to stop immediately. The same with me accompanying you at respectable events . . . though you've no need for me anymore."

"The other night at the Imperial," he said, self-loathing bubbling up acidly, "I went too far."

"We both wanted it to happen, and I don't regret it."

A thread of relief unwound in him, yet she wouldn't look him in the eye. "Whatever it is, just tell me. We'll find some way to face it."

She was silent for a moment, and she was somewhere distant, somewhere he couldn't touch. "Lord Montford knows. About Salome. He knows I'm her, and he'll expose me if I don't stop."

Anger the likes of which he'd never experienced erupted within him. The urge to hurt, to destroy, pounded in his blood.

"I'll fucking murder Montford," he snarled.

"If you hurt him," she said, her voice weighted with exhaustion, "the scandal would make you untouchable. No one will consent to have their daughter wed you. And if you don't marry, it doesn't just affect you, but Dom and Finn, too."

Goddamn his family and hers for forcing them into this unwinnable situation. Yet the solution was there, a solution that would break them free—and bring a lifetime of paradise.

"Marry me," he said, taking her cold hands in his. When she stared up at him, he spoke urgently, doggedly. "It solves all of our problems. I need a respectable bride, and if you're married, you'll be safe from the blackmailing bastard. And . . . I care for you, Celeste." His throat was raw as words he'd wanted to say finally came pouring forth. "You've become the world to me, and I want to be yours for the rest of our days. I will do everything to bring you the happiness you deserve."

He drew in a ragged breath, and his body shook. "Celeste, I love—"

"Don't." With a cry, she tore her hands from his. "Please don't say that."

"You don't feel the same," he said hoarsely. Something shriveled inside him.

"It doesn't matter *what* I feel," she answered, her voice so low he had to strain to hear it. "It can't happen. If I marry you to escape Lord Montford, he's going to go to the papers and let everyone know what I've done. Married or not, I won't be respectable anymore, and the conditions of your family's ultimatum won't be met. You'll be cut off without a cent."

"I don't give a fuck about the money," he ground out.

"What about Dom?" she fired back. "And Finn? Can we in good conscience consign them to poverty merely so we can get what *we* want?" She shook her head. "I can't."

The misery on her face, the bitter resignation nearly sent him to his knees.

She was being forced back into the box she hated. The independence that meant so much to her would be ripped away by a hand that wasn't hers. All the things that she prized, all gone in the course of a night.

He fumbled in his pockets before pressing a handful of coins into her palms. "It's not much, but I can find more. Take it. Book passage on a ship that leaves tonight. Just run, love. Run as far away as you can." It meant losing her, but she'd gain the freedom she needed, and that would have to be enough.

"It's not so easy." She pulled away so he was left holding the money. "What befalls me stains my family, and if I flee, Dom and my father will suffer the consequences of the scandal."

The night gaped all around them. Distantly, a heavy cart rolled by, and there was the harsh burst of laughter as a group of drunken young men staggered home from their evening's debauchery. It was like any night in London, perfectly ordinary, no one aware of the fact that Celeste was in agony, and Kieran suffered, too, because he was powerless to stop it—both of them burning bright at the center of the darkness.

"I have to do *something*," he said, roughened voice grating in his throat.

She shook her head, already backing away toward the street. "Even the wild Kieran Ransome can't rebel against this."

He stared at her retreating form, wanting to snatch her back, to tuck her into the shelter of his arms and run like hell into the night. Yet there was no way out of the snare Montford tangled around her.

That son of a bitch. The urge to commit violence seethed through Kieran's body. He'd never wanted to hurt someone more.

"I'll see you home, at least." It wasn't much, but it was something.

She shook her head as she continued to back away. "What we had together will sustain me for the rest of my life. Goodbye, Kieran."

Celeste started to turn, then hesitated before she launched herself at him. Her lips fastened to his in a hard, desperate kiss.

He had a moment with her in his arms, a moment to savor the feel of her, before she tore away and sped off.

Chest ripped open, he remained alone in the mews and stared into the shadows. The hours past midnight used to be his favorite, ripe with possibility, unhindered by expectations. He was the most himself when the good people of London were snug in their beds. When he'd shared that potential with Celeste, she'd grabbed on to it eagerly and flowered into her full self. He'd been lucky to watch her realize all that she was, and the night had belonged to them, at least for a time.

But now . . . now there was nothing but emptiness.

Kieran had no desire to go about his ordinary life. Nothing held any interest to him, and he consigned himself to prowling around his rooms, with forays to the pugilism academy to pummel his fists into anyone unlucky enough to be his opponent in the ring. Even the pain that shot up his arms from his ferocious blows barely registered.

Three nights after losing Celeste, however, Finn appeared in his bedchamber and threw a dark evening coat at him.

"Father commands us to attend him at the theater," his brother announced. "Bathe, for the love of God, and get dressed."

"I've no desire to play lapdog," Kieran said, wadding the coat in his hands. "On this or any other night."

"What you desire has no impact on Father's demand," Finn replied. "Either you voluntarily come with me to the Imperial Theatre or he'll get those burly footmen of his to drag you there."

What sodding choice was there, given that threat? Muttering, swathed in a foul humor, Kieran grudgingly cleaned himself and put on his evening finery. He and Finn rode to the theater without saying a word.

The last time Kieran had been at the Imperial Theatre, he'd barely paid attention to the performance. Then, he'd milled in the pit, hot with the awareness that later that night, he'd be showing Celeste the hidden side of life at the theater. Yet he'd also been afraid because his intention had been to reveal the secret of his poetry to her. Never in his most fevered, desperate imaginings had he anticipated that that night would end with her acceptance of him. He'd never believed that they would make love, or expected how it would alter him. Or show him what he'd lost.

Everything was colorless and flinty without her—he couldn't remember the last time he'd finished a meal, or slept more than a handful of hours. He was merely the framework of himself, empty on the inside.

"The melodramas haven't even begun and you're already looking tragic," Finn muttered to him now as they sat waiting for the performances to start. "If we're to enact the roles of dutiful sons for Mother and Father, we'll have to plaster happy grimaces in place and pretend we're exactly the respectable offspring they demand."

Slouching in his chair, Kieran glanced at their parents seated in front of him. They sat at the rail to observe all the other important people coming into the theater. There was the usual distance between his mother and father, and the typical lack of conversation. His mother shot him a pointed look and he reluctantly straightened, which earned him a nod of approval.

On edge, he glanced at the other boxes filling with the elite of English Society. Hard to give a damn about any of them, so his gaze continued to roam around the theater. The pit was its usual morass of bucks, dandies, courtesans, and other fast-living people all running from one sensational experience to the next. A few caught his eye and waved at him, urging him to join their company.

Yet even if he wasn't obliged to remain with his family tonight, what the fuck did it signify if he wagered at a gaming hell or took part in an orgiastic party? If he wasn't tasting Celeste's lips, why kiss anyone else? Why touch someone who wasn't her?

Moodily, he moved on from examining the pit, and he looked toward the tiers of seats reserved for the better-off audience members who didn't have quite enough prestige or finances to secure them a private box. Prosperous bankers and brewers, their wives and offspring. Some of them possessed substantial fortunes that enabled them to penetrate the ranks of the ton, and a few were recognizable to him. There was one bloke he'd seen at Jenkins's, and a couple he remembered from the musical recital, and then there was—

"Oh, fuck," he growled.

Celeste was there. She sat with Miss Carew and they appeared to be conversing as they also took in the scene.

Even across the span of an entire theater, he saw the purple smudges of sleeplessness beneath her eyes, and how in just a few days, her cheeks were hollow. She fanned herself lethargically, and her eyes were dull, despite the fact that she was surrounded on all sides by stimuli. Wasn't anyone looking out for her? She needed rest, and sustenance.

"Don't," Finn warned, clamping a heavy hand on his shoulder.

Kieran glanced down, only then realizing that he'd tried to rise and go to her.

"I have to—"

"Whatever it is that's happened between you two," Finn said lowly in his ear, "you're in no fucking state to be seen together. Christ, the way you're looking at her."

At that moment, Celeste's gaze found his. She went ramrod straight as color flooded her cheeks. The longing in her eyes ransacked him—and the sorrow in her face nearly made him crumple.

Then she murmured something to her friend, who in turn looked concerned. The two of them rose and made their way down the row until they reached the aisle. Celeste paused for a moment to look at him, her chest rising and falling as if she held back tears, before Miss Carew shepherded her out.

"Stay. Here," Finn said, his voice taut with warning and his fingers bruising with the amount of force it took to keep Kieran in his seat.

Kieran's legs burned with the urge to run after her. Yet he stayed where he was, partly because Finn possessed an unholy strength, but mostly because there was nothing he could offer Celeste except the bloody and useless fragments of his own shattered heart.

Heavy footsteps thudded in the hallway, but Celeste didn't stir from her seat beside the fire in the library. The footfalls drew closer until they entered the chamber and stalked over toward where the whisky was kept in a polished mahogany cabinet.

Saying nothing, she used the poker to stir the fire's embers. Flames rose up, brightening the room.

"Jesus God, Celeste," Dom snapped in surprise from the other side of the room. "You nearly gave me the apoplexy."

"You don't bat an eye at brawling with an entire taproom," she noted. "So, it's doubtful that the appearance of your sister would engender any fear. Bring me a glass of that, too," she added when he approached with a full tumbler of whisky.

"Since when do you drink spirits?" Despite his question, he did as she requested, and poured her a drink before carrying it to where she sat slumped in an armchair.

"Oh, I've been sneaking drams of father's whisky for years," she said, taking the glass from him. "You simply haven't been home to witness it."

She sipped at her drink, leaning into its burn, yet the spirits did little to warm her, just as the fire hadn't done anything to chase away the chill. It had accompanied her ever since she'd asked Rosalind to take her home from the theater . . . was that tonight? It seemed as if decades had passed, not hours.

"Who's hurt you?" Dom demanded. "Give me their name and I'll shred them into mince."

She almost smiled at that. It seemed as though the men in her life believed that physical violence solved any and all problems.

"Make yourself easy, Dom," she soothed. "There's naught you can do."

"But someone *has* hurt you," he said grimly. "I refuse to let that stand."

"You're going to have to."

Dom growled, but she stared at him, unmoving, until he relented and lowered himself down to sit on the rug. This did make her smile, how little he'd changed since their days in Ratcliff. The clothing was all Saville Row, and some of the Cockney had been smoothed out of his voice, but there was always something untamed about her brother and its origins didn't spring from where he was raised. No, Dom was a wild creature at heart, and always would be.

Especially now that Willa was gone.

She inhaled, catching the fragrance of night air and tobacco and harsher drink that clung to her brother's clothes and hair. Tears filmed her hot eyes—she knew those scents from her evenings out with Kieran, all the secret and wild corners of the city that had been, for a brief time, her kingdom.

She'd never again go to those places, just as she'd never again be alone with Kieran. Never share a private smile when doing something particularly forbidden. Never know his taste, or touch. Was it worse never to have known those pleasures, or was the pain all the greater because she'd experienced and lost them?

Three nights ago, he'd been on the verge of confessing his feelings for her, yet the elation she might have once felt to hear those words was gone, replaced by bitter heartache. It had been even worse tonight as they'd stared at each other across the theater, the naked yearning in his eyes stealing her breath and rending her into shreds.

She took another drink, yet it didn't soften the edges of her sorrow. Seeing the brooding way Dom nursed his whisky, he surely dwelt in his own misery.

"High times at the Kilburn household," she said wryly.

"Da always said that blunt would make us happy," he answered, staring into the fire. "All we needed was to get out of Ratcliff, buy ourselves a fine house, wear the right rigging."

"We'd dine on venison and drink smuggled French wine, and that would be enough."

He snorted as he looked at the bottom of his glass. "What'd blunt get us? Ma died, I'll never be good enough for Willa, who rightly despises me now, and you're here downing whisky like a longshoreman." He was silent for a moment, then, "Tell me who—"

"No, but thank you." She looked at the hard line of his profile that had only grown sharper and more imposing with the passage of time. He'd always frightened her a bit, her brother, and the seven years between their ages seemed to contain lifetimes she'd never fully understand. Shadows lurked behind his eyes, too, and she could only wonder what he did whenever he left the house.

Despite this, or perhaps because of it, love for him was a keen ache lodged between her ribs, made all the sharper by the despair that clung to him now that he and Willa had parted.

"Do you remember back before we came to Hans Town?" she asked. "I couldn't have been more than six or seven, and I'd found a ribbon, a blue satin ribbon. I tied it in my hair. Then someone stole it, and I came home crying."

"You didn't tell me the thief's name."

"If I'd peached, you would've skewered them on the spire of St. Dunstan's. You pounded on each door, looking for them."

"Everyone on the block was shitting themselves in fear." He chuckled darkly. "Wound up with my pockets full of buttons and baubles they threw at me."

"Attempts to appease the avenger of Ratcliff."

"Never did find the thief—but someone left the ribbon for me on a stoop, and I brought it home to you."

"I still have it," she admitted. "It's in a box with that hair comb Da gave Ma for her birthday."

He nodded and gave a tiny, sad smile, and her heart lodged firmly in her throat.

She couldn't have Kieran, and would have to endure a lifetime without him—to protect Dom, just as he'd always protected her. But a poisoned thorn of resentment lodged in her heart. Without her consent, she'd been tasked with upholding her family's social status, and because of Dom's spectacularly poor judgment in jilting Willa, Celeste paid the price.

It hardly seemed fair. But who had promised her fairness?

"A toast," she said, lifting her glass.

He looked at her dubiously. "What are we toasting?"

"You and me. Every material thing we might desire is ours for the taking, and yet we still suffer, unable to share our burdens, alone in our anguish."

Raising his glass, he said, "To us. The cursed Kilburns."

They drank in silence.

Chapter 21

✤✻✤

The conversation in Lord Hempnall's dining room bubbled as effervescently as the sparkling wine circulating the table. Esteemed guests supped upon fine food, prepared by the host's Continental cook, and Kieran had caught the daughter of a marquess casting curious but interested glances in his direction.

Kieran sat in the chair that, a month ago, wouldn't have been made available to him, surrounded by the respectable people his family so desperately wanted him to be a part of, receiving the welcome that should have been the fulfillment of his desires.

"Are you not enjoying your grouse, Mr. Kilburn?" Mrs. Cadleigh said from her place beside him. She eyed his plate, which was almost completely untouched.

He nearly bit back a retort that he had a mother, thank you very much, and didn't need anyone to remind him to eat.

"It's excellent," he said with a semblance of politeness, "but my luncheon was woefully substantial, unfortunately leaving me with too small an appetite to enjoy this superb meal."

Jesus. He nearly gagged at the obsequiousness in his own words.

And why did it have to be so damned *bright* in here? Did Lord Hempnall have a surfeit of candles that needed burning? Everyone's faces resembled elegant ghouls—no doubt he looked just as grotesque.

"After dinner," the host announced, "our gathering will grow. I've invited more to join us for music and dancing. It should be a capital evening."

"How delightful," Kieran muttered. Perhaps then he might be able to make his escape, slipping out with the influx of new guests.

Where was Celeste now? God, he burned to go to her. Yet that wasn't possible, and so he brooded through the remainder of the meal, barely speaking to anyone unless directly addressed. Doubtless he was undoing the hard work Celeste had done to rehabilitate his reputation, but it was hard to give a damn when Celeste herself was miserable.

If only he could beat Lord Montford senseless. Yet retribution had its costs, and he'd more than himself to think about. There was Finn, and Dom, too.

Goddamned ethics complicating everything.

At last, the meal concluded, but because more guests were expected to join the gathering, the after-dinner cheroots and brandy were curtailed and everyone went upstairs to the drawing room. Lord Hempnall's wife took her place behind the pianoforte while the others sat on sofas arranged around the room just as the newcomers began filtering into the chamber.

Kieran stood with a glass of port, attempting to determine when and how he could best make his escape. Perhaps he could light a small fire and, in the chaos, slip out.

Just then, Celeste stepped into the drawing room, and all thoughts of flight scattered.

It had been two nights since the theater, and she'd grown even more pale. She smiled as she entered the chamber, but the smile resembled one of the painted scenery flats used at the Imperial Theatre. The vibrant woman who'd stolen his heart was nowhere to be found.

Across the room, her gaze found his. A tremor worked its way down her body.

He took a step toward her, but she gave a minute shake of her head. There was nothing to do except watch her as she circulated through the party. Could no one else see how unhappy she was? Clearly not, because no one seemed to express any concern for her, only chatting blithely and laughing heedlessly—damn them all.

He should leave. There was nothing to be gained by remaining. Yet he stayed precisely where he was, staring at her as if she were a distant star whose warmth he'd never know.

"I'm grateful for the invitation, my lord," Celeste said to her host, but what she truly wanted was to curse Lord Hempnall. He'd inadvertently brought her to a gathering where, for entertainment, the guests could be diverted by watching her soul break apart.

No matter where she was in the drawing room, she felt Kieran's gaze upon her. Part of her wanted to beg him to look anywhere else—surely people would see the longing in his eyes—but to have him nearby was torture. To be close to him, yet separated by the span of the drawing room, soothed and tormented her in equal measure. At least he was nearer than he'd been at the theater—twenty feet rather than two hundred.

An acrid taste climbed into her mouth when Lord Montford entered the drawing room. He said something to Lord Hempnall that made the older man beam munificently. Lord Montford was always good at saying the right things to people, so he knew precisely how to manipulate a situation to his advantage. Of course, what Lord Montford had said to her had been pure contamination, but she didn't matter to him so much as reaching his objective.

After bowing to Lord Hempnall and greeting several other guests, Lord Montford made his way to her. She ought to have expected him to search her out.

Her worried gaze shot to Kieran. He stared at the earl and went very still, like an arrow about to be shot from its bow.

Fervently, she prayed he wouldn't do something that everyone would regret.

"Enough prevarication," Lord Montford said without preamble once he reached her side. He kept a smile on his face, yet spoke low so only she could hear him. "You've had enough time to recognize that what I'm doing is for your benefit."

"Is that what this is?" she asked with forced sweetness. "Your charity? I never asked for it."

He exhaled with irritation. "I see you're determined to cause yourself and your family grievous injury. Don't trouble yourself any longer. I've the situation well in hand."

Before she could ask what that meant, he called out to a passing Lord Hempnall, "On behalf of myself and my intended, I wish to thank you for your hospitality."

Celeste's stomach plunged. He'd done it. The bastard had gone and done it.

"Your intended?" The viscount's eyebrows rose as he looked to Celeste, then he laughed. "How utterly charming, that you two are to be married."

"What's that, my lord?" Lady Hempnall said from her place at the pianoforte. "Lord Montford and Miss Kilburn are affianced?"

"It appears so, my lady. This is the first I've heard of it, Lord Montford," Lord Hempnall said in a playfully chiding tone.

"She has just accepted my proposal," Lord Montford answered, looking at Celeste with fondness.

A mixture of rage and despair choked her as she stared back at him. How did she keep discovering new depths of unhappiness?

"Felicitations, my dear," the viscount said, patting Celeste's icy hands. He grimaced. "Goodness, you are chilled. Here, stand by the fire and we shall toast your upcoming nuptials."

Celeste glowered at Lord Montford, yet if she dared to contradict him, he'd waste no time in exposing and ruining her.

"Engaged." Kieran's voice cut across the room like a saber. He stared at her, eyes blazing, jaw taut. His fists opened and closed, the veins on the back of his hands standing out in stark relief.

He had to contain his fury—for his sake.

Terror made her dizzy as she silently pled, *Don't do anything. I beg you.*

"Congratulate us, Ransome," Lord Montford said affably, but there was no mistaking the threat in his gaze.

Fury burned in Kieran's eyes and for a moment, Celeste truly feared that he'd leap across the room and slam Lord Montford's head into the fireplace's marble mantel. But then, without a word, he paced toward the hallway. At the threshold, he swung around to send her one final, searing gaze, before stalking away. A moment later, the front door slammed shut—the sound of her heart breaking.

The room was silent, until Lord Montford said heartily, "Clearly, Ransome doesn't admire the institution of marriage."

Laughter erupted and people gathered around them. Celeste barely choked back bile as guest after guest offered her and Lord Montford best wishes on their impending nuptials.

Chapter 22

❧*❧

"I will fucking kill him," Kieran snarled as he slammed into his rooms. Fury coursed through him and his hands throbbed with the need to inflict pain.

"Kill who?" Finn asked. He stood in the doorway of his bedchamber, clad in a shirt and breeches, and rubbed a damp cloth across the back of his neck.

"Lord Fucking Montford," Kieran spat. He kicked a footstool, and the piece of furniture flew across the room to splinter against the wall.

"Granted, the man's a prig, and dull as Sunday afternoon, but does that warrant swinging for his murder? And I liked that footstool."

"I'm of a mood to tear this whole goddamned place apart, so consider it fortunate I stopped when I did."

Planting himself in front of the fire, he explained as concisely as possible Lord Montford's blackmail of Celeste. Kieran did omit the fact that he and Celeste had been intimate, but other than that, he included all the relevant details about what had transpired. As he spoke, his brother grew more and more still, until Finn just stared at him, his expression grave.

Finn leaned against the wall, his fingers steepled against his mouth. "Hell," he muttered. "There's no hope for it. She'll have to marry that bastard."

"He's not going to rob Celeste of her choice," Kieran said tightly. "That isn't going to happen."

Finn narrowed his eyes. "You've something in mind?"

"Haven't figured out all the steps yet," he said, and added grimly, "but if it's to work, I need to tell Dom everything."

His brother whistled. "He wasn't especially delighted by you being involved in any capacity with his sister. You could be inviting your own demise."

"Possibly. But if it means helping Celeste, I'll take that chance." He didn't care whom or what he faced, or what it cost him to do so. He had to help her. There was simply no other alternative.

Finn stood and walked quickly into his bedchamber. He emerged, slipping his arms into his waistcoat and holding his jacket in his hand. At Kieran's questioning look, his brother explained, "Someone's going to need to sit on Dom to keep him from eviscerating you with his pinkie finger."

Kieran nodded his thanks, and though he was grateful that his brother was essentially acting as his second, he tried to smother his impatience as Finn finished dressing. Once his brother was fully clothed, they headed out of their lodgings. It was just after midnight, the pavement slick with late-night fog, but in this part of the city many young men kept rooms, so cabs were fairly abundant and it didn't take long to hail one.

"Where to, gov?" the driver asked.

"The Foxhead Tavern," Kieran answered as he climbed into the vehicle. "You know it?"

"Bit of a rough place, eh, gov?"

Which was precisely why Dom liked it. He'd never taken to the more polished and sumptuous watering spots favored by the sons of the elite, and with the Foxhead located close to the docks near Ratcliff, it seemed to remind him of earlier times. Perhaps they were simpler times, too.

But as the cab headed south toward the river, and the air grew heavier with the scent of the thick water, Kieran mused that if the Foxhead Tavern was a refuge for Dom, he was about to ruin that sanctuary.

Hard to think of these grimy run-down streets as anyone's place of refuge, but they seemed to be for Dom. What vastly different lives they'd once led, the Ransome brothers and Dominic Kilburn. But they'd been drawn to each other because none of them had ever quite fit in to Society.

Thinking on it now, Dom had been largely absent from all the places the three of them used to frequent. Ever since the wedding, he'd kept himself scarce. Perhaps he blamed Kieran and Finn for enabling him to leave Willa at the altar, or perhaps he'd another motivation for being scarce.

Kieran would brood on that later. Right now, he needed all his focus on helping Celeste.

"I ain't waiting for you, gents," the cabman said once they'd arrived. He glanced at a trio of men slouching in a doorway, all of them watching the vehicle with sharp eyes.

"Not even for this?" Finn asked, discretely flashing a crown.

"You could throw a pound note at me and I'd still run like hell. G'night, gents." The driver flicked the reins and the cab trundled away as speedily as its rather rickety construction would permit.

"Inside," Kieran said. "I don't relish the prospect of being stabbed in anything significant." And he wanted to lay everything out with Dom as quickly as possible. The sooner he could apprise his friend of the situation, the sooner he'd endure his justifiable beating, and then he could enact his plan to help Celeste.

The inside of the tavern was only marginally more inviting than its shabby exterior. Even in their wildest nights, Kieran and Finn didn't accompany Dom to the Foxhead. There was wild, and then there was outright brutal. Heavy beams that dated from early in the previous century were low overhead, smoke and other substances stained the plaster walls, and people of surly disposition hunched over their tankards at scarred wooden tables.

None looked surlier than the wide-shouldered figure sitting alone in a corner settle. Dom cradled his tankard closely, and Kieran almost felt jealous that his friend seemed to trust the mug more than any human.

Warily, Kieran approached, with Finn close at his heels.

"If things go awry," Finn muttered, "I'm leaping out the window and running home."

"I thought older brothers looked out for their younger siblings."

"This one knows a losing bet when he sees one."

"My soul is at ease with you beside me," Kieran grumbled.

Dom glanced up through his brows as Kieran and Finn neared his table. He grunted, which might have been a greeting or a warning. Difficult to tell the difference.

"Ain't you supposed to be polishing some toff's arse in your bride quest?" Dom asked snidely.

"We thought we'd spend some time with your arse instead," Kieran answered. "Is there a private room where we can talk?"

Dom snorted. "That's where they keep the bodies."

"We'll sit with you, then," Finn said, sliding into the opposite settle. Kieran joined him, and perhaps this was what people felt as they approached the gallows on Old Bailey Road. It was both terror and a macabre eagerness to get it over with.

The publican came over and without asking for their order, slammed two tankards down in front of Kieran and Finn before stomping away.

Torn between drinking the suspect liquid in his mug or offering Dom a full confession, Kieran chose the less dangerous option and sipped at his beverage.

The best way to handle the situation was to come straight out with it.

"I'm in love with Celeste," Kieran said, looking Dom straight in the eye.

It felt terrifying to speak the words aloud, but also marvelous. Saying them calmed all of the vortices of emotion in him, as if uttering them was an enchantment.

A moment passed as his friend simply stared at him. Dom's jaw looked made of iron, and his voice was likewise full of rust when he finally uttered, "How does she feel about you?"

"She may care for me, too," Kieran answered, then added fervently, "I hope like hell she does. But even if she doesn't, I have to help her. She's in trouble."

"What kind of trouble?" Dom demanded. He reached across the table and grabbed hold of Kieran's neckcloth, which he used to shake Kieran like a sack of bones. "Is it your fault? Is it?"

Though Kieran was strong, Dom was stronger, and it took some strength to pry Dom's hand off his neck.

Flopping back against the settle, Kieran coughed as he dragged in a breath. But the air in the tavern was rancid and smoky, and set off a new round of coughing. Finn pressed a tankard into Kieran's hand and he took a reluctant drink.

When he felt somewhat certain that he could talk without hacking up one of his organs, Kieran rasped, "It's everyone's fault. Mine, yours. Your father's. Do you know that Ned's made her responsible for maintaining your family's reputation? Even when you were brawling in taverns, Celeste was the one who had to ensure that the Kilburns were accepted in the right circles."

"I didn't know," Dom said broodingly. "Damn. I never would have tasked her with that, had I known."

"She's been caged too long," Kieran persisted. "She needed a way to break free. In exchange for getting me into respectable gatherings where I could meet potential brides, I agreed to take her to some of London's less reputable corners."

"You. Did. What?" Face turning purple, Dom ended his sentence on a roar.

"I helped her live the life she wanted," Kieran threw back. "You and your father keep her chained to respectability. It was killing her."

Dom sneered. "And you were motivated by pure charity?"

"Admittedly," Kieran allowed, "my thoughts were at first only of myself. Celeste was the most respectable person I knew, and I wanted something from her. I figured it would be harmless—and not much trouble for me—to take her to a gaming hell, and one of Longbridge's parties. But," he went on resolutely as Dom growled, "I saw what it meant to her. That she could be responsible for herself, and no one made her decisions for her. She got to *live*, Dom, outside of the prison of respectability. And her happiness . . ."

He swallowed, his throat burning, but not from Dom's prior grip. He recalled her growing confidence at Jenkins's, and how she reveled in her freedom at the party.

"It was a beautiful thing to see. *She* was beautiful. Free and fierce and I couldn't help it—I fell in love with her. There was no way *not* to love her. To see her become all that she was, all that she could be, it was the most incredible thing I'd ever seen."

Dom's jaw was rigid, but he didn't speak. Neither did Finn, who watched him with curiosity, as though observing a wolf suddenly learning the power of flight. Speaking of Celeste *did* make Kieran feel as though he could fly, with all plummeting lows and soaring heights. Falling didn't frighten him nearly as much as never getting high enough.

Planting his hands on the tabletop, he leaned forward. "But Lord Fucking Montford is going to steal all that away from her if something isn't done."

"Always knew that sniveling fop was trouble," Dom said through clenched teeth.

"He's blackmailing her into finally marrying him," Kieran said. "He says he has proof of these midnight adventures and he's going to ruin her if she doesn't agree to become his wife. The hell of it is," he went on through a haze of fury and misery, "she's going along with his scheme to protect you. To protect me and Finn. Because if she's dragged down, so are we, and she's too good to let that happen."

Guilt enclosed him with its spikes, and he cursed himself again for inadvertently making Celeste accountable for someone else's wrongdoings.

"Goddamn it." Dom dragged his hands through his hair. Self-recrimination twisted his features. "I didn't know. I never would have made her sacrifice herself for the family."

"I love her, Dom," Kieran said hoarsely, "but what she needs more than anything is to be set free. At the end of this, if she wants nothing from me, I'll let her go, but it must be her choice to make."

"Can't we just go and beat Montford to death with his own skeleton?" Dom rumbled.

"He's put safeguards in place. Anything happens to him, word will still get out about Celeste's ruination."

"Hell." Dom's hands clenched and unclenched. "What if she ran away? America or Australia?"

"Already thought of that, and the consequences are the same."

"Montford is playing moves ahead," Finn said darkly. "Who knew the jackass was such a strategist?"

The three of them were quiet for a while, brooding over the ugly business of blackmail. Rain spattered against the grimy windows, while the other patrons continued the serious endeavor of getting drunk.

Kieran would have joined them, but he needed sobriety for what had to happen next.

"I'm formulating a plan," he said into the silence. When Dom and Finn looked at him, he went on, "I'll need your help. It's a risk, but if it comes off, then Celeste is free. She can go wherever she wants, and do whatever she wishes."

He hauled in a jagged breath. "If it means she can live on her own terms, I'll strew rose petals on the road away from me and watch her go without a moment's regret. It'll kill me, but whatever has to be done to make her happy, I'll do it."

Chapter 23

Seated at her escritoire, Celeste stared down at the beautifully engraved invitation, trying to make sense of it. The lovely script was legible enough, but its contents baffled her.

Mr. Kieran Ransome requests
the honor of your presence

Wednesday, the 20th of May, at the
home of the Earl and Countess of
Wingrave, 9 o'clock in the evening,

Music, dancing with a collation to follow

Then, beneath that, in scrawled handwriting, *Please come. What was damaged will be repaired. —K*

What could it mean? Now *Kieran* was hosting social events. Everything for him truly had changed, thanks to her efforts. Yet try as she might to feel a sense of elation or happiness for him, she'd alternated between incandescent rage at her situation and smothering sadness that all freedom was lost to her. She'd thought and thought, and had been utterly unable to find a way to disentangle herself from Lord Montford's venomous web.

There was a knock at the door to her bedchamber, and her father poked his head in. He brandished a piece of heavy paper that looked exactly like the one she now held.

"You get this, too?" he asked.

"I did." But why, and what Kieran hoped to accomplish with it, she'd no idea.

"Ransome himself wrote at the bottom asking me to come," he said in puzzlement. "What's it about, Star?"

"No idea." Which was true enough. "Will you go?"

Her father shrugged. "Suppose so, if Ransome's personally extending the invitation." He was quiet for a moment before asking, "Is Lord Montford coming?"

"He hasn't said anything to me about it." Ever since that awful evening at Lord Hempnall's three days ago, the earl had been calling with infuriating regularity. He insisted she accompany him on a drive down Rotten Row, or a promenade at the park, and an outing to Gunter's—despite her preference for Catton's. He'd accepted congratulations on their impending nuptials, and though Celeste hadn't also accepted the felicitations, she hadn't contradicted him, either.

In a week, he'd said at Gunter's, the banns would be read for the first time.

"You might've told me," her father now said, a touch of resentment in his voice. "About making official your engagement."

"It just sort of happened." Which was a rather mild way of saying that she was being blackmailed into marrying a man she despised, but she couldn't tell her father that.

Taking a step toward her, he said, "Thought when he finally proposed, you'd look a mite more pleased about it. We come from Ratcliff and you've truly landed an earl. That's a fine prize, my gel. Your ma and I had such dreams for you, and he can make them happen."

Celeste said nothing. It was either that or flip her escritoire across the room, which she couldn't permit herself because that would call for an explanation, and if she explained her circumstances to her father, everything would collapse from the collective weight of anger and sorrow, including herself.

"We can take the carriage together to Mr. Ransome's party," she said finally.

"You got a dress for the party?" her father asked.

"I'm certain there's something in my wardrobe that will suffice."

"Get yourself a new one," he said gruffly, stuffing his hands into his pockets. "Let my Star outshine all the toffs."

"The party is tomorrow," she reminded him. "That would be a difficult feat for Madame Jacqueline to create a whole gown in such a short amount of time." And the thought of going through a fitting exhausted her. She'd never enjoyed the process, yet now she could hardly stand the thought of picking out fabric and trim and a host of other details that didn't bloody matter.

"Pay her extra. Whatever it takes. Nothing but the best for my Star." He patted her cheek with his calloused hand. It had been years since Da had lifted a crate, but his work-roughened hands were still part of him. They always would be.

He lowered his hand and left her bedchamber.

Alone, she dropped her composed mask. After rubbing her face with her hand, she picked up the invitation again and studied it. One more day. Kieran had some kind of plan in motion, but didn't say what it might be. A tiny bud of possibility tried to sprout within her, but she tore it up before it could take hold. She used to do that in Ratcliff with the little dandelions that tried to poke their way through the dirt and cracks in the road—pluck them and dig around to pull up their roots. It hurt too much to see them struggle to bloom in such a despairing place, where they would only wither or be trampled under passing feet.

When there was so much at stake, she couldn't permit herself any hope.

Anxiety and uncertainty wedged in close beside Celeste as she, her father, and, surprisingly, Dom all made the journey to Wingrave House. Attempts at making idle conversation quickly died out, and, as her father and brother weren't naturally talkative, most of the journey was made in silence.

"You've no reason to be nervous," Dom said, breaking the quiet.

"Why would she be?" Da asked querulously. "She's gone to nearly a hundred of these blue blood parties, and her behavior's always sodding perfect. Isn't it, Star?"

Before Celeste could bite out that she was ruddy sick of behaving perfectly, Dom said, "It's them other toffs that need minders."

To her astonishment, he reached across the carriage and enfolded her hand in his own massive one.

"A little faith, Star," he murmured.

"In what?" she asked.

Her brother glanced at Da, who watched them closely. "In *who*" was all Dom said, and then sat back, releasing his grip on her.

Mind spinning with all the possibilities of what her brother meant, she tried to distract herself by fussing with the skirts of her new gown. It had been foolish, but she'd selected it specifically with Kieran in mind, knowing that a sensualist such as he would enjoy the luster of deep teal watered silk in the glow of candlelight. Unfortunately, when she'd glanced at her reflection before leaving her bedchamber earlier, she'd seen that the vivid color hadn't alleviated the new pallor of her face. Dolly had done her best to cover the circles beneath her eyes with powder. Yet some battles couldn't be won.

She could try to be optimistic. Perhaps Lord Montford would be at the gathering tonight—though it was unlikely Kieran would invite him—and see her looking so poorly that he'd end their farce of an engagement. But that was a fantasy. Lord Montford believed that he was somehow helping her, and, in his eagerness to play the rescuer, he'd surely see her declining health as yet another sign that he ought to intercede on her behalf.

The gall of that man! Many, many violent scenes had played out in her mind, and continued to do so, all of them ending with Lord Montford's grisly demise at her hands. Sadly, she was unable to enact any of those scenarios, and so all she could do was pray that whatever happened tonight, there would be an abundance of wine to numb her emotions.

When the carriage stopped outside Wingrave House, Celeste alighted, her father and brother at her heels. They entered the imposing mansion, where a footman divested Da and Dom of their hats and coats, before the butler directed them to an upstairs saloon.

As she climbed the steps, Celeste looked around at the expensive furnishings that had the well-burnished look of family heirlooms passed down through generations. This was the world into which Kieran had been born, and it was sumptuous beyond imagining, yet there was something distinctly cold about all the objects and portraits, as if they deliberately encouraged distance between themselves and the viewer.

No wonder Kieran eagerly searched out sensation and pleasure. If his parents were present tonight, it would be a challenge not to glower at them, knowing how they'd tried to suppress his poetic, emotional self.

"Ready, Star?" her brother asked as they neared

the saloon. Voices and music floated out, including Kieran's distinctively deep tones. Her stomach leapt at the sound, but she pressed her gloved hand to her belly in an effort to calm herself.

"Ready, Dom," she answered.

All three Kilburns stepped into the large, open chamber. It didn't have the massive proportions of a ballroom, but was substantial enough to contain a seating area, a pianoforte, and a decently sized space where a number of couples danced a gavotte.

Clearly, the reformation of Kieran's reputation had been a success, as evidenced by the number of virtuous members of the ton filling the chamber. She saw the Duke and Duchess of Greyland, and Lord Hempnall, as well as members of esteemed, landed families such as Mrs. Lapley. Even Mr. Longbridge was there, though he was considerably more respectable looking tonight than he had been at his party. He looked in her direction, but if he recognized her from that night, he gave no sign.

Celeste's gaze skipped over all these people as she searched out Kieran, and when she saw him, all the love she felt for him roared to life. He was clad in a midnight-black coat, with his cravat, waistcoat, and breeches a snowy white, and was so handsome her throat burned. He conversed with his brother, father, and a dark-haired woman with her back to the door, but when Celeste entered the room, he left the discussion and strode right to her.

"Mr. Kilburn, Dom," he said, visibly tearing his attention away from her to give a quick bow to her father and shake her brother's hand. With a bow to her, he added, "Miss Kilburn."

"Ransome," her father replied, his tone slightly terse. In a somewhat warmer manner, he said, "Been making yourself respectable, I hear."

"I've endeavored to, sir, but my efforts would've been in vain had it not been for your daughter's kind intercession."

Her father grunted before heading toward the earl, who hailed him in greeting.

"Everything ready?" Dom asked Kieran.

Celeste whispered urgently, "What do you have planned?"

"I—" He ground to a stop when Lord Montford appeared at the entrance to the parlor. Both he and Dom went rigid as marble. Clearly, then, Dom also knew about the earl's blackmail. It was close to miraculous that her brother didn't immediately charge Lord Montford and pin him to the floor as Kieran hammered him with punches.

The earl entered the room, his expression decidedly smug as he looked at Celeste standing with Kieran and Dom. It was the visage of a man who believed himself the untouchable victor—and the hell of it was, she couldn't dispute that. Lord Montford *had* won.

"Go get a drink, Dom," Kieran said under his breath.

"Like hell I will," her brother fired back.

"Please, Dom," Celeste said lowly. "There's murder in your eyes and I won't have you brought before a magistrate on my behalf."

"Go, Kilburn," Kieran added. "Everything's in place."

Her brother grunted, but walked away.

"What's in place?" Celeste demanded of Kieran.

Before he could respond, Lord Montford strutted over and proprietarily tucked her hand into the crook of his arm. A muscle in Kieran's jaw flexed.

"There you are, my dear," Lord Montford said indulgently. "I hope you were extending an invitation to our wedding to Mr. Ransome."

"I wasn't," she clipped.

"Then I shall. Ransome, do say you'll come. Though perhaps a morning ceremony might be a little early for your attendance. The wedding breakfast should be at a more reasonable hour for you."

Fury flashed in Kieran's eyes, his hands forming fists at his sides. Words hard as steel, he said, "There's someone I'd like you to meet, Lord Montford."

The earl raised one of his brows. "Indeed? I feel I know everyone in this room. Some I know more intimately than others," he added, glancing at her with the look of a man inspecting a favorite cow.

She ground her teeth together. Why wasn't it acceptable for young women to publicly scream in rage?

Kieran bared his teeth in what might have been a smile but looked more like a predator flashing its fangs before snapping the neck of its prey. "Oh, that may be the case. You may already be acquainted with her. However, indulge me for a moment. And please, Miss Kilburn, come with us."

He gestured for Lord Montford and Celeste to accompany him, and walked with purposeful strides across the saloon toward where his father and brother continued to talk with the dark-haired woman. From the back, she appeared to be about Celeste's height, and their proportions were likewise similar. Her bronze gown was a trifle snug for an assembly of this size and with this esteemed company, with the added effect of drawing several gentlemen's gazes toward her.

Heads turned to follow Celeste, Kieran, and the earl as they neared the dark-haired woman.

Kieran approached and cleared his throat. The woman turned, and Celeste stifled a gasp.

It was Lottie, who had been part of the gathering at the Imperial Theatre. But why would she be here?

Lottie smiled at her and Lord Montford.

Celeste glanced apprehensively at Kieran. What was he playing at, inviting Lottie here?

"Lord Montford, Miss Kilburn," Kieran said, his eyes gleaming sharply, "may I introduce Miss Salome O'Keefe? She's a good friend of mine lately returned to London from the Continent."

Celeste stared, but the cogs in her mind turned quickly.

"Miss *Who*?" Lord Montford sputtered.

"Salome O'Keefe," Lottie said, dipping into a curtsey. Her voice was pitched low, matching the same tone and accent that Celeste had used when *she* was Salome. Now that Celeste recalled it, many had remarked at how when she was disguised, she and Lottie looked almost identical.

Hope reared its head, and Celeste was half-afraid to embrace it. What if this scheme didn't work?

"But we've met before, Lord Montford," Lottie went on. "In rather faster company than this, though discretion prevents me from saying more about it. I was raised abroad, you know, and standards of conduct are a touch less restrictive than they are here in England."

Elation burst in Celeste's chest. Trying to speak as calmly as possible, she said, "You must find life here very quiet, Miss O'Keefe."

Lottie gave an appealing laugh. "I do, but Mr. Ransome has been gracious enough to escort me so I do not find myself the object of unwanted attentions. Still," she added, eyeing a reddening Lord Montford, "I am surprised that some individuals frequent places of wildly disparate character."

"I have introduced Miss O'Keefe to my family," Kieran said silkily, "as well as the rest of the company in attendance tonight."

"That surely includes Mrs. Lapley," Celeste said with a smile. She finally permitted herself to feel the possibility of freedom, and it made her lightheaded.

"Indeed, yes," Kieran replied. "Such a respected figure, and someone whose word is widely circulated amongst the ton." He looked directly at Lord Montford, who gaped inelegantly. "Mrs. Lapley will be certain to report that Miss Celeste Kilburn met Miss Salome O'Keefe tonight, and in front of many other esteemed personages."

"We met at the theater, didn't we, Miss O'Keefe?" Finn added, stepping forward with Dom at his side. "You recall Mr. Kilburn?"

"I'm frequently seen at the theater," Lottie said, smiling. "And I recall the pleasure of making both of your acquaintances. Keeping yourselves out of trouble, I pray?"

"Never," Dom answered.

Celeste couldn't stop herself from smirking, but she didn't care. Kieran had manipulated the situation so that Lord Montford could never accuse her of being Salome, not when "Salome" herself stood six feet away from her. And with an abundance of witnesses, including the lights of London Society, a duke and duchess, the earl and countess, and Celeste's own family.

She watched gleefully as Lord Montford turned red, then purple, and then the color leeched from his face.

"Excuse me . . ." he muttered. "I'd completely forgotten I have another engagement, and . . . your pardon."

His movements stiff, Lord Montford bowed before heading toward the door.

"A moment before you go, if you please," Kieran said, striding after the earl. He clamped his hand on Lord Montford's arm and hustled him into the corridor.

Celeste murmured an excuse to the assembled company and swiftly followed after Kieran and Lord Montford. In the hallway, she caught sight of Kieran shoving the earl into a room, then something heavy slammed into the furniture before falling to the floor.

Whatever came next, she needed to be a part of it. She hurried into what appeared to be a small sitting room, and saw Lord Montford sprawled across the carpet with a ferocious Kieran looming over him, hands knotted into fists.

"It's done, Montford," Kieran said, his voice cutting as flint. "Your accusations are baseless now."

Celeste's shadow fell across Lord Montford, who looked to her wildly.

"I was trying to *help* you." The earl sounded desperate, wounded.

"What you call *help* was never wanted," she fired back. For good measure, she added, "You son of a bitch."

"Scoundrel I may be," Kieran said, words low and almost languid, "but now I've many powerful friends. Dukes and earls who can make your life very, very unpleasant if you aren't careful."

Kieran took a step closer to Lord Montford, who scrambled back like a crab.

"This gambit you attempted," Kieran went on idly, "is never again to be repeated. Not with Miss Kilburn, not with *anyone*. Am I making myself understood? Am I?" he repeated when Lord Montford was silent.

"Y-Yes," Lord Montford stammered.

Kieran actually chuckled. "Playing on the dark side of the street wasn't a good idea, Montford. That's where *I* live, and that's how *I* play. You're nothing but an amateur."

"One other thing," Celeste added, leaning down. "You are to tell everyone that the engagement has been ended on mutually amenable terms. There's to be no retribution. No cuts direct, no gossip or slander toward myself, my father, or my brother. Is that understood?"

"It is," the earl said, his face pale.

"Now," Celeste commanded, confident that she'd secured her family's safety. "Get. Out."

Lord Montford lurched to his feet, before scurrying out of the room. His hurried footsteps tapped down the hallway, descended the stairs, and then out the front door.

She faced Kieran. The only illumination in the chamber came from the fireplace, casting one side of him in golden light, while the other half was bathed in shadow. His chest rose and fell as he stared at her. Something wild and wanting careened inside her, yet she couldn't quite liberate it. She'd been trapped by circumstance for so long that its absence nearly frightened her.

How could she trust this moment, or believe it was real? Especially when he made no move in her direction.

"What I did was to set you free," he said, his voice low and resolute. "Only that. Whatever choice you make, I'll respect. This wasn't about having you for myself."

"Meaning," she said cautiously as her heart pounded, "you don't want me?"

He stared at her with such intensity, she trembled.

"I want you, Celeste," he said hoarsely. "God, how I want you."

Elation was a flock of birds taking flight within her. "I want you, Kieran." She hauled in a rough breath, gathering the courage she now knew she possessed. "I love you."

He strode to her, and cupped her face with his hands. She soaked in the pleasure of his touch, and clung to the deep timbre of his voice as he spoke. "Before you, I thought my life was good enough. I did what I pleased, and didn't give a damn about anyone else."

"That sounds rather nice," she murmured.

"I believed it to be," he said wryly. "And I thought, when our families made their ultimatum, that I could find a way to exploit the situation to my benefit. My only intention was to use you to get what I wanted."

"I knew that I was merely a means to an end. I had no illusions about you."

"But *I* had illusions about *you*. Misbegotten notions that you were simply a prim and proper miss, perhaps a trifle bored, looking for something to break her out of routine. I was a fool, Celeste," he said, his words a rasp. "Because you . . . you're a hurricane contained within the structure of a woman. You're a force more powerful than anything else, and when you impelled me to accompany you out into the larger world, it was like beholding the birth of a whole new universe. I was merely the lucky bastard to witness it.

"Yet I meant what I said." Solemn, he looked deeply into her eyes. "If what you want is your freedom, I'll step aside."

She sucked in a breath, stunned at the enormity of what he offered her. "You aren't going anywhere," she said, leaning into his touch. "I choose you, for always."

Tremors shook his body, and his eyes shone wetly, yet a wondering smile touched his mouth. "When I'm with you, my muse doesn't just speak to me. She sings. Yet never believe your sole purpose is to be my inspiration. Let *me* inspire *you* to reach the heights you were destined to climb. If I can be the smallest part of your journey, I'll die a man fully content. Because I love you."

She let the tears run freely, and he didn't try to stop her from weeping. "Kieran."

"Celeste," he answered, her name a vow on his lips. "I was made to love you."

"Will you . . ." She inhaled, yet she wouldn't let trepidation hold her back, not when what she desired was so close. When *he* was here with her. "Will you marry me?"

"Oh, yes." He squeezed his eyes shut as a shuddering breath coursed through him, and her own elation made her light enough to fly.

"But there's a condition," she added.

He opened his eyes, all seriousness and gravity. "Name it."

"If we *are* to wed . . ." She spread her hands on his chest so she felt his heart pound beneath her palms, the heart that was hers, just as her heart belonged to him. "I don't want a tamed, reformed rake. I want *you*. My wild poet. I want to share adventures with you. I want us to take on the world, hand in hand. We'll experience everything—together."

His smile was brilliant, and sinful. "Precisely what I want, too."

"Kieran," she said urgently.

"Love?"

"Kiss me."

A fierce, joyous fire burned in his eyes. He tilted her head up and brought his mouth to hers. They kissed ravenously, driven by need that had been too long denied. She pressed herself into him, his strength meeting hers, as it was meant to be. Her body flared to life, demanding more and more.

She broke away with a gasp. "Thanks to you, I've just skirted scandal, but it wouldn't be the sagest decision to make love to you here when our families are right down the hall."

"When have we been wise?" he asked wickedly.

"Fair point."

"But," he went on, stepping back, "our next time together, I plan on being *very* leisurely and *very* thorough."

Heat coursed through her, yet she had to hold herself in check. For now. She glanced toward the corridor. Nervousness at what was to come skittered along her limbs. "We ought to rejoin the others. There's more work to do tonight."

"I'm with you," he said, steady and secure.

When he held out his hand, she took it.

Together, they entered the saloon. Much as she wanted to keep her fingers intertwined with his, such public displays were not well tolerated, so she tucked her hand into the crook of his arm as they rejoined his guests.

Many faces turned toward them, including their respective families. Both Dom and Finn wore self-satisfied smirks—she'd have to thank them later for their part in tonight's scheme. But for now, there was one person that needed to be dealt with.

Kieran must have been thinking the same thing, because he asked lowly, "Shall I talk to your father?"

"We'll *both* speak with him."

Kieran nodded in approval, and together they headed toward her father, who watched them with a touch of bafflement.

"Might we have a word with you, Mr. Kilburn?" Kieran asked politely.

"I'd like that, too, Da," Celeste added, holding firm to her courage.

Still looking perplexed, her father inclined his head and the three of them moved to a quiet corner of the saloon.

"What's this about?" her father asked, frowning.

"Da, Kieran and I are going to be married," she said.

Her father's brows climbed. "Thought Lord Montford was marrying you."

"He never asked formally," she explained, "and I never agreed."

"But . . ." Her father frowned. "He's an *earl*. Montford is going to be a marquess one day. This bloke," he added, glancing at Kieran as his frown deepened, "is just a third son. He's the heir to nothing."

"That doesn't matter," Celeste insisted. "What matters is a person's heart, and no one has a better heart than Kieran."

Kieran sent her a look full of pleasure and gratitude. "My thanks, love."

"He won't take kindly to you jilting him," her father pointed out grimly. "We won't be welcome in the ton."

"I am *so tired* of being this family's social savior," Celeste said fiercely. "I never asked to be the sole defender of our reputation, and it's bloody unfair that you've pinned that to me. If being accepted by Society is so important to you, Da, then *you* go to teas and balls and make meaningless conversation with the toffs."

Her father blinked, clearly surprised by her outburst.

Yet she wasn't done. "Who gives a goddamn what they think? What does it matter if they accept us or not? They aren't better than us. And I'll tell you something else, Da," she continued passionately, "I'm *proud* of being from Ratcliff. Good people live there, hardworking people who love their families. I refuse to be ashamed by who I am or where I'm from. And neither should you."

"They'll scorn us," her father protested.

"It doesn't matter," she insisted. "All that matters is not doing harm, and caring for others. I'm working with the people of Ratcliff now. Helping them learn to read and write, and if anyone sneers at that, then I say with all sincerity, *I don't bloody care.* If you're ashamed of our past, that's *your* battle to fight, not mine."

Her father stared at her in astonishment.

"You should be proud of her," Kieran said in the silence. "Of who she is and what she wants to accomplish. She's the best person I know," he went on, voice thickening, "and if that doesn't thrill you, then you deserve pity, Mr. Kilburn."

Celeste smiled up at Kieran as a grateful tear tracked down her cheek. Tenderly, he swiped it away with his thumb.

"I . . ." Her father seemed to struggle with comprehension, and she feared his response. But no matter what he said, she was doing the right thing. She followed her heart, and no one, not even her own father, could lead her from that path.

Then her father exhaled, and he slowly nodded.

Her own exhalation was a long, serrated breath of relief.

"I'm . . . I'm sorry, Star." Da sounded truly contrite. "I was too busy reaching for something I thought was valuable, but if it costs you your happiness, then I've truly failed as a father. I love you, gel. You and your brother. You're all that should matter to me."

He took her hand in his, and squeezed it. Moisture glossed his eyes—the second time Celeste had ever seen Da cry.

"But," her father added with a glare at Kieran, "you sure about wedding this rogue? He ain't good husband material."

"My past conduct has been a bit . . . unrestrained," Kieran said, yet added earnestly, "but, Mr. Kilburn, I love her."

"Love ain't always enough to keep a scoundrel at home," her father answered.

"When Celeste is home," Kieran replied, "I'll be home with her. When she's out, I'll be out with her. Wherever she is, that's where you'll find me."

Her father's expression warmed, but he turned to Celeste. "Is this what you want, Star? Do you trust him?"

"I trust him, Da," she said with complete sincerity. "He has my heart, and I know he'll keep it safe."

"Not every moment of marriage is awash in joy," her father cautioned. "There's anger and heartbreak in it, too."

"It's better to have someone beside you to face them," Celeste said. "And I choose him to have at my side."

Her father said nothing for a long moment, but then, eyes continuing to shine, he said, "Then you've my blessing. And your ma's, too. She might not be here, but she's here, where it matters." He tapped the center of Celeste's chest, and Kieran's, as well.

Her ribs were tight as she pressed a kiss to her father's cheek. "Thank you, Da."

"Thank you, Mr. Kilburn," Kieran added, shaking her father's hand. His voice thickening, he added, "She's a gift, your daughter, and I thank you for bringing her into the world."

Da dashed his knuckles across his eyes. "Everything she is, she owes to no one but herself."

Celeste swallowed hard around the lump in her throat. "We ought to tell everyone."

Kieran and her father nodded, and they rejoined the group. His family all watched them approach, and Dom looked as pleased as she'd seen him in months.

"As it turns out," Kieran said in a voice pitched so everybody at the party could hear, "tonight is an engagement party."

"Mr. Ransome and I are to be married," Celeste added.

There was a brief, stunned moment before the assembled guests broke into applause and cries of felicitations. Most likely, they were a trifle confused as to how Celeste had begun the evening as the supposed fiancée of one man, only to announce her engagement to another within the span of an hour, but sometimes the best strategy was to brazen it out, and others would fall in line.

Kieran's parents both beamed and clapped at the announcement, perhaps the happiest Celeste had ever seen them whilst also in each other's presence.

"But this is wonderful," Lady Wingrave said proudly. "You cannot find a more respectable young woman than Miss Kilburn."

"At least *one* of you is attempting to meet our requirements," Lord Wingrave added. He sent a pointed glance at Finn, whose gaze slid up toward the ceiling as if a ladder he could climb might descend from it.

"This has nothing to do with you or what you want," Kieran said to his parents, his gaze direct and unsparing. "It's for myself. Myself and Celeste."

His parents stammered and looked abashed, as if they couldn't understand how anything their son did could exist independently of them.

Celeste leaned close to him to whisper in his ear. "You're extraordinary, you know. And worth celebrating. They're fools if they cannot recognize that. But I do, and I always will."

His dark eyes were deep and full of love as he lifted her hand to his lips and kissed it. If the public show of affection was considered gauche or crude, neither she nor Kieran cared. All that mattered was the future that lay ahead of them, the future they would share.

The company took celebratory drinks. Celeste and Kieran shared a knowing look. To the world at large, she *was* perfectly respectable.

Yet she and her intended knew better.

Chapter 24

❧✻❧

Kieran padded through his rooms, shucking garments as he went. He dropped his coat, waistcoat, and neckcloth to the floor, then thought better of it and scooped everything up to deposit the garments on a chair in his bedchamber. It wasn't precisely putting his clothing away, but it would make Wesham's job a trifle easier in the morning. And if Kieran *did* attempt to stow his own garments, his valet would be insulted by the insinuation that he couldn't do his job properly and sulk for at least three days.

"Joining me?" Finn asked from the doorway. He'd changed from his slightly brighter outfit worn at Kieran's party into the dark ensemble he preferred for nights out at gaming hells.

"I'm reformed now, remember?" Still, Kieran grinned. "And Celeste would be most irritated if I were to venture somewhere scandalous without her." He sobered. "My thanks for tonight. We wouldn't have been able to sell our tale nearly as well without your assistance."

Finn merely shrugged. "Bluffing is an essential skill, but it's not so difficult to master with a little practice. Congratulations on your engagement," he added with unusual sincerity. "I'd despaired that you would never find someone to match you step for step, but Miss Kilburn will do all of that, and more."

Warmth spread through Kieran's chest at the thought of his intended. She was indeed his perfect complement and he was grateful he had enough wisdom to recognize that. Yet the lion's share of his thankfulness was for her, and that she could ever care for a scoundrel such as himself.

Walking over to a table that held a decanter, he poured himself a glass. He offered whisky to Finn, who waved it off. "And what of you, brother? Time is running apace, but you aren't going to locate your respectable bride at a gaming hell."

"You did."

"Celeste is one in a million," he said with sincerity. "In gaming hells, virtuous brides are scarce."

"Precisely why I'm going there. But," he went on before Kieran could voice an objection, "Dom's in a bad way, and the best answer to his bleak humor is finding *him* a woman who meets the criteria. I've just the woman in mind, too."

"Who might that be?" he asked with curiosity.

"Miss Tabitha Seaton, the bluestocking we met at the Duke of Greyland's ball. She's cool and rational enough to manage his wild impulsiveness."

Intriguing. "Have you a plan to bring them together?"

"I do—and it's going to require your assistance. Miss Kilburn's, too."

Before Kieran could demand elaboration, a knock sounded at the front door. He frowned. The party at his parents' home had ended shortly after midnight, and an hour had passed since then. It seemed unlikely that Dom would come around, given that he'd disappeared into the night long before the last guest had left Wingrave House.

"Expecting anyone?" he asked Finn.

His brother shrugged, and headed toward the door. Kieran followed, though he lingered at the entrance to his bedchamber.

Finn pulled open the door, but his sizable frame blocked Kieran's view of whoever stood on the other side.

"For you," his brother said over his shoulder. He stepped aside to reveal the late-night visitor, who had the slight stature of a woman.

Kieran's pulse raced when the figure pushed back the hood of her cloak, displaying her face. Celeste.

"Taking a chance." He couldn't resist her magnetic pull, and crossed the room in three strides. "Being out sans disguise. Coming to our bachelor lodgings."

"One of you isn't going to be a bachelor for long," she replied, tipping up her chin. Mist clung to her hair and her eyelashes and he wanted to lick up every droplet. It didn't matter that they'd be together for the rest of their lives; he wanted all of her all the time.

"In any event," she said, "Salome has done enough for us tonight, and who could fault an engaged couple for being overly eager to spend time in each other's company?" Her gaze heated as it traversed the length of his partially clothed body, down to his bare feet.

God, how he loved seeing how she desired him, and that she didn't try to disguise her passion.

"Seeing myself out . . ." Finn muttered. He exited their lodgings, shutting the door behind him.

Kieran and Celeste met in the middle of the room. Her arms immediately looped around his neck, and his hands splayed across her lower back as their bodies came together. She fit to him flawlessly, as though they'd been fashioned for each other.

"How I adore having you in my arms," he murmured, nuzzling along her neck. She smelled of the night air and beneath that, the tender musk of her skin. He inhaled, drawing her in as profoundly as he could. "And out of disguise, too. Finally."

"A good thing?" she asked breathlessly when he bit her collarbone.

"Very good. Because I'll never take this for granted. It'll be a continual, delightful surprise."

She stroked her hands across his shoulders, and he leaned into her touch, desperate for the feel of her.

"I was infatuated with you," she admitted huskily. "My brother's friend, a scandalous rake. Good girl that I was, how could I ever hope to attract your attention?"

Her confession undid him. "I'd no idea. How delightful to think that beneath your reserved, decorous exterior, you had wicked designs on my person. Yet you said you *were* infatuated with me. That girlish infatuation is no longer?"

"It's matured into full-blown love," she said, pressing a kiss to the corner of his lips.

He turned to take her mouth with his. "I'd read so many poems about love, and pretended to know what it was when I wrote my own verses, but nothing could prepare me for what it truly means to love someone the way I love you."

They kissed deeply, each kiss a vow.

His body was already aflame, but he held himself back enough to growl, "I want you so much, love. If you want to wait until our wedding night, I will."

"No waiting," she said huskily. "We can be careful, but I need you, Kieran. I need all of you." She dragged her hands down his back and clutched at the cheeks of his arse.

He made a sound that was part laugh, part snarl. How he adored her passion. "You might be a bigger glutton for sensation than *me*, and that's no small feat."

"I do love experiencing new things, but I love experiencing *you* more. And there's something that would give me both . . ." She moved one of her hands from his buttocks to the front of his breeches, cradling his straining erection.

He hissed with pleasure from the eagerness of her touch. Then he rumbled when she tore at the fastenings of his breeches to reach in and wrap her fingers around his bare cock. Her skin was a little cool from the night air, but it only added to his excitement. "Oh, God."

"There's something I want to try," she said throatily.

"Anything you want to do to me, I'm yours. *Christ*," he said, hoarse, as she pumped him.

"I was taught many things to be a proper young lady," she whispered, breathless. "How to embroider. How to pour tea. But not this."

"You're . . . *hell* . . . doing a marvelous . . . *God* . . . job." He tipped his head back, lost to the pleasure his beloved gave him.

She lowered to kneel before him. He could only utter the coarsest of profanities as the best way to express his gratitude.

He'd never seen anything so wondrous as Celeste on her knees, angling his cock to her mouth. Her shy, excited gaze met his. He loved that they could share more new experiences together.

"I've only read about this," she whispered. "How do I . . . ?"

The prospect of telling her in explicit detail exactly what to do made his already stiff cock rigid as forged metal. "Wet your lips, my bride-to-be."

She did, and looked up at him for more guidance.

"When you're ready, lick the head."

She followed his guidance, moistening her lips before she leaned closer so that her breath was warm against the crown of his cock. The first swipe of her tongue against him shot lightning through him. She was tentative to start, just little licks that were deliciously maddening, but then she asked, "There's more, isn't there?"

"Yes," he grated, "take the head into your mouth."

"Not all of it?"

She was determined to kill him. "Start slowly," he growled, "and make yourself comfortable before moving on."

"Always so considerate." She gave a tiny smile before she dipped her head low and drew the crown of his cock into her hot, welcoming mouth.

"I love your passion," he gasped. "Your courage."

She gave a sound of pleasure, and he fisted his hands at his sides, fighting like hell to keep from thrusting into her as his body demanded. She licked and sucked him, growing bolder and more assured, until she took him in deeper. Yet she could only take half his length and made a noise of frustration.

"Easy," he managed to say. "You can use your hand for the rest."

"Like so?" she murmured, pumping him before lowering her head to suck him again.

"*Fuck*, just like that."

Through slitted eyes he watched her throating his cock, the gorgeous view of seeing his length disappear between her lips. The pleasure was so intense he could hardly remain standing, yet he planted his feet to anchor himself as she devoted herself eagerly to this experience, just as she met everything in the world with bravery and ardor.

Celeste's chest rose and fell, and her cheeks were flushed, revealing her arousal.

Her excitement stoked his higher, until the rising of release began to gather at the base of his spine. Yet he was determined to last as long as possible for her, and so, with the greatest of regret, he pulled from her mouth.

"Love," he rasped, "if I don't fuck you, I'm going to lose my mind. Any objections?"

"None at all," she panted.

He could have shouted with gratitude, and helped her to stand. They removed their clothing with desperate haste. When they were both naked, he stepped back in admiration. A flush stained her cheeks and chest, yet even after all they'd shared, she still lowered her lashes as if slightly abashed to be seen in the nude.

"You're as luscious here as you were in the Imperial Theatre's dressing room," he said, his voice deep. "Now it's even better because there's no disguise, and we're promised to each other. At last, I can take my time with my intended."

Weaving his fingers with hers, he led her into his chamber, then swept her up into his arms to carry her the remaining distance to the bed. He laid her down upon the counterpane, and she looked perfect there, body lush and gaze replete with love.

"A bed," she said huskily, lifting on her elbows. "How novel."

"We'll soon have one of our own. Our private kingdom." Climbing onto the mattress, he kissed her. She met his searing need with her own, the kiss voracious. He stroked her breasts, teasing them into sensitive points, and committed her body to the memory of his hands. Every inch of her was exquisite, this wondrous woman who brought ferocity and bliss to his life.

When she was gasping, he stretched out onto his back.

"Put your cunt on my face," he commanded huskily.

"Oh, yes," she said breathlessly.

He helped position her, placing her knees on either side of his head. She gasped as he nuzzled against the soft, silken flesh of her thighs that so delightfully imprisoned him. The most magnificent sight of all was her flushed, wet quim just above him, so slick with desire. His hands cupped her hips, and together, they lowered her down, until his mouth met her pussy.

The taste of her . . . He could exist on nothing else but this. She was molten and spiced, delicate and yet unafraid as she chased her pleasure, grinding against him as he flicked his tongue against her clitoris and sucked at her opening.

"Kieran," she moaned, "I'm—" She cried out, her whole body growing taut.

But he wasn't appeased. He had to give her everything, so he slid one hand down her belly and then worked it between them until he was able to plunge two fingers into her passage. He stroked into her, finding the place within that was so swollen with arousal. She shuddered once more as she gasped his name, and gave another cry as he urged her to another climax. Then she pulled back.

"Please, Kieran," she pled. "I want . . . I want . . ."

"You want me to fuck you." He flipped them so that she lay on her back and he lay between her legs. This was where he wanted to be for the remainder of his days. "The respectable girl insists she wants my cock."

"I want you forever." She gripped his arse again.

"God, how I love you." He sank into her with one hard plunge, and she arched up to meet him.

He'd intended to go slowly, to draw out each stroke, but control slipped from him as she writhed and moaned with each thrust of his hips. The feel of her around him was bliss, like coming home, and he panted like a beast as he lost himself to the task of pleasuring her. She hooked her ankles around the small of his back, her movements frenzied as he fucked her with wild adoration.

He spun them so she straddled him, and he watched the determined ecstasy on her face as she rode him, chasing release. Love for her filled him, along with the need to give her as much ecstasy as she could stand. When she cried out with another orgasm, he pulled out a moment before his own climax.

They panted together, until he lowered her back down to the blanket. She was boneless as he slid from her arms to cross the room on shaky legs. He found a cloth, dipped it in the water-filled basin, and then returned to clean them both. Each stroke of the cloth over her body was reverent. With that task taken care of, he lay down once more, cradling her close.

She spread her hand on his chest, lightly scraping through the hair that curled there.

"Didn't think I'd ever find this," he said softly.

"Find what?" she asked, drowsy.

He searched for the right word, but in the wake of such extraordinary pleasure with such an extraordinary person, syllables were in scarce supply.

"I'd say *contentment*, but that's too still and static. It's like . . . it's like the whole world has opened up to me in a way I've never experienced, but that world is here, in my arms." He pressed a kiss to the crown of her head.

"It's ours to explore, you know." She snuggled closer, the fit of her body to his perfect in every way. "That world belongs to us, the day and the night. We never have to adhere to anyone's definitions of who we are, or who we ought to be. We're simply *us*. In all our imperfect, searching, wonderful beauty. So long as we see each other as we truly are, we need nothing more."

"I don't know how I existed before you," he said, voice thick, "but now that you're mine, and I'm yours, all I want is to take the next step."

She smiled up at him, infinite love in her eyes. Love, and acceptance.

"And the step after that," she said, rising up for another kiss, "and the one after that. Our road is endless, my love. We'll travel it together."

Epilogue

Two months later

Do you think we'll have enough?" Celeste asked Susan, surveying the books piled on every available surface. She leased an empty room in the Ratcliff tenement strictly for the storage of teaching materials, and the chamber was stuffed full of hornbooks, chalk, paper, quills, and an abundance of books.

"Believe so, miss," Susan answered. She handed a child's primer to her grandson, who toddled it over to a stack of similar texts. "Between Her Grace, your father, Lady Ashford, and the other patrons you've gathered, we aren't wanting for more books. Besides," Susan added wryly, "there ain't room to accommodate more."

"My father *does* own several warehouses nearby," Celeste pointed out as she piled up more books in anticipation of the first lessons. Nervous anticipation gathered in a ball in her stomach. Tutors had been hired, and in two days free schooling for whoever in Ratcliff desired it would begin.

"Let's start with what we've got," Susan advised warmly. "You've already done so much, miss."

"Do you think anyone will come?" Celeste asked anxiously.

"I know they will. Half the families in Ratcliff have pledged to bring their children, and there's more than a few adults who mean to learn their letters, too. Including me," Susan said with shy pride.

Celeste wove around the books to give the other woman's arm a squeeze. "You'll do splendidly. And I'll be here, cheering you on."

"Be sure to bring that handsome fiancé of yours, too," Susan suggested with a wink. Then she added thoughtfully, "Though, he might prove a distraction. Lord knows he turns *your* head whenever he's around."

"Untrue." Kieran stood in the doorway, and his smile flashed—which never failed to make Celeste's heart race. "I've been standing here a full minute and my bride-to-be hasn't noticed. I shall be forced to retreat into manly brooding."

"Yet you look so gorgeous and Romantic when you do." Celeste crossed the room and went straight into Kieran's waiting arms. He clasped her to him as though he'd been waiting a lifetime to hold her, even though he'd seen her hours earlier. "I'd hate to deny all of us the pleasure."

"Minx," he chided her affectionately. He tipped up her chin and pressed his lips to hers. Though they were in public, the kiss was deep enough to steal her breath.

"Once you're done ravishing Miss Kilburn before my very eyes," Susan said with humor, "I hope you're taking her home for some supper. She's been working all day and needs a rest."

"Is this true?" Kieran asked, his assessing gaze moving over Celeste's face. "You *do* look tired."

"Nothing a bit of time with my intended cannot alleviate," she answered honestly. Every moment with Kieran invigorated her, including now, when she was indeed weary from hours sorting teaching materials.

"Then I shall take you home posthaste," Kieran said with a grin, "and let you bask in the revivifying remedy that is me."

"Go on, the pair of you," Susan said and laughed. "I'll see you in two days, Miss Kilburn."

Hand in hand, Celeste and Kieran made their way to the ground floor, and then out onto the street. She was met with salutations and many people expressed their eagerness for the tutoring to begin. Kieran was greeted with familiarity, too, since he'd been providing tireless assistance with the literacy program and was now well-known in Ratcliff.

Her pride in him couldn't be surpassed.

As they made their way down the narrow street, he asked her, "Are you *very* weary? There's something I'd like to do before we go back to Hans Town."

"I'm never too tired for you," she said with a smile.

"This way, then." His own smile was warm and intimate as he led her southward, until they reached the river. The water was thick and dark, and gave off a dank smell, especially in the heat of high summer, but she knew this view and this place too well to be disappointed that it wasn't particularly picturesque. With Kieran beside her, every view was beautiful.

"It's not my intention to steal glory from your project," Kieran said once they stood on the wharf. "But . . . I thought you might like to see this." With a shy smile, he pulled something from his coat pocket and handed it to her.

"Your book," she exhaled in wonderment. She opened the slim, leather-bound volume to its title page, and there in elegant copperplate print it read *Verse, Songs, and Dreams: Poems by Kieran Nicholas Ransome.*

"Oh, this is wonderful," she exclaimed, touching her gloved hand to the paper. Seeing his name printed there, for all the world to see, was a marvel. "How you amaze me."

"There's more," he said softly. "Turn the page."

She did, and it read *To C. K.—Every line is for you.*

Tears welled in her eyes, and she clasped the book to her chest. Kieran gazed at her with happy apprehension. "It's true," he murmured. "There is no poetry in my life without you, love. There is nothing in my life without you."

"Oh, Kieran." She rose up to put her mouth to his, and he cupped her jaw as he kissed her with adoring sensuality. No matter how many kisses they'd shared, each one set her aflame with need and possibility.

"I sent a copy to my parents," he said when they finally surfaced.

"What if they don't like it?" The earl and countess had been relatively welcoming to her when she'd dined with them over the course of the last two months, and though things weren't precisely warm between Kieran and his parents, there was a degree of cordiality. The earl had even invited Kieran to his club with him, which, Kieran had told her later, had never happened before.

"It doesn't signify." A corner of his mouth lifted. "*I* like it, and so do you, and that's all that matters. This is *our* journey. Speaking of which . . ."

He drew her even closer as he spoke in a husky tone. "I have an evening's jaunt planned. An artist's salon in Bloomsbury that promises to be quite disreputable. Will Salome be there?"

"She wouldn't miss it," Celeste answered, her pulse kicking with anticipation.

Their nocturnal escapades hadn't stopped since their engagement. She still went out as Salome, and since it would be too scandalous for the engaged Kieran Ransome to be seen in the company of a woman who was, for all intents and purposes, *not* his bride-to-be, he also wore a disguise. To her delight, he usually lined his eyes with kohl, just as he'd done at Mr. Longbridge's party. And when the evening was done, she and Kieran returned to his bed and made love until the sun stole beneath the curtains. They were careful, of course, but it would have been impossible to wait until their planned late autumn wedding.

Every time she and Kieran went out together, exploring the wild and wicked side of London, was as exciting as their first foray. It didn't matter where they went—the most exhilarating part was being with Kieran. He encouraged her, celebrated her, and together they learned all of the world's mysteries. And every time in his bed was more pleasurable than the last.

He now cradled her close and kissed her again. "There's my daring love."

"I'll go anywhere with you," she murmured against his lips. "My wild poet."

"There are so many blank pages ahead of us," he said throatily. "We'll fill them all with our adventures."

One Scoundrel down, two more to go!

Don't miss Finn's story . . .

THE WALLFLOWER WINS

✤✲✤

Coming Fall 2022!